MW01171084

The End of Nobility

The End of Nobility, Book 1

Michael Green Jr

Published by Lynit Publishing, 2024.

THE END OF NOBILITY

This is a work of fiction. All the characters and events portrayed in this book are fictional, and any resemblance to real people or incidents is purely coincidental. While every precaution has been taken in the preparation of this book, the publisher assumes no responsibility for errors or omissions, or for damages resulting from the use of the information contained herein.

Published by Lynit Publishing

Lynit Publishing
99 Wall Street #689
New York, NY 10005

ISBN: 979-8-9862547-2-2

Cover art by Xavier Comas

Written by Michael Green Jr.

First edition. May 3, 2024.

To my 15-year-old self, who struggled to imagine black and brown kids using magic.

Prologue

The red light of a spell surrounded Mira, reflecting a soft glow off her dark body. It pulsed to the rhythm of her shifting, swollen belly, but the stubborn woman wouldn't die. She lay sweat-drenched in a hospital bed, clenching her fiancé's hand.

"That…that isn't a strong heartbeat," a protector said as he pulled his head back. The red tint washed from his white robes when he released the sphere of energy enveloping Mira. "It's two weak ones. I will inform the head protector." He hurried out of the room.

Slithlor jerked away from the back wall. He placed his cup of tea on a nearby counter. It was finally time to terminate this monstrous child. It had been a gift, but not every experiment would succeed and failures were dangerous. In the same way that he would question what went wrong, so would another person. The head protector would not let this oddity go unstudied, and there could be no trail back to him. His experiments on foreigners were tolerated, but he would be executed for what he did to Mira's child. Fortunately, there was no way to study the magic of a dead baby.

The father dabbed Mira's forehead. "First extra limbs, now two hearts?"

Mira propped herself up on her elbows. "It doesn't matter what Alaandre looks like," she said. She pulled his face to hers. She kissed him. "I love you."

Invisible psychic energy leapt from Slithlor's head. It disturbed the air in a way that only he could sense. He maneuvered it around the father and touched the woman's belly. She fidgeted but didn't cry out. Inside her womb, however, there weren't only two hearts—there were two minds. Interesting. He pulled back his energy.

Several people in white entered the room. The head protector stepped to the front, wearing large blue and red earrings. "I understand that many have come to see you over the past few weeks and have told you many different things. It is normal that expecting parents are wary of new technology during pregnancy, but in your case, it is most important that we get a clear image of the baby."

"Can't you check with protection magic?" the father asked.

"Yes, but we are experiencing something we have never seen before. This device will give a second opinion." She placed a hand on a shiny metal machine next to the bed. "Magic imitates the world, and this machine imitates magic. The ultrasound will not harm your child." She tilted her head from side to side. An emblem of six overlapping circles within a seventh circle was carved into her earrings. It was the symbol of Lynit. Six people: Vous, Yordin, Cast, Pol, Palow, and Finrar, discovered six forms of magic, and Kertic, the only person ever able to wield all six as an adult, brought the desert people together under one banner. Kertic had only one law: Magic must be shared. Then, Lynit was formed. The descendants of the six became the nobles, and the descendants of Kertic became the kings and queens. The head protector was a Pol, a descendent of the creator of protection magic. The colors of her earrings, blue and red, were Pol colors. Her family was praised for being so dedicated to helping others, but their bloodline didn't make them all-knowing.

"The ultrasound will not harm your children," Slithlor said. He kept his face blank as the parents and protectors turned to him.

"What do you mean?" the father asked.

"There are two minds in her womb," Slithlor said.

"Are the babies healthy?" Mira asked, straining to see him through the clump of perplexed healers.

"Two children? Human twins?" a protector said, shaking her head. "That's impossible."

"Who are you?" the head protector asked.

It was a tricky question. Slithlor knew Mira. They had gone to the same school for a few years as kids. It was enough of a connection that she didn't question when he showed up in her life a year ago. But as a colleague warned him, he wasn't close with anyone who didn't serve a purpose and was starting to develop a reputation for that. Any answer he gave now would be scrutinized in the years to come.

The room quieted.

"A researcher," Slithlor said. "I first identified the anomaly several months ago and have been monitoring it ever since."

"Months?" the father said. "You've never said anything before."

Slithlor kept his eyes on the head protector.

Mira grabbed the nearest arm. "Use the machine."

Ten faces crowded around a small screen. Someone flipped a switch, and the device whistled to life. A few seconds later, the thick sound of a heartbeat filled the room. The bass rattled the machine. The head protector adjusted a few knobs, and the sound resolved into a lighter syncopated beat—two amplified heartbeats pumped in almost perfect unison. White lines traced two identical forms.

"Congratulations, you discovered the first case of human twins," a man said. He shook the head protector's hand.

Slithlor would have been annoyed that a noble was credited for his work, but in this instance, he didn't want credit; he only wanted results. "Will their magic be different, more powerful?" he asked.

The head protector turned from the screen. "Unfortunately, we won't know until they are older."

"But are they physically healthy?" Mira asked.

"Yes," the head protector said. She tapped the screen, then explained some medical jargon.

More protectors flooded the already-cramped room, some arriving from different hospitals, some from different cities via matter shift.

After fourteen hours of loud labor and magic, Mira gave birth to two boys, Alaan and Dre, the first twins ever. Slithlor slipped out of the hospital and returned to his office. A large metal board hung on the wall. Small magnetic blocks lined up on a grid. He grabbed the third one down and slid it over to the column labeled Pending. Then, he turned his attention to other projects.

Chapter 1 - Rye

"You stab me this time," Rye Ternitu said. He panted. Adrenaline flooded his veins, preparing his body for flight, but he held his welt-covered hand against the stone wall.

He was the last in line outside the exam room. Down the hall, a group of kids laughed and toyed with the green and white circular pins fastened to their chests. They had proven themselves as ordinary animalists. Those ahead of Rye mumbled to themselves. Not one animalist had been drafted from this school, but the students averted their eyes from the exam room door as if looking at it made them more likely to be selected.

"Hurting yourself won't get you out of it," the girl ahead of him said. She wore oversized square glasses. Her black hair was braided into long, thin plaits that reached her hips. They rustled as she shook her head.

Rye's hand trembled. It was swollen. The red lumps from his previous attempts looked like infected insect bites. He always flinched when he stabbed himself, but he didn't move out of the way. He passed her a thin metal rod. "I need to try when I am not causing the threat. I'm practicing instinct control."

Flinching was an involuntary physical response. It was the instinct to avoid harm. Every creature alive survived because of

5

instincts, but for an animalist, it warped their logic. Sophisticated plans could be wiped out by a scent or color that triggered a primal rage in a creature. The best animalists thrived by mastering control of their body and their reactions.

"Practicing? Are you crazy? You want to get drafted?" the girl said. She tossed the rod. It slid down the hall, scraping against the stone floor.

He nodded, but he wasn't crazy. If he were drafted into the Guard, he wouldn't see his mother and brother again until he was nineteen, but he would have access to information that wasn't in any public library. The Guard was Lynit's army and the training ground for the most powerful animalists. Lynit was a nation of four domed cities in a desert full of dangerous creatures. He was safe as long as he stayed inside, but that was boring. On the edge of the horizon was a forest full of countless undiscovered insects and furry critters. He could discover them one day. The world was so big, but it would be out of reach until he was strong enough to survive in the wilderness. Joining the Guard was his best route.

One of the boys with a green and white pin approached. He was taller than Rye, with a round face covered in light stubble. His almond eyes carried a brightness they didn't have fifteen minutes ago, before he had failed the exam. "You are here to declare your magic. Don't worry about the draft. Remember your mistakes and you will be fine."

From early childhood, every Lynitian could use all six forms of magic: protection, wizardry, sorcery, elemental, psychic, and animalism. But by the time they reached adulthood, they lost the ability to use more than one. Today was the day to declare the single magic to continue into adulthood. Each one had its own colored pin. It took most kids years to decide. Each magic was different and fun to use, but Rye had known his choice since his first morph at seven. Animalism was encoded into his bones.

The exam room door creaked open. A short, skinny boy exited wearing his green and white pin but wasn't smiling like the others. He carried a crisp brown sheet of paper. Not only was real paper expensive, it was proof that someone had left the desert to get it.

"I was drafted," he said, his voice almost a whimper.

The other students pulled back. Rye stepped around his stunned classmates. He slipped the letter from the boy's fingers with little resistance. In a few lines, it explained that Oron had been accepted into the Guard's draft program. His training would begin in two weeks. A handwritten note at the bottom explained the draft reasoning.

"Oron has potential for instinct stacking," Rye read aloud. It was the ability to combine the instincts of multiple creatures. Rye's father had been an expert at it, but Rye never got a chance to learn it from him before he died. The paper crinkled in his hand.

"She said my mistakes were too identical to the two students' before me. It was obvious that we rehearsed them," Oron said. He leaned against a wall, then slid to the floor.

Rye squatted next to him. "What did you do, exactly?"

Oron's head sank between his knees. "I'll never see my family again." He sobbed.

Rye sucked his teeth. The ones who passed the exam were taken away, and those who failed only gossiped about how not to use animalism.

A girl wearing several silver bracelets shook a fist and said, "We are here to declare ourselves as animalists. We know how to adapt. Divvy up the mistakes."

One boy failed to morph into a bird by making his bones too dense. Another boy turned the outside of his body into a black wolf but kept all of his organs human. Three girls made variations of blood mineral concentration mistakes. A large boy with a gapped tooth morphed perfectly but couldn't maintain his shape for long.

He didn't coordinate his organ functions and passed out.

The students continued sharing their mistakes, and Rye checked them against his list. They were all tricks he'd used to float through school with a barely passing grade over the years. A good grade ended in a lecture from his mother. She didn't want him anywhere near the Guard and was willing to sacrifice his education because of it. Somehow, she forgot that magic was the foundation of Lynit. The region wasn't always a wasteland. It used to be a grassland a thousand years ago. People from all over the world lived here. Six different races and cultures merged. None of them had magic, but the vegetation and docile wildlife were enough to support them. When the rain stopped and the quitols arrived, everything changed. Rocks and slingshots weren't enough for the eight-foot-tall creatures. Food and water became scarce. They would have all died if the first nobles didn't invent the six magics. Lynit thrived because everyone was given access to magic. Now, no one in Lynit was helpless, though, since the start of the draft, there was fear.

After the girl with braids returned with a green and white pin but no sheet of paper, it was Rye's turn. He carefully slipped his aching hand into his pocket and entered the room.

The tables from his third-period classroom were pressed around the edges. The vials of preserved creatures in milky white liquid were packed in the back corner. Of all the posters lining the walls, the best one was of a flock of birds in V formation. They flew for thousands of miles in an efficient pattern that they knew from birth. Instincts were cool.

Currently, the poster was obscured by the head of an unimpressed soldier seated behind a child's desk. Her dark blue eyes were half open, and blonde hair hung loosely around her face. She wore a standard-issue green overcoat fastened by white buttons down her sides. She was an animalist guard. She had the skills to morph into hundreds of creatures, traverse the hazardous desert, and explore the forest.

To her right sat another guard, a blank-faced man in black and gold. He was a sorcerer. He didn't need to travel to explore his magic. He saw all the rules of the universe in this room. In his special vision, strings of golden words raced in all directions, creating hyper-dimensional shapes and intricate structures. Rules described gravity or the density of rock. With precise edits, he could temporarily rewrite a physical constant. If the melting point of stone were lowered, the whole school would become a lake of dead children.

And at the end of the short line of desks sat a friendly face, that of Mr. P, Rye's third-period teacher.

"Rye Ternitu, this room is for animalism. Are you sure this is the magic you wish to declare?" Mr. P said.

Rye grinned finally and fully. "I was born to be an animalist."

"You'll have to demonstrate that you can use animalism in any capacity, and then you'll receive your pin. It's that easy. Secondly, and separately, these guards will test your magic further to determine if you qualify for the draft. It's the Guard's involuntary training program for children. But first, I have a few simple questions for you. Five years ago, you chose animalism, protection, and sorcery during the first magic selection. Can you use any other magics?"

"No."

"Which magics can you still use?"

"Animalism and a little bit of protection."

"You must only use animalism from now on. Don't risk being stuck with a magic you don't want."

Rye nodded.

Mr. P turned to the guards.

"Ternitu?" the sorcerer said, slowly turning to his counterpart.

"Yes, I am Barin Ternitu's son," Rye said, holding his head high.

He knew that with his hair cut short, he looked just like his dad, crooked nose and all.

His father perfected instinct stacking and was the first non-noble elite, a personal guard to the king. The fact that he had failed to protect the king during the last war was sad but not shameful, like how the Guard tried to frame it. No one had been prepared for spirit fiends, beings of pure magic from the spirit realm. They leveled an entire city in a matter of hours. Tens of thousands of people died that day. The other five elites were noble and they, too, failed to protect the king. Nobles were the descendants of the original inventors of magic. If they couldn't keep the king alive, no one could.

The guards' posture tensed. The animalist calmed after a bit of effort and returned to business. "The goal of the draft is to identify top talent and accelerate their growth. Though participation is involuntary, we see an eighty-eight percent enrollment rate of draftees voluntarily joining the Guard after they age out of the program at nineteen. It was created by Slithlor, who used his vast knowledge of foreign magics to design material to train a new set of warriors deft at exploiting enemy weaknesses and keeping Lynit safe. The exam will consist of five scenarios. For each one, you will take on a form you think is best equipped to handle it. You will be judged on creativity, speed, and technical execution. Any questions?"

Rye shook his head.

"Any level of animalism will be enough to declare your magic and receive your pin," Mr. P said. He held up the green and white piece of metal. It sparkled in the light.

The animalist lowered her clipboard. Her eyes were serious now. "You are standing on a low cliff. In front of you is a clear body of water. Behind you, three unknown individuals are approaching, carrying weapons made of metal."

Rye dropped down and placed his palms on the ground. He hoisted himself into a handstand, legs straightened and toes pointed. He calmed his breathing as he separated his legs into a split. The memory of a tipit—a large bird with silky brown feathers and sharp talons—rose to the surface of his mind.

First, he protected his consciousness by compressing his brain to fit in his shrinking skull. The process rarely required thought since the brain always protected itself, but Rye moved through the steps carefully. Next, he twisted and reshaped his intestines, swallowing back the bile rising in his narrowing throat. It was like spinning and falling.

His fingers curled into claws. His legs bent and cracked painlessly. Tiny bumps flushed across his pale skin then burst into feathers. Once his body understood the shape, it continued undirected. Extra mass was released as energy that glowed about him. When he was done, he stood with his chest out, his shiny wings raised.

The sorcerer scribbled something, pausing only to scan Rye with emotionless eyes. He slid his notes over to the animalist. She frowned and an accidental squawk escaped Rye's beak. She instructed him to twirl, run, flap, and act like a bird. He did as told.

"Return to human, please."

Rye released the details of the creature from his mind and his body remembered that this wasn't his body. The morph reversed itself. His clothing, a green shirt and brown pants, returned intact. That was one strange aspect of animalism. His clothes weren't part of him but were preserved during his morphs.

Whether there was uncertainty or danger, a bird fled to safety. They weren't smart, but their instincts were strong. From the ground, movement meant danger. From the air, ground movement meant prey. The tipit was one of the first creatures he learned and had executed it perfectly. He grinned.

"Thank you," the animalist said. She wrote something down. She reviewed her notes with the sorcerer, who nodded in agreement. Then she clasped her hands together. "The draft will not need your service at this time."

Mr. P jumped to his feet, clapping. "Congratulations, Rye. Come get your pin."

Rye didn't move. The guards were being unfair. They punished him for his father, but he had already been punished enough. His father died, too, during the war. He was strong but not omnipotent, and the Guard blamed him for it. "You said there were five scenarios."

"There are five for those who make it that far," the animalist said.

"My organs formed properly," Rye argued. "My blood pH levels were perfect. All my feathers were the same length. You couldn't see from all the way over there."

She squinted. "Your feathers were all the same color as well, but all three breeds of tipit have white tail feathers and wing tips. Your morph took over a minute. Your return to human was sloppy. It looked like you didn't even manage the process at all and depended completely on the Correction Factor."

The sorcerer nodded.

Rye jerked his head back. Everyone relied on the Correction Factor. It was the only reason children were allowed to practice magic. It was a safety net that fixed simple spell mistakes and handled necessities like returning an animalist to human if they failed a morph instead of letting them die in a malformed body. The hope of making it to the forest was dimming. "I can't practice at school. I can barely practice at home. I didn't make any of the major mistakes."

"Come get your pin," Mr. P said, shaking it at him. "Other children are waiting to declare their magic."

"I want to join the Guard," Rye said. It was the first time he'd said it aloud since the draft started two years ago. The guards whispered something back and forth. Despite their prejudice, in a time when children were terrified of the organization, he was the best they would get. "I can't do instinct stacking yet, but I have good instinct control. I promise I will be stronger than my father."

The animalist's eyes softened for a moment. "It is refreshing to see someone eager to contribute, but your speed is too slow. It's not your technique. I'm sorry."

"We lost a lot of people in the Battle of Ki, but they can only be replaced by those with sufficient strength," the sorcerer said.

Mr. P stood up, holding out the pin.

Rye backed up until he hit the wall. "No, no, no, no, no."

"Welcome to animalism," Mr. P said as he clipped the green and white pin to Rye. "You're supposed to be happy."

It was the first time he had failed anything unintentionally. He failed many school exams to please his mother, but he wasn't supposed to fail this one. It was like a morph. He had pretended to be bad at magic for so long that he was now bad at it. He transformed into a horrible animalist. He would never be a guard. He would be trapped under the safe and boring dome for the rest of his life.

He wiped the tears from his eyes before he left the room.

Chapter 2 - Dre

The angle was all wrong. It was too narrow. Dre Word brushed the marking off the ground and drew another one. Dirt and chalk caked on his hands. Alaan stood at the focal point of the angle, tilting his head from side to side. His ridiculous hairstyle looked like a fin hidden under a thin layer of a dark bush. It was called a mohawk or something similar. Alaan thought he was trendy, but he wasn't. He changed his hair every year, and no one bothered to copy it. At least he was still cute with smooth dark skin, dark eyes, and high cheekbones. Other than the hair and the scar over his right eye, he was the mirror image of Dre. He was his twin.

Behind Alaan, sewing machines and mannequins lined the back wall. The floor mats and metal rings hanging from the ceiling poorly concealed that the gym used to be a garment factory. Dre wheeled a mannequin to one end of the V. He moved to the other. "Look between us. Turn until we are both in view," he said. Dre held up three wiggling fingers. "How many?"

Alaan wrinkled his forehead. "Two? No, Four?"

"The angle between the mannequin and I is one hundred twenty degrees. It's the field of vision. You see us at the same time, but not our details." Dre slid to the side, away from the mannequin.

Alaan turned to him. "Aah...more than that, and I am forced to attack one of you at a time."

"Exactly, divided attention is key."

"Sneaky, sneaky."

"It's just geometry." Dre bent his arms and wrists at ninety-degree angles. He framed his face. This dance style started in clubs but was now taught at the prestigious noble dance academies.

"That's not geometry. It's how our eyes work," Alaan said.

Dre rolled his eyes. "Whichever."

Alaan laughed. "Was this in the Magic and Martial Arts material?"

"Of course not. Those lessons are for normal people. We aren't normal people," Dre said. The twins were born with a magical deficit. Despite being only a couple of years away from becoming adults, they individually had the magical strength of preteens. Wizardry was about balancing light energy that lifted the caster and dark energy that pressed them down. Instead of being ineffective at both, they decided to specialize in one. They had to create new tactics to compensate. "When we end the draft, the history books will say that we did it with style. Besides, two years surrounded by mannequins who don't applaud is enough for me."

Alaan smirked. "You're right. We have it so hard with our private gym."

Dre drew more lines. "We'll review angles for two opponents. We can't leave anything to chance. We'll likely have to carry the group's average."

The MMA was a new home study program out of the Guard aimed at replacing the draft that required kids to leave their families. Years ago, most kids wanted to join the Guard. The original entrance exam was the biggest competition in the country. Only the best were accepted. Now, children failed in school to avoid service, and those who showed an ounce of potential were reluctantly selected. The draft wasn't working, and finally, the

Guard realized it. Dre and Alaan were part of a group of testers for the MMA and today was the first review of their progress.

When the twins finished the angles exercises, Alaan left the gym, carefully sneaking out the back door. Dre waited a few minutes, then followed after him, pulling up his hood. Trash bins formed a corridor down the alleyway. The stench of rotting meat burned Dre's nose. The backs of the buildings were various shades of blue, red, yellow, and green. Some were factories. The others belonged to nosey neighbors who didn't know there was a back exit to their house. He slid along bricked walls and double-checked around corners. The paparazzi usually camped out in front, but every once in a while, someone was adventurous.

He crept down a side alley that ended in an old, forgotten stairwell without a sign. Alaan's head dipped out of sight as he descended. Dre checked one last time over his shoulder before going down himself. There was no one following him. The stairs were metal, but the tunnel walls were grey stone. Sunlight dimmed until everything faded to black when he reached the bottom of the third flight. He steadied himself with a hand on the wall.

A slight pull on his skin preceded his brother's use of wizardry. Bits of magical light flickered to life, the white dots illuminating Alaan. They fluttered around him like insects. Then he stretched his arms wide, and the warm energy brushed against Dre, expanding and brightening the tunnel. It had been years since Dre last tried light energy. That half of wizardry was for Alaan. Dre practiced exclusively with dark.

Furry rodents with long tails scurried out of sight along the brick pathway. The tunnel was constructed before the dome, when the city was exposed to the desert heat. Now, it was their private passage.

They traversed the city unnoticed and resurfaced in the center of Poli at another stairwell that people ignored. Tall metal and glass buildings stretched to the sky, nearly touching the dome. They were all black and didn't match the colorful palettes of traditional buildings, but they were the city's pride. They were a testament to technology. They challenged the old theory that science imitated magic. Magic couldn't make structures that big alone.

The oldest structure in the city was a fat white marble Castle, the home of the Guard. The Lynitian emblem of six overlapping circles within a seventh circle was chiseled on the front. A waterless moat surrounded the Castle. A stream of people crossed the bridge that connected the antiquated building with the only city in Lynit that didn't worship it. It was the most people Dre had seen in a long while.

Alaan crossed the bridge first. He shouldered through a mix of civilians and guards in uniform. Dre kept his head down and trailed a safe distance behind. He almost made it inside before someone snapped his photo. The man pushed his small glasses up his nose, a broad grin on his scruffy face. His press badge hung around his neck.

"I can't believe it. You're one of the Poli Twins," he said.

Dre nodded but continued walking.

The reporter caught up. "Have you returned? What brings you to the Castle?"

Other people on the bridge noticed the exchange, too, and stopped.

Alaan backtracked. "A little visit," he said to the small crowd.

Dre hummed for a moment, then tilted his head to the side. "A little performance." It would be their first one in two years. They used to train publicly and participate in tournaments before the draft started. Their last fight was part of a two-versus-two tournament against adults. They were only fifteen but managed to come in second place to the Balison sisters. Fans chanted "Poli Twins." Everyone had heard of them because of their birth, but now they were more famous than any noble because of how they performed together in the ring. Despite their low magical strength, they discovered a wizardry skill that more than made up for it.

The reporter dug into a satchel and pulled out a small grey orb. "Are you performing for the Prince and Princess?"

People cheered.

"Sorry, gotta go," Alaan said as he pulled Dre along.

They slipped inside the Castle. Guards stopped anyone who didn't work there from following. The hallways seemed smaller than they used to be. The chandeliers were only a jump away. The floors were still as reflective as a mirror. Dre waved at himself. He was over a foot shorter the last time he was here.

"We aren't performing," Alaan said in his ear.

"Anytime we are in public, it's a performance," Dre said. "We are the Poli Twins. It's a role."

"Don't get us in trouble," Alaan said.

"I didn't show any magic, only words. It was like flirting. I can't help that I'm a flirt," Dre said, then winked. Alaan shook his head and pulled Dre to the front desk.

The receptionist greeted them, asked for an autograph, then escorted them through the building. Curious guards followed.

"Were you drafted?" someone asked.

"No," Dre huffed. Not only would he not turn himself into the Guard if we were, but he failed the exam like everyone else. He tried his best during the exam because it didn't matter. His magic was well known. There was nothing he could hide. Since each child was tested individually, Dre and Alaan had nothing to worry about. The Guard was impressed by their skill but valued power more.

"What are you doing here?" Someone said.

"Don't answer that," Alaan said in Dre's ear.

Dre locked his lips shut with an imaginary key.

"Here we are," the receptionist said as they approached thick stone doors. A sign on the wall read, "Magic and Martial Arts Personnel Only."

A psychic guard in purple robes waited on the other side. His dark eyes glowed against his brown skin. A neat shape-up framed his face. This man was fine.

"Hi," Dre said, pitching his voice flirtatiously.

The guard glanced at Dre. He checked his clipboard, then waved the twins through.

Dre pouted. "He could have at least smiled. I am seventeen. I am practically an adult."

Alaan snickered.

The exam room was really two rooms. The main room was rectangular. Twelve guards, two of each type of magic, stood in neat lines at the center. Their uniform colors identified them. Purple was for psychics; black and gold for sorcerers; green and white for animalists; blue and red for protectors; blue, green, red, and white for elemental mages; and black and white for wizards. Behind them, small window cutouts looked into a second room of gigastone, the most magic-nullifying material in the world.

Dre and Alaan joined the clump of fourteen jittery MMA participants packed on the left side of the room. The youngest boy, Gron, was a fifteen-year-old newly minted sorcerer with arms too long for his body and a cute fuzz growing on his upper lip. At the introduction to the MMA program, Gron screamed and begged for a picture with them, but no one had a camera. Today, he had a camera.

The oldest participant, Zalora, was taller than Dre. Her hair was pulled up into a neat top bun. She wore a loose jumpsuit cinched to her waist by a large belt. Boredom covered her face like a mask, but she watched the guards. The other students ranged between the two but were all from Poli South Academy. It was the loose connection they shared, though Dre hadn't been to a class since he and Alaan started homeschooling almost five years ago.

Alaan approached the handsome psychic. "Do we all have to pass, or is it on an individual basis?"

"The program's success is based on how well you all perform throughout all the exams. The first exam is unique, however. We know that you have spent years hiding your magic and that it will take a little time for you to adjust to rigorous training. The minimum requirement for this test is that everyone doesn't fail it," he said.

"And if we do all fail?" Zalora said.

"Then you will all be removed from the MMA," the psychic said.

"And eligible for the draft again?" Zalora said.

The psychic nodded. A few of the participants gasped.

"We'll be fine," Dre said. When he was placed into the program, he had only one question: Would he and Alaan be tested together? An old man, the head of the MMA, responded, "There would be no point in including you otherwise."

Alaan turned around. "But everyone prepared, right?"

"I have studied secondary and tertiary disruption in the gravity and spatial rule sets," Gron said.

"I read through all the material twice. Psychic magic helps," a small girl with large dimples said.

"I learned eight new creatures," another girl said.

"I can track two locations without a communication orb," a protector boy said, tapping his chest.

Someone one-upped him and the competition continued. Gron held up a grey dilo coin and it became a betting match on who would do the best. The pot grew to thirty-five, enough money to eat off of for a week. Dre and Alaan didn't participate because no two children were better than them.

Then, the tests began. Dre slipped behind the guards. He pressed onto his toes to reach the highest viewing slit. Three large electric lampposts on the far side of the room illuminated the black space.

An elemental mage strolled to the center of the room like she owned the place, all while wearing an impractical bright yellow dress. Two elemental mage guards took their place at the front of the room. Two sorcerers went to opposite corners carrying gold paddles. They would signal when someone used the Correction Factor. The psychic waited off to the side with his clipboard.

The girl started the exam with a stomp. She punched the air and whirled her other arm around. A slight haze blurred above her. The guards ducked. One of them responded by lifting both hands quickly. Something socked into the girl, wind maybe, and knocked her off her feet. Her dress flipped over her head.

"I thought she was an elemental mage. Why can't we see her fire, electricity, or whatever element she uses?" Gron asked.

"The gigastone nullifies magic. If the lampposts in there were magical, we wouldn't be able to see them at all," Zalora said.

After a couple more minutes, the elemental mage exited the room with the psychic, who said that she had failed the test. She quietly walked over to a table of refreshments and poured a glass of water.

The next test didn't go any better. Gron and the two sorcerer guards faced each other. Their mouths moved, likely casting and counter-spelling each other, but all the while, the guards held up the gold paddles. Gron failed because he depended too heavily on the Correction Factor. The next seven children failed after that. None looked Dre in the eye. They joined the yellow-dress elemental mage.

For Zalora's test, a protector pulled a wollopin out of a small cage. It was as long as a hand with a humanoid shape and wings. Its body was covered in a bone-like exoskeleton. The creature flapped erratically in the protector's grip as she raised it high, then slammed it on the ground. Dre flinched even though he had seen this before and wollopins didn't feel pain. The imagined crunch rang in his ears. Protection magic was divided into two major areas: shielding and healing. Unfortunately, the only way to test healing skills at will was to injure another living thing.

Zalora moved quickly. The red glow of healing magic didn't show, but the creature responded to the effects. A moment later, it shot up to the ceiling and out of reach. The next creature was a ten-foot-long sedated serpent with two tails. Its black head was shaped like an arrow and used for digging. The protector cut it with a blade, then Zalora stitched its flesh together.

When they moved on to shielding exercises, Zalora struggled. The guards threw metal balls at her. The first few ricocheted off the normally blue but currently invisible barrier she held up. After she was directed to shield herself and two other spots, the metal balls passed through all three of her shields. And that was enough to make her fail.

"I can't tell if the test is difficult or if they are all bad at magic," Alaan said.

"Mmmhm," Dre said. "Whichever the case, the draft is not going to end at this rate."

"You're not bad at magic," someone said. Dre spun around, then jerked his head back, banging it against the wall. Three well-dressed civilian nobles were close, too close, too creepy. He couldn't tell whether they wanted to eat him or kiss him. Somehow, they had bribed their way into the MMA area.

"Hello," Dre and Alaan said simultaneously. The nobles flinched and backed away, as many did when the twins acted as one, which was why they did it.

The woman in a red dress with white shoes and a blue-green bracelet was a Cast, a descendent of the inventor of elemental magic. Her family managed the weather inside the dome and owned almost two-thirds of farmable land. Her eyebrows looked as if they were held high by her tight cornrows. She held her pregnant belly as she grinned. The man in the white robe fanned himself. A round green hat adorned with embroidered patterns sat on his head like a toy crown. He was a Finrar, a descendant of the inventor of animalism. His family was an odd mix of spies and diplomats. They mimicked foreign customs to perfection and dodged uncomfortable situations. The third man nodded at Dre. He wore all black.

"He's Yordin," Alaan whispered. "His skin is the whiteness."

"Clever, clever," Dre said. The inventor of wizardry family's colors were black and white. Though wizardry made them the most versatile fighters, they equally kept their ear in politics. They started the Guard, which turned out to be the balance they were looking for. "Noble fashion rarely disappoints." Magic colors were really noble family colors. Children wore them on their pins and guards on their uniforms, but for nobles, it was a way to flaunt their heritage. So they did it as tastefully as possible.

"I am sure you are well prepared for the test. The Poli Twins always give a good show. I have seen you perform several times when you were younger and mixed animalism, elemental magic, and wizardry. Can you still use all three?" the Finrar asked. He adjusted his hat.

Alaan sighed. "We are seventeen."

"When was the last time you tried?" the Cast said as she leaned in. The fragrance of momonut oil wafted from her. "Nobles keep a second magic longer than average. The real cutoff, the Kertic cutoff, is nineteen."

"Did you declare animalism?" the Finrar said, smiling.

"We declared wizardry. I assumed anyone who wanted to know, knew," Alaan said.

"It would be terribly impolite not to ask you directly," Finrar said, mimicking a forehead wipe.

"I always knew you would stick to wizardry," the Yordin said.

"So did most people," Dre said. Instead of balancing light and dark energy internally as everyone else did, the twins figured out how to share it between them.

"It wasn't because of your ability. It's the way you use magic. The Yordin in you is clear," he said.

A shriek slipped from Dre and he fell into Alaan. The two erupted in laughter. The nobles frowned.

"Wait, wait, wait, wait, are you serious?" Dre said, holding up a hand.

"I am sure of it," he said.

Dre pulled up his sleeve and stretched his dark arm next to the pale, freckled Yordin. "The Cast tried many times before to convince us, themselves, the world, that we were Cast. At least that was plausible. But Yordin? We aren't this dark by chance. Have you seen our parents or grandparents? Actually, we have sketches of our great, great, great, great grandparents, and they look just like this. Our respect was earned, but nice try," Dre said. Nobles couldn't stand that Dre and Alaan were so talented, so famous, and had no connection to them. The Yordin were willing to bend backward to resolve that dissonance since the Poli Twins were another proof that nobility wasn't that special after all.

The Yordin's eyes leveled and his jaw tightened. "And what of your lineage one thousand three hundred ten years ago?"

Dre rolled his eyes.

Alaan threw up his hands. "No one has records that far back, not even you."

"That's the point. Lynit was founded by magic, shaped by it, and will end by it. You lived your life surrounded by people who take for granted the magic that was shared with them, but you respect the craft. You bring a fresh take to the meaning of balance and creativity. It is in the way you move together with an organic harmony of opposite styles. You add a performative flare that makes your work seem easy and unbelievable all at once. That's how a Yordin uses wizardry. That's what makes you Yordin. Magic is passed down, but not through blood."

The Finrar covered his mouth.

"That's enough," the Cast said, grabbing the Yordin's arm.

"Ahh..." Alaan said, nodding at the Yordin. He docked his chin in the crux of his thumb and pointing finger. "Dre, this is like the time you said that you were changing your last name to Sass because you were convinced you were channeling it from some distant ancestor."

The Cast's and Finrar's jaws dropped. Dre was to sass what Alaan was to sarcasm. They could have been known as the S and S Twins just as easily.

"Word," someone called. The psychic waited at the entrance to the exam room.

Dre waved goodbye to the dumbfounded nobles. The Yordin had said something he probably wasn't supposed to say. Nobles never officially said that magic passed through blood, but they acted like it did and the general population believed it so. It was one of the reasons Dre took being a Poli Twin so seriously. Like the first non-noble elite, he and Alaan were more than just celebrities. They were examples that didn't fit into the noble narrative. Maybe six people one thousand three hundred years ago were special because they each invented a magic, but definitely not their entire lineage. Even Kertic, the source of the royal line, was the only person ever able to maintain the ability to use all six magics into adulthood. His descendants did achieve great things, but nothing that merited them inheriting the throne by birthright. And all this time, the nobles knew it too. Magic didn't pass down through blood because blood was made of matter, and magic was made of spirit energy.

The psychic scratched his neck, then checked his clipboard. "Which one of you is Dre?"

"I am."

"You will go first, then Alaan."

"What do you mean?"

The psychic repeated himself. Dre shook his head, then repeated himself more slowly.

"Ohhhh," Alaan said. "We have to take it separately."

"But we are supposed to be tested together," Dre said. It was the one thing the old man who ran the program had promised. "Where is Elite Palow?"

The psychic held up the clipboard. "I have sixteen names on my list. I will do sixteen tests."

Alaan steadied Dre's shoulders. "Listen. To end the draft, we have to prove that the MMA works for everyone. It's meaningless if we can't pass it separately. We are already extraordinary together."

"But, but..." Dre said. He looked around. Everyone was watching him. It was like when he was ten and his year-end exams were held on the school field. He was tested in each magic. Slithlor, the then head of foreign magic research, had come to watch. Thousands of others gathered to gawk at Dre fail every test thrown at him. It was the second time Dre was in the news since birth. All the children laughed while the adults took notes.

"We'll do fine," Alaan said, then backed away. His smile reached his eyes, but he wasn't showing any teeth. It was the smile he gave to fans he didn't like or when he thought he had gotten away with something.

Dre squinted. "You've been practicing with dark energy." It was the only way Alaan could have maintained any ounce of confidence.

His smile stretched into a grin. "A little."

"Not this again." Dre slapped his forehead. Alaan was awful at dark energy. Every hour spent not practicing with light was a waste. "We're doomed. The draft is going to last forever."

Chapter 3 - Rye

Chalk dust wafted around Mr. P as he drew, erased, and redrew a brist on the board. The canine was small, with thin red fur that blended with the desert dirt. Rye lazily copied the image onto a metallic sheet of paper with fast-drying ink. He didn't bother with proportions, nor did he use multiple shades to capture the depth of the fur.

Mr. P returned to his desk and flipped through a stack of crinkly folders. He placed his chalk-covered hands on his waist. "Anyone complete last night's homework?"

Silence. The other students hadn't done their homework from their first day as fully-fledged animalists either. Rye wanted to do it, but his mother came home late from work and he was stuck babysitting his brother. He only had enough time to practice his tipit morph a few times. The animalist's remarks during his exam had been harsh but true. He had confirmed average morphing times in a textbook. He lacked speed. His morph was nowhere close to under a minute, though he had shaved off about five seconds last night.

"As I said, even if you don't turn in the paperwork, please practice magic at home. These courses are critical; if you don't learn the skills now, it will be more difficult to pick them up later. I understand that you are afraid of the draft, but don't limit your future with magic. Unless, of course, you are all content with magicless careers. I hear that there has always been a shortage of librarians."

Rye raised a hand. "How could someone increase their morphing speed?" If he wanted to attempt the regular Guard entrance exam in four years, he needed to focus on that.

Mr. P dropped his arms. "Well, it depends on your magical strength, but there are anatomy tricks to speed it up."

"How do we measure our strength?"

Mr. P stepped around to the front of his desk. "Unlike the other magics, ours is internal. The only measure is morphing speed."

"How do we improve it?"

"Practice."

"Great." Rye leaned back in his seat. Practice, practice, practice. It was all the teachers said. But there was no place to practice. He'd broken his bed twice already. If he morphed in a public park, he would probably make the news as the first child in years to use magic outside. Oron would have tips, but his seat remained empty in the room. He hadn't returned to school. He was likely on vacation with his family, enjoying their last days together.

"Have you ever tried to explain to someone how to separate a creature's instincts from your own?" Mr. P asked. "There are some things you can't read in a book."

Rye tried to explain it to his brother once. Felix kept comparing it to separating thoughts, but instincts weren't thoughts. Instincts were a combination of biology, habits, knowledge, experiences, fears, and repeated neurological pathways in the brain. And this influenced thoughts. Separating instincts was more about understanding behavioral patterns and subtracting the pieces that didn't serve the situation. It was a case-by-case reevaluation of the self.

A knock clanked against the classroom door. Two psychic guards waited in the hall. Dark purple overcoats fitted neatly against their torsos and draped over their legs. Their mouths and chins were tucked behind high collars that obscured spell words, though psychics didn't need their mouths to spellcast or speak. For them, it was a tool of intimidation.

Mr. P touched a hand to his chest, leaving a chalk print. He stepped out. A few seconds later, his arms flew about as he spoke and his voice rose almost to the point of clarity behind the closed door. Some kids whispered.

Mr. P returned. "Rye," he said. His voice was soft.

Several people gasped, including Rye. Not only was he not a psychic, it wasn't even one of the three magics he selected years ago. Rye had only seen a kid get drafted once. Almost two years ago, a sorcerer handed a draft order to his friend Drime, who was also a sorcerer. But maybe the matching magics was only a coincidence.

Rye stood up. The Guard could have observed his morphing practice somehow and was impressed with the progress. At that rate of improvement, in a few years, he could be the first to achieve instant morphs. That would make him an elite, for sure.

He walked smoothly out of the room. When the door clicked shut behind him, he said, "What made you change your mind?"

The women shared a glance.

The larger one with wide eyes and a curved nose leaned in. "Follow us, please," she said, her words clear through the fabric around her face.

He searched their hands, but neither held a brown slip of paper.

Something pressed against glass. Behind him, his classmates watched. A few shamelessly flattened their ears against the window. Mr. P stood in the background, on the verge of tears.

Rye's voice dropped to a whisper. "This isn't the draft?"

The guards shook their heads. Rye bit his lip. This was very odd behavior. Today wasn't career day and Rye wasn't a psychic.

Nothing had happened to his mother or brother because civilian protectors would deliver that news.

Rye followed them. They ignored the white archway that led out of school and went deeper into the building past more windows packed tight with terrified peers and frustrated teachers. His instincts sensed something, but it wasn't danger. The Guard was the definition of safety. If anything, he was lucky. They had selected him for an important task and he didn't need to know the facts to obey. It wasn't his place to question their motives.

Down the hall, a boy sobbed. He hobbled behind another pair of psychics. They were headed in the same direction, towards the auditorium, though the boy's feet were bound in purple chains. The hallway echoed with footsteps and sniffles, the chains ringing a lullaby. It was like an unknown ceremony, a procession. Rye lengthened his stride and mimicked his escort's still shoulders.

A man and woman, also psychic guards in purple robes, stood post outside the tarnished silver auditorium doors. Their collars were up as well. They opened the doors wordlessly when Rye arrived. Inside, the crying boy's chains softened into dough. The links weren't made of metal but of condensed mental energy. Slowly, they dissolved into purple vapor, then faded away as if they never existed.

The boy didn't run because there was nowhere to go. A clump of guards in identical purple overcoats waited on the stage where the principal gave the yearly address. They didn't talk amongst themselves, as trained soldiers didn't when on a mission. Over a dozen children were also in the room. Their faces were wet. Rye controlled his smile and started down the steps. The audience turned back to the mass of guards, but two faces stayed on him.

The first one was his friend Hila. Her curly hair fuzzed around her face and the "C" shaped birthmark along her jaw looked like a stain. Her usually confident eyes were wide and soft like a toddler's.

That look of despair pierced him. He grabbed the rail to steady himself.

Lakree sat next to her. His neatly twisted dreads were oddly tied up into a playful bow that didn't match his permanently serious face. His skin was a light brown, a mix of the dark and pale complexions of his Cast and Yordin parents, and his coarse blond hair was another mix. They first met seven years ago in the Castle. Rye's parents were guards and Lakree's were noble, so they were always there. Lakree greeted him one day and Rye stared back dumbstruck.

noble guards were generally friendly to Rye because of his dad, but rarely civilian noble adults, and definitely not their children. Lakree started talking about comic books and magic. He fantasized about traveling the world. Rye used to have such a crush on him back then. It took Rye years to get over it.

"You didn't get drafted, right?" Hila said when he sat down.

Rye shook his head.

She hugged him and rubbed his back. Her pin clinked against his.

He flicked the red, white, blue, and green pin, an elemental mage's pin. "You are fully Lynitian now."

She was the only foreign-born person in the school, likely the nation. After the Battle of Ki, her father was deported, along with all other foreigners. Her Lynitian mother wasn't enough rationale for her to be allowed to stay, but her ability to use Lynitian magic was. Now, she was a declared elemental mage. There was no better proof of citizenship.

"And now I have the same problems as everyone else," she said, turning her gaze back to the guards.

"Were you drafted?" Rye asked Lakree.

Lakree pointed at the crying boy who had entered with Rye. "That's what it looks like when someone is drafted."

"How could you fail?" Rye said.

Lakree's family didn't fear the Guard. They were top government officials who created the laws that the Guard enforced. They didn't ban him from public displays of magic like most parents did to their children. That was his own rule. "At the least, they would have known you were faking it."

Lakree tapped his chest. A black and gold pin blended in with his dark outfit. "I confused them. I picked sorcery."

"No way," Rye said slowly. Lakree pointed at his complex hairstyle. Bows and knots were sorcery symbols. He always liked sorcery, but it was invented by the Vous, not his parents' Yordin and Cast families. His connection to wizardry and elemental magic was in his blood. "Unless you are part Vous too somewhere down the line."

Rye didn't have that special connection to magic, but the Guard was the bridge between an ordinary civilian and excellence. His father was proof, despite what the Guard said about him now. The Guard was the only reason Lynit survived. With everyone trained in one of six forms of magic, the nation could destroy itself overnight, either by accidental spells or fanatics. That's why there was the Guard, to protect Lynit from itself and then from others.

Lakree held up his hands. "No, no, I am not a Vous yet. I still have to do a Verbindous. I have to prove that I deserve that name. The Vous can manipulate gravity and molecular forces while counterspelling another sorcerer at the same time. They predict foreign political evolutions by analyzing complex chains of cause and effect. They are the ones in the Guard that maintain the Correction Factor. To be a part of that family, I have a lot of work ahead of me. I am just a regular sorcerer for now."

"You won't be just a sorcerer," Rye said. In ten years, Lakree would probably break new ground in sorcery like his ancestors did before him. The Verbindous was just a fancy noble ceremony for acknowledging the skills they were born with.

"But he will always be our Lakree," Hila said. She plucked a dread hanging on the side of his face.

He winced. "I am transferring to a Vous school soon," he said in a single breath.

"No," Hila said, her voice shooting up an octave. Everyone turned around.

Rye huffed. "That explains it. You didn't want to be drafted because you always had something better waiting for you." noble schools were the only education better than what the draft offered.

"My parents are liberal, but I pushed it by picking a magic neither can help me with. They will make sure I get a proper education. If I don't make Vous…" he said.

"You can't leave us, too," Hila said. It wasn't a command. It was a plea. The three of them used to be part of a group of four until Drime was taken. By now, he would be in shape and able to use sorcery like a soldier.

Lakree shifted in his seat. He fidgeted with his fingernails.

This was the start of the splinter that would divide Rye and Lakree, even though they both wanted to leave the dome. Lakree was destined for whatever he desired, but Rye had to work for it. Now that Rye wasn't drafted, his chances of meeting up with Lakree in the Guard faded to zero. The gap in their skills would grow until Rye couldn't catch up. A noble guard who traveled the world protecting Lynit and an ordinary civilian wouldn't be able to maintain a friendship. It was probably why the other noble kids didn't bother speaking to Rye in the Castle. If he didn't prove himself, he would only waste Lakree's time. Rye blinked back a tear.

A professorial man sifted to the front of the stage. He was significantly older than the rest of his colleagues and a white "E" was stitched on his chest. He was the replacement for the previous elite psychic who'd died during the Battle of Ki and the only guessable noble of the group. At least in the Guard, nobles looked like everyone else. Nobles didn't wear additional pieces of their family's colors when in uniform. But, if a second elite weren't noble, it would have made the news. Therefore, the old man was Palow, a descendant of the inventor of psychic magic. His family was full of judges, interrogators, and therapists.

He approached the podium, a wooden structure and the most expensive item in the stone and metal school. He surveyed the room for a few minutes, drinking in the sobs until the students tired or acquiesced.

"Thank you all for coming," he said, his voice deep but soft.

Hila shifted in her seat. "We didn't have a choice," she said. She rubbed at her bruised ankles. She must have tried to run. Rye tapped his head to her shoulder. He wouldn't have expected anything less.

"Will the sorcerers raise your hands, please? I can't see the pins from here," he said. Three nervous students raised their arms. "In the yellow shirt, what is the shortest spell you know?" He signaled her to stand.

She started shaking. She rose but didn't answer.

"Dead," the old man said.

She dropped back into her seat. She wasn't harmed. She simply looked confused.

The raised hands fell.

"Keep them up. If you are alone and your opponent is an arm's length away, what do you do?" He glided his arm over to Rye, no, to Lakree.

"You run," he said through clenched teeth.

"They attack and you are dead. Would it not be best to hinder their ability to use magic? A sharp blow to the throat or head disorients. It may provide enough time to cast a spell," he said.

Sorcerers' ability to see and edit the universe's rules was powerful, but the universe fought them every step of the way. When they changed something, the golden rules broke out in chaos, symbols whipping around angrily, smashing into each other and the effect rippling down onto other properties. This could trigger unexpected responses that could either undo the change or tear a hole in the fabric of space. As they patched these side effects, they were completely vulnerable. They couldn't see the rules and the physical world simultaneously. During battle, they would never let anyone get close to them. This old man's suggestion would never apply. Rye tilted his head.

"Protectors, your difficulties with shielding lie in accurately tracking the relative locations of those you wish to protect. What happens when you have shielded a fixed position, but your position is not static?" he asked. He nodded encouragingly at a girl two rows down.

"Think of them as your center point and that you are moving around them," she said.

"Correct. What do you do if both parties are moving?" he asked. No one answered. "If they have a communication orb, the signal it emits does the tracking for you."

"Ahhh," two protectors said.

"What is this?" Rye asked.

Hila and Lakree were silent as if transfixed. In the several years of their friendship, it was a first. A moment rarely passed when neither tried to contradict whoever was speaking. More than thirty guards had been involved in bringing these children together. They hadn't come to casually discuss magic. Today wasn't career day.

"And psychics, you have it the hardest. You can practice manipulating mental energy to lift objects, perceive everything covered in your energy with your eyes closed, and render the mental energy invisible to the eye if you are skilled. However, navigating a person's mind is tricky and dangerous to practice. You have always needed an expert psychic to guide you through the process. Now, we plan to change that. You will have your own personal tutor with you at all times."

The students with purple pins sat up straight in their seats.

The old man continued. "Over thirteen hundred years ago, before the founding of Lynit, we struggled in the desert. Water was scarce and our greatest enemy was the sun. We found ways to co-exist with the powerful quitols and hunt the tasty brist. At a population of only a few thousand, we managed to survive. It wasn't until the well-known six individuals: Vous, Cast, Palow, Finar, Yordin, and Pol discovered the six forms of Lynitian magic that we began to grow as a people.

"After Virt was founded, a new era began, the era of discovery. We learned more in those first three hundred years than in the remaining one thousand. This is true for every domain, from politics to philosophy to physics. The key ingredient was an environment that encouraged us to test any imaginable theory. This is what we need now.

"You were all selected to be in a new program called 'Magic and Martial Arts.' It is a home study program where you train in your free time. You won't have to leave your family or stop going to school. If this program works, we will end Slithlor's draft. The challenge is that we need a new generation of guards but aren't receiving enough qualified candidates through current channels. The Correction Factor allows children to practice magic safely but creates a handicap if proper technique isn't learned. Most of the Guard's work is abroad and there is no Correction Factor outside Lynit. We are testing the MMA on a few cohorts to determine if this can be rolled out to everyone. To ensure the quality of the experiment, all eighteen of you are now exempt from the draft."

Rye jumped to his feet. This was perfect. It was a second chance to get properly trained. He threw his hands into the air. "Yeeessssss."

He wasn't the only one. The other kids screamed, too, all except Hila and Lakree.

"They trust me?" Hila said as she leaned back in her chair. Until yesterday, she had barely been classed as Lynitian. Now, she was in a Guard pilot program.

After everyone calmed down, Lakree stood up. "You are Palow. My parents are Cast and Yordin. You cannot lie to me." His tone was different, a little deeper. It was his noble voice, which usually got him whatever he asked for.

The old man said, "Official documents stating your exemption status will be delivered to your homes this evening."

"What's the new technique?" Lakree said. "There must be a—"

Hila slapped a hand over his mouth. She twisted his head towards her, but he kept his wild eyes on the elite. The room quieted.

Rye grabbed Lakree's hand. "Don't ruin this for everyone else." One word to his family and this fledgling program could be canceled. Most of the captains were noble.

"We are using a new process. These psychics will implant the curriculum into your mind. It will be dense. It will be challenging. But if I am right, it will be faster to learn than reading a book and bring some of the advantages of having an instructor with you. However, the one caveat is that the material is temporary. It will begin to fade from the moment it is placed. You must not only read the material. You must study it and ingrain it in your reflexes. We don't have the bandwidth to train the number of children we would like to, which is why we are giving you a chance to train yourselves. And I believe you can do it. You were all good students once." He winked. "We will have exams every month to review your progress. This could become the largest scale training program conducted by the Guard."

"But why us three?" Lakree said, pointing to Rye and Hila. He seemed not to care about the other children. "We don't have anything in common."

They didn't. The son of a disgraced guard, a foreigner, and a noble made for an unlikely friendship. Being placed in the same Guard program was odd.

"Who cares?" Hila said and hugged him. A grin broke across his face. She rustled his hair and they laughed. Rye hugged them both. He hugged the kids in the row below.

"Now open your minds," the old man said.

Purple snow, speckles of psychic energy, rose above the guards, then blew out. Rye closed his eyes, imagining a black door on his forehead nestled between his equally dark eyebrows. He put in white marble hinges and a green knob. The handle twisted and the door swung open. Inside was empty, like a tunnel stretching to infinity. Outside, a blip of light hung in blank space.

He filled in the rest of the image with his memory of the room, gray stone benches and the children seated on them. He pushed his vision further, encompassing more and more rows of empty seats until it reached a purple mass, a heap of bodies and mist. A spark floated off to the side. As he focused on it, the image of a woman resolved, her face uncovered by her collar.

Her cheeks were flushed and she looked less cold than when she pulled him from class. The light propagated from her, rising and falling in a wave. Colors flickered from within, maroon, cyan, and yellow, mingling, separating, like vibrations. When it reached his door and blocked the view of everything else, it stopped. A string of images, flat motion, rotated in place. The first picture was of a torsit, an orange and brown furless creature with two long legs and small arms tucked close to its slender body.

Rye pulled in the figure. It warmed his forehead with a rippling pulse. The other images zipped past behind it, too fast to be identified. The torsit's angled head bobbed as if it was counting or setting a tempo. Around the sixth beat, it crouched low, head still bouncing. Three counts later, it leaped into the air. As it reached the jump's apex, it bent at the waist and flipped forward. Rye cringed as his sternum tightened with the pang of falling. With a foot extended, the creature hit a dark figure that appeared. The shape crumbled and the creature landed, frozen again.

The image flipped around. On the backside, anatomical diagrams panned and zoomed. Rye released the card and it joined the blur. Colors, sounds, and instructions danced through his endless tunnel, storing themselves somewhere in his mind. This was one of the most amazing things he had ever experienced. He was searching for access to the secret Guard libraries, but now loads of their information was in his head. He clenched his fists. When the images stopped, he opened his eyes, panting.

"It is done. Go home and practice. Your first test will be in a month," the old man said.

The guards exited the room, filing into neat lines, uniforms flapping out the door. The old man thanked his audience before he crossed the threshold, concluding the ceremony.

A chant started.

"We will end the draft."

"We will end the draft."

"We will end the draft."

"We will end the draft."

"I will be a guard," Rye said, then joined in with his new brothers and sisters.

The torsit danced, flipping around in his head, tempting him. Small lizards with camouflaging scales and white felines swished about, luring his attention into the bright spaces of his mind. He followed them and explored. Magic was safe again. He wouldn't have to pretend anymore. The road ahead was long, but the forest and the unknown creatures beyond were within reach.

He skipped all the way home.

A thin letter waited on the copper table in the foyer. It was the second one from the Guard and the seal was broken.

He searched the living room, the kitchen, and his mother's room, but she wasn't home. He soon found Felix playing with a metal block in his bedroom. Felix pushed it across the floor with mental energy, then heated it with light energy. He spoke a long stream of sorcery spells, but the spell failed. He surrounded it in the red glow of a healing spell.

"If you had to pick your three right now, which would it be?" Rye said.

Felix whirled around. His face lit up, then he jumped on Rye. "What does 'Exempt' mean?"

"It means I don't have to worry about the draft."

"Oh. I thought it meant you were gone, like Daddy," Felix said as he released his hold. "How did you pick animalism?"

Rye's favorite part about animalism was that no matter the situation, there existed a creature that was naturally capable of handling it. If he fell into a lake, he could turn into a fish. The water was still there, but it was no longer a problem. Or if he were cold, he would grow fur. "It picked me. You will feel it, too. You just need time."

Rye returned to the letter in the living room. He pressed it close to his chest. Whether he was drafted or in the new Magic and Martial Arts program, it didn't matter. Practicing magic mattered. Morphing in under a minute mattered and so did reducing his dependence on the Correction Factor.

Dad's portrait hung on the wall. He grinned big. He was always smiling, whether in his green and white Guard uniform or his favorite old shirt. Once, in a park, a man played with his grandson. While chasing after him, he tripped and his toupee fell off. The grandson laughed, then kicked the hair around as the man chased after him. Rye and his father couldn't stop laughing until the man approached. They quickly apologized, then Dad said, "We can't control the world, but we can control ourselves." It was an animalism phrase. They couldn't stop that moment from being funny, but they could stop themselves from laughing at that man in public. Later, it became a joke in formal situations. Rye and his father would look at each other and say "toupee," then they tried their best not to laugh, though they usually failed.

"I'll make you proud," Rye said. The MMA gave him a head start on his career. It was a reorientation to compensate for the shadow of the draft, which ended up limiting his magic progression.

He went into his mother's room. An expansive map covered a wall. The three continents, El, Aminal, and Davi, were thick with cramped writing identifying geological features. The highest peak in the world was north of Lynit. The longest river divided Aminal into two unequal pieces. Seven shaded regions defined the territories of the nations. Everywhere else was city-states. In those places, citizens elected anyone popular to be the leader. Then, those leaders selected regional representatives who brokered trading deals across the globe.

He traced his finger around the continent of El. There were no nations, no city-states, and an unknown quantity of undiscovered creatures. Along the coast, a note marked the sleeping grounds of diamond-backed natsin. They were the largest known land creatures in the world and more magically resistant than a quitol. The wild owned that continent. And one day, he would explore it.

Mom came home, her keys jingling as usual. He scurried out of her room. She stopped at the entrance. She was still in her work apron with a splash of yellow stained on the front. Joining the Guard was for her, too. She used to be a captain but left soon after Dad died. Rye could restore her love of the organization and create a new legacy.

Her keys clattered against the floor. Her hand trembled as it pointed at his brown letter on the table. "What is that?"

"It's not the draft."

She let out a tight breath, then read the notice. At first, she laughed, then she reread it. "No. They will use you up and throw you away like they did your father." She chucked the letter away before walking into the kitchen.

"But I'm exempt. I won't have to leave. They are giving me a chance to learn," he said.

She opened a cupboard and pulled out two jars and a loaf of bread. "You hungry? I'm starving."

He raked his hands over his head. It was like the day the draft was announced and she banned him from practicing magic in public. Her instincts were still fried by grief, though Dad had been dead for five years. She was overly sensitive. In a way, his father, or at least the memory of him, was the barrier she used to keep Rye away from the Guard.

"The Guard is my only chance to see the world, too," he said. His parents brought back stories of strange creatures and foreign magics. The world was big because of them. "And I can't do that if I can't morph in under a minute." But, more importantly, he wouldn't see Lakree again. He huffed and crossed his arms.

She cupped his face. "The Guard can turn a man into a warrior, but not a child into a man." It was a phrase his father had said many times. To new recruits, he meant it as a promise, a challenge. To Rye, his mother meant it as a warning.

Chapter 4 - Dre

The not-so-handsome psychic ushered Dre into the MMA exam room. Four guards waited inside. The same two Correction Factor expert sorcerers were in the far corners. Two wizards, a man and a woman, in different robes waited to test him. One robe was all black with white accents on the collar, shoulders, and buttons. It was the old style of guard robes, which looked like an uglier copy of the sorcerer's black and gold robes. The newer wizardry robes were pure black on the outside and all white on the inside. New guards wore their uniforms depending on their mood. This was proper Poli style.

"The exam is broken down into three sections. Two will focus on single wizardry energy usage and the third will involve both. Which do you want to do first?" the psychic said.

Dre picked dark. The wizards created a cloud of light energy and a solid dark energy disk high above themselves and a second set above Dre. The heat of the light energy warmed his head.

"The first section is simple," one of the wizard guards said. "Destroy our targets before we destroy yours. Each time you destroy ours, you move to a more difficult round. When we destroy yours, we move to another section, which means changing the wizardry energy you use."

Dre clenched his teeth and extended his senses. A soft pressure caressed his skin like he was naked in a brewing storm. It intensified slowly, then subsided like a wave. As it rescinded, a force pulled on his skin, bones, and blood. The tug peaked, then the pressure returned. It repeated in a cycle, the pulls and pushes in equilibrium. It was the exchange between the two wizardry energies.

On the next push, he pulled with his mind. Above his hand, dark energy ripped free from the light energy that held it inert. Black specks crowded his vision, growing in thickness as he pulled harder. The light dimmed around him in response. The heat behind him dampened. Soon, a thick smoke hung suspended, still. Free of its opposite, the dark energy was a cloud of pressure pushing frantically against him, trying to ground him to dust. He blocked its path back to balance, back to light.

A force, a vacuum, sucked the dark cloud together. He clenched a fist and the energy condensed into a thick vertical slab. The pressure focused into a sharp point on his arm and the energy stuck there like a shield.

"I'm ready."

The round started. The wizards summoned a small cloud of light and a solid black ball. The dark sphere zipped across the room while the light drifted. Dre stepped in their path, angling his shield. The fast ball rebounded up with a resounding clang. It hit the ceiling, cracked, and disappeared. He swiped at the light energy with the top of his shield. There were no sparks or sounds as the opposing energies collided. A small hole was dug halfway through his shield. The energy rejoined peacefully, returning to the invisible substance that permeated the universe, floating around harmlessly in the air and ground, mixed with all matter. It was the natural response when light and dark energy touched. They were harmonious opposites.

The wizards repeated the same attack. Dre deflected the dark ball again. He pushed softly against his shield with his mind, and it floated off his arm as if a tight wire tied the two together. There was a potential energy building in that distance. He twisted his hand and the shield spun. It chopped the air like a fluttering bird. He aimed it, then clipped his connection.

The dark energy was no longer his, no longer pressed against his body. The force turned into a repulsion and the whirling blade shot forward. Once clipped, dark energy couldn't be adjusted or controlled. It hit the light energy and didn't slow. The wizards stepped aside. It smashed the black disk on impact and nullified the light energy. What was left of the attack crashed into the wall.

"Round one complete."

"That was easy," Dre said. "How did everyone else fail?"

The wizards replaced their targets and Dre generated another shield. The wizards fired quadruple the energy as the first round, four dark spheres and four clouds of light. The first three spheres clanked against the shield. The fourth one broke through, socking Dre in the chest. It knocked him over, but it was more surprising than painful. The new attacks were denser. The difficulty was ramping up.

He rolled to his feet as he made another shield and four spheres. The wizards sent another volley of dark balls that zipped again past their slow-moving light energy. Dre calculated the angles and fired his attacks. He hit two of the dark balls. His energies cracked and faded on contact but knocked the approaching balls off course. He blocked the remaining two with his shield, then shot it at the approaching light energy.

The four balls of light moved in a box pattern, but then three slowed, leaving one to collide with Dre's shield. That one ball of light shrank into itself, reducing its size by more than half but doubling its brightness. Then, it exploded. Light energy didn't like being compressed like dark. It was too hot. The force blew the shield back at Dre. He snapped and the dark energy puffed into a mist before evaporating. The remaining three balls of light hit his dark energy target disc and ate it up. The wizards had already fired their new set of dark energy spheres.

"Uh oh." Dre ran forward. He condensed and shot a spray of dark pellets. They rattled the oncoming attacks, knocking all four off course. One wizard dodged the remaining pellets, but the other was hit square in the face. She staggered back. Using the distraction, Dre planted his feet. He fired a wide disk and ball at the targets. He destroyed both.

"Round two complete."

Dre panted a little. He cracked his knuckles. As long as he didn't let down his guard, he should have no problem passing this test. The familiar buzz of a victorious performance flowed through him. For the third round, the wizards didn't stay still. They darted around each other and fired double the energy from the previous round from many different angles.

He attacked their feet. One wizard tripped over a low bar. He tumbled forward, converting the fall into a roll. He landed unharmed but evaporated all of his energy as a courtesy. Dre deflected attacks from his partner and launched two spheres of his own. He cracked the dark energy target. The wizards didn't let Dre trip them again, but he cleared their light energy target anyway.

"Round three complete."

The fourth round was a flex of power. It started with a wall of dark energy halfway to the ceiling and just as wide, more energy than Dre could produce and in a useless shape. Dre condensed his energy carefully, compacting it tightly into a spear. He charged. The tip of his spear stabbed into the less dense wall, shattering it. Behind it, however, was another wall, a sheet made of light.

He threw the spear. It whistled as it flew, thinning slightly as it cut through the light. It hit the black target on the other side. Dre backed up to the wall as the heatwave from the light energy hit him. He braced himself and pulled as much energy as he could grab. The weight crashed into his body. It was like the air punched him. His feet slid apart, but his stance held. He pictured a shape in his mind: a thin, long, angled blade. He clenched both fists and created twenty identical copies of it. They were organized in two circles, like the spokes of a wheel.

Before the now blinding light reached him, he spun the blade like the great turbines underneath the city. A gust picked up into a steady stream, scattering the light energy.

The wizards gasped, and in their distraction, their wall faded away. Dre released his connection to a blade one by one and aimed it at the light energy target. As one shrunk the target, he replaced it in his turbine. After ten hits, the target was gone.

"Round four complete."

The wizards applauded.

"Well done."

"I've never seen dark energy used like that," the other said. "Very creative."

Dre released his energy with a snap and cracked his neck. He dabbed his forehead. If they were impressed with that, there was plenty more amazement in store. When he and Alaan fought together, they never won a match based on strength. Their specialty was using wizardry in ways that others didn't expect.

"Now, the same thing again, but you only use light energy."

"That's it for dark?"

"We didn't expect anyone to get past the fourth round this early into the program."

"Make something up then," Dre said. "I'm just getting started." He stretched his arms.

"What matters is that you did well enough. We will move on to light," the psychic said.

"Can I skip that?" Dre said. "My skills with dark should be more than enough to pass."

"You have to make it to at least the second round using each energy and then again on the combined round," the psychic said.

"I can't," Dre said under his breath. Over his shoulder, the eight small windows were like eyes with head-shaped pupils. His hands dropped to his side. There was no point in making a fool of himself.

"I am excited to see what you do with light," one of the wizards said.

Dre gritted his teeth. If he didn't pass two light rounds, he would fail the test. He would be eligible for the draft again and his parents' mandated house arrest would continue. He could move about the city unseen through the tunnels, but there was nowhere to go if he couldn't train in a park or participate in a tournament. He extended his senses. This time, he focused on the pulls against his skin. The tiny hairs on his body stood on end as if they didn't belong to him anymore and were returning home. He pushed his mind into the strange sensation.

Flickering beads of light sparkled in the air like insects. As the light moved across his body, each point pulled on him so delicately that it tickled. Bits of the energy whizzed off, repelled by each other's heat and faded. The sorcerer in the back raised a golden paddle. Dre activated the Correction Factor because there was no other way for him to use light energy. He didn't even know what his mistakes were.

The psychic wrote something down. The wizards fired two simple attacks and flashcards surfaced in Dre's mind. Usually, the MMA material didn't bother him because his dark skills were beyond everything it covered. Now, it suggested all kinds of maneuvers he couldn't do. His targets were destroyed in the first round.

"What?" Everyone else in the room said.

Dre shrugged. "That's the tradeoff Alaan and I made. Better to be great at one energy than mediocre at both."

"The rest of us have to maintain our own balance. That division is only practical for the two of you," the other wizard said.

"But it is not practical for the MMA," the psychic said. "You failed."

Alaan placed a hand on Dre's shoulder as he exited the gigastone room. "It's okay. Apart, we're just like them."

"Shared failure shouldn't be what brings people together," Dre said, knocking away the hand. He had failed the draft exam, but this was supposed to be different. The MMA exam was supposed to reveal how he and Alaan had grown over the years rather than being a reminder of the deficiency he was born with. The Poli Twins had a whole host of new maneuvers to show.

"If we all fail the test, the problem isn't with us. It is with the test."

Dre pushed past Alaan. The test was obviously flawed. There was no point in testing them separately. Now, everything hinged on Alaan. "You better pass," Dre said.

"I would never miss the opportunity to show you up," Alaan said.

The guards and nobles watched Dre, but the other children averted their eyes. They didn't mock him after all. The room was silent. Gron scooted over, clearing a spot at one of the viewing slits.

"He will pass," Zalora said. "He has to."

Alaan started his exam by floating up. He planted his feet on the dim ceiling. Invisible light energy held him there like a lonely stalactite. Then, he ran across the room with poise.

Where Dre broke up all his movements with a short pause or shift in weight, Alaan flowed through transitions seamlessly, as if every dodge was part of a more extensive routine. And it likely was. He had guessed the exam format by watching his brother. Dre relived the moment by watching him. The way Alaan moved his arms and his distance from the wizards told a story. Dre had fought with

Alaan so many times that, based on Alaan's reactions, he traced back to the cause. All of their previous battles sat at the front of Dre's mind. All the possible enemy attack patterns and all the ways to respond were like roads on a map. He usually didn't even need to look at Alaan to know where they were and what they should do next.

For the dark energy round, Alaan returned to the ground. He moved differently, awkwardly. It was like watching a drunk child juggle. None of it made sense. It was difficult to read. There was nothing to compare it to. Alaan hadn't used dark energy in a long time, well, not at least in front of Dre. However, there was something familiar to his movements. It was like squinting into a dirty mirror far away. Alaan attempted to mimic Dre's movements, but he didn't know which ones actually helped control dark energy and which ones were simply for show. But he completed the first two rounds somehow.

Dre hummed. Alaan had been practicing dark energy more than a little. Ever since they selected wizardry and divided up the energies, Alaan has been curious about using both. Since Alaan liked winning fights, he hadn't wasted much time on dark energy before. But that seemed to have changed. Dre liked surprises, but not this one. Alaan was supposed to be predictable, at least to Dre, but Dre didn't see this coming.

"Can you feel his wizardry?" Gron said, his eyes wide.

Dre leaned back. "That's gigastone."

"You are the Poli Twins. You can do special stuff," he said.

With enough time not actively displaying his magic in public, kids started to make up new things that he could do. "Special maybe, but not impossible," Dre said. Everyone turned to him. "Well, ah...if we could use magic through gigastone, we would have been drafted on day one."

"If you could do that, we would call you the Gigastone Twins,"

Gron said.

"No, they would still be the Poli Twins," Zalora said. "We don't call them the Eclipse Twins."

"That would be cool," Gron said.

"Stick with Poli Twins, please," Dre said.

"How did you get that name anyway?" Zalora said. "You're the only twins."

Dre reached down to his waist, but he wasn't wearing his blue suspenders, his gift from King Kertic. The royal family traveled once to see one of his matches. While the nobles fought over which family he belonged to, King Kertic said that it only mattered that he was Lynitian.

"It's what King Kertic called us and it stuck."

"Wow," several kids said.

Alaan started the combined energy portion of the exam unbalanced. He zipped up to the ceiling again. Before the exciting idea that Alaan would be the first to pass the exam could take hold, he failed the second round.

"If only I had started practicing dark energy earlier," he said as he exited the room. He shook a fist in the air. "I was so close."

"So close to such a low bar," Dre said.

"You failed, too," Alaan said.

"Ah duh," Dre said. Alaan was calm as if their lives weren't ruined for the next two years. This test was stupid. Everything was stupid.

"If the Poli Twins can't pass, we have no chance," the girl in the yellow dress said, pointing. Dre wanted to respond, "No, you failed because you dressed like you were going on a picnic," but he didn't.

Gron shrugged. "I would have passed if I had practiced the creatures I read about." He lifted his camera. "Can I still get a picture?"

"You didn't practice?" Alaan said.

"My parents wouldn't let me," he said. He handed the camera to Zalora, stepped between Dre and Alaan, and grinned.

"Mine wouldn't either," a lanky boy said as he scratched an elbow.

"Mine neither," another boy said. Ten more said the same thing.

"But we are all exempt," Alaan said.

Zalora snapped the photo.

"Can I have one, too?" The lanky boy said.

"We can't end the draft until we find a replacement and everyone is afraid of the replacement because the draft exists," Alaan said softly. The other children shrugged. Even the nobles were baffled by that conundrum.

"My parents said that I could practice if the Poli Twins returned to training in public," the girl in the yellow dress said, then pointed at Alaan. "But you didn't risk it. Why should we?"

Maybe Dre's parents would have let him risk it if Slithlor wasn't the head of the draft. He was public enemy number one in the Dre's household. Dre's mother was still mad that Slithlor had been studying her pregnancy longer than he had initially let on. "If you don't practice, this program will fail," Dre said.

"My father said that the MMA is a trick to test our magic," someone said.

"The only way back to freely using magic without the fear of being snatched from your family is this program or age nineteen. Gron, you're only fifteen. Do you want to wait four more years?" Dre said. Gron shook his head. "I want to be on stage performing, competing with Alaan. I want a rematch with the Balison sisters. I want Alaan and I to be the best fighting duo Lynit has ever seen. What do you want?"

A few of the kids murmured to themselves. The guards leaned in. The Yordin wouldn't stop smiling.

"Did you hear about the girl who died yesterday in the magical accident? Andela Passin, she was a sorcerer and disintegrated her own body," Zalora said. "We have to be careful practicing this risky material on our own. She isn't the only one. An animalist boy died a couple of weeks ago when he didn't return to human after failing a morph. There have been only five accidents in almost ten years since the Correction Factor was upgraded and all of them happened within the last year. Something new is happening."

Dre shuddered. He always considered the safety net a handicap that the nobles created to slow people from learning how to use magic properly. Noble kids were trained off of the Correction Factor by the time they were twelve, probably accounting for seventy percent of their higher skill level. They spent more time perfecting the basics of single magic instead of dabbling across multiple until they were fifteen. But despite all of that, the nobles needed to fix their system. Lives depended on it. Fortunately, Dre and Alaan never produced enough energy to endanger themselves.

"I tried a spell at home and set my room on fire," the girl in the yellow dress said.

Dre nodded. "Elemental magic isn't an inside-the-house sort of thing." The girl didn't understand her own magic.

"It doesn't matter how much we train. We won't ever be as good as the Poli Twins. They failed and they are noble," Gron said. The students nodded.

"We aren't noble," Dre said, rolling his eyes. "Everyone knows that we weren't born with our wizardry ability, but that we had to discover it and create our own way to make it useful. Otherwise, we would only be as good as a single wizard together." Lynitians had been practically trained since birth to associate anything extraordinary with nobility, and it was annoying.

"We trained for four hours a day nearly every day since we were eight. If any of you worked that hard, you'd be famous, too," Alaan said.

"These years are the most important when it comes to magic. We set our magical foundation that will stay with us for the rest of our lives. If you don't practice magic enough, you can lose the ability to use your primary magic as well," Dre said.

"I think I am losing my magic," the lanky boy said as his voice cracked and he hunched smaller. "All that comes out are small wisps of energy."

Dre hugged him. The other kids did, too. They were silent for a moment. It was the danger teachers warned about, but no one believed it actually happened. It was supposed to be a trick to motivate children to do their homework.

"If your parents will let you, come train with us. We have our own gym. You won't have to worry about any guards watching you," Dre said. "This is an invitation to all of you."

The last of the tests finished and all sixteen students failed. The problem wasn't the test. It was the draft and that would always be the problem until it was ended. The fear of it was too great.

The guards lined back up in the center of the room. The psychic with the clipboard stepped to the front. "Everyone failed. You will be removed from the Magic and Martial Arts program."

The guards moved as one and marched.

Dre sprinted for the door. "Wait, wait, can we retake it together, please?" He blocked their path, fingers interlaced at his chin. "Our magical strength is low because of our birth, not from a lack of effort. You know this. Everyone knows this."

"I was the one who asked for sixteen tests instead of fifteen, and it was a mistake," Alaan said.

Dre blinked twice, then three more times. Alaan stood back with the other children and out of Dre's punching range.

"If you are dissatisfied with the exam, feel free to submit a complaint."

"Have other MMA cohorts failed the first exam?" The Finrar

asked.

"No," the psychic said. "This is by far the worst cohort I have seen. Even if the children are still weary of the Guard, they select one person to pass."

"A Cast wouldn't have let their peers down," the Cast said.

"Nor would have a Finrar," the Finrar said.

"Wait," the Yordin said, raising a soft hand.

"What did you do?" Dre said as he approached his brother, grabbing his collar. Alaan had gone behind his back and did something stupid.

"I…I…," Alaan said. He dropped his head into Dre's shoulder. "I was curious to see what I could do by myself." Dre resisted the twitch to flick him away.

"The MMA needs a fair chance to succeed. It is the noble solution to the silly program started by Slithlor. We would have never suggested a mandatory program to train a new army. You can't force someone to be extraordinary. They have to want it. They have to believe it," the Yordin said

"I have my instructions," the psychic said.

"…instructions that were edited based on the words of a child," the Yordin said. "I am asking you on behalf of my family to give these boys a fair chance, all these children, another chance. If the Poli Twins fail out of this program, it will be the end of the MMA. After this hits the news, do you think any child will even try to make the program work? Almost sixty-five percent of nobles join the Guard, but we aren't enough. We need everyone's participation if we are going to be able to defend ourselves in the next war."

Dre turned around. The Yordin was right.

The psychic pressed his lips tight. He looked to the other guards, but they didn't even blink.

"And, the Yordin would be in your debt."

The psychic raised an eyebrow, then called the wizard and

sorcerer guards back to the gigastone room. "The Poli Twins will take the test together as originally planned," he said. "I am sure that is what Elite Palow would have wanted."

The Yordin placed a hand on Dre's shoulder, then leaned beside his ear. "Can the Sass do that?"

Dre looked at Alaan, who wasn't smiling either, though what the Yordin had said was funny. Getting something they wanted from a noble was a trap. The psychic would later approach a Yordin to cash in his favor and someday, a Yordin would sneak up on Dre and Alaan for a repayment.

Chapter 5 - Dre

Dre and Alaan went back into the exam room. The stakes were final now. There would be no third chance if the twins failed together. The Yordin followed them in with a smile, though. He was cashing in his favor now. Nobles have been requesting private performances since Dre could remember. They have offered money, items from foreign nations, and to marry him, but he always refused. It was an agreement that Dre and Alaan made. They were celebrities who monetized their brand, but they only performed for free and in public. This exam wasn't technically private, but the Yordin would consider it so because he would ignore all the non-noble people there. His repayment for helping was a front-row seat to the Poli Twins' magic. And he would receive the show of a lifetime because Dre was in the mood to show off.

Dre elected to start with dark energy. Alaan stepped to the side. The angles and frequencies of the wizards' attacks were the same. Dre repeated his maneuvers. He deflected dark energy with his shield. He nullified light energy. He attacked the wizards' feet. He launched his spear and completed the fourth round.

"Impressive," one of them said. "The ability to repeat a sequence on command is a stronger sign of skill than a flare of brilliance."

Alaan summoned light energy, floated up to the ceiling, and

completed all four rounds.

"Now, both energies," the psychic said. "For this section, there will be no targets. Instead, you will pass if you hit the wizards three times before they hit you thrice."

"They have to make it to at least round four to pass. Together, they have to be as good as two wizards even if they aren't as good as one alone," the Yordin said.

"Ah, okay," the psychic said.

Dre tapped two fingers to his forearm and slid them down to his wrist, keeping them together.

Alaan shook his head. "The Yordin didn't do this because he likes us. He wants to study us."

"Oh, there really is no such thing as a free lunch," Dre said.

"If I didn't think it'd count as a point for them, I'd chop you in the head right now."

Dre pouted, then created a shield.

In the first round, eight dark spheres and eight blobs of light were above the wizards. They fired half of each energy as offense and kept the rest hovering as a defense.

Alaan nullified the four dark spheres that reached them. As each one of them disappeared, the wizards created replacements. The second wave of dark energy arrived before the first wave of light energy.

"Get close," Dre said. They walked side by side down the middle of the room. A small black cloud followed on the right and a white one on the left. They nullified all attacks flung at them. It took four waves of attacks before they were ten paces away. Then, they hit the wizards three times.

In the second round, there were sixteen of each energy. The wizards' arms whirled as they manipulated each ball independently. This was already more energy than Dre and Alaan could cancel out and there were two more rounds to pass after this.

Alaan jumped to the ceiling and half the attacks followed him. Dre circled the wizards slowly. He spiraled inward, which only made the dark energy harder to avoid. He spiraled out and the wizards negated his attacks with ease. He circled several times with no progress.

Alaan screamed. Dre strained to spot him through the clouds of light energy hovering near the ceiling.

"One hit," the psychic said. The ceiling cloud energy moved, revealing Alaan rising to his feet upside down.

Dre fired all his energy and the weight lifted off his body. The wizards blocked all of it. He circled the wizards faster. Only one wizard watched him while the other whittled holes into Alaan's descending cloud. Dre's attacker, the woman in the new wizard robes, blocked his attacks and fired new ones while still chasing him with light energy.

Then her energy changed direction and moved opposite to the circle he ran around her. It cut off his path. The light shrank momentarily and Dre created a shield just in time to block the explosion. His feet slid across the floor until he hit a wall. He was in a corner, and now both wizards' attacks were being directed at him. The dark balls rattled his shield, but the approaching balls of light were the real threat.

The exam wasn't going as well as Dre expected. He reached out his senses, not for wizardry, but for his brother. Alaan responded. He exploded his remaining light, which caused the wizards to pause and turn around. From above, Alaan fell like a needle. Before he hit the ground, he summoned more light, which slowed his landing. Dre pulled as much dark smoke as he could. He formed it into an angled wedge to seal him and Alaan into the corner. It was dim in the enclave, but it wasn't quiet. More explosions boomed and bits of light flashed around the edges of the black wall. Dre and Alaan took a moment to breathe.

"Stop playing around," the Yordin said.

"He's right. I know this feels like a private show for a noble, but we aren't going to win at this rate," Dre said.

"We don't have to give him what he wants," Alaan said.

"What other choice do we have?" Dre said.

Alaan sucked his teeth. "We have to outsmart them. Kill the lamps," he said, then pulled so much energy that he zipped up like a bird. Dre released his wedge and dashed to the right. On the other side of the room, the three lampposts provided the only non-magical light. He circled the wizards again.

Then he dashed for the lights. A few black spheres whizzed past him. One hit the lampstand, but it didn't even shake. It was made of heavy metal. Dre solidified a black camp over the first bulb and the room dimmed.

"No tampering with the lamps," the psychic said.

"Leave them," the Yordin said.

Dre ran along the wall to the next two and capped them.

The wizards were bathed in their own energy. They circled each other back to back. Balls of light roamed the space, searching. Alaan killed his energy and faded into the darkness. Dre moved back to a wall. He was quiet as he crept to a new position.

Then, a flash of light revealed Alaan. He was in a far corner, near the door. During a second, longer blink, an illusion of Dre shined next to Alaan. Not only was light energy hot and able to lift a wizard to the sky, but it also created illusions. This illusion, however, wasn't a perfect copy since Dre wasn't even wearing the blue suspenders his illusion wore. But the wizards didn't notice. They directed all their attacks in that direction.

As Alaan distracted them with the fake, the real Dre crept into their blind spot. He waited until he was only a few steps away before summoning energy. The wizards turned to Dre, but it was too late. Dre formed a bar of energy and shot it at their legs. They fell over and before they could get up, he shot them twice more.

"Round two complete," both wizards shouted. Dre snapped and released his energy. Real light returned to the room. Under its judgment, the copy of Dre was transparent. It looked more like a phantom than a boy. It wavered and flickered. Alaan snapped and it vanished. Illusions didn't usually work in battles because there was sunlight to reveal the truth.

"That was an illusion?" The old robe wizard said. "How did we fall for that?"

"Tampering with the lighting is not allowed. Don't do that again," the psychic said, shaking his clipboard.

"Oh, sorry," Alaan said.

Dre joined Alaan at their starting spot. "That was nice. I give you that, but we aren't going to make it to the fourth round with only tricks," Dre said.

Alaan looked back at the windows. "No, we can do it. Give me your best and I will give you mine."

"But this isn't our best," Dre said.

"Then give me just enough," Alaan said as he rolled his sleeves.

In the third round, the wizards fired more attacks than Dre could track. Alaan jumped to the ceiling and a wizard followed him. Dre ran wide. Dark energy hit the ground behind him. The new robe wizard adjusted her attacks. She shot where he was headed. He zigzagged. She fired where he might pivot. He jumped and flipped in new directions. He did aerials and side tucks, and fired beads of energy during layouts.

Heat socked into him anyway. It was like a slap from the sun. His breath rushed out of him. He banged into a wall or the floor or the ceiling. Everything spun. There was a sound, a muted noise, almost like yelling, but underwater. He picked himself off the ground and propped himself against the wall. He skittered along it as the wall vibrated from hits of energy. Alaan cried out.

"Two hits," the psychic said.

"Wait, wait," the Yordin said. "Your technique and coordination are unmatched by any pair of wizards, any two people of any magic. You are holding back."

"We are trying to be as close as possible to two regular wizards," Alaan said, panting.

Dre furrowed his eyebrows. This wasn't his goal. He not only wanted to win, he wanted to amaze. Failing seemed to be Alaan's goal. He was trying to test how good they were if they didn't use any of their gifts.

"But is this your limit? Was taking this test together a waste?" the Yordin said.

"Start the round again," Alaan said and huffed. The psychic allowed it.

Dre checked his body. His shoulder was sore and he had a soft ache everywhere else, but it was nothing serious. He had been in worse shape many times before. Alaan helped him to his feet. Dre tapped his forearm with two fingers and slid them down to his wrist. Alaan repeated the same movement but kept his two fingers separated.

"Why are we holding back?" Dre said.

"Can't you tell? This is a Verbindous. We aren't following MMA protocol anymore. The Yordin are testing us," Alaan said. He repeated his hand gesture.

The Verbindous was the noble ceremony at nineteen that welcomed them into adulthood. They still had two more years before that time. "I don't care if this is a noble's birthday party. I want to win. And remind everyone who the Poli Twins are."

"We beat many adults with shared balance alone. It's more than enough," Alaan said. It was true, but he was playing too carelessly with their only chance of ending the draft. "If they truly determine that we are Yordin, then what? There will be nothing that we can say to the public to undo it."

Dre grunted as he summoned dark energy in small bursts, the pressure distributing across his body. It was a small massage for his aches but also kept the heat in his chest from getting out. Before he reached his max, Alaan summoned light energy. There was usually a slight vibration when someone used wizardry nearby, but when Alaan did, there was a firm tug.

Underneath Dre's pressure, there was a new invitation to balance. He didn't need to reach for light himself. Through Alaan, he found that connection and leaned into it. The weight of his dark energy lessened as he shared the burden with Alaan. A vast cloud of light swirled overhead and Alaan's feet stayed firmly on the ground.

Dre then pulled more energy, more than he could alone without flattening himself. Without the weight, he pulled until the pushes and pulls of the universe were numb against his skin and a new pull produced nothing. A dark cloud the size of a house floated above him. It was still less than another wizard his age could produce, but it was his true limit. He could only reach his maximum energy while sharing balance with Alaan.

The wizards launched energy galore. It was still almost double what the boys had out together. Dre bolted at the wizards. He weaved around the dark energy attacks. He fired his own, but as spikes. They zipped across the room faster than a sphere. Two hit spheres and cracked them but were knocked off course. By the seventh one, Dre's feet lifted off the ground. By the twelfth, he soared over the guards, firing attacks from a new angle. He didn't land a hit, but that wasn't the goal. When the last of his dark energy was used up, his feet slammed into the ceiling. Alaan was up there waiting for him.

For a moment, the wizards' attacks froze. Hearing about the shared balance between the Poli Twins was one thing. Dre had risen without any light energy of his own and witnessing it had to be a shock.

Most of Alaan's light energy was next to him, but a small puff on the ground near the wizards went unnoticed. It exploded. The blast hit one, but the other snapped away dark energy and sprung out of the way.

Dre summoned more energy and eased off his balance with Alaan. He dropped. He breathed calmly as his stomach fluttered from the sensation of falling. He slid past the rising wizard. Her eyes widened as she spotted him. He clenched against Alaan in time to soften contact with the ground. From this angle, the woman's surprise was menacing. He created two thick spikes and fired them. She blocked effortlessly with light energy, which dampened her ascent.

Dre summoned more energy and swirled it around himself. It distracted her enough that she hadn't noticed Alaan. He pulled on Dre's balance and kicked her in the back with the weight of a boulder. She grunted but caught herself before hitting the ground like a pro. She was a guard, after all. She bared her teeth. The wizard hit by Alaan's earlier light energy blast groaned and cursed as he struggled to his feet.

"Two hits," the psychic said.

Dre fell up. Dre fell down. His body barely knew the difference. He swapped ground for ceiling every few seconds. Alaan was his counterweight. The wizards lobbed energy, but Dre dodged all of them. They couldn't predict his movements because they couldn't read his energy to understand his imbalances.

The wizards adjusted their strategy. Dre winked at Alaan and they adjusted theirs. Dre tested the wizards. He fired attacks angled slightly off, but they both responded to block them. Alaan flashed bright lights and the wizards attacked with their eyes closed. The guards ended up nullifying most of their own magic.

Dre and Alaan adapted to everything the wizards tried with little more than a hand gesture and eye contact or less. A tug on each other was a sign, too. Winning a fight depended on exploiting the enemies' weaknesses and for most in paired combat, it was their teamwork. Dre delivered the third hit and ended the round. It was like old times.

Dre gripped his shaking knees and panted. Sweat drenched his sweatshirt. "We still got it," he said.

Alaan lay on the ground, gulping air. "We will always have it."

At the start of the fourth round, Dre's heart jumped into his throat. The wizards produced a wall of energy but in an attack formation this time. The center was a black circle. It was a nest of black spheres. The rest of the energy radiated out in alternating concentric rings. Each zone could attack or defend. It stretched to the ceiling and the walls. There was no way around it. It was as much an exhibit of guard precision as an instrument of death. It was enough heat to kill Dre twice over and incinerate his remains.

"We forfeit, we forfeit," Alaan said, flailing hands.

"No, they don't," the Yordin said. His padded shoes thudded up from behind. "If you do not complete this round, you will fail the test."

"Only trained guards could handle that," Alaan said. The energy hung in the air, waiting. Black and white whirled in a dizzying dance.

"Trained guards, nobles, and you. The only reason you weren't drafted already is because that program doesn't have a curriculum for you. There is no curriculum for you. You must discover your own path and that path is made of combined energies," he said.

"That's not fair," Alaan said.

"It's not fair getting a second chance at this exam, but here we are. Either you pass this round or I will make sure every one of you is drafted," he said.

Dre straightened up. Being drafted meant that the two would

become Slithlor's personal test subjects. "Okay, Alaan. Let's give the Yordin what he asked so nicely for."

Alaan labored to his feet. His face was stone. "Give us a minute to catch our breath first."

"No," the Yordin said. "At the point of exhaustion, all your learned behaviors erode and your true self is revealed. I want to see that."

Alaan flicked a glance at Dre. That was precisely what the nobles said about the Verbindous. Alaan was right. The nobles came to this exam because they wanted one last attempt at claiming the Poli Twins. There was no way to prove blood relation to the original nobles. There was only this tradition. But it didn't matter what the nobles said. Dre's and Alaan's last names would always be Word.

Alaan tapped his forearm and slid his fingers to his wrist, keeping them together, which was the sign for using combined energy, but then he clenched his hand three times.

"Are you sure?" Dre said, grabbing his brother's shoulders. That additional hand gesture indicated that they might hurt someone.

Alaan clenched his jaw but kept his eyes neutral. It was the look of an angry Alaan. He would destroy anyone who stood in his path. It was Alaan's best look.

"If he wants a show, we will give him one he won't forget," Alaan said. He took off his shirt. Stretch marks looked like scratches on his shoulders and back. He had grown a head taller in a single year, just like Dre.

"Finally," Dre said, wiggling his hips. He reached out his senses. There was a buzz on his skin, but no pushes, no pulls. It was like a static that numbed his connection to wizardry. He was exhausted. He pulled and a pitiful puff of dark energy winked in and out. Alaan didn't do much better. After a couple more tries, Dre and Alaan produced three head-sized clouds each.

Dre pushed the first one into Alaan's. The energies flowed into each other, then vanished. Dre jerked back his head. He looked from Alaan to the air and back again. That wasn't supposed to happen, at least not to them.

King Kertic's voice played in Dre's head: "Don't become dependent on that ability. It may not last past your Verbindous."

No one had ever learned a new magic or maintained a second one past nineteen except for the first king of Lynit. Most people's magic settled much earlier than that.

"This can't be happening," Dre said as he dropped to the floor. Without joining energy and sharing balance with his brother, Dre was nothing. All of his skills were based on having Alaan beside him. Alaan covered for his weaknesses. Now, there would be a hole. He would be forced to compete with fourteen-year-olds for the rest of his life. He wouldn't be famous anymore. It was like a blow to the chest. He couldn't breathe.

"Am I supposed to believe that?" the Yordin said. He pointed at the sorcerer in the back corner, who held up a Correction Factor paddle. "Stop the games. The sorcerers can see it."

Dre patted his drying throat. "I need water. Can I have water?"

"Join the energies or fail," the Yordin said. Dre and Alaan had never used this ability in a fight before. They only discovered it three months before the draft started and stopped appearing publicly.

"No, Dre, it must be a fluke. We are tired. It worked yesterday. Do it again," Alaan said.

Dre's last two puffs of energy were like a lifeline, his last chance to remain famous. He focused as he pushed his energies into Alaan's. As the flecks touched, they blinked a few times, then merged. Each droplet looked like a tiny eclipse, a dark circle surrounded by a ring of light. The soft pushes and pulls from the universe faded. There was only Alaan. Every movement of Alaan's body pulsed in Dre. They were connected. It was like being an island, surrounded by an expansive presence and proud of the isolation. The world was shut out.

Dre and Alaan closed their fists and the energies condensed into two dark pebbles bathed in light. The wizards attacked with their oscillating wall of energy.

The first pebble whipped across the room. It punctured a hole in a black sphere, causing it to shatter. Dre and Alaan lifted their left arms and the pebble changed course, hitting the next one. It moved just as fast as dark energy alone but with the control of light energy. They intercepted each dark energy attack, shattering them like glass.

Then, they switched to light. The wizards tried to spread the energy out but were too slow. The pebble collided with a part of it, setting off a reaction that caused the light energy to explode in growing, expanding concussions as it traced the room.

Neither wizard noticed the second slower pebble. It stopped between them. Dre snapped, releasing his dark energy. Now, the bead was only light energy and packed tighter than any other wizard could compress it. A blimp of light flashed several times, followed by a boom that shook the room. The wizards flew like cloth. The shockwave knocked the psychic into the wall. His little clipboard snapped. Dust and black debris rained out.

"Did we pass?" Alaan said.

The Yordin clapped. "Yes."

"Get out," the psychic coughed. A cocoon of purple energy surrounded him. "This is the last favor I do for a Yordin."

Dre and Alaan left the Castle, ignoring everyone's questions. Mommy waited outside. She was in her floppy brown teacher's robes and carried a thick book in one arm. She was allowed past the line of guards holding back the mob of men and women holding communication orbs and cameras, though she stayed the mandated fifty feet from the entrance.

"What are you doing here?" Dre said.

"Did you end the draft?" she said.

"Not yet. We have a lot of work ahead of us," Dre said. The next test would likely be more demanding and require more children to pass.

"Was Slithor there?" she said.

"You made it clear that he should stay away from us," Alaan said. When Dre and Alaan were on a tour of the Castle in Virt, Slithlor pulled them aside. He pressed them into a corner, his huge frame casting them in shadow. His breath smelled of candy and he said that if they didn't come to him when they turned nineteen, he would find them. Afterward, Mommy charged into the Castle, threatening every person she passed. She was later banned.

"He's not crazy," Dre said. The presence of the head of the draft would have been the only way the exam could have been worse. Dre and Alaan wouldn't have taken it together.

"You're all over the news. Supposedly, you are giving a performance," she said, pointing over her shoulder. Fans were sprinkled in, holding signs and shouting for autographs.

Dre shrank a little.

Off the side of the bridge, tucked between two buildings, was the small stairwell to the tunnels.

"We can lose them there," Dre said.

"If they report that, the tunnels will turn into a hip new spot. I'm here now. Let them blame me for being rude," she said.

"Oh no," Dre said.

"What's wrong with you, Alaan?" she said.

Alaan's gaze was distant. He shook his head. "Nothing. Let's go." She then turned to Dre.

"He's mad that we couldn't pass without taking the test together," Dre said.

The guards stepped aside to let them pass, but the mob didn't move. There were people from big-name places like the Poli Times,

Virt Express, Lynitian Post, and a couple from celebrity gossip networks. Cameras flashed. Dre leaned into Alaan and posed. He clenched Alaan's hand until he smiled. There was a duty to being the Poli Twins.

"Excuse us," Mommy said, but the reporters would not give them space.

"Is it true the Poli Twins were drafted?" a woman said.

"No," Dre said.

"Did you perform for the Guard or the Kertics?" she continued.

"We need to get by," Mommy insisted.

"What do you say to all the fans you've abandoned?" The reporter with small glasses from before said.

"Abandoned?" Dre said. They didn't abandon anyone. They did exactly what the other kids did after the draft started: they hid their magic. This meant no more competing in tournaments or putting on performances in Co Park. And they always traveled through the tunnels because they drew a crowd. "We are kids, too."

"Can you still join your energies?" someone said.

"Is that all people care about?" Alaan said in Dre's ear.

"Your matches attracted people from all over Lynit. Your public appearances dominated the media after the war. It gave many people something to look forward to after losing so many. Then you stopped, but now it seems you are only sharing your gifts with the Guard," the reporter said. He fixed his glasses again.

"If you spent more time reporting on the draft, maybe you would know that no children practice magic in public. If you want to see the Poli Twins perform again, end Slithlor's program," Mommy said.

"Are you saying that Lynit doesn't need more guards?" someone shouted.

"Ninbod Volitum," Mommy said. A dark blue light started above her head and expanded into a shell. With her magic, she defined a boundary that blocked physical things from crossing the threshold. The shield also sealed in Dre and Alaan.

"What are you doing?" A woman said.

Mommy moved forward. Several protectors put up their shields, but she pushed them aside. Cameras flew into the air. Reporters fell into each other and cursed. They crawled after rolling communication orbs. The fans laughed and chanted, "Momma Word."

Dre, Alaan, and Mommy crossed the bridge. The questions didn't stop, but no one else tried to block their path. The crowd followed them all the way home, which surprised the paparazzi posted up out front.

"I wish 'Poli Twins' would die already," Alaan said when they entered the house. He took off his shoes and tossed them into the corner.

"You don't like it?" Dre said as he pulled off his smelly sweatshirt.

Mommy shook her head. "Dad and I give you leeway because you paid for this house, but that isn't permission to be messy. Don't leave your clothes in this hallway." Dre nodded as she walked down the hall.

"You know I don't like it," Alaan said. He took off his shirt and pants. "It's just like being thought of as noble. We are a thing to them, not real people. We sound like mutant creature half-breeds."

"There is no other word for human twins," Dre said.

"They could call us by our names. Everyone knows them."

"You don't want that," Mommy called out, her voice carrying from the living room. "You want the distance the title gives you. Let the fans obsess over the Poli Twins—the idea of you. The more they know about the Poli Twins, the less they know about Alaandre."

"We've had two years out of the public eye. We can start fresh. There could be a positive side to the draft," Alaan said.

"When you are nineteen, we will start up the PR team again. They will build you whatever brand you want," she said.

"What if we end the draft sooner?" Alaan said.

"I'll believe it when I see it," she said. "I doubt Slithlor will let that happen."

"All of this is his fault, but the reporters aren't accosting him," Dre said.

"They don't want to make an enemy out of him. He is close to the king regent," Mommy said.

Dre showered and changed, then went to find Alaan in the gym, which was connected to the rest of the house by a large metal door in the kitchen. Dad installed it when they bought the factory next door. Chalk covered half the floor and mannequins were toppled over. It looked like a circus.

Alaan sat on a large hoop dangling from the ceiling. It was the largest in an eleven-ring obstacle course meant for light energy control exercises. He condensed, then shot three small balls of dark energy at one of the upright mannequins and missed.

"How did you pass the dark energy round?" Dre said from the doorway.

"The targets were bigger," he said. He fired more balls and missed again. "Could you tell when we activated the Correction Factor?"

Dre leaned against the doorframe. "With dark, yeah. When I am exhausted, my senses are numb. I pull and hope for the best, but it never feels right. With light, that's just the norm."

"I can teach you how to pull it properly," Alaan said.

Dre sighed. "Why did you ask to take the test separately?"

Alaan jumped from the ring and summoned just enough energy to drift down like a feather. "I have a better question. Do you think the MMA will replace the draft if we pass the test together, but all the other students continue to fail?"

"It won't matter if we pass it separately if everyone else still fails."

"It would motivate them if we pass alone."

"I invited them to train with us. If they are serious, they will come."

"Will their parents let them?"

"So the program is doomed." Dre panned his hand across the room. "At least we have this and each other."

"We can inspire them. Inspire their parents. We can practice in public."

Dre laughed. "Do you want to die? Mommy would kill us or worse."

"You don't really believe that she can 'Slap the magic out of you?'"

"She grew up in Wrinst before there was a dome. She lived through quitol attacks and the sun beaming down on her. I wouldn't put anything past her. Don't let those teacher's robes fool you."

"True, true." Alaan fired four more dark spheres, hitting the mannequin once. "Aiming is hard."

Dre created three spheres, fired them, and hit three mannequins in the forehead. "Yeah, it is," he said, then stepped back into the house.

He ran into Dad in the kitchen. Two tattooed black lines peeked above the collar of his shirt. A small gold hoop earring hung from his left ear and short stubble texturized his usually bald head. A large metal box hovered next to him on a bed of purple energy. "How did it go?" he asked.

"Two steps below great and one step above awful," Dre answered, and Dad raised an eyebrow. Dre crossed his arms. "We had to take the test separately."

"That is a surprise, but you like surprises." He winked.

"Not when they come from Alaan."

"Oh, so he did do it," Dad said.

"You knew and not me." It was a low blow. He was really going to chop Alaan in the head. "Ever since we stopped competing together, it's been difficult to predict what Alaan is up to."

Dad nodded at the box. "Another batch of fan mail."

"There is going to be a lot more after today. Mommy picked us up from the Castle."

He smirked. "Should we throw it out? We have so many unopened boxes as it is."

The reporter's words replayed in Dre's head. Maybe he had abandoned his fans. "You know what? I will read some now."

"Really?"

The Poli Twins' office was on the other side of the house. Boxes were stacked against one wall and six desks lined the opposite one. Dust covered everything. There used to be three employees and Dad who worked under the Poli Twin brand. They replied to fan mail, corresponded with the press, scheduled tournaments, and designed apparel. Now, there was only Dad, who stacked mail once a month. After the draft started, they shut down shop. A planned new line of eclipse-inspired merch was put on hold. It was hard to be celebrity tournament fighters when they rarely left the house.

"Wait a sec," Dad said. A light purple mist tickled Dre's face. It swept across the room. The chairs spun as they were wiped down. Dad squeezed the dirt into a tight ball and dumped it into the trash.

Each box was labeled with a date. Dre unstacked a few until he found the oldest one, from over a year ago. He flipped up the lid. Hundreds of metallic letters glinted. Brown ones made of expensive paper were sprinkled throughout. Dre pushed aside the ones from nobles and grabbed a small silver letter at the bottom. He sat down in his chair. His father stacked the new box before leaving.

Dear Poli Twins,

Thanks for your response. I didn't expect to hear from you. I took your advice and entered into the Gigasphere Tournaments. I am still a little nervous, but I started training three days a week after work. I am exhausted all the time, but I am motivated. I was wondering if you would be at the tournament this year. I think it would be safe for you to compete. Everyone knows your skills and about your ability, so if the Guard hasn't drafted you already, you should be safe. Or just come to cheer me on.

Animalist Vin Gammol, Wrinst

He grabbed another letter.

Dear Poli Twins,

I received a draft notice today. My parents think we should leave Lynit, but where would we go? Everyone is so afraid of it because you seem afraid, but could it really be that bad? You have to leave your family, but the Guard trains you. Isn't that a good thing? I am seventeen, so it should only be two years, and then I will be an adult. I would rather stay and get it over with. What should I do?

Psychic, Poli

"Oh no," Dre said as he put the letter down. He and Alaan were why no one was practicing the MMA material and why everyone feared the draft. The programs were going to fail because the Poli Twins were in hiding. If only Slithlor specifically weren't the one who ran the draft, Dre's parents wouldn't have been so paranoid. Dre and Alaan would have never stopped competing in tournaments. There was nothing wrong with joining the Guard.

He opened another box. He read several more pleas for advice. The abandonment wasn't just that Dre and Alaan weren't performing anymore, but that they weren't talking to the people anymore. Dre and Alaan had a lot of access and connections but freely shared their advice and insights. They didn't carry themselves with the air of mystery that nobles did. Even when it came to magic, they explained what they did when asked. Nobles trained in private because they were full of magical secrets they didn't want others to learn.

He rubbed his neck. He grabbed a big stack and took them to his room.

The walls were covered in autographed posters of every male member of the Poli Silvercats livit team, all eight of them shirtless and sexy. The sport was played on a field divided into three zones: two outer black rock zones for using magic and one grassy magic-free zone in the middle. The game started with three balls on the painted center line. Dre tried to play the game when he was younger, but since it required him to play without Alaan, he wasn't strong enough to make a team.

But other trophies cluttered his dresser. They were from matches won against Alaan. His father made them. Alaan had about the same amount in his room. Before their wizardry joined, the only person who was an appropriate competition for Dre was Alaan. After school, they sparred in Co Park. Others came to watch. By the time Dre was ten, it was as much about putting on a show for the fans as it was winning the fight. This was when their real fame started. Then their energies joined and they were able to fight other people. The paired combat in the Gigasphere Tournaments became the new showcase.

"We'll win the next one," he said, circling a spot for the trophy. He sat on his bed. He selected a letter.

Dear Poli Twins,

Something weird is happening with my sorcery. I noticed some symbols that appear to be changing on their own. Other sorcerers don't see it, but every time I cast any spell, those symbols activate.

Sometimes, it makes my spell more powerful or uses less energy. I tried to manipulate the symbols directly, and it made more symbols appear. Now, my spells don't behave at all as I expect. I could ask the Guard, but what if they draft me? What do you think I should do? Should I stop using magic?

Sorcerer Andela Passin, Virt

This was the sorcerer who disintegrated her body. She trusted the Poli Twins even though they had never met. He could have helped her or at least introduced her to someone else who could have. Maybe she would still be alive. Tears rolled down Dre's cheeks and ticked against the metallic paper.

He sniffled at a tap on the door. He wiped his face. "Come in."

Alaan entered. "So I was thinking…" He paused. "What happened?"

Dre lifted the letter. Alaan climbed onto the bed next to him.

"I had a whole argument prepared, but this trumps that," he said as he grabbed Dre's hand. "We have to start using magic in public again."

"Yeah, I know," Dre said.

Chapter 6 - Rye

Mr. P droned on at the front of the classroom about amphibians while Rye flipped through the MMA materials in his mind. There were two hundred and six creatures, thirty-one textbooks, and thousands of flashcards of fight sequences. There was a chapter on increasing morphing speed, one on instincts, and one on morphing with injuries. Rye was pretty sure there used to be a chapter on increasing muscle density, but he couldn't find it. The material was already fading from his mind. His first exam was in two weeks, but he still had no place to practice. The elite who ran the program said that there were several cohorts of children participating, but if their parents were like Rye's mother, then the program was going nowhere.

Through a window, pass the schoolyard, and high above the city, a semi-clear dome separated Virt from the world. It kept out the desert heat and roaming creatures, but Rye's parents were like environmental factors he couldn't escape. On one hand, his father was a motivation. The Guard only valued strength and wouldn't value Rye until he had it. On the other hand, his mother didn't value the Guard anymore. Both smothered him.

Animalism philosophy was rooted in adapting to the environment, but there was no form he could bend into that would allow him to study magic freely. However, if he twisted the mentality on its head and changed his environment, he could follow his own rules. Daily training would be the law. With his own gym, he could train all night. Or even better, he could leave Virt. If his mother couldn't find him, she couldn't stop him. All he would need was money and Lakree had plenty.

Several snaps broke his attention.

"Maybe it would be best to spend your last days at home," Mr. P said. He stopped wiping down the board. He dropped the rag on his desk. All the other students were gone.

"I wasn't drafted," Rye said, a tinge of annoyance in his voice.

"Oh, I assumed…never mind," he said. He stacked metal tablets onto a cart. "Then what has had you so distracted?"

"I'm in another Guard program," Rye said as he slid his papers into his backpack.

Mr. P wrung his hands. "I knew it. This needs to stop. Schools aren't schools anymore. Kids are too afraid to learn."

"That's everyone else's problem. I am exempt from the draft now. My problem is my mother."

Mr. P leaned closer. "Exempt? What is this new program?"

"It's called Magic and Martial Arts. We don't have to leave our homes or school. We are just expected to train in the evenings. I have animalism textbooks and moving pictures that explain fighting sequences stored in my head," Rye said.

"What do you mean by 'stored in your head'?" Mr. P said.

Rye tapped his head. "A room full of psychics put it here."

"What?" Mr P's face went slack.

Rye shrugged, flung his backpack over a shoulder, and left the room. He cut through the auditorium. The wooden podium looked lonely in the grey room. The chanting celebration of the MMA echoed in his mind. The program was larger than his mother's fears. It was a potential replacement for the draft, a chance to train children who were wasting their magic otherwise.

At the bottom of the stairs, doors opened onto a grass field. He hurried past a group of students chatting about everything except magic. The scent of sweets wafted in from the vendors stationed in the yard. Hundreds of kids milled about. Lakree waited next to the white awning of a cake shop. He hadn't changed his clothing style to match the Vous yet, but his hair was still tied up. Today was his last day at school. His last guaranteed day with Rye. After he crossed the noble threshold, Rye would have to fight for an overlap in their lives. At least through the MMA program, they would see each other once a month during exam time.

"I need your help," Rye said.

Lakree perked up. "...with what?"

"Could I have a piece of wood?"

Lakree's house was near the center of the city. There was so much wood there that his parents wouldn't notice if a fist-sized block worth a few hundred dilo went missing.

Before Lakree could respond, someone called out, "Noble Boy."

A small girl disturbed the flow of students around her. It was Astor. She wore a slim black dress that was inappropriate for school. Her hair was newly styled into two big braids and she carried a stack of papers. She always made a point to carry her schoolwork in her hands instead of a backpack. She was a year older and flaunted that she wasn't afraid of the draft. She had the best grades in the school, but the Guard still didn't want her, making her reckless. The crowd parted for her.

Lakree shrunk in on himself. Astor cut to the front of the line for cold teas. The people behind her didn't say anything. They didn't even look at her. Rye tugged on Lakree.

"This is where you have been hiding?" she shouted. "We are supposed to get lunch."

Lakree mumbled before saying, "I already have plans with Rye. I can't today." He put his arm around Rye's waist and pulled him close.

Astor sized up Rye. She pressed her lips tight, then turned her gaze back to Lakree. "His father was an elite, but he failed the draft like everyone else. I'm the best you'll get at this school," she said. "Give me a shot. We'll do lunch tomorrow."

"Yes, tomorrow is perfect. Let's meet here," Lakree said. He gripped Rye tighter as he said it, but it only made Rye cringe. It wouldn't be funny when she turned her anger or affection to Rye when Lakree was gone. Rye would really need to leave the dome.

Astor pulled out a piece of metallic paper, scribbled something down, then handed it to Lakree. "Call me," she said.

"I think that was a threat," Rye said under his breath.

Behind her, a boy ran into the cake line. He hugged another two boys there. "I took the exam late and I failed too," he said.

His friends and all the surrounding kids who heard congratulated him. He opened his arms wide in a grand gesture of triumph. He was an animalist. He might fill the empty seat in Rye's class left by Oron.

"They can still draft you," Astor said. "Starting today, any guard who thinks your pee looks magical will draft you." The boy clamped his arms around himself as if he were naked. She laughed, winked at Lakree, then turned away.

"The guard can't possibly track everyone's magic," Lakree said and it calmed those in earshot.

Someone bumped into Astor. Silver paper flew into the air. Her tea sloshed over her hand. She slammed the empty cup.

"Idiot," she said. "Did a psychic shrink your brain?"

"Sorry," Hila said. She clutched a book tight to her chest and looked over her shoulders at the papers on the ground as if she had no idea how they got there.

All other conversations stopped. No one stared directly because

Astor didn't like it when people stared, but they stood as if frozen. Astor shoved Hila. It was her signature response. Whatever could be done to resolve an issue, she did the opposite. Hila stumbled back and fell but still held on to her book.

"Fiiiiiiiiiiiiiight."

It broke the moment. Everyone scrambled. Rye pushed past the excited faces. A circle formed around the girls.

Hila placed her book on the ground and rose, her face rigid. Rye swallowed as he took a tentative step into the ring, prepared to beg Astor to forgive Hila. It was up to him to de-escalate this. That wasn't Hila's strength. But before a sound could escape his lips, she flicked him a glance that stopped him in his tracks.

"Pick them up," Astor said, pointing at the littered ground. Hila walked up to the older girl. She reached her right hand to the left side of her body. Then it shot up and backhanded Astor.

"No, she didn't!" some boy said; others whooped. Rye's jaw dropped.

"Triminara latinvitri phista," the bully screamed, holding out her hand. Tiny white strings fizzed in and out of the space surrounding her. The electricity waves spooled together, creating larger strings and pulling in more charges from the air. It was an elemental magic spell. Aster lifted her other hand and sparks flashed. Then, a line of lightning fired at Hila. It was slower than actual electricity, but Hila barely dodged it. The strike cracked against the school wall.

Protectors shouted. Blue lights flickered—shiny spheres of warding energy surrounded the bystanders. The fear of using magic was gone. Witnessing a fight was worth it.

"Fedelilo portantri ki." Hila responded with a shouting spell of her own. Wild flames curdled in front of her.

Rye's nose wrinkled at the stench of burnt metal and grass.

Astor repelled it with a rush of air, ripping a path through the flames. She flung her arms about, directing the magical winds. The gust gained strength and she curved it into the structure of a cyclone. Dust lifted into the air. Rye coughed, covering his mouth with his shirt.

A mist thickened above Hila and dew collected on her face. She shivered as the water droplets crystallized into snowflakes. A cold wave washed over Rye, reaching through his clothing like a knife. Protectors said more spells and the cold was banished.

As Aster pressed her now-roaring whirlwind forward, Hila pushed back with frigid air. It was difficult to see the collision through the blue-tinted shields and swirling debris, but Rye heard it. A deep roar and high-pitched whistle wrestled for dominance, grunting girls fueling the struggle.

Hila created soft shapes with her flowing arms and steps, giving instructions to her spells. Her movements were entirely unlike every other elemental mage's and unlike her personality. It was the only way to tell that she wasn't born in Lynit. She spoke and acted like an average girl from East Virt, but this was her accent. Her use of magic didn't follow the sharp movements used by the Cast family, the inventors of elemental magic.

Astor pressed further still and Hila slid back. Students shuffled out of the way as Hila was pushed against a wall. Her curly hair was pressed flat. She slid up the wall like a piece of cloth. Rye shouted uselessly in his mind for a teacher to break up the fight, but he didn't turn to look for one. This was the most magic he had seen in a long while. Not using animalism freely was a burden, but there were five other magics that were wonderful to see in their own right.

"You seem to have the adults fooled, but not me. You aren't Lynitian. You are a spy," Astor said. She launched the same taunt anytime she saw Hila. Usually, Hila did her best to ignore it, but this time, she smiled—no, she laughed.

Her lips moved and her cold spell intensified, picking up speed. It sounded like a whistle rising step by step until Astor's wind attack lost its luster. Hila lowered off the wall. She lifted a hand high, then sliced it down. Sleet flung Astor against a wall of students, knocking them over.

Rye whooped. There was likely a floating card that told her about cold magic and not backing down from a fight. The MMA material had changed her. It would change Rye, too.

Enough. The telepathic message cut through the noisy crowd. A short woman in brown robes floated overhead. "What happened?" she said, her round face pinched into a frown. She looked down at the girl covered in snow. Everyone looked away. The blue shields popped.

Astor charged at Hila, but a wall of purple mental energy stopped her. The teacher shook her finger.

"The draft will love that move," Astor said. This silenced the whispers.

Hila tilted back her head. "I am exempt," she said slowly, panting.

"There are only forty minutes left for lunch. Go eat," the teacher said, fanning away the crowd. "I want to see both of you in my office after school." She waited for Astor to calm herself and led her into the building.

Everyone cheered for Hila. Some chanted her name. Most would try an extra spell before bed tonight.

Rye ran up and hugged her. "No matter what happens, you are going down in history." He paused. He turned his gaze to the dome. "I should start a fight." He scanned the crowd. All the kids with green and white pins were potential sparring partners. His mother couldn't be mad at him for defending himself.

"Have you lost your mind?" Lakree said. His noble voice was back.

"She didn't start it," Rye said. After the draft started, Lakree harped about not using magic outside of class. He didn't think the school grounds were safe because one of the wizardry teachers used to be a guard.

"I did it on purpose," Hila said, crossing her arms.

"Oh," Rye said.

"I was never scared of her. I wasn't even afraid of the draft because my accent made people uncomfortable. The Guard wouldn't want me. But I didn't do my homework and failed the draft exam as we had agreed. I didn't draw any attention to myself. But now that I am in the MMA program, I don't have to take slack from anyone. My parents didn't raise me to cower," she said.

Rye snorted. They, more likely, had raised her to ask for help, but Hila chose to attack first and ask questions later anyway.

"You caused a scene," Lakree said. "I could have figured out a way-"

"For me to do what?" she snapped. "Run?"

"She's not going to leave you alone. That is how bullies work. You were lucky."

Hila shrugged. "It was worth it. My hand still tingles. I've never hit someone before. I haven't used magic so freely in a long time."

"It's not safe. I feel like there's something the elite didn't tell us," Lakree said.

"Of course there is," she said.

"So why did you fight her?" Lakree paused, then leveled his gaze. "I'm not paranoid."

"Everyone else is afraid of the draft because the Poli Twins are, but you are simply suspicious of everything. At most, ten thousand kids have been drafted out of millions, but you're always worried they will get us. Just because they took Drime doesn't mean we are all special," she said. She rubbed her collar, fingers playing on a simple necklace made of twine and three green stones. It was Drime's necklace. He had given it to her before he turned himself into the Guard.

"We must do the minimum until we know more," Lakree said. "I can't see the sequence of cause and effect. I don't know why the three of us were selected. It's the one question the elite didn't answer and it's a big one."

"No," Rye said. The minimum wasn't acceptable anymore. That's what his mother wanted for him, too. But it was his right to morph wherever and whenever he wanted. The Guard selected him to participate in the MMA program because they saw his potential. He would not let this opportunity go to waste.

"If she avoids me, I promise I won't look for her," Hila said.

Lakree stomped off, kicking up loose dirt.

"I'm going to learn all of it," Rye said, his voice small. If he planned to leave the dome, he had to tell someone. Secrets never flourished, but dreams did because they could be shared.

Lakree turned around so fast that he whipped himself in the eye with his hair. "I can't keep you safe if you don't listen to me. Trust me. There is something else at play."

"You don't want us to use magic, but you practice freely at home. Your parents encourage it, especially now. You learned to matter shift this week," Rye said.

"That's the problem," Lakree said. "I knew the technical aspects before, but I didn't have the strength. That day you came over was the only time it worked. But I have been able to cast other powerful spells sporadically. And now Hila. She overpowered Aster, who should have easily beaten her."

Hila swelled. "You've been practicing secretly while berating us for practicing too much."

"I have to prepare for my Verbindous," he said. "I have no choice."

"I can't believe you," she said, poking him, breaking his anger.

"No one saw it," he said with a slight chuckle, the tail of his words dropping off. He skipped ahead, trying to get out of range. She chased after him.

Lakree hopped onto the cobblestone pathway that separated the north and south campus. "I could matter shift us outside the dome," he said as his gaze turned up. "No one will see our magic out there."

The wrinkles on his forehead relaxed. His eyes were wide in wonder instead of narrow. He wasn't calculating risks. For a brief moment, he looked like a carefree younger version of himself, back when he had two-strand twists and wasn't consumed by paranoia. He looked like the boy that Rye used to dream about. Lakree was the first person Rye ever liked. When Rye told his parents, they were encouraging, but even at twelve, he knew that unless he became a captain or elite, there was no way Lakree would consider him. Their worlds were so distant. He was lucky to be his friend.

"We'll leave right now and get back in time for Hila to go to detention," Rye said.

No one complained about missing afternoon classes.

After stuffing down a few dishes, Rye slipped off campus. Lakree and Hila followed. The first several streets were narrow, lined with identical red stone houses. The buildings were smooth, almost single-piece structures that stretched the length of the block. They were built before the dome. A whole community lived inside. Rye lowered his head to avoid the gazes of old couples seated on the porches. Lakree spoke loudly about his relatives who were running for various government offices, being particular about repeating their last names often. Hila nodded along. None of the adults asked why they weren't in school.

The neighborhood changed to a mix of wooden and marble homes. The Lynitian symbol was carved into the pavement at every intersection. City workers in white jumpsuits installed thick rods that reached up to the dome. Long wires stretched from rod to rod and home to home, connecting telephone to telephone.

"This technology is eroding the traditions of magic, but it cannot replace it. Protector-encrypted communication will always be superior," Lakree said. Several nobles walking down the street nodded in agreement and also didn't ask why they weren't in school.

The dome sloped sharply at the edge of the city. There were no buildings within one hundred feet of it. There weren't any people either. It was quiet. Rye walked up to the thick glass. He tapped it. The dense material absorbed the sound. Outside, a ring of man-made cliffs surrounded the city, tiered into rows of increasing height. Two ramps outlined in white stones ran up the side of the cliffs, separated by a slit wide enough for two people to fit through. A pale red color swished on the wind. He rubbed the dome. The world his parents told him so much about was so close.

"Lakree, you're up," Rye said.

Lakree rubbed his neck. His hands were shaking. "Maybe this is a bad idea. The only thing I've moved before was a spoon. This may not work at all," he said.

"We are only moving two feet. You can do that," Rye said.

Lakree turned around, facing the city. The worry lines on his forehead were back. "If the Guard detects the matter shift, they might come to investigate."

"You said it yourself. The Guard can't possibly monitor everyone," Rye said.

Hila pointed at the blurry mountainside. "You can study how I overpowered Astor out there."

Lakree blinked, then searched the air for the invisible rules of the universe. His lips moved, forming various shapes as he read.

"Scard pert invid craimum ordum sansi frasit vidid manpri crip," Lakree said. His eyes darted around. Black specks circled him initially, then the radius expanded to include Rye and Hila. They started low, blotting out Rye's feet and legs. It was like standing in a murky pool he couldn't feel. He leaned in close. At his waist, some of the black dots shot away. It was as if they repelled each other. The spell stopped rising.

Lakree stomped a foot. "It didn't work. I can't do it."

"Try again," Rye said. He tried to scoop the black bits up, but his fingers moved through them to no effect. The rest disappeared as the universe corrected itself.

Lakree's eyes hardened. "I will be a Vous in four years. I can do this." He repeated the spell.

"Come on, come on, come on," Rye whispered. His future rode on this spell. There was no other place for him to practice. His home and school were off-limits. Running away was an idea but not the best option. He only needed to move two feet.

A thicker swath of black specks appeared as Rye imagined the respectful nods he would receive when he wore his green and white robes through the marble halls of the Castle. Even nobles respected him. He was an elite, just like his Dad. Everyone knew his name and they celebrated it. The echoes of Rye's boots resounded in his ears.

A burst of darkness raced up his chest and he held his breath. Outside the dome, black dots formed in the air, swirling. Lakree explained once that the spell worked by bending the destination space to him, then, when the universe corrected itself, sent him along with the bent space back to its original location. Rye closed his eyes before the spell swallowed all of them whole.

Chapter 7 - Rye

Heat stung Rye's face. His feet dangled. He opened his eyes and screamed, flailing as the bright world fell up to greet him. He hit the red ground. He was outside. The dome was a few paces behind him. Lakree's spell had transported him two feet forward and four feet into the air. The last black specks fluttered for a few more seconds, then evaporated.

"It worked," Lakree said, his voice breathy.

The uneven ground poked Rye's feet through his soft shoes. He lifted a hand over his face. "The sun is more yellow." He squinted up against the brilliance. It stung a little.

"Stop, don't stare at it," Hila said.

Rye dropped his gaze, blinking furiously. Dots drifted in his vision like after staring at light energy. "Why is it so bright?"

"It's a ball of fire in the sky," she said. "The dome dampens it and alters the color."

"I need to rest," Lakree said. He was hunched over, his hands braced against his legs. He hobbled to the shade of the cliffs and plopped down.

Rye ran up the ramp to the top of the cliff. The Winder Plains stretched out below. Bursts of rock formations populated the desert. Some were thin needle-like rock towers; others were complex networks of caves. The maze of pathways etched into the hillside of Virt was a natural defense.

"I am finally outside," Rye said. This was the beginning of the rest of his life. His mother couldn't yell at him about any magic he used out here because she wouldn't find out.

"I haven't been outside in so long. My mother's been saving for an escort for us to visit my dad," Hila said, then pointed to the East. "That's Poli over there." A silver dome sat low on the horizon, reflecting the yellow sun. It was the largest city in Lynit and a hub for merchants. They traveled the world discovering new treasures and brought back the best of the best to Lynit. The telephone wasn't invented in Lynit. It came from a nation to the North. They used science like Lynit used magic and lived in snowcapped mountains. There were so many places in the world to see.

A MMA flashcard surfaced in Rye's mind. It was a small white bird. Its anatomy was standard, but its long feathers were bushy. It lived in environments that were well below freezing.

"Whoa," Rye said, shaking his head. "The MMA material suggested something based on what I was thinking about." That was new.

"It recommended the cold spell during my fight with Astor," Hila said.

He grinned as he dropped down into a handstand. Blood, bone, organs. He pushed aside the flashcard for now and focused on the tipit anatomy. His wrist thinned and his mouth stretched into a beak. He color-corrected his growing wing tips. His vision honed and the tiny lines within Poli's distant dome resolved into tall metal buildings.

He flapped, lifting himself off the ground, leaving Hila and Lakree to wander without him. He sliced through the wind. The sky was a vast blue that belonged to him. The higher he climbed, the more the air thinned. Each beat of his wings was easier than the previous one. He relaxed into a soar. A human fear of heights flashed over him, but he reminded himself that he was a bird and that the sky was freedom.

The two other cities of Lynit, Wrinst and Nintur, were small and to the south, both built atop the only other fertile grounds of the region. They were both farming cities. Nintur was along the southern border of Lynit. It was a culinary center specializing in foreign cuisine until Sewit attacked with spirit fiends. Further east, past Poli, was a green line. It was the edge of Winder Plains and the beginning of a forest full of life. Spangots, big blue wolves, roamed the area. They were blind but had the best tracking skills in the world. Rye's dad promised to take him to see one after he selected his magic. Now, he would have to find his own way.

With a warm current, he could tour the world from the sky. No one would find him. In the forest, he could hunt, build shelter, and adapt. Survival skills were implanted in his head. He didn't need the Guard anymore. He would build his own strength. He could catalog new creatures, learn from them, break them, and then tame them.

Colors shifted on the ground. Red, black, brown, and gold. His eyes locked onto the movement. Two bodies huddled next to a cave on the side of the Virt. His descent was silent. His feathers flattened and his talons extended. A thirst to sink his claws into unsuspecting flesh rumbled in his stomach. The features of his prey resolved into a familiar boy and girl. He opened his wings, breaking off his attack. Thankfully, his humanity prevailed and he suppressed the creature's instinct to eat his friends. His unconventional training at stabbing his hand paid off. Lakree and Hila jumped back in panic. Rye landed gracefully between them. He released his morph.

As his human brain returned, he dropped the thought of escape. Any serious revelations made as a bird were skewed. Its escapist instincts distorted logic. It was an honor to serve in the Guard, to protect its citizens from those who would destroy them. Other nations had their own magics and Rye wasn't prepared yet to defend Lynit. And he couldn't abandon Lakree and Hila to stumble into a danger.

Hila held a finger to her lips. Her collar was damp with sweat and her sleeves and pants were rolled up. "We heard a noise inside." The cave opening was twice as tall as her and a few times wider. All three of them could stand fingertip to fingertip and still not touch the sides. The view inside was shallow, however. There was a sharp turn a few paces in. Lakree inched into the cave.

"If it's a quitol, it already smelled what you ate for lunch on your breath," Rye said.

"We can outrun them if we need to. They are slow," Lakree said.

"Their bodies are built for strength over speed and their skin is resistant to magic," Rye said. It was what was written in the textbooks, at least. He had never seen a real one. "If they catch us, one could pull our limbs off without much effort."

"The MMA material is suggesting several new spells to me. I want to try them," Lakree said. He crept closer.

Rye grabbed his arm. "Are you crazy? Quitols are the reason we first built the dome."

"I need to see you and Hila at your limits. Hold nothing back," Lakree said, an unfiltered curiosity in his eyes.

"I want to know, too," Hila said.

"But you can't slap it, Hila," Lakree said, a playful grin darting up the side of his face.

It was the final proof. His fear of using magic was gone. He was acting like his old self again, someone who shriveled up with puberty or the start of the draft. Leaving the dome fixed him. Everyone believed Lakree was wise and cautious, but Rye was the serious one. When they were little, Rye often stopped Lakree from running through restricted Castle areas. Lakree was just a boy who loved magic, too. Rye's grip loosened.

"But I can slap you," she said, raising the back of her hand. Lakree squealed.

A low growl followed by three quick barks echoed from the cave. It was a quitol. Rye motioned for them to back away. They were better off running, but Lakree rattled off syllables. Hila prepared her spells. Flashcards surfaced in Rye's mind. The MMA program recommended four different creatures. He grabbed the diagram of the torsit.

A brown and orange-spotted quitol stepped out of the cave. Its hide was shinier than Mr. P's imitations. It stood upright with two thick arms and four legs connected to its torso at different heights. Its three nostril holes sniffed.

Threads of electricity swelled in the air. The spell was the same one Astor used earlier. The creature howled as lightning cracked into its chest, but the attack didn't leave a mark. It charged at Hila.

Rye started with his skull, enlarging and thickening it, elongating his jaw and widening his smile. Color flushed over his skin and his ribs expanded. His arms shriveled and tucked close to his chest. It was his first attempt at this creature, but the transformation was familiar to his body. Those psychics had done more in his mind than store text. This program was amazing.

Before the quitol reached Hila, its feet lost purchase on the ground. It tried to take another step, but instead of moving forward, it rose a foot into the air. It flailed, tipping over and spinning in place. It was weightless. Lakree chanted. Hila danced around it, attacking with fire, water, and ice, all to little effect.

Rye wheezed. His lungs were collapsing. The morph had failed. He was too distracted by the fight. He wasn't acting like a proper animalist. He stepped back as his body returned to human. He shut his eyes and morphed again. His bones stretched and reshaped. Sound muffled into a monotone buzz as his ears shrank. He ignored the blips of quitol barks. The morph wasn't smooth, but it was completed.

The quitol's body jittered as if in a rapid pulling match between gravity and Lakree's spell. In the end, gravity won. The quitol hit the ground on its side. As it pushed itself upright, Rye charged. He leapt and his new powerful legs launched him high. At the crescent of his jump, he flipped forward, bringing the heel of his extended foot down on the quitol's head, just like in the flashcard.

The quitol did not buckle, though. Rye landed awkwardly, with one leg on the ground and the other stretched into nearly a split and still on the creature. The quitol grabbed his leg and spun him. A quick pressure pounded in his head. It released him and he soared for a moment before slamming into the cave wall. Air exploded from his chest. White spots clouded his vision. He cried out. He rubbed the back of his head. It was wet. His shoulders ached.

The sun's heat diminished and a shadow loomed. A high-pitched shrill triggered his instincts, or it was something from a flashcard, but he rolled to the side and tossed himself. The quitol landed where he had been. Its claws scraped away a chunk of rock. It growled. This fight wasn't fun anymore.

Hila waved her arms as a wind picked up. Red dirt stirred. A blinding cloud thrashed. The quitol barked. Rye picked a direction and moved slowly with his tiny arms extended out front. A whiff of the quitol whipped past him and he jumped. But it wasn't there. Lakree's and Hila's scents were all around him, too.

Rye called out to them. He yipped, howled, and barked but couldn't form words. The wind stopped, but the dust still hung in the air. He gritted his teeth and ran. A few seconds later, he burst out of the opaque nexus. He was the only one outside.

He skirted the edge until he spotted the path back to Virt. When enough dust settled to reveal the quitol, it wasn't alone. There were three more with it, one adult and two adolescents. This was why children didn't roam the Winder Plains and there were safe paths between the cities. It was his fault for not stopping their fight when the first quitol stepped out of the cave. Quitols were community creatures. There were always other quitols nearby.

Lakree and Hila were huddled together, shaking but safe. Rye ran. Though his hands were small, he scooped them up with ease. He zigzagged through a collection of rock formations that he could have avoided. The barks and stampede of the pursuing quitols softened as they struggled over the awkward terrain. He skirted around the jagged rocks on the hillside, then slipped through the slit between the two cliffs. Torsits were the fastest bipedal creature in the world. He stopped at the edge of the dome.

"Quickly, Lakree," Hila said.

His mouth moved. Black bits swirled around them. Specks rose to Rye's knees, then faded. "Not again," Lakree said. He clenched his fist and repeated the spell. Two puffs of white smoke flittered for a few seconds, then shot away. He tried the spell again. Only a few black dots formed.

Rye turned around at a cacophony of noise. The quitols arrived. They barked and banged against the rock. The two adults tried to fit through the slit but were too big. One of the smaller ones pushed its way to the front. It pulled its body in tight. Its knees scrapped as it dragged itself forward.

"Hurry up, Lakree, or this is it," Hila said.

One of the larger quitols started climbing up the cliff. It moved out of view, but the scrapes of its claws still echoed. The younger quitol was almost through. The second was climbing in behind it. It growled. Rye growled back. He put Lakree and Hila down.

Lakree took a slow breath and rolled his neck. He spoke the spell more carefully. Black dots faded in and out of existence.

"I promise I will stay away from Astor," Hila said.

More black bits swirled as the adult quitol crested the top of the tall cliff. Then it leapt. It soared right for them, traveling more than fifty feet. In all that he read about the creatures, nothing ever mentioned that their powerful legs, which usually enabled them to lift large rocks, also allowed them to practically fly.

A fast burst of darkness blotted out everything. Sound sloshed away and the heat ended. The matter shift worked. Panting breaths disturbed a new silence. Rye's feet were still on the ground, which was a bonus. The ground was marble, however. He was in a ballroom. Hundreds of small chandeliers lined the edge of the room. The ceiling was covered in a painting of the Winder Plains, the four cities of Lynit outlined with broad strokes and pale colors.

Portraits of pompously dressed men and women lined the walls. There was an uncanny similarity from frame to frame but, at the same time, distinct features in each face. The royal line married into a different noble family each generation. The Kertics were a mix of all Lynitians. A vast wood panel covered in markings spanned an entire wall. It was a mosaic. It told the story of the verdant Winder Plains and the cataclysm that had transformed it into a desert. The largest etching was a symbol of Lynit.

"I shouldn't have been able to do that," Lakree said softly. His legs flopped, but Hila caught him.

The wooden mosaic narrowed down to the back of a chair, the only chair in the room.

"This is the throne room," Rye said. This was the most protected place in the city. The Guard would not be happy to see intruders. Maybe kids shouldn't practice new spells outside the dome after all. Rye released his morph.

Chapter 8 - Rye

The man seated at the throne almost blended in with the wood. His hairless head was the same color. He slouched to the side with an elbow resting on the armrest. His narrow chin and lips lifted in a slow smirk that didn't reach his eyes. He wore purple robes and he wasn't the king regent, who was appointed to serve until the Prince turned nineteen.

He was Slithlor, the head of the draft. He wasn't exactly a family friend, but was one of the few who attended Rye's dad's funeral. Standing next to Slithlor was another psychic, a woman with wide eyes and a curved nose. She had pulled Rye from class for the MMA.

"There is always more than one way to know," Slithlor said as he slowly rose to his feet. It was a psychic saying. The woman tucked her face deeper into her high collar.

Several high-pitched whistles sounded in the distance. Large doors on the opposite side of the room flung open and the noise came in with it. Voices shouted. Boots pounded as a mass of colorful guards poured in. One shot up to the ceiling, white light swirling around her. Dark smoke surrounded Rye's hands, but it wasn't Lakree's spell. This energy was more controlled. It tightened on his wrist and yanked him to his knees. More wrapped around his ankles then condensed into a cast that clamped his arms and legs in place.

Flashing colors pummeled his mind. He couldn't concentrate enough to count the growing angry army that filled the room. He clenched his eyes shut, but it didn't help. He pictured a door on his forehead, then shut it. The images stopped.

"We are Lynitian. Don't hurt us," Rye gasped. It might have been better to have stayed with the quitols. At least the creatures would have been clumsy in their anger. These guards were calm and precise.

Lakree was on his side, hair sprawled around him like a mess of wires. His eyes were closed and he winced with each breath. Hila was bound on her knees like Rye. She had the face of a child caught stealing a snack.

An elemental mage with three earrings and a large afro approached with a hand raised. Rye's lips buzzed with the taste of a charge in the air. "Any attempt at magic will be considered a threat. Identify yourselves."

"I'm Rye Ter—" he said, cutting himself short. "I'm an animalist." His full name would not help the situation. His magic was the most important.

"I'm Hila Kolit, an elemental mage," she said.

Lakree didn't introduce himself. His head slouched over.

Hila spoke for him. "He is Cast and Yordin," she said, but it didn't seem to relax the guards. More continued to pack the room. Now there were more than ten wizards on the ceiling and just as many psychics who floated atop purple clouds.

"How did you get here?" the elemental mage said.

"A matter shift. It was an accident," Hila said.

"Get Captain Carnius Vous. They are Lynitian," she said. She lowered her hands and the static hum subsided. The other guards seemed to calm, too.

Rye sighed. The main crisis was averted. The Guard wouldn't kill him.

Captain Vous arrived. His face was flat with thin eyebrows. His long black hair was tied up in a top bun. His black and gold robes brushed against the ground, giving him the appearance of gliding. He checked his metal tablet. His gaze swept over Rye, then the room. "A matter shift? Impossible. Where did you come from?"

"You can ask Slithlor. He saw us," Rye said. He turned to the throne, but it was empty. Both psychics were gone.

Lakree wheezed as he lifted his head. His eyes were red. "I didn't mean to come here. I don't know what happened."

Captain Vous lifted Lakree's head higher and inspected his face. "You are the Oldenfoot who picked sorcery." He turned around. "Is this supposed to be some sort of joke? These kids did not break through four layers of security. Someone must have sent them."

"No one sent us," Hila said. "We were attacked by quitols and Lakree matter shifted us away."

"You were outside the dome?"

The guards tensed again. A new buzz of electricity hummed. Rye kept licking his lips as if he could eat away the threat. He was in deep trouble.

The sorcerer's face didn't change, however. "Take them."

Two guards hoisted Rye out of the room with Hila and Lakree behind him. Whistles echoed in the distance as the alarm repeated throughout the Castle. Stray guards stopped and watched.

"Rye?" A man said. A soft face gleamed amongst the hard ones. A single thick eyebrow stretched across his forehead. It was Captain Tamor Finrar. He gave Rye's father's eulogy. Rye tried to tuck his head away, but there was nowhere to hide. His short-lived training outside the dome was over forever. This fiasco would make it to his mother for sure.

Tamor pushed past a couple of guards. "Carnius, what's going on? Are they the intruders?"

Captain Vous didn't slow. "It's being handled."

"I know him. He is Rye Ternitu."

Rye winced.

"Ternitu?" Captain Vous said, raising a hand to stop the procession. "And with an Oldenfoot?"

"What happened?" Tamor said.

"They matter shifted into the throne room from outside the dome or somewhere underneath the Castle," Captain Vous said, then glanced an eye back at Rye. "Though it is likely the former."

Tamor stepped close. Small bits of grey flourish around the edges of his hairline. Though his teeth showed as he smiled, his eyes were sad. He placed a hand on Rye's shoulder. "Tell me what happened," he said, brushing Rye's cheek.

"I forgot that quitols lived in packs. It's my fault. They surprised us. We almost died."

"Is your father Barin Ternitu?" Captain Vous asked.

Rye nodded weakly. His father prided himself on reducing the family morning routine to a little under an hour. He led the training of new recruits with the same vigor and efficiency. But now the guard knew that none of his lessons trickled down to his son, who skipped school, sneaked outside the dome, and broke into the Castle. His father would have been ashamed. "Take them to Lieutenant Dormin Palow."

Tamor spun around. "You cannot read their minds. They are children."

"We thought Barin was a coward, but maybe he was a traitor after all. This could be part two of his plot," Captain Vous said.

"Traitor?" Rye said. It was one thing to be disappointed or even angry that his father wasn't strong enough to protect King Kertic. It was another thing to call him a traitor. This was uncalled for. He had died protecting the king.

"Have some respect, Carnius. You weren't there. You don't know what happened," Tamor said.

"You weren't there either. King Kertic was there, and where is he now?" Captain Vous glanced down at Rye. "Are you here to assassinate the Prince and Princess?"

"Assassinate?" Rye said. This line of exaggeration was too far. The Guard still didn't like his father and were now turning their ire to Rye. It was exactly as his mother had warned. This was why she didn't want him in the Guard. His instincts flared. MMA flashcards recommended six different birds. It was time to run, but he couldn't possibly escape Guard custody.

"Carnius, these are children. You are a Captain now. Don't embarrass yourself. There are protocols for intruders and protocols for children. Make sure they are followed."

"Yes, I am a captain and I won't overlook anything when Lynit's safety is at risk."

"You can read my mind," Rye said. He opened an imagined door on his forehead wide. Maybe the guards were scared, which was understandable. Children shouldn't be able to break through their wards by accident. He had nothing to hide.

"You can't agree to that," Tamor said, then squeezed Rye's shoulder. It was sore but he didn't shrink away. "Everything will be okay. Answer all their questions. I will be waiting for you when this is done."

"Tell my mom that I'm sorry," Rye said.

He was separated from Lakree and Hila. He was placed in a windowless room with a single desk and two chairs. A wizard snapped away the cast on his arms and legs. Someone handed him a glass of water, but his hands were shaking too much to drink it. A tall woman sat across from him with a slim folder, her posture square, elegant. A long scar ran down the side of her face, the mark curving away from her eye.

"Do you understand that trespassing in the throne room is a serious offense?" she inquired.

"It was an accident."

"Did you cast the matter shift?"

"No."

"Are you a sorcerer?"

"No."

"Then how do you know it was an accident?"

Rye shrugged. Sorcery rules were organized in complex sequences and affected each other based on their location in the endless strings that looped and knotted. There was no way he could guess what accidental changes Lakree made to circumvent the guards' protections. Only another sorcerer could figure it out.

She read a long list of names from her folder. They were all criminal sorcerers who might be capable of such a hack.

"Why won't you believe us? Lakree did the spell. He is noble. He will be a Vous soon."

"I am going to be frank. Things aren't looking good for you. Trespassing in the Castle is a serious offense. You will have to give me information or you won't be going home tonight. Do you know what it is like in prison?"

Rye shook his head. There wasn't much crime in Lynit because it was difficult to get away with it. But the ones who did it anyway didn't care if they were caught. They were the disturbed murders that even psychics couldn't fix. "Read my mind. I've told you everything."

"You haven't told me everything," she said, lowering her clipboard. "You haven't told me where your father is."

Rye clinched his hands and placed them on the table. She knew very well that his father was dead. All guards knew that. Something was wrong. He couldn't put his finger on it, but guards were saying too many wild things.

"He is buried here underneath the Castle, where all guards are buried," he said.

"I didn't ask about his casket. I want to know where he is. Was he outside the dome with you?"

Rye shifted in his chair. His father's body wasn't technically underneath the Castle because it was never found. The spirit fiends that attacked during the Battle of Ki leveled a city. Brick and metal evaporated from their pure energy attacks. Beings from the spirit realm didn't belong in the material world. Many bodies weren't found. But there was something extra in her tone. She was implying that his father was alive even though he had been very dead for over five years.

Someone entered the room, but Rye didn't take his eyes off the woman. This must be the intensive guard interrogation techniques he had heard about. She was good. He couldn't tell what was going on.

"Slithlor wants to speak to him," the new visitor said. He handed a brown paper to the woman. She read it slowly before sliding it to Rye. It was a draft order with his name on it. It explained that he had been placed in the MMA program through a paperwork mixup. He was originally supposed to be drafted. At the bottom, it said that his performance on the draft exam was outstanding.

"Outstanding?" Rye said. Maybe guards simply used dramatic language. When his room was a mess, his mother would say 'No one is going to marry you if you live like a copin.' She definitely picked up that phrase here. Or the guards that examined Rye were harsher than they should have been. They were just like the guards in the Castle. None of them liked his father and took it out on Rye. Despite Rye's slow morphing speed, he was a good animalist. He had what it took to be a guard.

The text about the two-week grace period was scratched out. This draft was effective immediately, and it was signed by Slithlor.

Rye looked up. "Is this about the matter shift?" There was no reason for an immediate draft unless it was meant to scare him. The Guard still wanted answers. "I really don't know how the spell works."

The man escorted Rye out of the interrogation room. The whistles were gone. A few guards pointed, but the fascination had subsided. The threat level was lowered. He scanned for Tamor but didn't see him. He was pushed into another room. It was all black. The walls, the table, and the chairs were carved from one continuous piece of gigastone. It was a hollowed-out boulder. It felt magically quiet. An electric light illuminated the space from a corner. Lakree and Hila huddled in another. They looked like the creatures at the zoo when an annoying kid banged on the cage.

"I think I didn't completely turn back to human. The torsit's brain must still be affecting me," Rye said. It was understandable that the Guard was on edge about the intrusion, but their comments about his father and the last-minute draft order were overboard.

Lakree started muttering. The words were almost familiar now. It was the matter shift spell.

Black mist swirled in a thick wave. It was barely distinguishable from the gigastone that canceled the stray bits that zipped too close. But more blackness flowed from Lakree. The spell moved from Rye's waist to chest.

Lakree was acting as crazy as the guards. He was put in the gigastone room so that he definitely couldn't matter shift. The spell would fail.

The door opened. Slithlor stepped in. He stared for a moment as if curious, before speaking. "I do commend your tenacity, but running is futile. That is not to say that you won't escape this room. Your potential is beyond anything most could imagine, but I deal in the unimaginable and I don't let it go," he said.

"Who's potential?" Rye said as the black mist jumped above his head. He didn't shut his eyes in time and a burst of images spun through his vision as his body was ripped away.

He crashed down on a wooden table. Two of the legs broke. His teeth rattled. His balance shifted. He gripped the sides as he slid backward. His elbows stabbed into splinters. The front legs of the table broke and the whole thing flattened out. It was thousands of dilo worth of imported wood destroyed. Rye was in Lakree's living room. A single chandelier jingled above; the rest of the sturdy home was unmoved. Lakree landed with a soft whoosh on a sofa next to him. Hila landed on a fluffy armchair.

"How did you do that, Lakree?" Rye said. Blood dribbled down his arms. Wood bits stuck out of his skin. Gigastone nullified magic. It was supposed to block any and every spell. Even the Vous were bound to that fact.

Hila jumped to her feet. "They tried to draft me."

"You too?" Rye said. He lifted the draft order still clutched in his hand.

Lakree wheezed, holding his chest. His face was twisted in agony. His skin blanched.

"He needs sugar," Rye said. Magic flowed from the spirit realm, but forming and manipulating it required nutrients in the body and Lakree's were all used up.

Hila went to the kitchen. Cabinets banged open. She returned with a waterberry cake and helped Lakree sit up. His eyes were barely open. "Did they draft us because of Lakree's matter shift?" she said.

Rye awkwardly maneuvered to his feet. "Or they didn't believe our stories and were trying to scare answers out of us. This was signed today." He handed it to her.

She sighed in relief. "I didn't even read all of it. I was too busy trying to bust out of the room."

Lakree lifted his head and finally took a bite of the pastry. Then he pointed at a bookcase. It was stacked with volumes of paper novels, though there were a few normal-priced metal ones. "Grab the wooden box on the end. The one with the sun etched on the top," he said, a breath for each word. Rye stepped over the broken table.

He grabbed the small box. "What is it?"

"We have to go to Poli," Lakree said. "My aunt will hide us."

Rye snickered. "You can't run from the Guard." Overexertion must have starved Lakree's brain of oxygen. He was delirious. Rye handed him the box.

"They aren't drafting us. It was a trick," Hila said.

"That's the problem. All of it was a trick," Lakree said. He checked the contents of the box.

Hila peered inside. "Including the MMA program?"

Lakree nodded. "Yes. Call your mother."

She leaned back, humming. Then she walked to the polished silver phone. She called home.

"Hi, Mom, I…" A low voice buzzed through the phone. "I'm at Lakree's house…I know…What? It isn't fake?"

"What?" Rye said. The surprise on the MMA psychic's face flashed in his mind. She was part of a competing program for the draft, but she met with Slithlor. She must have spotted the paperwork mix-up.

"No, I didn't do anything. Lakree said we need to leave. Huh? Now? Go now? I love you, too." She hung up, eyes wide.

Rye shook his head. "No, no, this is crazy. You did not get drafted, nor did Lakree, and nor did I. Isn't it weird that they only realized it today? They just want to know how Lakree matter shifted into the throne room," Rye said, then turned to him. "Did you tell them?"

Hila plopped down next to Lakree. "She told me to go to my father."

"No, no, no," Rye said. He lifted his hands in the air and pain pounded in his shoulder. "I know you're afraid of the draft, but you can't run. Lakree will pass out from the heat."

"Give me a few minutes and I will matter shift us there," Lakree said.

"To Poli?" Rye said, the inflection in his voice exaggerated. It took multiple guard sorcerers to travel to another city.

"I just matter shifted into the Castle and through gigastone. Don't question what I can do."

Rye closed his mouth.

"Now you call your mother," Lakree said.

"If they did draft us, we are supposed to have two weeks. That's the law. It doesn't matter what Slithlor scratched out. Take some time to think before you do something stupid," Rye said.

"Call her," Hila said.

Rye hesitated before he dialed home. His mother probably already knew that he was in the Castle, but he needed to make sure she was sitting down before he told her about the draft notice. He wanted to be drafted from the beginning, but these weren't the circumstances he had dreamed of. Despite what the draft notice said, it felt like the Guard didn't want anything to do with him. They didn't trust him or his father.

"Hello," his mother answered.

"Mom."

"Where are you?"

"Lakree's house."

"They said you broke into the throne room."

"Lakree did it. It was an accident."

"Come home now. I will handle it."

"Tell her you were drafted," Lakree shouted.

"What?" Mom said. "Why would they draft you now?" She paused, panting for a moment.

"There was a paperwork mixup, but Lakree doesn't believe it. He says that we need to go to Poli. His aunt will hide us."

"Yes, do that. Go with him. Tamor was right."

"Run from the Guard? Mom, tell me what's going on. Too much is happening too fast."

"The Guard is not through with tormenting our family."

The facts didn't line up, but there was more to the Guard's dislike of his father than his failure to protect King Kertic. They called him a coward, implied he was a traitor, and wanted to know where he was. Rye swallowed, and the sound rang in his ears. He licked his lips. With a slow, ragged breath, he said, "Did Dad run too?"

The phone went quiet. She breathed three long breaths before she spoke again. "They found the king's body and everyone else's in his personal guard, but not your father's. But it doesn't—"

The phone cut out. A second later, something slammed into the front door. The metal rods that anchored the stone door to the wall bent. Dust puffed in. People shouted. Lights flashed through the cracks around the door. Hila pulled Rye to the couch. The phone flew from his hand.

"Now," Hila said.

Lakree swallowed the rest of the waterberry cake whole and started his spell.

Another softer bang and the thick stone door fell off its hinges. The first man through the door said something, but it was distant, drowned out by a wind. Red spots mixed in with the swirling blackness. It was like the desert was being brought to them instead of the other way around.

The spell was so slow that the man, an animalist, grabbed Rye. On reflex, Rye wrapped his legs around Lakree. It was like his little brother's grip when Rye didn't want to carry him anymore.

The guard yanked and threatened him. Rye's aching body begged him to let go. He couldn't run, or he would be just like his dad. His father faced a similar challenge. An elite's duty was to protect the king, but his instincts must have told him something else. Spirit fiends' magical presence disturbed the reality around them. Deep terror sprung from understanding what they were. There was no preparation or training for that level of fear. Animalists knew to suppress their creature instincts, but they were slaves to their human ones, like everyone else.

Hila grabbed his shirt. "Remember our pact." Her eyes locked onto him. Another guard grabbed her and she screamed, but she didn't let him go. Darkness swallowed half their bodies and Hila's gaze held him in place. She pinned him with a force stronger than magic. They made the pact after Drime was drafted. His parents cried and pleaded, but it didn't matter. It was the law and Lakree, Hila, and Rye agreed that they would look after each other because the adults were useless.

Alone in the Winder Plains, Lakree and Hila wouldn't survive. They had MMA flashcards related to their magics but didn't know how to adapt to a new environment. Rye did. His animalist training prepared him for it. If Lakree's spell didn't travel as far as he expected, Rye could escort them to Poli. Rye knew how to avoid every creature in the desert.

The guard yanked again and Rye's fingers slipped apart. There was so much sweat and he was shaking and thirsty and so tired, tired of pretending not to want to join the Guard despite what they thought of his father, tired of living by the fears of his mother and Lakree. To make it to the forest outside of Lynit, to remove the disgust at his last name, he had to join the Guard. He would build the skills to protect the Prince in the next war. He couldn't let his human instincts dictate his life any more than a bird's. As the world blurred with darkness, Rye closed his eyes and bit down on a meaty hand holding his shirt until it let go.

Chapter 9 - Dre

Six black pillars curved from the edges of the stage, creating an apex. It was a cage for magical energy, a gigasphere. There were two more like it in the park that could hold fifty thousand. The ground was gigastone, too. This park was a deep crater, the remnants of a meteorite that pummeled the region a thousand years ago. A single defiant tree grew through the stone.

"I missed this place," Alaan said as he circled the closest stage.

The last time Dre had visited Co Park, temporary bleachers were stacked high with screaming fans. There was music and food. One bakery sold gigasphere-shaped sweet bread. The Gigasphere Tournament was the biggest event of the year.

"We could win the next one," Dre said. He held an invisible trophy in his hands. He waved to imaginary fans.

"The Balison sisters will have improved too. They are adults. They haven't stopped training," Alaan said. He walked over to a metal bin next to the stage. He lifted the lid and a soft glow reflected off his face. Dre moved along the edge of the park to another box. Inside, a pile of public communication orbs shined. They looked like a galaxy. He continued around the park in one direction and Alaan went in the other. Dre checked three more metal boxes. Most of the orbs were still powered. The first hundred arriving fans could spread the news of the twins' appearance.

"The reporter is late," Dre said when he met back up with Alaan.

"We have time. Mommy doesn't finish proctoring exams for another three hours."

"We could do a press release instead, ask the other parents to let their children practice with us."

"Words will help, but they're not enough. They need to believe that our parents let us practice in public. They need to see other MMA children practice in public and the Guard not show up to draft them. We won't get another opportunity to show up. Dad doesn't leave Poli often. It is now or never."

Today's challenge was to put on a public performance that didn't look planned, generate a large crowd of spectators, and get home before his mother could murder them in public. "Gah." Dre shook his head free of the image of her bursting through the crowds in a blue shield, then yanking him off the stage. She would slap the magic out of him, but he preferred it to happen in private. Crying outside was not a good look. "What if this isn't enough? It could take months for a parent to trust the draft exemption and our MMA cohort will fail the next exam if they don't start practicing soon. We won't be able to carry them again. The first exam was a special case, not the rule."

"Look at me. Relax. Breathe," Alaan said. "We are the Poli Twins. They will listen to us. We just have to perform well." He stepped back. He swept a foot across the ground in an arc, then lifted the opposite leg.

Dre smirked, then did the same. He leaned forward, balancing his body into a 'T.' Alaan did the same. Dre stepped through more movements. Alaan mirrored each breath, punch, and lean. Dre reminded Alaan that his kicks were low and lazy. Alaan pointed out when Dre's foot was turned in. They both corrected the mistakes, then finished the routine forty paces apart.

"I remembered more than I thought," Alaan said.

"No, you didn't. We mixed up two different ones. We were following each other."

"Heh, I thought I was real-time remembering."

"Real-time copying is just as important," Dre said. This skill was how they moved together in a fight, even without a plan. It was also supposed to be why Alaan never surprised Dre, but Dre didn't see that Alaan kept a secret from him. Maybe they were out of practice. "Do you remember the one with the lift?"

"The one with our eyes closed?" Alaan said. Dre nodded. "That was dangerous. Why did we do that?"

"Magic is dangerous. Do you remember it?"

Alaan nodded and rubbed his hands together. "All of our routines are burned into my head."

"Good." Dre counted aloud. On ten, he sprinted forward. Alaan ran to meet him. He dove high and Alaan dove low. His hanging suspenders slid against Alaan's back. He hit the ground, then rolled back to his feet. He closed his eyes.

Alaan swept his foot against the ground. Pebbles scrapped a few paces away. Dre moved slowly through a combo of punches and kicks. He ducked low and fabric brushed across the top of his head. He moved around his brother, working through a routine that required perfection from both of them.

A hand pressed against his right thigh, then he reached up to grab Alaan's waist as he cartwheeled to Dre's left thigh. For a moment, Alaan's weight was his. As kids, they trained with weight sharing before they knew they would need it. It was as if their subconscious was preparing them for what was to come. For the last move, Dre stepped in front of Alaan and grabbed his hands.

Alaan tensed. "I'm ready."

Dre jumped, pressing his hands down. His body was rigid. Alaan lifted his hands to hold the weight on his shoulders. Slowly, Dre unfolded his legs into a handstand as Alaan extended his arms above his head. Dre held the pose upside down and connected to the earth through Alaan, but Alaan's arms wobbled. He adjusted himself, forcing Dre to shift his body's angle. Alaan's hands moved again, which started the balancing act all over.

Dre opened his eyes. "Are there any other secrets you are keeping from me?"

Alaan flinched and his arms dipped. Dre yelped and dropped his legs. Alaan caught them and placed Dre on the ground.

"What is it?" Dre said. "Does Dad already know it?"

"Sorry, don't mean to interrupt," a voice said. A man with most of his face buried underneath a thick beard stood beside them. His pale bald head glistened with fresh beads of sweat. He wore multiple black and white rings. "I am Homin Yordin, civilian liaison to the Guard."

The Yordins would never leave the twins alone now that they knew the boys could still join their energies. It was a wizardry feat, in addition to sharing balance, that the family couldn't replicate. There had been a cascade of letters from Yordins after the MMA exam. They all personally requested to see the boys' magic.

"Hello," Dre and Alaan said together. Homin twitched slightly.

"I'm Alaan. Long 'a', long hair. This is my brother, Dre."

Homin patted his belly and cleared his throat. "What was that maneuver? Is it from the Magic and Martial Arts program?"

In any other situation, Dre would have ignored him, but right now, all fans were welcome to this impromptu Co Park show as long as they spread the news of the event. "No, it's our own thing," Dre said.

"Will it help you pass your next test?"

"No," Dre said.

"What if you didn't need to pass your next test?"

Dre checked his surroundings. There was usually an accomplice in a setup. Homin didn't want to ask them about magic. He was part two of the plot to get the Poli Twins indebted to the Yordin.

"What do you want?" Alaan said.

"From my title, you can guess that I am in constant contact with the Guard. As a government official, I have access to information and conversations that aren't open to the public. It is my duty to use that access to champion civilian concerns," the noble said. "Do you remember the woman fourteen years ago who was arrested at the border for refusing to cast a spell to prove her citizenship?"

"We were three," Alaan said.

"They don't teach that in public schools? It was an important moment. It sparked a debate around magic and identity. I worked with her to build a landmark case that declared the test discriminatory to the magically inept and that it was a right to keep our magic private. Now, we have the identification card and the Guard no longer has access to school records. The draft is the next big issue. By working together, we can end it."

"Sounds like a plan," Dre said. "You go do your job and leave us to do ours. We have to finish practicing the MMA material."

"Yes, of course. However, given that the other children in the program aren't practicing, it will be a struggle. Hopefully, your demonstration today will inspire them," he said.

Dre bit the inside of his lip to stop his face from changing. Yordin had done his homework and saw through this stunt.

"If your plan is to wait for the reporter from the *Poli Times*, well, he's not coming." Dre grabbed Alaan's hand. "The Poli Twins asked a junior reporter to bring a broadcast orb to Co Park. Did you seriously think he would keep it a secret?"

"He said he would," Dre said under his breath. If the parents of the MMA kids found out that this whole display was staged, they wouldn't trust Dre's and Alaan's message.

Homin pulled out an orb. "I have their broadcast orb, though. The

Editor-in-Chief owed the Yordin a favor."

"Excuse us, we have to go," Alaan said.

"You didn't use your PR team to organize this event. If your parents don't support this, how long will it last? If pressure is applied in the right places, we can stop children from having to leave their families. There is a Gigasphere Tournament in a couple of weeks. You would feel safe enough to compete again."

"You can apply your pressure without us. You only want to further associate us with the Yordin name," Dre said. "Don't think we didn't recognize that little Verbindous the other Yordin put us through."

Homin tilted his head to the side. "Lucky for you, it wasn't one or you would have failed. Yes, we are impressed that you can share balance and join energies, but that isn't enough. You're still missing some important ideas. Fortunately, we have plenty of time to train you. There are still two more years until you are nineteen."

Dre rolled his eyes. "We can literally do the impossible, but you think there is something you can teach us."

"You spoke to the other Yordin," Alaan said. "Did he tell you that we laughed at him?"

"To end the draft, you will need a lot of support. Yes, your brand is strong. It will sway the general population to your side, which will force most elected officials to at least publicly support you. However, changing a policy within the Guard takes powerful people working together, most of whom are noble. If potentially Yordin children were not receiving the proper preparation they needed for a Verbindous because of these Guard programs, there is at least one family that would support ending this mandatory training."

Dre dropped his smile. "Public opinion should matter more than a few nobles."

Homin shook his head. "Lynit doesn't work that way. The government makes the laws, not the people. Our case is that the

Guard's program infringes on civil rights."

"Which rights are those?" Dre said.

"The right to practice magic," he said.

"Hmm..." It was the first law of Lynit—every person, no matter their circumstances, had access to learn and use magic. "So you are saying that the draft makes children too afraid to practice magic. This was the situation from the beginning, but only now do you happen to notice this injustice when you can use it to get something out of us."

"We are minors. We can't agree to any deals," Alaan said.

"It's not a deal. I am only offering my help. A case like this will be sent to the council and king regent, the arbiters between the Guard and government. They will review every detail and interrogate everyone involved. Neither organization wants that level of scrutiny," Homin said. "Nobles may be the minority, but they represent about eighty percent of leadership roles in both organizations. If we get four families to support a change, we can broker a deal before the council and king regent address the case. "

"We change laws by threatening people with an audit?" Dre said.

"Exactly. The challenge with getting nobles onboard is that protecting the right to practice magic could mean that the MMA couldn't be mandatory either, which means that there would be no working program to rebuild the Guard. Not many would easily support that. Therefore, one path forward involves me only doing what is expected of my office. The other path involves having the Yordin on your side from the beginning. In the meantime, all you have to do is learn to integrate a few Yordin principles into your wizardry," Homin said. He lifted the orb to his head. "While you think about it, I will tell everyone that the Poli Twins are boldly practicing magic in Co Park."

Homin's eyes glossed over as the communication orb blinked to life.

"These Yordin," Dre said.

"Perform first and worry about him later," Alaan said. "For now, we only need to sway the people."

They left Homin and climbed into a gigasphere. Dre rubbed a pillar for good luck out of habit. Hopefully, it would shield him from the drama that came with nobles.

Dre and Alaan practiced a few spells from the MMA flashcards. After a short while, the first people arrived in Co Park. Middle-aged adults quietly watched from afar, pointing and nodding. Then the crowd went from thirty to a hundred to two hundred. It was still primarily adults, but a few children who should have been in school were sprinkled throughout. Light twinkled across the park as people used the public communication orbs. Within the next hour, there were over a few thousand. Hundreds stood on the elevated rim of the park. A few wizards and psychics floated overhead.

Blue and red lights flashed in another gigasphere. A girl stood in the middle of the stage. Two shields circled her. The lights flickered as they passed the spokes of the gigastone.

"It's Zalora," Dre said.

Alaan jumped up and down. "Yes. This is going to work. It will work." The crowd noticed, too. A soft roar grew.

Five more MMA participants eventually joined her. They crowded on one stage and manipulated magic around each other. Other people climbed onto the furthest stage. They were too tall and spun magic too quickly to be children, but Co Park was alive with energy.

When the park was half full, Alaan raised a hand. The chatter slowed to a halt. All their faces locked onto the stage. "It is a pleasure to see so many here, especially other kids. This used to be our park. Any day of the week, someone was in a gigasphere practicing a new spell. School provided us with knowledge and techniques, but this was where we developed our skills. I know it has been a long time, but Dre and I are back. Like our friends over there, we were put into a new program administered by the Guard. If we prove that this program's training is sufficient, we will end the draft for everyone. However, some parents are afraid of the program. They think it is a trick. We are here as proof it is not."

Alaan touched his necklace. Six overlapping wooden hoops rested on his chest. "King Kertic gave me this. He said that being Lynitian was about fighting for what you believe. He believed that six warring families could be brought together to make one great nation. Dre and I believe that the days of the draft are numbered."

There was more cheering and applause. A chant started. Other noise muffled it until the fans synced up to a beat.

"Twin magic," they said. It was the popular term for the Dre and Alaan's wizardry ability.

Alaan shook his head. Softly he said, "No, not that. We are practicing MMA material."

Dre spread his arms out. "Oh no, but that is what the crowd wants." He moved a cloud of energy to the center of the stage. The crowd chanted louder. "We don't want them to think we are hiding it because we are afraid. It is out of our hands now."

"Mmhmm," Alaan said. He shook his head for a few moments, then he caved. He backed up. He summoned light energy with a large wave of his hands. The crowd roared even louder.

As the pieces collided with Dre's, they flickered for a moment, then winked out. The energies canceled each other. The crowd gasped.

"No," Dre said. He pushed more energy into Alaan's, but each time, it vanished. It didn't make sense. He wasn't exhausted or numb. There was no disturbance in the pulses of wizardry. After the MMA test, they tested their energy joining and it worked fine.

When they were first interested in wizardry, their father warned them against it. He was convinced the boys only liked it because they had recently discovered their unique ability. "Your ability will manifest itself in any magic," he had said. But that wasn't the reason.

Wizardry was meant for them. It captured what being a twin meant. They were conceived as one but separated to achieve their best. Through rigorous training, they were able to move as one. But now, that togetherness wasn't reliable. Without the ability to share balance and join energies, being a twin was just an unfortunate birth defect. Dre sank to the floor.

The crowd didn't laugh. Instead, they shouted.

"Dre, cover us," Alaan said. His face was blank. He wasn't crying. He wasn't even looking at Dre. And his tone said that they were in danger.

Dre turned around as he summoned dark energy. A clump of guards penetrated the edge of the crowd, uniforms ranging across all magic types. They approached the farthest gigasphere, though everyone else resisted their movement. This was not part of the plan.

Dre pushed his energy low against the ground, fanning the darkness into a ring, the energy tugging on him like a belt. It condensed gradually as he swooped his arms over his head, thickening as he added more energy. When he finished, a heavy black dome thumped against the ground, blocking out all light.

Alaan stepped away and speckles glittered in his wake. The light moved around the small space in a wave, growing larger and brighter until it created another smaller bright dome around the boys. Alaan slid around the edges, coaxing the light to spin faster. It looked like the inside of a tornado with rugged streams racing together. The treads and lines thinned until only pure white surrounded them, no beginning, no end.

A pale blue seeped from above, bleeding into the mixing bowl. To the side, red expanded out. The colors didn't stay against the walls but moved into the air, blocking Dre's view of Alaan. Finally, green joined and divided the entire space into trisections of color. Dre lifted his hand but couldn't see it. He moved about, but the direction and intensities of the colors never changed, like a long-lost property of the universe.

Then, the world shifted. The colors mixed. They folded over each other like dough, making patterns of light and cross-sections of hues. The patterns multiplied and stretched out to distances beyond where Dre could see. It was like the infinite space between mirrors, always another pattern, always a deeper level. Dre shut his eyes against the nausea, thinking of his feet and the pressure of gravity.

"Look," Alaan said.

Dre opened his eyes to an illusion of Co Park. Everyone in the audience wore the same clothing and had the same hair. It was the same person copied over and over. Certain angles were off, too, like the curvature of the gigasphere pillars and there wasn't much depth in the park. It looked flat, like a picture. Though the guards' faces were blurred, their uniforms were crisp. They represented the six disciplines of magic.

"You can't do this!"

"Leave these children alone!"

"Run, Poli Twins!"

"Bullies!"

When Dre imagined them being kidnapped by Slithlor, nobles, or some obsessed fan, he assumed it would happen at night. These guards approached too openly with their collars down to fit that scenario. Whatever they wanted, they had the law on their side. "Do we run?" Dre said. If the Guard wanted him, they would have to work for it. He wiped his sweaty palms.

"Let's see what happens. They could be here for someone else. Be ready. Release it."

Dre snapped. Natural light pierced through and mocked Alaan's magic. The image of the park paled, hollowed. The copy of the guards wavered, looking more like a mirage than soldiers. Under the judgment of sunlight, the illusion didn't hold up. It hung in the air, silly. Alaan snapped and it vanished, emptying the stage of all magic.

The crowd fanned out around the pack of guards, but one man in black and white entered the circle.

"It's the Yordin," Alaan said.

"I doubt they are charging him with harassing minors," Dre said.

"If he is stepping in, then the guards must be here for us," Alaan said. "He doesn't care about anyone else."

The noble and guards spoke for a few minutes, then a guard pulled out a communication orb. After a long moment, all the guards retreated. The crowd cheered.

Homin turned around with a smug smirk on his face. Even his walk was smug. He created black steps up the side of the stage. The true power of the nobles was never their magic.

"There was a mix-up with your files. It seems that your group of Magic and Martial Arts participants was never supposed to be in the program. You were supposed to be drafted."

"This is crap," Alaan said.

"A mix-up? Ha," Dre said.

Homin handed Dre and Alaan the draft orders. Dre read his. The two-week notice period was scratched out. He was expected to present himself at the Castle immediately. It was signed by Slithlor.

"He really tried it," Dre said.

"I challenged Slithlor's authority to overrule the MMA's draft exemption. Correcting an administrative mistake is not sufficient grounds. He will have to get special permission from the head of defense, who is conveniently a Pol while Rigmen serves as the king regent. We already need noble support for the main case, so we'll start courting that family."

Dre sucked his teeth and crossed his arms. "Or is this blackmail?" The Yordin at the twins' MMA exam had threatened to make sure they were drafted if they didn't show him what he wanted to see. And this Yordin could be using the same threat to get the boys to join their family.

Behind Homin, a MMA participant floated above the crowd. A blanket of purple energy surrounded her small frame. On another gigasphere, Zalora placed an arm around Gron, rubbing his head.

Alaan raised a thumb, which caused everyone else in the park to clap. "It's not just us in danger. The other MMA participants would be taken, too," Alaan said.

"I know this looks bad, but I had nothing to do with these draft orders. If our relationship started with blackmail, it would end with blackmail. I wouldn't have made it this far in my career if I dealt in that. To prove it, you have the Yordin's full support to beat Slithlor's attack and end the draft for everyone. And I know the perfect Pol to talk to," Homin said. He nodded at his makeshift steps. The Yordin had the twins as puppets and knew it.

Chapter 10 - Rye

Rye didn't scream or flail as he bumped into the red ground of the Winder Plains. His elbows stung, but he stayed low. Black bits loomed above, billowing, blocking the sun. Lumps swelled and folded over themselves, growing in some spots and shrinking in others. They looked like dark fingers knuckled within, threatening to break the surface and snatch him back. The taste of a dirty hand soured on his tongue.

The last droplets fizzled out of existence and sunlight warmed his face. Nothing else came through the portal. The finicky matter shift succeeded again at exchanging one location for another, one problem for another. His father ran, and now he was on the run, too. It was a family trait. But it was difficult to imagine his father older, possibly with a wild beard, and hiding somewhere. It didn't fit in with his personality. He was brave enough to admit when he made mistakes, but he had abandoned his family without a word. There had to be an explanation and Rye would find it. He stood up, folded his draft notice, and slid it into a pocket.

Hila stomped about, her hair bouncing. She kicked up dust. "That spell," she said. "They almost had us. They grabbed us, but we got away." A purple finger-shaped bruise rested across her collarbone. She flinched as she touched it.

To the west, atop a rocky hill, was the silver dome of Virt. It looked like a fortress, a flag that claimed the desert for Lynit. Behind him was Poli, less than a mile away. The whole of the Winder Plains was reflected at warped angles. The top of the dome was transparent. Inside, the tips of black towers reached up to the sky.

"He was right all along. Something is going on with the draft," Hila said.

Lakree was still on the ground. His skin was translucent, and green veins branched underneath. His face wrinkled in strain. Hila called his name and shook him, but he only moaned. His chest rose and fell in sharp jabs.

"Why didn't he say anything before?" Rye said. He met Lakree when his father was a promising captain, which may have made Lakree consider talking to Rye in the first place. If every guard knew what happened with his father, so did every noble. The fact that only a few showed up at his dad's funeral hurt in a new way. Everyone knew except Rye. The snide remarks and silent glares were all justified. For five years, he missed the signs. After his father's disappearance, Lakree should have abandoned Rye, but he didn't. He'd done the opposite. He moved closer by transitioning to a public school. He was the best friend Rye could ask for. There was no way Rye could have left him in the desert to die.

"We wouldn't have believed him anyway," she said. He nodded.

She lifted and maneuvered Lakree onto Rye's back. His head drooped over Rye's shoulder. Rye adjusted his grip. He placed each step carefully as his ankles threatened to send them tumbling. Lakree sneezed, but it sounded more like a cough. Gross spray sprinkled on Rye's neck. They walked only a few minutes before Rye was exhausted.

A crater separated them from Poli. It stretched around the city, shallowing from the north to the south until it leveled out. It looked like the grove from a finger raked across dirt. A wide bridge arced like a bow across the crater. It was lined with floating orbs grouped in sets of three: blue, red, and grey. It was the only path across. A few paces away, a smooth road led to the bridge. It was a deeper red of compressed dirt stacked shin high off the ground. Sets of orbs stretched along the path that connected Virt and Poli. Hila took a step towards it.

"Wait," Rye said. "The road will activate." The blue orbs fired beams at each other. They grew until they formed a tunnel that protected travelers from roaming creatures. The blue streak was visible from Virt, even in daylight.

Hila re-examined the crater. "It will take hours to walk around but only five minutes to cross."

"But then the Guard will know where we are headed."

A gust of wind swooped from the crater, puffing up a cloud of dust. He squinted and turned his back to it. Hila did the same. Lakree's dreads whipped out in front, slapping him in the face. Lakree sneezed again.

"The red orbs can heal him," she shouted over the noise.

"He isn't injured. He's exhausted." By now, his body was drained.

"We can't get into Poli without him," she said. The wind broke. A dust cloud rose above them, twisting on higher currents, obscuring the sky.

Rye grunted. Sorcerers were packed inside Lakree's house, surveying the place with their magical eyes to decipher where Lakree's spell had sent them. It was only a matter of minutes before a new black mist appeared in the desert. A sleeping Lakree was a useless Lakree. "I'll take us into the crater."

It was deep, deep enough to kill anything that slipped into it. A ledge jutted out several arm lengths down, and below that, another ledge. It was like the tiered rows of cliffs that surrounded

Virt...maybe they weren't man-made after all. The Winder Plains had a style of its own. Abrasive winds designed the landscape.

"The orbs can temporarily stimulate his body. I have seen them work before. They are fast," she said.

"Even if it only takes one minute, that's too long," Rye said.

"But, the..."

"No," he said. In hunting, a critical moment came after the prey realized it was in danger. This was when instincts told it to retreat to a hiding place or run off in panic. Lakree, Hila, and Rye were somewhere in the middle, but they had to remain unseen. Hunters captured the prey they classified correctly. The Guard would lay a trap for them, but they won't know which to use.

"We are taking the bridge. You've never left Virt before. I have."

"Argue with me in Poli, not here," he snapped as he turned around.

She crossed her arms. "I knew you wanted to join the Guard, but I didn't think you would sink to sabotage to get it. You want us to get caught."

"I bit a man's hand for you," he said. He was a fugitive because of them. It was the opposite of joining the Guard. "Why didn't you conjure up a dust storm to hide us? Why didn't you cover our footprints? I am the one carrying Lakree. You could have done something useful. I will morph into a torsit, then carry you and Lakree into this crater. You aren't contributing anything."

She drew in several breaths, nostrils flaring. She evaluated him, Lakree, and the road. Arguing with her was tricky business. It hinged on the tone of voice—too gentle and she ignored it, too insulting and backlash was guaranteed. If he overshot the mark, she would hold her tongue until she was ready to strike, just like she had for Astor.

She tossed her chin up at him, giving him the go-ahead. He awkwardly shuffled Lakree onto her back. He checked his arms.

Splinters stuck out of his skin. They throbbed, but the bleeding had stopped. He picked at them, flicking hundreds of dilo worth of wood into the wind. A few pieces were too deep to pull out.

He surfaced the torsit diagram in his mind. Some of the details had already started to fade, but luckily, he remembered the important bits. A blimp in the back of his mind drew his attention away. A new MMA suggestion presented itself. It was a reptile with a bulbous knot on its tail. He twitched as a metallic blur sliced away one of the lizard's limbs. Black blood dripped into the blackness around it. Then, the appendage grew back.

He shook his head. His arm pained him, but cutting it off was not the best way to handle it. He shoved the MMA proposals away and morphed.

The pressure building in his forehead eased as his skull grew. As his limbs joined the transformation, the soft pulse in his elbows grew into a stab that shot up his arms. It was like hot needles in his skin. His eyes fluttered and the world tilted. He leaned forward, but a rough hand pulled him back from the edge.

"Don't kill yourself," she said.

He held up a hand as he caught his breath and returned to his human form. Morphs weren't supposed to be painful. It was a simple and essential property of animalism. Bones shattered and limbs atrophied, but changes were never painful, no matter how abrupt. The MMA material suggested a chapter on the Correction Factor that explained that injury management wasn't in the scope of its protections. Rye was in uncharted territory.

He dove back into the morph. The pain returned, but he pushed through it, forcing every muscle fiber and bone to stretch and thicken. He synced his heartbeat with the counts listed in the torsit diagram. His body resisted him, then obeyed. His clothing melded into his expanding form and his vision worsened. The splinters lodged themselves in the nooks between his muscles and bones. The pain swelled and his grip on the morph wavered again. He couldn't recall anymore what metabolic processes he needed to activate next. They were written on the information card, but the wording fuzzed in his mind. Everything fuzzed. As the next wave of pain pulsed, an idea rode the current. He shut down his nerve receptors. The pain dampened along the left side of his body. With the next pulse, he focused on the right side. His limbs prickled. He had created a flaw, something he had never done on purpose before, but it worked. His body felt like a swollen blob.

He picked up Lakree, and Hila climbed onto his back.

He peeked into the crater once more before he jumped the ten-foot distance. Hila yelped. He landed safely on the ledge, his backward-facing knees absorbing the shock. She hopped off and they walked north, passing cautiously underneath the bridge. Metal beams reinforced the arch. The orbs remained dull. They were safely out of the Guard's line of sight.

Poli rose over the crater wall, creeping closer as their path curved towards it. They stopped at a second ledge that jutted chest-high from the crater wall. It looked like a flat plank of stone wedged into the wall. The path he stood on dipped lower underneath the overhang, creating a shaded alternative to the road above.

Rye put down Lakree and released the morph. He didn't rely on the Correction Factor but carefully returned to his natural form. He shrunk and the brown colors of his pants returned to his legs. Tiny pieces of wood ticked against the ground. The splinters were expelled from his body.

Hila picked up Lakree's feet. Rye grabbed him under the arms. Lakree winced. At least he was responsive now. They ducked under the ledge and Rye's lower back screamed. Several shuffles in, he was panting.

"I need a rest," Rye said. He flopped down. Hila sat next to him and pulled Lakree's head into her lap. Rye leaned back; he ached all over.

Metallic hinges squeaked. Hila held a wooden box above Lakree's head. It was small, barely larger than her palm. A piece of paper nestled in a corner on top of a photograph. A rough red stone weighted the two down.

Hila rolled the stone between her fingers. Rye pulled out the picture. The edges were crisp, but the ink was faded. A woman dressed in guard attire with an "E" on her chest smirked. Her dreads were black and she had a few small moles on her face, like Lakree's father. Her collar was pressed flat and stripes stretched vertically over her shoulder. It was an old uniform he didn't recognize.

He checked the back. It was blank. "Half of Lakree's family is in the Guard. Why would she want to keep Lakree away from it?"

Hila swapped the picture for her paper. It was a note written in slick penmanship. It outlined how to contact Juli, but Rye looked away at the mention of Co Park, a place in Poli. He put it back into the box. He didn't want to know the details. His gut wouldn't let him abandon Lakree and Hila, but he would turn himself in after they made it to Poli. The draft orders had to be real if his mother told him to run. He would be stronger than his father if he returned. Whether the Guard forgave him or not for the bite, when they asked about Lakree's and Hila's whereabouts, he could answer honestly. He wouldn't know.

Hila passed the stone. "I bet Lakree has a complex plan in that sorcerer brain of his."

Rye scuffed as he dropped the stone back into the box. Lakree was passed out in the Winder Plains. He didn't have a plan. "You weren't in Lynit when the monsoon hit, but one random sunny day, the sky turned dark and millions of droplets splashed against the dome. It lasted for a month. The sound was deep, louder than thunder, but after two days, most people continued their normal lives. Not one droplet entered the city, but the Winder Plains was flooded. Whatever plans Lakree made inside the dome don't matter anymore. We are in the storm now."

Rye stayed awake each night during the rains, listening to the ruckus, imagining the water drenching his body and his primal instincts urging him to seek cover. But there wasn't any cover when every divot was filled with water. Many creatures of the Winder Plains drowned. And the intensity of the guards after Lakree would be more devastating than the rains. Lakree not only broke into the Castle, but he matter shifted through gigastone. The Guard was concerned and intrigued. Fleeing to Poli would not save him from pursuit, but Rye said nothing and drifted to sleep.

Later, he awoke to a sharp jab in the side. He moaned but didn't open his eyes. His head rested on Hila. A few stones tumbled in the crater, echoing all the way down. Another jab, and he sat up. He wiped the drool from his face and her shoulder. "Sorry."

She pointed at the lip of the overhead ledge. He squinted against the bright light. Something slithered against the roof, a hand, a hand with thick claws. They dug into the roof as something snorted above. A second claw gripped the side of the wall.

A smooth head peeked down, orange and brown spotted skin pulled tight across a giant skull. Its hallow red eyes glinted. It was a quitol. A smaller hand reached past the head, extending from its back. Its three slender fingers wiggled playfully as if they were only curious but were strong enough to crush a windpipe.

Hila struggled to pull Lakree's body away as the hand groped for his feet. It barked, then dipped lower, increasing its range. Its support hands clenched tighter. The black marks on its chest and neck were put there by Hila. It was the same quitol from before. It had followed their smell. It must have wandered for hours.

Images of birds and rodents popped into his mind. Each one was small and quick. He pushed them aside because he would only be able to save himself. Then, a bulky beast sprang to the front. It was covered in thick fur and its jaws were strong enough to break rock. Unfortunately, it was too big for the cramped space. Rye flipped through his personal repertoire, but it was too late. The creature was too close. Morphing quickly was his weakness. There was no form to take.

Hila lifted a hand. "Triminara latinvitri phistavado." The air buzzed deep, like a drum. Rye's mouth vibrated. He crouched back into the corner, dragging Lakree with him. Saliva dripped from the quitol's lips, spilling into an eye. It sniffed and growled.

The air blurred. It looked like the mirage above a hot surface, but this heat moved with a purpose. A slow path of disturbed currents reached from Hila to the creature, moving around its hand. She lifted her second hand and a boom cracked in the tiny space. Rye screamed, his voice quiet in his ringing ears. A light flashed and a bolt of white lightning shot from Hila. It followed the blurred path and struck the quitol in the face. Wind backlashed from the impact. Gelatinous bits of eyeball splattered everywhere.

The quitol fell into the crater, tumbling like a stone.

Rye shuddered, then crawled to the edge. Limbs molded neatly around rocks. "Good job," he said. A quitol tried to kill them, but they killed it first. This was the original purpose of magic.

Hila was frozen, palms still up and her gaze vacant. She inspected her hands before dropping them to her side.

Lakree sat up, wiping something from his cheek. The veins in his face were no longer visible. His breathing was even. He yawned and cracked his neck. "What was that?"

"Is it dead?" she asked.

Rye nodded. It was the deadest thing he had ever seen.

Lakree peered over the edge. "You did that, Hila?"

She didn't answer, but Rye responded for her. Lakree picked up his wooden box. "During the Battle of Ki, my aunt, Juli, came to see us for the first time in my life. She was panicked, scared. I didn't hear what she told my mother, but I know she gave her the red stone and never came back for it. My parents told me about the box and stone a few days after the draft started. They didn't mention what my aunt told them but said if there was an emergency, I should find her. It should be impossible to matter shift through gigastone. Even the Vous can't do that. Juli may know why I was able to."

Rye glanced back at the mangled quitol. They were resistant to magic, but they weren't impervious. "But why do they want to draft me?" His magic wasn't extraordinary.

"My parents have been speaking to both of your parents more often since the draft started. Drime's parents, too." Lakree sighed, then rubbed his face. "When we were put in the MMA program, I knew something was wrong. It didn't make any sense that they selected the three of us. I thought keeping our magic hidden by training outside the dome was safest, but that backfired."

"My mother would have told me if she knew that the Guard was interested in me," Hila said. "It was something we talked about often."

"Parents are good at keeping secrets," Rye said. His mother was never angry at the Guard, but she was angry at his father and didn't want Rye to learn the truth. The Guard wanted Rye because they thought he knew where his father was.

"If your magic is different, wouldn't that benefit a noble?" Hila said.

"Not when Slithlor's involved," Lakree said.

All this time, Rye thought Lakree was afraid of being drafted, but really, he was afraid of his aunt's conspiracy. If this elite didn't trust the Guard, maybe it was for a good reason. And maybe that was the same reason why Rye's father ran. It wasn't cowardly to flee when fleeing was the best option. "How long before you can matter shift us into Poli? I need to know what Juli knows."

"I might faint again," Lakree said, stepping from underneath the shade of the overhead ledge. "We have to sneak in."

Chapter 11 - Dre

Cordera Square was as Dre remembered. A few restaurants were new, but the strip of themed dining experiences was still as tacky as before. The servers at the Quitol Express dressed as smiling quitols and served racks of brist. A small girl banged on the table as her father tried to calm her. A woman walked towards them, nodding at the man as he held his daughter's hands still. A waiter noticed Dre, then froze. Dre waved. The woman tripped over the inflated legs that dangled off the waiter's hips. She fell into him, sending this platter airborne. The ribs tumbled next to the little girl and she clapped.

"Ooh," Dre said, wincing. He still had that effect on people.

"Greet the nobles," Homin said softly in his ear.

Two women sat cross-legged on a stone bench. The gold collars of their sorcerer overcoats were folded back. Their hair was braided in two different looping patterns emblematic of the Vous. One of them gasped and the other laughed, clasping her hands together.

The noble guards stopped talking when they spotted Alaan and the new disciples, the other six participants in the newly coined Gigasphere Showdown. Zalora, Gron, and four other kids moved like a swarm, circling Alaan, diving in to ask questions, smiling, and laughing at things that weren't that funny. They were excited to be walking in public with celebrities.

The women searched for Dre until they found him next to Homin at the back of the group. With each blink, the sorcerers likely switched between their natural and sorcerer's eyes. They read things about him he couldn't see or cover. Rules explained the laws of his body and his magic. They were probably searching for proof of the hilarious news that the Poli Twins were just two brothers now. The Verbindous came for everyone. Dre wished that he could disappear into the tunnels.

"I'll pass," he said. "My focus is on convincing the Pol to protect us from Slithlor's draft attempt. Who is this person we are going to meet?"

"Kalin Pol is a professor at Sepotine University who was consulted in creating both the draft and MMA. She was the one who suggested a draft exemption be part of the MMA program. All you need to do is remind her that she was right to add that barrier between the programs. Show her how that clause brought the Poli Twins out of hiding," Homin said.

"That shouldn't be so hard," Dre said.

"Yes, but why not use this time to lay the groundwork for the main case? It doesn't hurt to have nobles who like you."

"Today is our first day back in the public eye after a long while. How we behave now will determine what people think of the Poli Twins. We have to project confidence despite knowing that there is a draft order looming over our heads. If parents think our confidence is from having nobles looking out for us, they won't feel sure that their children will be safe. We have to balance the optics," Dre said.

"Balancing your efforts doesn't mean evenly dividing your attention. It means focusing your attention where it is most effective. To make the MMA a success, it will take a year or more. Are you confident that no new surprise will spook children out of training? Are you confident that the quality of the MMA educational material will be successful as a teaching method? I hear that the content starts to fade within days after implant. But, if you win the lawsuit, which would be over in a few weeks, none of that other stuff will matter."

Dre tried to think of a witty comeback but came up short. He sighed. "Fine."

"Greet every noble you pass since any of them could be the one that commits their family to support you," Homin said.

"There's not a specific person that makes these decisions?" Dre said. The council Members were the highest-ranking nobles but were busy overseeing the entire nation. Dre had assumed there was a second-in-command who handled family drama.

"It would erode the definition of our families if there was a hierarchy. If someone is a Yordin, they value balance at their core. Therefore, they wouldn't commit to a stance they weren't knowledgeable about since they'd risk unbalancing the Yordin's standing with the other nobles. If they attempted such a move anyway, they aren't Yordin. Nobility is not a one-way designation. Each family pursues its own philosophies. Ultimately, it boils down to sweet-talking a clever person into believing it is in their family's best interest to support you, then leaving them to convince the rest of the family."

"Then what do you need us to do? We already have the Yordin's support and I am sure you have experience in sweet-talking," Dre said, but in his head, he added, "and blackmailing."

"You are not only the new face of ending the draft. You control whether any training program will work. Children stopped practicing magic because you non-verbally warned them against it. But today, children practiced magic in public because you asked them to. If we end the mandatory nature of the draft and MMA training programs, nobles need to believe that the Poli Twins will continue to motivate children to rebuild the Guard. The issue is that you are known for only caring about your tournament fighting and fame. If you seemed more Yordin-leaning, they would know which principles guided you and they would trust that."

"And what does that entail? Wearing black and white?" Dre said.

"No, being a Yordin is about your magic. You would have to improve how you use wizardry. There is an excellent balance between you and Alaan. We admire it. This is where your fame comes from, but individually, you are still stunted. It seems like-"

"Well, we can't do anything about that. We were born with half the strength of the kids our age."

"Strength is a consequence of balance, not the cause."

Dre grunted. "If we hadn't chosen to focus on different energies, then we wouldn't have won any tournaments and you wouldn't have ever wanted us to be Yordin."

Homin smiled. "And there you have it. Your fame is still your primary concern."

"No, that is only what nobles think of pride when it doesn't involve them. To everyone else, we are two brothers who persevered despite having a handicap," Dre said. "We inspire kids to challenge themselves."

"I understand that it was difficult to arrive where you are, but there is more for you to learn, like all children," Homin said. "You can enroll in a Yordin school to pick up the lessons you haven't figured out during your home-schooling."

"That's not happening," Dre said. The official process to become a Yordin was the Verbindous, but the unofficial one that the public would identify was how Dre and Alaan behaved. If Dre and Alaan seemed like Yordin, then they were Yordin and it would reignite the idea that all of the twins' wizardry skills weren't learned but a product of what they were born with. "The only option left is to threaten the nobles, tell them that we will scare all children out of using magic even in the privacy of their own homes if the draft continues. I bet nobles trust that Lynit wouldn't survive with a generation of magicless children."

"We can try that," Homin said.

Dre stepped onto Dime Street. Stores selling expensive merchandise, from personal clocks to typewriters to knives, lined the road. The constant chime of opening doors echoed off the buildings. Teens roamed in packs, toting several bags each and talking nonstop. Every year, new entrepreneurs were awarded one of the twelve storefronts on this famous block to launch their businesses.

The biggest name in fashion, Victoria Finrar, started here. Even Alaan knew who she was. She was the first noble to stop wearing her family colors, even though she supported her family closely. To her, clothing was meant for expression, not designation. And that idea put her at the heart of Poli fashion. It was the reason Dre cut his belt from King Kertic into suspenders. He respected the royal family but had to make any gift from them his own.

If Dre were awarded one of the shops, he'd sell suspenders. The tables would hang from the ceiling on metal cables twisted with fabric and no two suspenders would be alike. He'd call the place Suspended. At first, people would buy them because of who he was, but after a few months, they'd sell themselves. Alaan would work the floor as he was the charmer and Dre would be in the back counting all the dilo. Dre had enough money left over from his performing days to buy a shop elsewhere, but Dime Street was the best place because it leveled the playing field. Any wealthy person could buy a shop. He and his brother weren't born into wealth, but new money and fame had similar benefits.

Tall gray buildings marked the perimeter of Sepotine University. Green and yellow vines draped from their roofs. Dre pulled up beside Alaan as they approached the front gate. Yellow flowers sprouted in a small garden below a statue of the university's founder, Alexandre Sepotine. His thick, wavy hair and the lines around his eyes were meticulously carved in bronze. Alaan circled it. He admired the man and this school. It was the first higher-level education institution that wasn't dedicated to preparation for entering the Guard and wasn't founded by a noble.

Gron read the plaque between the statue's feet. "For every ten problems that magic solves, there is an eleventh that it doesn't."

With a flash of Poli Twins' identical smiles, the MMA participants and their chaperone were granted entrance to the campus. Healthy grass covered most of the grounds. Large circular slices of stone punctured the green with gray. Students congregated around these spots. A large block of dark energy sat on a stone platform and a woman flicked it with light energy, shaping it into the shirtless man sitting next to her. A patch of hair on his chest trailed to a thin stream at his navel and beyond. His abs flexed as he laughed.

"Yes, please," Dre said. The other downside of being cooped up in his gym was that no boys were there. At least in the draft or Slithlor's lair, there might be shirtless, sweaty men. "Do you think someone would give me their number? We are seventeen now." When he was fourteen and smiled, the university men patted him on the head and said that he was adorable. But he wasn't adorable anymore. His voice was deep and little hairs grew on his chest. Though, he still wouldn't approach anyone first. After the third boy he pursued turned out not to even like boys but was a fan trying to give Dre what he wanted, Dre decided to wait for the men to come to him. At least so far, no one had ever initiated a fake romantic interest.

"Stop trying to get people arrested," Alaan said.

As they continued across campus, the men Dre passed who weren't already focused on their communication orb were happy to see him and wished him well but then quickly returned to searching for an orb instead of asking for an autograph. Word traveled fast in Lynit, almost instantaneously through communication orbs, but this was too fast. At Co Park, the crowd had been alive with excitement. Here, the return of the Poli Twins was old news.

A few paces away, a short, red-haired man ran up to a public communication box. He clenched his fist in excitement before pulling out an orb.

"Hi," Dre said, stepping closer. "Are there any more left in there?"

The man scanned the group. "Oh, wow. Hello," he said. "Ah, ah, no, there aren't any left. Sorry. You have to check another box. Good luck with your training." He moved a few paces away.

"Do they not remember what we look like?" Dre said.

"They know who we are but don't care," Alaan said.

"He should have offered me the orb," Dre said.

"Your new fixation with pretending that your energies don't join anymore backfired," Homin said, but Dre hadn't been pretending. His ability, his twinness, was disappearing. "Now we'll have to make our conversation with Kalin Pol more of a performance. She must believe that you will pass the next MMA exam."

When a child lost the ability to use the other five magics, the fade was unidirectional. Once it dried up, it never reverted course. Dre's ability could be on the same route. Yordin's have tried to replicate sharing balance and joining energies, but they never managed it. There was no definitive proof whether the ability was something the twins were born with or developed from their extensive practice. If it was the latter, then the Verbindous couldn't touch it. Therefore, Dre and Alaan couldn't attempt another performance until they answered that question.

Dre pressed his palms over his eyes to massage the forming headache. "They can't expect us to show them everything all at once. That has to be the reward for ending the draft. The Yordin are already on our side and the other families should trust you," he said. "For now, we only flirt."

"People should be celebrating the Poli Twins' return or gossiping about the guards who showed up at Co Park. This disinterest could destroy the only leverage that you have against the nobles. And for Kalin Pol specifically, we have to make sure she sees that you still have the clout to motivate children to practice magic," Homin said.

"We made it clear that we don't do private shows," Alaan said.

"Sepotine has an outdoor gigastone field," Homin said. "All of Lynit needs to see the full you."

Alaan sucked his teeth. "Okay."

But a public performance would be worse. Not only would the twins lose their fame and noble's support to end the draft, but Dre wasn't sure he would be able to stop himself from crying. Newspaper clippings of him balled up on the ground would be titled "The End of the Poli Twins."

Gron held up a finger. "If your energies stopped joining for real, would you be able to compete against each other like you used to? I liked those more than your fights against other people."

Alaan didn't answer.

Back then, they mixed wizardry, elemental magic, and animalism. This drew their first crowd. No one else would waste time practicing a dynamic that wouldn't last long, but Dre and Alaan had to explore every possible avenue to make up for their handicap. It drove them to rethink magic. Dre experimented with covering dark energy spheres in flame, while Alaan used light energy to float when in the form of a canine. But a win against children a few years younger never felt good and kids their age wouldn't give Alaan and Dre the time of day. An artificial rivalry grew between Alaan and Dre that limited both of them. They actively deceived each other in everyday life so that they could surprise each other better in the ring. The only positive outcome was that it led them to discover that their energies joined.

Dre shrugged. "It doesn't matter."

"But hypothetically, who would win now?" Gron said. He elbowed Dre.

"We are even. He is better in certain situations. I am better in others," Dre said as he darted a glance at Alaan, whose face was unreadable. Alaan's strength was supposed to be sweet-talking their way out of embarrassing situations, but he wasn't doing a great job of it. A public performance could destroy them.

"I mean, if Alaan decided he hated you, and you two fought, not holding back, who would win?"

"That would never happen," Dre said. Gron and most people framed them like close brothers, but they were more than that. Siblings went through life at different speeds, learning life lessons at different times. Dre and Alaan learned to walk the same day, got their first chin hair the same week, and were dumped by their first crush within the same month. They lived life as one across two bodies.

"Pretend. I'm sure you know his weaknesses."

Dre rolled his eyes. "There is no riff between us. There will never be one. But let's talk about you. Why is your sorcery so bad, but the Guard is interested in you?"

Gron raised his hands in defense. "I was just playing around."

Dre motioned to the group. "These are the questions we should be asking. Why were all sixteen of us supposed to be drafted a month ago? Maybe we shouldn't be performing for anyone until we answer that."

The MMA kids shrugged or shook their heads.

"Or, why was the mix-up discovered today?" Homin said.

"What if that is what the news is about?" Zalora said. "I'll check." She cast a spell and a grey light blinked in the air. It thickened as she shaped it with her hands. It solidified into a communication orb. She closed her eyes and didn't move for a moment. She blended in with the news junkie university students.

Dre shook her. "What is it?"

"Sorry," she said when she opened her eyes again. She extended her hand. "Connect to this one. I will manage the transmission."

Everyone touched it. A soft energy pricked Dre's fingertip. His body's natural resistance kept it out, but he pulled it in. The sensation slid up his arm, settling neatly in the center of his head. Voices mumbled, then clarified in his mind.

"What happened next?" a reporter said.

"I followed them," a girl said.

"Did you know where they were headed?"

"No"

"What made you follow them?"

"I was curious."

"Did they head towards the Castle?"

"No, they went to the edge of the city, to the west. They crept behind the Alphe Museum. I waited for a while, then peeked back there. I saw Lakree slumped against a rock outside the dome. I tried getting his attention, but after a few minutes, I left to get help."

"Interesting. According to your timeline, they left the dome over two hours before appearing in the throne room. That critical window may hold answers as to their motives for the intrusion. Hopefully, someone else will come forward with knowledge of what they did out there."

The male reporter signed off, then a woman's voice hummed in Dre's mind.

"For those of you just joining us, a few hours ago, three suspects illegally matter shifted into the throne room. Lakree Oldenfoot, of families Cast and Yordin, is, oddly, a sorcerer. He is fifteen years old and five foot ten. Hila Kolit is an elemental mage, fifteen, five foot seven. Rye Ternitu is an animalist, fifteen, five foot eight, and the son of the former Elite Barin Ternitu.

"It's not clear whether they matter shifted from within the Castle or the spell was cast from outside the dome. No one was harmed during the intrusion. The suspects were temporarily taken into custody but later escaped. No formal charges have been announced yet, but the incident has raised concerns about city defenses. If anyone has information on their whereabouts, please contact the Guard."

Dre lifted his finger. "Oh, good," he said. "That's why everyone is so distracted."

"What would drive Lakree to break into the Castle and then flee?" Homin said.

"Those three kids were in the MMA program. The news anchor said it earlier," Zalora said.

"This new generation of noble kids is picking magic that is different from their parents and these are the consequences. He wouldn't have qualified for the MMA if he'd picked wizardry or elemental magic," Homin said.

"They said that he matter shifted out of the Castle from inside a gigastone holding room," Zalora said.

"Then how did he end up in any Guard program?" Homin said. "The only way to make it into the MMA is if you aren't good enough for the draft. And there is an upper limit to the draft as well. Above a certain skill level, there is nothing new that the draft can teach you. Noble kids are also tested for the draft but almost always test out."

"He has an extraordinary ability and it sounds like he learned about a paperwork mix-up," Alaan said.

"Why is he afraid of the draft, though? noble kids love the Guard," Dre said.

"Unless he is afraid of Slithlor," Alaan said, then subtly sketched an "M" in the air. When Dre and Alaan were ten, they competed individually in their first Gigastone Tournament and lost to seven-year-olds. The following year, when they were eligible for paired combat, they won their first match against two fourteen-year-olds. Then, at twelve, they defeated two eighteen-year-olds with a combined light and dark energy attack. Within three hours, they met with a group called Medina that offered protection. They said that there may come a time when someone in Lynit decided the twins' unique ability was more important to them than the boys' freedom or lives. Dre didn't know of anyone else with a unique ability until now.

"If we could talk to those kids, they would be strong support for our case. We would have a Vous-in-training who is in danger of being trapped in a Guard program and not receiving the proper education he deserves," Dre said as he turned to Homin.

"His mother is a Yordin. She would help us," Homin said as he rubbed his beard.

"The nobles won't need to trust us if we prove that Slithlor is the real threat. He has found a loophole to snatch up any kid he wants," Alaan said.

Homin nodded. "I'll go to Virt to meet this boy's parents right now. Their emotions are still raw. I'll see if I can get the Cast parent to commit his family to ending the mandatory guard programs," he said.

"In the meantime, find another Yordin here to help you. They will introduce you to Kalin Pol and set up a space for you to perform, but as Dre said, hold back on joining your energies. She'll be hopeful for Lynit's future by seeing the Poli Twins return to practicing magic in public, but she may have missed the news of your earlier performance because of the Castle break-in. It should be easy to get her to uphold the draft exemption, if not also support ending the program altogether." He walked away.

Dre turned to Alaan. There was no telling what worked or didn't work with their magic. "We shouldn't do any sort of performance right now," he said.

"It'll be fine," Alaan said and smiled, but it didn't reach his eyes. There was no reason for him to be so confident unless he was up to something. In another circumstance, this would have comforted Dre that Alaan had a plan, but Dre didn't like spotting another secret. "I'll get us a Yordin."

Dre rubbed his blue suspenders. They were made of spangot fur. The creature was the best hunter on the planet and the most difficult to hunt. It was visually blind, but each follicle of fur was a sensor. It detected smells, vibrations, heat, light, magic, and some said even thoughts. But it still hadn't sensed its demise. Even the best could be defeated if not careful. There's always another angle. Outside the dome, every angle tried to kill. Inside the dome, every angle plotted.

Chapter 12 - Dre

Dre stood on the sidelines of Sepotine University's gigastone field, which was really meant for livit. Two strips of grass divided the rock into three rectangles. Opposing teams of six competed to score three forty-pound balls into goals. There were only two rules: only players touching a ball could use magic and no magic was allowed in the grass zones. A common strategy was to hold one ball for defense and send the rest of the team to score the other balls. Dre always wanted to play the sport, but Alaan had no interest, which meant Dre was never good enough to join any team.

Sepotine's team wore unadorned orange and brown quitol leather suits. Each player used a different magic, which was the more common pattern in recreational games. Though this team was balanced magically, they weren't any good. The protector shielded herself and tried to score points, which hadn't worked once the whole game. The wizard and animalist, the two most agile players, played defense instead of mid-field. Sepotine was thirty-seven points behind the opposing team from Wrinst. The chances of coming back in the last few minutes of the game were close to zero. There was one person on Sepotine's team who had skill, though. It was their sorcerer. He played mid-field, which was difficult for slow-cast magic, but he maintained a decreased friction spell going, which caused many comical slips and slides. Only MMA participants laughed at those as everyone else was still focused on the news of what happened in Virt. The question that still lingered was how Lakree matter shifted through gigastone. It was a new thing that went from impossible to rare.

"I used to play livit professionally before I retired to teach," Kalin Pol said. She was more than a head shorter than Dre. Her face was round with puffy cheeks. Two short, thin braids hung in the front while the rest of her head was buzzed. She wore the typical brown teacher's robe, but it was barely noticeable underneath the blue chains that looped around her neck, wrists, and ankles and were connected by strings of red beads.

"I would have thought you were in the Guard," Alaan said. He scratched his head, then immediately fixed his hair fin. This detail conflicted with Homin's intel. She wouldn't commit her family to a stance within the Guard since she wasn't part of it.

"Oh, I was, but I had fun, too. After the first few years in the Guard, you are either stressed because you barely survived a fight against an odd flavor of magic you have never seen before or are filling out paperwork about that fight. Maintaining a hobby other than war and bureaucracy kept me sane," she said. Dre never considered joining the Guard. Sleeping in the wild with bugs sounded awful. "But let's get to business. I only have a few minutes before I am needed to supervise an experiment after the game."

Alaan told her about their participation in the MMA program and their plan for a public performance. "At first, Dre and I thought the fear of the draft despite the exemption was unfounded, but then we practiced magic in public today to inspire other kids to do the same, and Slithlor drafted us," he said.

Kalin's brows knitted together. "He can't do that."

Alaan explained the ridiculous paperwork mixup. "Luckily, we are working with the Yordin, who challenged Slithlor's authority to override the exemption even for a clerical mistake. We think the same may have happened to a noble kid in the MMA who fled capture earlier today."

"Ah…" she said, nodding. "Slithlor will be forced to get approval for the irregularity from the head of the defense, who is Pol, which explains why you have come to see me."

Dre's eyes darted away, which was likely a sign of weakness. He had hoped her excitement at seeing the Poli Twins would have stunned her stupid. After the boys showed her a few tricks, she would plead for the end of the nasty programs that scared children from using magic. But she was already on to them. Dre brushed his arm with two fingers. He and Alaan would have to up their plan of attack.

"Dre and I are scared that if we are drafted, it will be the end of the MMA. Many believe that the MMA is a funnel for the draft and most parents don't want to be separated from their child for years," Alaan said. "Do you have any children, Kalin?"

She smirked, then sidestepped his question. "Most nobles said that the draft was bad when Slithlor first suggested it. The debate went before the council and the king regent. Council Member Yordin was the only one to side with the king regent to support the draft, but she stipulated that it was only acceptable until an alternative was found. If Slithlor is attacking the children in the potential alternate program, there will never be a replacement."

"So you'll help us?" Dre said, but in the back of his mind, he noted that Homin had left out an interesting piece of information. The Yordin initially supported the draft. Homin probably didn't care about infringements on the right to use magic. He just wanted to rebalance a mistake his family made.

"Any Pol would uphold the separation of the two training programs. It's not about helping you specifically, but it is because the MMA cannot function without clear boundaries. If you cross a boundary once, it will be broken later."

Dre had heard that protector's proverb before. It meant that any weakness in resolve or magic would be exploited. And this applied to laws, it seemed, for the Pol. Homin had said that if Dre were Yordin, the other nobles would know what he believed in, but the other side of that was that Dre knew what the nobles valued. There was a pattern to their behavior. It wasn't that they were serving themselves; they were serving the principles of their magic. The Yordin loved a redemption arc and the Pol valued clear definitions. Dre could use those angles. Being famous came from more than being the best at something. It took a sensitive ear to understand what people wanted and the skill to give it to them. Dre flicked a glance at Alaan. They were safe from Slithlor's attempted draft. Now, they needed to switch the conversation to getting the Pol's support to end all mandatory Guard programs.

The livit game ended. Sepotine lost. One of the players approached, his attention focused on Dre. He removed his helmet and jostled his shoulder-length hair, which covered part of his face. His pink lips parted in a smile. Above the neckline of his livit armor, he wore a black choker studded with gold rings. He was Jamil, Dre's ex. Years ago, Jamil didn't seem to care for his family's style, but all he needed to do now was braid his hair into a knot and he would be a Vous model.

"Dee," Jamil said, then gripped Dre tight, pulling him onto his toes. For a moment, Dre was weightless by way of a different sort of magic. His mind snapped back to the last time he was called that. He was at a professional livit match, the Silvercats versus the Quitols. The crowd sang chants. Dre's face was silver, but Jamil hadn't painted his, though he was more of a fan than Dre. He was serious that day. He didn't even heckle.

The game screeched to a halt when the sirens blared. It started as a deep rumble that vibrated in Dre's chest. People screamed. A

Quitols fan nearby pulled out a communication orb. She was in her forties. The wrinkles on her forehead showed through the orange paint. "Lynit is under attack," she said. That was the day King Kertic died. It was also the day Jamil broke up with Dre.

"It's good to see you again," Alaan said, shaking Jamil's hand.

"What are you doing here?" Dre said. Most noble kids set their goals on joining the Guard or government. This university was not a feeder school for either.

"I will join the Guard in the end, but I took your advice. I'll play some livit before I do," he said.

"Smart man," Kalin said.

Dre smiled. "…and music? Are you still singing?" Jamil's voice was always low, but his falsetto rose into the clouds.

"Yeah, still singing, but not writing any of my own stuff. And you? How have you been?"

"You don't listen to the news? We're back," Dre said, shaking his hands at his sides.

"That's great," Jamil said. "And besides training?"

Dre furrowed his brows. There wasn't anything else to his life, not anymore. There was Tess until she got drafted and Jamil until they broke up. "Until today, it had only been that."

Jamil pouted. "So still no time for yourself, huh?" he said. It was something that Jamil used to say. He didn't like that Dre rarely told stories that didn't involve Alaan, but what else could Dre do? He lived and worked with his brother. They were like binary stars orbiting a common center. Everything held together by their gravity was shared. He never wasn't thinking about Alaan.

"That's not fair," Dre said. "We are training to protect Lynit while you get to play sports."

Alaan explained their situation.

A girl ran up behind Jamil. "Can I still borrow your gear?"

"Oh, sorry, I forgot," he said. He unfastened the rest of his quitol armor.

She put it all on. "We are ready to start," she said to Kalin, who nodded in response. The girl joined about ten other students in armor who waited in the center of the field. They performed the experiment that Kalin spoke about.

Part of the group started with a soft chant. Syllables strung together to make words that Dre didn't know, but the language was familiar. It was sorcery and sounded almost like a song. The rhythm of their voices was practiced. The remaining students read aloud from thick tomes. They were sorcerers working a massive spell. They formed a circle. A small distortion writhed in the center. It was a dark hole that absorbed the light around it, but the edges weren't stable. It flexed and bent, sometimes swirling around itself. It partially collapsed before tripling in size. Everyone stepped back.

"What are they doing?" Dre said.

The distortion wiggled and twisted. It chewed, swallowed, and spat back out a pocket of reality. Several quick bursts of light flashed, followed by a boom. Everyone previously too busy for Alaan and Dre crowded the field. Four protectors joined the circle of spellcasters. They created blue shields with symbols rolling across the surface. As the distortion flashed again, they pinned it with the shields at its corners.

"It's the Spirit Club. They have been trying to open a portal to the spirit realm all year," Jamil said.

"Isn't that where spirit fiends live?" Alaan said.

"It's just a window," Kalin said. "We still know little about spirit fiends. We need a way to study them."

"That's still dangerous," Dre said as he slowly stepped back. If they saw the spirit realm, then the spirit realm saw them. The last time spirit fiends knew where humans were, they killed seventy thousand people, leveled a city, and killed a Kertic. The first international law banned tampering with the spirit realm. There was no way this experiment could be legal. Alaan didn't move with him, however. His face was focused.

"My research domain is into the origin of magic. We are all born with a connection to the same spirit energy, but the magics practiced in Lynit and the rest of the world are so different from each other. Magic is a translation process that is learned. Foreigners can't reconstruct our magic even though they have seen it. It is like a language that must be taught in childhood by a native speaker. I believe that understanding the spirit realm itself could be the key to unlocking how Kertic managed to stay fluent in six different tongues," she said.

"If the spirit fiends have crossed the boundary into our world before, does that mean the boundary is broken?" Jamil said.

"Yes, Sewit broke it," Kalin said, causing Dre to shudder. "Not in the sense that the spirit creatures will spill over here at any moment, but in the sense that we now know what is possible. The boundary in our imaginations has been broken. The nations may be locked into laws that ban experimentation, but a small village looking for power might risk it."

"In that case, we need more than just replacements for the soldiers we lost in the Battle of Ki," Jamil said. She nodded.

A fully implemented MMA program was a solution, but Dre agreed with the Yordin that they couldn't force children to train. The MMA was another form of school but without the typical motivation of getting good grades or passionate teachers that made learning fun. If the MMA were to meaningfully work, children needed to train for years, then funnel into the Guard for even more training. They had to be excited about learning and nothing was exciting about worrying that Slithlor might use another loophole to snatch up a child.

"And when will we know we are safe?" Dre said.

"There is no absolute safety. It is only a relative concept. All we can do is to evolve our defenses faster than everyone else's offenses," Kalin said.

"But the cost of that is the right to practice magic," Alaan said. His gaze was on the experiment, but he still followed the conversation.

"What do you mean?" Kalin said.

"Well, the fear of these mandatory programs has caused some kids to lose the ability to use magic," Alaan said.

"We made the MMA to combat the side effects of the draft," she said.

"But it is still happening," Alaan said. "There is a new lawsuit between the Guard and government over this."

"If your public practices work, the current cohorts will practice MMA material. Then we expand the program to all children," she said. The nobles were indifferent about ending the MMA because the twins had done what they wanted.

"That's an unfair burden on two children," Jamil said.

"We aren't ordinary children," Dre said, clasping his hands behind his back. He was famous, and like nobles, he knew how to make it work for him. "We must balance our fame with service. There should be no boundary between the two."

Kalin turned away from the field to watch Dre. His twist on the Yordin and Pol ideologies surprised her. He would continue to frame their plight as a challenge to the core of Lynit and, therefore, the nobility. This was a better strategy than threatening the nobles.

The distortion on the field boomed, which sent ripples into the shields that held its corners in place. It was now more of a window. The edges were sharp. It was an arm's span in width and as tall as a person. With the next boom, blue washed across the surface of the window. The crowd ahhed. The back of Dre's left ear tingled. The sensation was like hearing his name in a packed room, but unsure where it came from. He took a step forward.

The sorcerers moved, rotating their positions and adjusting the rhythm of their voices. The song slowed into a sad hymn. Dark streaks of blue moved across the pane. The edges of something round and dark slid into sight. It swiped from the bottom corner to the top. Green hills spilled into the frame, providing perspective. In the spirit realm, the sun was a deep blue ball in the sky. People clapped.

"I can't believe it. It worked," Kalin said.

"If we have figured this out, imagine what someone else will achieve in five years," Alaan said. "We won't get the best out of children in a forced program."

"The MMA is not the ideal solution. It is only an improvement over the draft. I don't know what the best solution is, but I don't believe putting all our hopes on the two of you is the best option," Kalin said.

"We already are the reason the programs don't work. Let us be part of the solution," Alaan said.

And then Dre heard his name again. It sounded like it came from behind, but it felt like it came from the window. The tingle had spread to his whole head and sank down his chest. Its progress was slow, but Dre took a few steps closer to speed it up. Alaan followed.

A brown flake of dust drifted across the spirit realm horizon. It climbed and descended the hills, growing bigger the closer it got. The tingling reached Dre's legs. It felt like prickling needles, not painful, but soothing. He wanted the sensation to engulf him.

"Alaandre!" a voice shouted, snapping Dre's stupor. He released his breath and whirled around. Behind four rows of unblinking faces was his mother. Her hands flew up in relief as she spotted him. Her clothing was clean, but sweat dripped down her face, and the top of her robe was unbuttoned. Dre tugged Alaan.

"Alaandre," she repeated, extending her arms.

"We need to get rid of her fast," Dre said softly. They were close to convincing Kalin but needed to position themselves as the critical boundary between the MMA's success and failure. Alaan nodded.

"Mommy," the boys called in unison. Dre weaved nervously through the crowd.

She hugged him. "I was so scared. What happened at Co Park?"

"Let's go over there," Alaan shouted over another boom, pointing to a spot well away from everyone. She followed. "We were preparing for the next MMA exam. We needed the safety of a gigasphere for a tricky new spell. Then, people showed up and it became a thing. It was definitely a bad idea."

Three quick booms rang. She wiped her forehead and smoothed out her robes. "Nice one, but try again."

Alaan opened and closed his mouth. That was the excuse the two had rehearsed, but somehow, she saw through it. Dre raised his hand like he was in school. "We practiced MMA material in public to motivate the others in the program. They were too afraid of the draft to practice at home. We barely passed the first test, but if the others don't seriously practice, they will fail the second test and the entire program will fail. We will be eligible for the draft all over again."

"I thought you two were planning something the past few weeks, but I trusted you. You took that trust and abused it." Her eyes fell upon Dre. He resisted the urge to squirm because he wasn't sorry for what he attempted. He only regretted the outcome. He described the guards showing up at the park. When he mentioned the draft orders and the supposed paperwork mixup, she held out her hand. He pulled out the brown piece of paper. She touched it with her fingertips as if it would burn her. He explained that things would have been worse if he had stayed home. Homin wouldn't have been there to save them from the immediate draft order.

"But we just convinced the Pol to uphold the draft exemption.

Now all we need are three more families to protect our right to practice magic," Alaan said.

"We'll leave Poli," she said softly, dropping the paper.

"No, Mommy. If we succeed, mandatory training programs for everyone will end," Dre said.

"We are trying to—"

With the next boom, she grabbed Alaan's arm. "You think I care about some plan," she said.

Alaan yanked free. "If we leave, the MMA will fail. More kids will be drafted. We have to try. This is not only about us."

"You think all of this is a game? Slithlor has been trying to study you since before you were born. Only the law has kept him from treating you like those people he tortured when he was head of foreign magic research. With the draft, he has the law on his side. This isn't the—"

"Wait, listen," Dre interrupted.

She paused for a moment. "Go ahead, explain to me why I should care."

"The Pol are protecting us," Dre stuttered. She only thought of them as her children, but they were more to the rest of Lynit. Before the Battle of Ki, their performances attracted people from all over the nation. Children, adults, nobles, and even the Kertics traveled to see them. They were the biggest entertainers. After the Battle of Ki, they became the Poli Twins, a symbol of Lynit. "When we hid from the draft. We made everyone else hide. Children are losing their magic. You and Dad panicked. Now, the rest of Lynit is paying for it."

"Oh," she said, nodding. "Because these people like you, it means you owe them something?" She fanned out an arm, then snapped a finger. "But look at that. No one is even paying attention to you, the most famous boys in all of Lynit. They have found something more interesting than you. Too bad you can't matter shift through gigastone."

"What do you want us to do? Hide in the house and never use magic again?" Alaan asked.

"Dad and I said you could participate in the MMA program as long as you trained for it in the house. You have a whole gym," she said.

"That's not enough," Dre yelled. It was the first time he had ever raised his voice in anger. Though Dre and Alaan trained daily, more of the same would not fix the problem of Alaan practicing dark energy behind Dre's back or their energy not joining. He hoped that the problems were connected. The only solution that he could think of was returning to tournament fighting. He never felt closer to Alaan than when they moved as one in battle.

She gasped. "Who do you think you're talking to?" she said.

The heat in Dre's face vanished as quickly as it had come. He wouldn't look away, but he did not answer that question.

Alaan grabbed his hand. "We will end the draft."

Dre clenched his body. His mind flashed with an image of Mommy and her magic-stealing hand raised for a death strike.

A slight smirk whisked across her face. Another boom rang a pitch lower than the previous ones, echoing off the buildings. She rose on her toes, her nose a finger away from Dre's. She pressed her lips into a tight line.

"There was a special power in being a parent. I had the power to say 'no.' nobles, elites, guards, and even the Kertics could all say 'yes,' but a simple 'no' from me negated all of it. This draft steals that away, but I don't accept that." Her gaze shifted to Alaan. "I suggest you have the best day of your life today. It's your last one in Lynit. I'll see you when you get home." She buttoned the top of her robe, then stalked away.

When Slithlor announced the draft, it was phrased as a better education system for the most talented children. Many celebrated the initiative. It seemed like the only logical way to rebuild an army. And in theory, it was true. There wasn't an outcry when the first batch of children were taken. Families were saddened but not distraught. Now, because of the twins, however, they were. Dre read more of the letters he had received, some from the parents of draftees asking what happened inside the Castle. In a way, the twins had become more famous and crucial to Lynit's culture, but simultaneously, they were more reclusive and noble-like. They had so much power between them but were blocked from using it to help others. The parental power that Mommy talked about was selfish. Parents didn't know what was best for the world. They only knew how to keep their children safe for one more day.

The booms of the Spirit Club's experiment drowned Dre's grunts and sobs. He buried his face in Alaan's shoulder. Alaan hugged him tightly through the shuddering. His chest caved as Alaan's expanded. They were in sync. At least he still had that.

When the crowd started to disperse, Dre and Alaan separated and wiped their faces. Dre didn't think he could put on a smile, but he at least didn't want to be seen crying. There have been articles written about him for much less. The experiment ended with a lot of noise but from more voices than booms. The conversations were discordant. Some sounded of joy, others of anger.

Zalora, Gron, and the other MMA participants hurried over. "The Guard is shutting down the school because of the experiment," Zalora said. The window to the spirit realm was gone. Dre glimpsed Kalin, who was in a heated discussion with three other professors.

"So I guess no performance then," Gron said.

Alaan shook his head. "And our parents are taking us on a trip tomorrow. We don't know when we will be back."

"What does that mean for the court case?" Zalora said.

Alaan rose on his toes and scanned the crowd. "The Pol will keep us out of the draft, but they don't like that Dre and I are at the center of motivating everyone to train. You have to show them that we aren't needed as long as you believe you are safe from the draft. Can you take the lead on finding more MMA children? Get them to practice in public?" Zalora nodded.

Dre excused himself and waded through the crowd. He found Jamil and told him what happened with his mother.

"That sounds like her," Jamil said.

"Before we go, can you study our magic? Our energy doesn't join consistently anymore," Dre said.

Jamil searched Dre's face, then his eyes softened. "Oh, that's big, like very big for you, for both of you."

"Can you look at it?"

"Right now?"

"The Vous are supposed to be the best of the best."

"It's not something that I can glance at. I'm not an expert in the proper behavior of wizardry."

"But you can spot what the disturbance is?"

"The rules a sorcerer sees encompass all the rules of the universe, from the speed of light through water to the forces that hold your atoms together. I need to know where to look. I have to research the symbols."

"If you studied us, could you learn to reproduce our ability and then figure out what is going wrong?"

"Every magic can theoretically be reproduced with sorcery since, by definition, magic is the manipulation of energy and even energy follows rules, but no sorcerer has ever been able to do it completely. "

"Okay, Vous. I am not asking you to pioneer a new field. I only want to know if the Verbindous has come for us."

"Oh, I can check that. That has nothing to do with your specific magic. But it still takes some time. I need to see you use magic until you are exhausted. Basically, I need to see a Verbindous."

"Why is nineteen the cutoff age?"

"It's the age after which no one has ever been able to use a second magic except the first Kertic. All magic comes from the spirit realm and our connection to that place is amorphous when we are young. Then, as we age, our connection stabilizes into a particular flavor. Foreign magic has the same cutoff."

"I know this may be a lot to ask, but could you spare a few hours to study us?" Dre said.

"Sure, I can try," Jamil said. "Classes are canceled for at least the rest of the week."

Dre, Alaan, and Jamil left campus without anyone following them. They went underground at the nearest tunnel. It opened up into a node, an intersection of six tunnels. Sunlight filtered through three glass circles on the ceiling. Small stone blocks covered the walls in symmetric patterns: rectangle, triangle, triangle, rectangle, circle. Barely visible in the dim lighting, the ceiling housed a faded map of the network. "Sepotine" was chiseled crudely into the ground.

A soft, singsong voice whispered, "Alaandre." The tone was familiar, but it wasn't his mother's. A girl entered from a side path. Her round face was set with a sly smile. Her clothes were dingy and her dyed purple hair desperately needed a pick. Her stance was relaxed. She looked as if she enjoyed the confusion.

"Tess!" Alaan and Dre shouted, their voices echoing down the tunnels. Dre covered his mouth. He checked above, but no one was there.

"I knew I could count on you taking this route," she said.

"What are you doing here?" Dre said. He hugged her, sniffed her, then regretted both. She smelled like the back alley behind the gym, like she hadn't showered since the last time he saw her a month ago.

"I came to see you," she said.

"They let you out?" Alaan said.

Dre squinted. "Read the room, Alaan. She didn't go."

"Didn't go where?" Jamil said.

"You ran away?" Alaan said. Her smile wavered for a moment, but she nodded.

"Oh," Jamil said. "She was drafted."

"I thought you were fine with joining," Alaan said. Dre had sparred with her often when they were younger and lost every time, though she was two years younger. She picked up training after school to stay involved in the twins' lives but became as dedicated as them over the years. She was committed to excellence. She didn't hide anything during her draft exam.

"I was. I went to the Castle," she said, eyes dropping to her feet. "I spoke to the person at the front desk. He called a guard to escort me. Along the way, I overheard a couple of guards talking about a Vous kid that was drafted. My escort heard it, too, and jumped into the conversation, demanding to know who submitted the paperwork. She left me there to stop that order from going through since nobles aren't drafted.

"I waited for a while, but she didn't return. Then I was angry. I couldn't believe that guards were more focused on ensuring nobles weren't drafted than drafting me. I thought we needed to rebuild the Guard, but I guess we aren't all needed. I walked right out of the Castle. My heart was pounding, but no one noticed me because I wasn't noble. That's how those kids broke into the throne room. They walked in and then walked back out."

"No way," Jamil said. "My cousin did say that the Guard tried to draft her, but I thought she was lying. Slithlor is full of himself if he thinks the first iteration of his new program is better than the education nobles have perfected over generations."

"A few days later, I met other kids at a food bank hiding from the draft. They took me with them," she said.

"Do you have money?" Alaan said, reaching into his pocket. He pulled out a stack of coins wrapped in a cloth.

Her eyes widened. "No," she said, staring at Alaan's hand. "But, but, but, that's not why I've come. I want to hear about the guards at Co Park. What did they want?"

Alaan held out the money until she accepted it. Then he told her.

"Oh, that's worse than I thought. I was afraid the guards would show up looking for me," she said. "I am known to be at your performances."

"And you came anyway?" Alaan said.

She asked, "Who was there when Stavender Il fired that bolt of lightning that gave Alaan his scar?"

"You," Alaan said.

"Who, on the first day of school, beat up Sol Hampa when she pushed you down in year four?"

"You," Alaan said.

"Who was there when you discovered your ability?"

"Yes, Tess, it was you," Dre said.

"So you must know that I was not going to miss anything I don't have to," she said, then smirked. "Also, I've told the other runaways about you and the MMA program. They all said they ran because the Poli Twins went into hiding at the start of the draft. Most kids were afraid of the draft because of you."

Dre nodded. "Seems that everyone is doing things because of us."

"If the draft is ended, it will be helping them, too," Alaan said.

"Some of them are losing their magic since we don't practice much," Tess said.

"Yeah, same for the kids in the MMA program and probably those who don't make the cut for either program," Dre said.

"It's that bad? The Vous must not know either. That is a problem we would get behind. Lynit is founded on magic. Our nation won't last if only a few have it," Jamil said. "Though in terms of solutions, it isn't clear that ending the draft will solve anything. The problem is a social one. If inspiring children by having celebrities participate will solve the problem, the issue isn't with the program itself. The Vous would say to focus on a better marketing campaign rather than ending it. We would need proof of a flaw in the structure of the draft."

"So, would you commit your family to help if you got that proof?" Alaan said.

Jamil shook his head furiously. "If a sorcerer disrupts a rule they don't fully understand, that could mean death for everyone in the vicinity. I know little about how the Guard works or should work; I can't risk disrupting Lynit by trying to change that. But I can help you prepare your argument for the Vous."

As Homin had explained, being noble was about more than magic. It hinged on representing their family's philosophy. Dre wondered if this meant that there were tons of descendants of nobles who never matriculated into a family. Perhaps some were too stubborn or free-spirited to stick to a set of rules, and they integrated into general society with new last names and never spoke of their past.

"What if you trained them and kept them busy in the meantime? Just enough that they don't lose their magic," Tess said.

"Train draft defectors? How?" Alaan said.

"In your gym. No one would know," she said.

The gym was a perfect training spot, but not for the runaways. Children without adults were like beings from the spirit realm— mayhem. Those kids would destroy that gym in a week since no one would be there to supervise. Reporters would run wild with the story.

"We can't train anyone. We are leaving Lynit tomorrow," Dre said.

"Why?" Tess said.

"Our mother is serious about keeping us away from Slithlor," Dre

said.

Tess pulled a silver ball from her pocket. It looked like an average communication orb but larger. She whispered something and pulled delicately at the hemispheres until it stretched apart into two separate balls. She handed one to Dre.

"These orbs are directly linked. We'll be able to talk in private," she said. "And now it sounds like your gym will be vacant, so maybe we could use it."

"I want a house to return to after our parents calm down," Dre said.

Tess pouted as she pulled out a piece of paper. Dre recognized the format without reading it. It was her draft order. "Have a drink with me while you think. Daramis Bar will serve a drink to a draftee regardless of age."

"Okay," Alaan said. He raised his draft order.

"No, we need time for Jamil to look at our magic," Dre said.

"What's up with your magic?" Tess said.

"Go with him, then," Alaan said, his voice flat.

"How about you change that tone?" Dre said, raising a finger. Again, Alaan was uninterested in investigating what was wrong with their magic. No, he was avoiding it. He acted as if he was unfazed by their predicament. Maybe it was hormones. While they made Dre want to make out with every other boy he saw, they muted Alaan's optimism. He was resigned. He had accepted that the inevitable had come and chose to move on. But Dre wouldn't without definitive proof.

"What if you got ahead of this and found the kids right after they received the notice? If no new kids joined the draft program, that would be another signal that they need to change it. You could start your own underground Poli Twin-approved training program," she said.

This would doubly prove that kids could organize and train when there wasn't fear. There would be two separate cohorts: the MMA participants and draft defectors. Dre crossed his arms, annoyed that he liked the idea. He lifted the orb. "What's the reach on this?" If he could stay in contact with Homin, there might be a chance for the court case. And if he could stay in touch with Jamil, he would have access to magic help.

"The Guard has communication orb relays along the border. Anyone can use them to boost the signal if they get in range," Jamil said. "And I can leave Lynit. I can research wizardry to understand what is happening with your magic."

"Marvelous," Dre said, pulling out his draft order. He was excited to get drunk for the first time, but more importantly, he wanted Alaan inebriated. First, Alaan asked for them to take their exams separately, then he was unconcerned that their magic was finicky. Dre had read that alcohol made people stupid. He could use that lapse in judgment to coax Alaan to talk. For Dre to maintain being the compliment to his brother, he needed to know exactly what was going on with him.

Tess beamed and hugged him. Alaan patted him on the back.

"I can drink, too," Jamil said, holding up his ID.

"Great, a double date of exes. No one would suspect that we are plotting to change the nation," Tess said, then laughed.

Chapter 13 - Rye

"I am going to sell it for four thousand dilo," Santi said, her tone deep. Her gray robes brushed against the ground, a ring of red staining the bottom. Her hair was short like Rye's, and long earrings hung past her shoulders.

"Four thousand?" Gamine said, her voice a little softer but raspy. She strolled beside Santi with a walking stick that ticked against the ground every few seconds. She hunched as if her neck was burdened by her thick gray hair wrapped loosely atop her head. On the side of her neck, she had a fading tattoo of a cloud. "No, baby, no one will pay that much. Last year, I sold three vials of ri venom for eight hundred each and that was after twenty minutes of bargaining. Who will pay four thousand for a sunstone?"

Rye rode inside a cart next to the two women who were smuggling him into Poli. It was a tin box on wheels, long enough for his legs to stretch out in a "V" but not high enough to sit up fully. His chest pressed against Lakree, who sat between his legs. The cart was dark save for two small slits, one on each side. The two women were visible through the right slit. Rye shifted his head to rest on Lakree's left shoulder to peer through the other. Hila was squished in an even smaller cart that rolled beside him, pushed by purple energy.

"It's all about the story, Gamine. I would not get more than one thousand if I sold it only as a sunstone. If I sell it as a relic from a temple in Ries, there is always a noble who will want to impress another noble," she said. The two women laughed, the sound ringing over the soft hum of a small caravan of carts, most stuffed with items, two stuffed with people.

"Santi," Gamine said and sucked her teeth.

"I already sold it," Santi said. "Someone requested it."

"Ah...I heard of something like this. What happens if you don't find the item?"

"I have to pay them back an additional ten percent of the price."

"You are a gambler, Santi."

"I only get locked into one or two of these a season. I make a good profit when I do."

"But the stress, Santi, the stress."

The cart bumped. Rye gripped his arms around Lakree, but they still both banged their heads. One small metal box in the cart bounced, popping open its lid. A bright yellow glowing crystal was inside. Rye reached a hand for it.

"Sorry," Santi and Gamine said.

"It's nothing," Lakree said. He slapped Rye's hand away and closed the box.

"If you need more ointment, say so," Santi said.

"I'm okay," Rye said. He released his hold on Lakree and inspected his arms. The pain in his elbows was gone, but his face, arms, and neck peeled while Lakree was only tanned.

"Have you seen anyone from our old crew?" Santi said.

"No, I haven't, but there is a gathering happening soon near Fits. You should come," Gamine said.

"The ban on foreigners is what helps me get away with these absurd prices, but I do miss everyone," Santi said.

They rolled up an incline. The angle increased until the sunstone box slid back. He grabbed a side and braced an arm against Lakree as his weight pressed back. Each bump in the road rattled everything and pinched Lakree further into Rye's crotch.

"Ahh," he hissed.

"Sorry, sorry, sorry," Lakree said as he tried to scoot himself forward, but his feet were already flush against the front.

Fingers tapped the cart. "Remember, don't use any magic until we are inside," Gamine said.

After a few minutes, the road leveled. The pinching lessened. Rye collapsed back onto Lakree's shoulders to rest. Other voices chatted ahead. Merchants argued with guards about their contents. Wheels bounced and compartments opened. Creatures hissed and barked. Two men with strange accents were turned away. The cart stopped.

"Santi, Gamine," a man said. "I thought I missed you. How was the trip?"

"I stuck to the east and south. I saw some friends, then met up with Santi in Zartum," Gamine said.

"We would have been on time, early even, if we hadn't spent so much time with her friends," Santi said.

"We are here now and have plenty of goods to sell," Gamine said. Fingers tapped the box.

"You have your licenses? Is there anything dangerous I should know about before inspecting these carts?"

"All of our merchandise falls within Lynitian import standards as usual," Santi said. "Here's the Declaration."

Boots scuffled around Rye. He wrapped his arms around Lakree again. If they were caught here, Rye wouldn't have a chance to talk to Juli and learn the truth about her conspiracy. He tried to calm his body with deep breaths as hinges creaked and metal slid against stone. Lakree mimicked his breathing. The man counted off items. Santi and Gamine spoke as he worked, recounting stories of their adventures. He told them about the festival and the newest shops in the city. He paced past Rye's and Lakree's cart but never stopped beside them.

"You're good," he said loudly, then in a much quieter voice, "I'll come by tonight."

"We will be in our usual spot," Gamine said.

"Unless it's already taken," Santi said.

"Aye, Santi."

"Lieutenant General Bon," a high-pitched voice said. Conversations halted. The man cursed. "Have you been inspecting this cargo or have you been chatting?"

"Captain, inspecting, of course. Did you not see me?" he said, his tone playful.

"I saw a lot of teeth," she said.

"I know these two, but I inspected their cargo like everyone else's. Here," he said.

The woman hummed. Something tapped against metal. "I guess you won't mind if I double-check," she said.

"Of course not, Captain, but I do not want to waste your time," he said.

"My time is never wasted," she said. A set of heavier boots scraped against the ground. Metal squeaked. "This one looks good."

Rye wrestled Lakree out of the way and pressed his eye as close to the slit as he could. The captain walked from one cart to the next. Red dust caked on the bottom of her black and gold sorcerer robes. As she stepped next to Hila's cart, creatures popped into Rye's mind, useless creatures. He squeezed Lakree tighter. No creature could help right now.

She grabbed the top of Hila's cart and tried to lift it. It didn't budge. "This one is stuck," she said, then grunted. She adjusted her grip.

Lakree wrapped his hands over Rye's and pressed him tighter into his chest. He couldn't see it himself, but he felt Rye's shaking.

Rye shut his eyes and pulled away. He nestled into Lakree's neck. Lakree leaned back into him. Rye knew that running from the Guard was a stupid idea from the beginning. Guards weren't just skilled at magic. They were also brilliant. They had procedures for handling fugitives on the run and checking the cargo that entered their cities.

"Captain," a new voice called out. "There is an urgent message from Virt."

"Check these carts carefully. If there is another voroborous infestation, Bon, you will be on the extermination crew," the Captain said. Footsteps stalked away.

Rye and Lakree exhaled, but neither one released their sweaty grip on each other.

"I hope you two aren't getting me into trouble," the man said.

"No rodents, I promise," Santi said.

The cart rolled again. Soon, they were through the dome. Soft music played. Large brass instruments thumped counter tempos and flutes trilled, the melody fluttering higher and higher. A few minutes later, the cart stopped again. Someone knocked.

"It is safe," Santi said.

Lakree tentatively pushed out the cart lid. Cool air washed in. He climbed out. Rye maneuvered onto his feet. His whole body tingled. He rubbed his arms as bumps broke out. This city was colder than Virt.

He was in an alley between two buildings made of red stone but with white lines crisscrossed like a grid. He climbed out, stepping onto the paved ground.

"That was scary," Hila said.

"More than I expected, but Rye kept me calm," Lakree said. Rye smiled back. Enduring the hot and sticky cramped box sucked, though being tangled up with Lakree was enjoyable in its own way. Rye wanted more of it, which was a problem. The old feelings for his friend that were supposed to have been stamped out and adapted around were resurfacing. Today was potentially his last day with Lakree until he was an adult and something inside dared him to make the most of it.

Lakree offered Santi the other half of the wooden box. One set of the metal hinges was twisted and dangling off. "Here's the rest, as promised."

"Keep it," she said, holding up a jeweled hand. "You have already paid enough."

"Santi," Gamine said, grabbing her arm.

"When I was a little girl, I sneaked into Poli more than once. They could have gotten in for free, had they known where to look." Santi turned back to Lakree and shrugged. "I would have told you, but you offered the wood."

"Thank you for your help," Lakree said.

"Which way is Co Park?" Hila said.

"Ah...of course," Santi said, shaking a finger. Gamine nodded. "Walk towards the center of the city. You will see signs."

Lakree ran a hand through his hair.

"What's the other way in and out of the Poli?" Hila said.

"You'll be able to walk right out of Poli just like you did in Virt, but to get in without an ID or a guardian, enter through the crater just to the south. At the bottom are several caves, but there is one marked with an 'M' etched into the roof of the entrance."

"Thank you," Hila said. The merchants waved goodbye and wheeled their carts away with mental energy.

Rye followed Lakree and Hila toward the music. Voices accompanied the song, some singing, some laughing. The alley opened into a market. Throughout the wide walkways, there were metal stands selling clothing, jewelry, strange plants, and art. One booth brimmed with colorful powders. Hundreds of people explored the different wares. They wore thicker clothing, more knitted sweaters and long dresses or robes.

Several performers, however, were dressed in minimal clothing. They danced in a small space that had been cleared for the purpose. They threw objects into the air, caught them, and balanced them on their chins and knees. They were like the circus in Virt, performing silly stunts without magic. Lakree oddly loved going to them. Pulling a creature out of a hat and sawing people in half without magic baffled him.

Lakree tapped Rye and directed him to a sign posted on a building. It was a small rectangular drawing of the three of them in their current attire. It read "Wanted" in bold black letters.

"They are overreacting," Rye said. This was another example of the Guard's dramatic responses. The last time there was a wanted sign, it was for the Nightmare Killer. He killed over fifty people before he was apprehended. Lakree, Hila, and Rye didn't deserve to be treated like murderers. Even Lakree's matter shift into the throne room and through gigastone didn't warrant this. Juli's conspiracy had to be deeper than unusual magic abilities. Slithlor had warned that he would not let their unimaginable potential go and it showed. It wasn't clear whether the Guard considered that potential a gift or a threat.

Hila ripped down the poster.

"No," Lakree snapped. He pointed at a guard at the end of the building. She was dressed in red and blue robes. She fussed as she applied glue and smoothed out another poster. Next to her was a cart stacked with signage. He pulled Hila away and they darted through the market. Rye lowered his head, weaving past the barrage of vendors shoving salted meats and trinkets at him. He slipped to the edge of the shops and ducked through a curtain that marked the end of the market. Lakree checked down several side streets they passed, finally turning down one with only a few people. They walked for several minutes until the music faded and the buildings changed from stone to painted metal.

Tall black towers packed the newest part of the city. They were primarily large tinted window panes separated by metal beams that stacked up forty or more flights. On the street, men and women in various shades of gray or black darted around each other. They didn't look up at the buildings. They were focused on navigating the fast-paced stream of bodies. The ones who bumped into Rye shouted at him for not paying attention to where he was walking. This city was nothing like Virt.

Hila waved a hand in his face.

"Huh?"

She pointed down a shaded walkway between two skyscrapers, which sloped up to the sky. He followed her down the corridor of tinted windows. In the distance, only the tips of other buildings were visible. Most were black, except for four white stone towers. A squat white structure connecting the towers rose into view. The Poli Castle was a replica of the one in Virt.

At the end of the street, a massive black crater separated Rye from the Guard headquarters. A small metal sign labeled the place as Co Park. It looked like an explosion of black rock leveled the city's center. Some of the rock was crafted into three gigaspheres. There weren't any in Virt, but he recognized them from the news coverage of the Poli Twin's old training sessions. After the draft started, the park was supposed to be empty, but currently, many people roamed about. A few played in the gigaspheres, but most were on communication orbs. The blips of light looked like stars against a night sky.

A thick brown trunk grew through a crack in the rock on the other side of the park. Tendrils of bark reached out and away from the base, long green leaves draped down like hair. Its roots threaded through the ground. A breeze rustled the leaves. It was a soft sound, unlike all the other sharp noises of the city. This was a real tree.

"Wow," Rye said. The first tree he had ever seen found a way to thrive in an unusual environment.

"There is a whole forest full of them outside of Lynit," Hila said.

"We can't go down there. We are the ones on the news," Lakree said. He stepped back from the edge of the park. "We have to hide until nightfall, then come back. I know a place. It's called Daramis."

Rye sucked his teeth. The longer he waited to turn himself in, the more annoyed the Guard would be, but it was worth it to talk to Juli. "Okay, let's wait then," he said.

Two guards, a psychic and a sorcerer, turned down the street, holding a sheet of paper between them. The psychic wasn't wearing his uniform but carried it over his shoulder. He was short and took three steps for each of the sorcerer's two. The sorcerer was in her black and gold uniform. She fastened the remaining buttons with one hand. They were like his parents, who multitasked as they dressed for work every morning, though his father was usually the first one ready. But unlike his parents, they wouldn't be kind when they saw Rye.

"This is ridiculous. All this noise over three children," the psychic said.

"That one is noble," the sorcerer said, tapping the paper. "Cast and Yordin."

The psychic lifted the paper to his face. "So double the family drama."

"Do you know what they did?" she said. She finished with her buttons, then twisted and tied her hair into a bun. She was only an arm's length away.

"A threesome," the psychic said and laughed. She elbowed him. He stumbled as he passed Rye. "Luri."

The woman glanced over her shoulder. Her light-hearted smirk dropped.

"Linti Dervi Boliva Transi," Hila said. Her arms swooped as a burst of wind shot out in response. It knocked the sorcerer into a window. The glass cracked but didn't shatter. She slid to the ground. The man shot out from between the buildings and soared over Co Park. His uniform fell as purple energy rushed from his head, surrounding him. He slowed to a stop in mid-air.

The image of the blackened-face quitol resurfaced in Rye's mind. He checked the woman's breathing. It was faint but steady. Rye wasn't so sure that the Guard would forgive him for this. Attacking guards was what criminals did. He backed away, trembling. "Hila, what's wrong with you?"

"I just...I...I...I..." she said. A whistle blew from the park. The floating man held a hand to his mouth and pointed at them with the other. Lakree pulled Rye and Hila into a run.

They cut out of the alley and down another. The whistling multiplied as other guards answered the call. This area of Poli was organized like a fake grid. Every other intersection was at right angles, but in between were narrow winding streets that sometimes abruptly ended at a wall. At one corner, there was a large map. A long obelisk next to it marked the area as the absolute center of the city.

Lakree traced a finger to a shopping district. "This is where we need to go."

After several more turns, Rye stepped onto a fancy street. Yellow and pink ribbons draped from building to building. Long, wiry collars spanned from lampposts, creating a see-through canopy. The ground floor of each building was a large storefront. Several "Wanted" posters tumbled underneath his feet.

On the next street, they went into a clothing store. Primly dressed customers exchanged looks. Rye slipped the first robe he reached over his head. It was knitted and patterned with orange and blue shapes. He grabbed another one and struggled to pull it over Hila. Her gaze was distant. She was still apologizing. Lakree wrapped his hair up in a scarf.

The owner of the shop stormed over, but it was almost elegant. Lakree thrust the wood at him.

"This is not a bargain shop. You pay in dilo here," he said. He leaned back for a moment. He grabbed Lakree. "Hmm...three children trying to steal clothing. Are you the ones who broke into the Castle?"

Lakree tried to pull free but couldn't.

A spark raced down Rye's spine, skipping his brain. "Get off him." He balled up a fist and punched the man in the gut. The shoppers gasped, but no one did anything. The owner crumpled over. Hila mumbled and Lakree pushed her out of the store. Rye followed after.

Something purple hovered over the square. Rye pivoted to face a clothing store window display. Rings and necklaces decorated headless metallic mannequins. Behind them, the patrons stared back at him in shock. "Stay inside," he said under his breath, threatening them with his eyes.

The psychic from earlier flew overhead in the reflection, whistling and asking the crowd if they had seen the fugitive children. No one answered him. After the shadow passed, Rye strolled behind Lakree and Hila, who pretended to argue over a telephone's colors in the shop window next door.

"Daramis is over there," Lakree said, flicking his head towards a bar on the other side of the square. One by one, they peeled off. The guard looped back over the park. He flew low, scanning the area. Lakree and Hila entered the bar, but Rye waited for the psychic to fly out of sight before he slipped inside.

The dimly lit establishment smelled of ash and old clothes. Rye's shoes squeaked on the sticky floor. A man behind the counter filled a glass with a brown liquid. He nodded at Rye, then returned to his task. A sign hung in the entrance. "No guards!" Rye walked past men and women drinking and chatting. Some of their greetings were slurred. He flicked a hand up in a quick wave and averted his eyes. Lakree and Hila sat in a booth in the back. He slid in across from them.

He pressed his hands flat against the rough table, but it didn't stop the shaking. The past fifteen minutes were like a blur, but the clear image of the injured sorcerer stayed with him. His feet bounced underneath the table as he waited for the adrenaline to subside. He wished he had stayed in Virt. "You attacked a guard," he said through clenched teeth.

Hila's already sheepish frown deepened. She sank her head into her chest.

"Whatever happened, happened," Lakree said, pushing one of his dreads back into the wrap. His white and gold scarf matched Hila's robes.

Rye rubbed a finger against the smooth table. "Running from the draft isn't worth all this."

"What's wrong with me?" Hila said softly.

"She did what she had to do. We aren't the only draft deserters, but they have wanted signs up for us. We have to contact my aunt, no matter the cost," Lakree said.

"We aren't noble, Lakree," Rye said, his voice louder than he expected. "We can't ask our parents, cousins, uncles, grandfathers, second cousins, or anyone for a favor. This won't go away. She injured a guard and I helped her escape by punching a man. I'm an accomplice. This will be on our records for life." He dropped his head into his hands.

Hila rubbed her birthmark. "I don't have any control." Tears rolled down her face. They dripped onto the table. "I'm sorry for what I said in the desert."

Lakree rubbed her back.

Rye stopped fidgeting. "When we finally return home, we all

have to answer for what we've done. Don't do anything you can't apologize. Don't follow your instincts," he said. Even if Rye's father's desertion was justified, after King Kertic's death, he couldn't return. There was no ordinary life for him to return to or level of apology that would bring back the dead. All Rye could hope was that it wasn't too late for him.

Chapter 14 - Rye

The bartender approached Lakree, Hila, and Rye. Her red hair was separated into two afro puffs and a sheet of black tattoos covered an arm. She tapped a hand on the table. "Welcome to Daramis. How can I help you?"

"Our friend was drafted today and we have come to share his first drink with him," Lakree said.

Rye flashed his draft order.

"I am sorry to hear that, young man. Be brave for Lynit," she said, then twisted around. "We have another draftee here. The first round is on the house."

Chairs squeaked. Conversations halted. Everyone turned to the table.

"I'll take the second," a voice on the other side of the room chimed. It was a woman in a dark leather jacket fastened with metal rivets. She held up two fingers.

"I'll take third," another woman said. She sat at the bar alone in a white dress.

"We'll take the rest," a girl in the next booth said. Her purple head poked above the divider. Next to her, two almost identical heads rose. The only difference between the dark-skinned boys was that one's hair was cut into a strip down the middle.

Rye hadn't seen pictures of these brothers in a long while, but their older faces were still recognizable. "It's the Poli Twins."

"What?" Lakree said. He stood up to check.

Ever since the draft started, headlines ran about the twins' disappearance. At first, the rumors were that the boys were drafted, but the reporters camped outside their house hadn't seen them leave. The twins were in hiding. They had a special ability and were an obvious target for the draft. It was odd to find them in this bar Lakree knew about. Rye pinched himself under the table. He checked the corners of his vision. He imagined a black door on his forehead and shut it. But the twins were still there. The purple-haired girl slid out of her booth. The twins followed. There was a fourth boy—no, a man—with them. From his black and gold clothes and oval-shaped eyes, he looked like a Vous, but his hair wasn't styled in knots.

"Can we join you?" the girl asked.

"Sorry, we are having a private moment," Lakree said.

The girl pulled out a draft order. "Us too," she said as she sat beside Rye, clanking her beer glass on the table. There was a sharp smell to her. "I'm Tess. That's Jamil, and I'm sure you already recognize Alaan and Dre." She motioned for Lakree to scoot over as she pushed Rye further in. Alaan and Jamil squeezed in. Dre stood on the side of the booth, now packed with six.

"Long 'a'. Long hair," Alaan said, pointing at his head.

Dre grinned. "That's not going to catch on."

"Hi," Rye said.

Hila wiped her red eyes but said nothing. Lakree introduced them but used fake names.

"Which one of you was drafted?" Tess said.

"Me," Rye said slowly.

The bartender returned with a glass of a dark, murky liquid. Foam bubbled at the top, a few streaks sliding down the sides. It smelled like poison.

"Four more," Alaan said. Lakree protested, but Alaan insisted. The bartender dipped her head. She dragged over a stool for Dre, then left.

"This is the only time they will serve you alcohol. Take advantage of it," Jamil said.

Tess raised her glass in the air, motioning for Rye to do the same. "To our crappy luck," she said and tapped his glass.

He sipped it. It was bitter, like the rind of a tree melon. During the week before his father's birthday, his mother came home late smelling of places like this bar. But all this time, he thought beer was delicious.

Tess laughed. "That face."

"Where are you from? Virt?" Alaan said.

"Why do you think we aren't from Poli?" Lakree said, adjusting his head wrap.

Dre laughed, then covered his mouth. "It is not common here to see such expensive robes on children in a bar. They are Polian style, but you obviously just bought them."

"You look like you were rolling around in the dirt, then put on new clothes," Alaan said.

"And you are all wearing your pins. They are popular in every other city, but not Poli. We don't define ourselves here by our magic. It's just a preference, like a career choice or favorite color," Dre said.

"Our parents are merchants," Lakree said. "We arrived today for the festival."

Rye kept his eyes on his beer. The foam fizzled. This bar was kind to draftees, but it didn't mean they could afford to be recognized.

The front door banged open behind Rye. The first image in his mind was of guards bursting in. The second image was a MMA diagram of a camouflaging lizard. It was a simple creature, possible to complete in less than a minute. Lakree perked up, peeked over Rye's head, then relaxed. Hila shut her eyes and grunted, shaking her head.

"Are you okay?" Alaan said.

"Ah, ah, cramps, I'm on my period," she said.

"Oh, sorry," he said.

"I'm a protector. I can help," Tess said.

Hila held up a hand. "I'm fine."

"Or are you afraid of who might enter the bar?" Tess said.

Rye gulped a mouthful of beer. Tess was perceptive. Even if she didn't recognize them now, it would be easy to connect the dots when she saw the wanted signs in the street. Whenever these kids left the bar, Lakree, Hila, and Rye would have to leave.

"Is this where you have been hiding the past few years?" Lakree said.

"We are back as of today. Last month, we were placed in a new Guard program. We practiced the material in public earlier, but things didn't go as planned," Alaan said.

"Hmph," Hila blurted.

Lakree tried to put a hand over her mouth, then poorly played it off by rubbing her chin.

"Does 'MMA' mean anything to you?" Alaan said.

Rye choked on his beer. Everyone turned to him. Lakree's eyes were daggers. The new people were intrigued. "Ahhhhh...nothing, nothing, continue. It just sounded familiar," Rye said. It was weird that the Poli Twins were placed in the same program as Rye. They were the definition of extraordinary. They competed against adults in tournaments when they were fifteen.

"Familiar?" Alaan said. He passed a slight glance to his brother. "Where did you hear about it?"

"Oh, I don't remember," Rye said.

Dre set an elbow on the table and dropped his head into his hand. "You don't remember?"

Rye averted his gaze. He fiddled with a napkin holder. Dre's eyes were like a sorcerer's somehow. They saw through him.

Tess drummed her knuckles on the table. "You plan to flee the draft order?"

"No," Rye said sharply. He could answer that question honestly. The idea sounded just as wild coming from her as from Lakree.

"Many kids in Poli do," Tess said.

"That's them," Rye said.

"What do you mean?" Lakree said.

"You're from Virt, aren't you?" she said. She paused and sipped her beer. Rye finished the rest of his. Tess placed her draft order on the table. It was crinkled, dirty, old. She flattened it out the best she could. "Check the date."

The date was almost five weeks ago. She had managed to hide from the Guard for three weeks. Maybe there was hope for Lakree and Hila.

Lakree tapped a finger on the table. "But you are in the MMA program. You are exempt."

"No, I'm not," she said with a sly smile.

"How did you know that we are exempt?" Alaan said.

Lakree looked at his hands, then at the wall. Dre rolled his eyes. Rye tried to take another sip of his beer, but the glass was empty. Luckily, the bartender arrived with a tray of four more beers. They weren't the same that Rye had before. They were a lighter brown, almost yellow. Hila took a sip, then gagged. Everyone laughed except for Lakree and Alaan. Lakree didn't reach for his glass. It sat there alone as Rye, Hila, and Tess drank theirs.

"I expected it to be sweet," Hila said.

"It does make you feel warm, though," Rye said, then swallowed a mouthful. Not only did his hands and legs tingle, but his head was a little light, too. The chill of the city felt distant. The danger of staying put in the bar still bobbed around his mind, but it didn't feel as urgent anymore. He was with the Poli Twins. This was a once-in-a-lifetime moment. "Could I have an autograph?" He placed his draft order on the table.

Alaan seemed to consider it.

"We can't sign that. We don't want evidence that we were with them," Dre said.

"If we wanted to hide from the draft, could you help us?" Lakree said.

"If the three of you were drafted, yes, I would help you," Tess said. She sipped her drink.

"The three of us were drafted and we need a place to hide for a day or two," Lakree said.

"Sure," Tess said. She pushed Lakree's glass to him. "But first, you have to tell us what happened in the Castle today."

Rye's beer slipped from his hand, hitting the table and spilling over. Everyone slid back. Dre stood up from his stool. The liquid soaked Rye's draft order. Tess was quick to yank hers out of the way.

"Sorry," Rye said. He snatched up his paper and patted it with napkins. The beer made his hands clumsy. No one spoke as the waiter appeared and wiped away the mess. Lakree gulped down his drink.

"You are all over the news. Today, you are more famous than them," Jamil said.

"This isn't fame. It is a fascination that can turn on you," Dre said.

"What are they saying?" Rye asked. If the Guard spoke about him the same way they spoke about his father, there was no hope of returning.

"Or is it infamy?" Tess said. "Depending on what you were really doing in the Castle, of course. So tell me, from one fugitive to the next. What does a noble have to do to get drafted?"

Lakree's eyes hardened. "Did the Guard mention that we were placed in the MMA last week and that they tried to draft us today after I matter shifted into the Castle?"

"What?" Dre said, his voice dropped to a loud, high-pitched whisper.

"We wondered why the Guard picked today. It wasn't because of our performance. It was because of them," Alaan said. He grabbed Dre's hand across the table.

"The same program that wants me, someone who failed the draft exam after a little over a minute, wants the most famous fighters in Lynit," Rye said.

This situation grew crazier by the minute. His paperwork couldn't have been a mix-up because he failed the exam after the first morph. There was no way that the animalist or sorcerer in the room with him wrote "Outstanding" anywhere in their report. Juli's conspiracy might not only be related to Lakree. Rye's mother knew that his father had run, but she still wanted Rye to do the same. This conspiracy could involve everyone at this table and even more who weren't there.

Dre pinched the bridge of his nose. "We failed the draft exam, too."

"Then Slithlor is after your wizardry ability," Jamil said.

"And Lakree's can matter shift through gigastone," Alaan said.

"I read about how there are fewer children with unusual abilities today than in the past," Jamil said. "Slithlor could be the cause."

"Of course he is," Dre said.

"You make it sound like he is doing something evil. He is following the law," Rye said.

A bell chimed behind again. Heavy boots entered the bar.

"Hey, read the sign. We don't want any trouble," the bartender

said.

Rye strained to see over the booth's lip. The shop owner he had punched stood with two guards, an elemental mage and the psychic Hila had attacked.

"There they are," the shop owner said, pointing.

Rye dropped back down. He reached across the table, grabbing Lakree's and Hila's hands. Lakree recited a spell.

A purple shadow moved over everyone. "They are attacking?" Alaan asked. He slid out of the booth. He raised a hand. Light flashed. The mental energy fizzled.

"Attempt number two," Dre said as he moved beside his brother. Black balls solidified around him.

Jamil jumped back from the table. He gripped his head, shaking it. "You can't attack children. My father is Lornius Vous. He is Deputy—"

A gust of wind blew everything off the table, splashing beer everywhere. The Guard could attack children who attacked them first. They were mad about their injured friend. This had nothing to do with the draft.

Tess covered them in a shield. The wind stopped. Lakree twitched, then scooted out from the booth. He moved outside the shield's range and restarted his spell. He could matter shift through gigastone but couldn't see through a magic shield.

Everyone else in the bar shouted. Some cursed the guards. Others complained about the draft. The bartender tallied the price of damages. Rye squeezed Hila tighter. He stared into her eyes. No matter what, they could not fight back. Escaping to talk to Juli was one thing. Being a fugitive for the rest of their lives was something else.

A whistle blew the same note that rang throughout the Castle earlier—the memory of the stomping boots played in Rye's mind. Then the whistle's pitch dropped, slowed to a rumble. The table vibrated. The bass chattered Rye's teeth. He scooted out of the booth with Hila.

"Whoa," he said. The psychic's cheeks puffed as he blew on a silver pipe. The elemental mage was in mid-stride with her hands raised, face set in determination. The guards weren't frozen, though their clothes rippled slowly.

"What happened to them?" A woman shouted over the noise.

"You did that?" Dre said. He turned to Lakree, who almost seemed frozen, but his lips still chanted the spell.

"Run. There's a back door," the bartender said.

"Go. I'll make sure my family knows that the Guard is being used to kidnap children," Jamil said.

"Tell my parents that we got away," Dre said. Jamil grabbed his arm for a brief moment, then released him.

Lakree pulled Rye out the back door of the bar. The whistle dropped to a barely audible hum as the door slammed shut behind them. The alley was quiet and smelly. Large trash cans overflowed with food scraps.

"Follow us. We know a place that will protect you," Dre said. The twins moved to the front of the group, leading the way to the end of the alley, then down another street. After the next turn, they ran down an old, dark stairwell. Before they reached the bottom, a mist of light rose around Alaan. They were in a tunnel underneath the city.

"You were right, Dre. We shouldn't have gone to their table," Tess said. No one responded as they ran to the end of the path. It opened up into a sort of hub that connected several other pathways. Sunlight filtered in through a few ceiling plates of semi-opaque glass.

They went down the hall two to the left, made two more turns, then reached another hub. It was identical to the first one, a six-way intersection. Alaan picked a path to the right and they continued like that for several minutes. The twins ran side by side, their strides and breathing in sync. Lakree's hair bounced on his head, unraveling his scarf, but he mechanically fixed it as if it mattered anymore. The crystals lining the walls activated, radiating a soft light.

"The guards are here," Alaan said, snapping a finger. His light energy winked out. They crossed a few more intersections. Some only had two connections. Others had up to six. One tunnel was collapsed, and another was closed off by metal bars, but otherwise, they all looked the same. It was like a maze and Rye was utterly lost. The only thing that grounded him was Lakree and Hila running next to him and the fact that if he was caught, he was going to prison with the psycho killers.

As they turned down a new tunnel, a dark-haired man in green and white animalist robes stepped into the far end of the hall. "Give it up. We have you surrounded," he shouted. Though his voice was too deep and he didn't have an "E" on his chest, Rye thought of his father, who could have a tangled beard like that man's.

"Go back," Dre said, throwing up his hands.

A perfect disk of dark energy sealed off the tunnel. Rye squished into Lakree and Tess as they turned back. A growl, a bang, and a screech of claws on stone reverberated through the wizard's wall.

"They are going to trap us down here," Rye said. The lightheadedness from before was gone.

"No, they won't," Dre said. "Come on."

They backtracked to a more prominent intersection and ran down a different path.

A whistle sounded and was answered by another. More tunes and the thump of familiar guards' boots joined in, echoing in all directions.

The next tunnel was twice as long. The crystals set into the walls were more spaced out, leaving dim patches of tunnel between them. The twins ran faster. They pulled a few paces ahead. They checked around corners before waving the others through. Lakree and Hila struggled to keep up. They were hobbling. Lakree had an excuse; he was still recovering from multiple matter shifts, but Hila didn't. Like most Lynitians who weren't animalists, she was in bad physical shape. They planned to run from the Guard but couldn't run a few miles.

"Lift your knees," Rye said. His breath misted. Lakree's and Hila's exhales were visible, too. A wave of cold air moved down Rye's body and flooded the tunnel with a chilly steam. Crackling ice rushed along the walls. At the end of the tunnel, the ice thickened. It built on itself, pulling the water from the air and freezing it solid.

The twins and Tess dove through the sealing hole. Lakree tried to dive but only got an arm through when the ice snapped shut in a burst.

He groaned. His arm was frozen in ice. He wiggled and jerked, but it wouldn't budge.

The elemental mage from the bar entered the tunnel from behind. Her overcoat was unbuttoned, sloppy. She pulled out a whistle and played two tones. Thick black dots formed in the air. She started running. The cloud solidified into a new wall, cutting her off.

"We got you," Dre said through the ice. The twins and Tess were distorted but visible.

"All exits are covered. There is nowhere to run," the elemental mage said, tapping on the wall. "If you cooperate, things will be easier for you."

"Not yet," Rye said under his breath. Lakree and Hila needed to be stashed somewhere safe first. Then, after Rye heard Juli's story, he could decide what to do next.

Light energy flashed on the other side of the ice. It spread out to a large disc.

"Concentrate the heat," Lakree said. He tugged on his arm but to no avail.

"You won't be able to climb through a fist-sized hole," Alaan said.

"Make a hole and put the energy inside it. Less heat will be wasted," Lakree said.

The temperature continued to drop as more moisture condensed in the air, thickening the ice wall and creeping up past Lakree's elbow.

"Ah," he screamed. "Hila, Hila, make a fire from this side."

She tensed. "A fire in this small space?" She shook her head. The ice crept up to Lakree's shoulder. He leaned his head away.

"Do it," he said.

"Fedelilo portantri ki," Hila said. Bluish red flames slammed into the ice like a punch, cracking it. They spread over the surface, some spilling up the ceiling. Rye dropped to the ground as the heat hit him. Lakree tried to drop, but his arm was stuck. His scarf caught fire. He patted at it with his free hand. Hila slapped his head. She ripped the scarf off, then stomped it out.

Lakree sniffed, then patted his head. "My hair!" A few of his dreads were missing from the right side of his head.

"Sorry," Hila said, her hands over her mouth.

Rye stood up. The top of the ice was gone, but Lakree's arm still wasn't free.

A small zap of electricity cracked and shattered Dre's wall. The elemental mage was close. The annoyance on her face was evident. She advanced with her arms extended low, palms up. "You are only wanted for questioning. What are you afraid of?"

A blue shield surrounded Rye, Lakree, and Hila. Rye backed up against the ice. The elemental mage shook her head. She then hit the top of the shield with a tiny bolt of lightning. Lines of energy rippled across the surface. Then she fired another one, slightly stronger.

"She is testing the strength of the shield. She wants to break it without hurting us," Rye said. She could destroy all their defenses with a single attack but kill them in the process. Her training guided her. Being a guard was about more than power. It was about precision and care. This was another example of why he didn't accept that Juli's conspiracy implied that the Guard was somehow evil. There were a lot of secrets within the organization, but that was how it should be. The Guard's duty was to protect Lynitians, even when they were criminals on the run.

The third attack broke the shield. Tess created another one, but the elemental mage destroyed it with ease. She understood Tess' strength. Lakree recited a spell and the elemental mage started running.

A dark blue shield expanded in the small space between Rye and the elemental mage. This shield was a physical barrier instead of a magical one. The type was distinguishable by the shade of blue, but it was too late for the guard to react. She crashed into the shield, bouncing off.

She grunted as she stood back up. "You are wearing down my patience."

"Come on. Come on," Dre said to Rye.

There was a big hole in the ice now and everyone else was on the other side. Rye mouthed "Sorry" over his shoulder as he climbed through. Tess placed more shields behind them as they ran. Footsteps, voices, and whistles echoed from every direction. At the next six-way intersection, the twins stopped.

"Calister," Dre said, pointing to a small sign on the wall. He and Alaan discussed a path through the maze. In less than thirty seconds, they agreed upon a path that didn't give away their destination.

The twins pointed at a tunnel. A loud growl bellowed from it before they could step down it.

Tess grabbed Alaan. "Let's split up. I'll take them with me. You can't be connected to this. You have important work to do."

"We are sticking together," Alaan said, then to Dre, "We have to use an illusion."

Dre shook his head. "We are better off running." He turned to another tunnel. "That way."

"Let's try," Alaan said.

Dre shook his head again, but his eyes were sadder. "Even if we manage to join our energies, we don't know if they will stay joined. We can't depend on that right now." He ran down the tunnel. Rye followed after him.

Down another long tunnel, the elemental mage from before stepped into view.

"This is your last warning," she shouted.

"How did she catch up?" Lakree said. "Are we going in circles?"

Dre and Tess threw up defenses.

A bright light exploded, flinging Rye off his feet. He broke his fall with his elbows, which reactivated the stinging from the splinters. The rush of air and heat held him down for a moment. Lakree and Hila crawled next to him, but they were okay—so was everyone else. The tunnel was clear again and the elemental mage wasn't alone. A wizard stood with her.

"Oh no, are you alright?" she said, stepping forward. She bumped into a new shield. "Just stop it. We don't want to hurt you."

Hila helped Rye to his feet.

"I will hurt you if I have to, though," the wizard said. The collar of his black and white robes cast his face in shadows. Three balls of light floated near his torso.

Rye backed into something solid. New bars of dark energy stretched across the tunnel, trapping them with the guards. The wizard fired a barrage of attacks. The twins danced around one another, nullifying the magic, but couldn't turn to dissolve the energy caging them in. Then, a sorcerer arrived and recited a spell.

"That's not good," Lakree said.

"Run," Tess said softly as she sprinted at the guards.

"No," Alaan said. He reached after her, but Dre pulled him back. The wizard paused his attacks. Right before Tess reached them, she covered herself in a physical shield. She didn't slow her stride and plowed through them.

"Run," Tess shouted, then turned the corner. Dre threw up a wall of dark energy, blocking the view.

"What have I done?" Alaan said.

"She knows what she is doing. We have to go," Dre said, tugging on Alaan.

"I got it. Let's go," Lakree said. Two of the bars were gone. Lakree pressed a small cloud of light energy into a third.

"Stop that. Are you crazy?" Rye said. It was the stupidest thing Rye had ever seen Lakree do. He slapped Lakree's hand. Lakree's father was Yordin, but he wouldn't be happy stuck as a wizard. He wasn't just running from the draft. He was afraid of something darker.

They slipped around the bars and ran back the way they had come. Every few steps, Dre created another black wall behind them. They returned to a six-tunnel intersection.

"Dre, we have to do it," Alaan said.

"But it didn't—"

"Trust me." A tear ran down Alaan's face, but he held Dre's gaze. "It will work."

Dre pressed his lips tight and then caved. The Poli Twins summoned energy. In the center of the room, wizardry clouds swirled in a blur. Light flashed and flickered shadows on the walls. As the energies condensed, they didn't fade away. Shadow and light dampened to a focal point. For a moment, it looked like an eclipse, a beautiful spinning black hole surrounded by a ring of light. Alaan and Dre moved around their creation. They swung their arms in unison, sidestepping in a circle.

Down another tunnel, voices grew louder. Two women complained about annoying children. Lightning crackled down the tunnel with the three guards.

The twins divided the energy into two forms of equal height. They were humanoid-shaped. Rye blinked a few times as the forms flashed red, green, and blue, then settled on exact copies of Alaan and Dre. They even sported Dre's blue suspenders and Alaan's wooden necklace. They were indistinguishable from the real boys.

"Wow," Rye said, looking up at the glass ceiling. Sunlight shined in, but the illusions were still solid. They even had shadows. Rye had often heard about the twins' ability but had never seen it. The copies shifted into a fighting stance.

The real Dre celebrated his work, then pointed at a space between two tunnels. Everyone squished tight. The twins covered them in another illusion that looked like the other gray bricks in the tunnel. It was dark underneath. Rye held his breath as boots entered the hub.

"Why are you helping the fugitives?" the elemental mage said.

"Which way did they go?" the wizard said. No one answered. More guards entered.

"Careful, you can't hurt the Poli Twins," a new voice said.

Dre and Alaan fidgeted.

"Stop running," the elemental mage said.

"I will stick with them. Check for the other three. They've likely split up and plan to regroup later," the wizard said. The guards left.

Rye waited thirty more seconds before breathing. The twins released the covering.

"It's not too late for us," Dre said.

Alaan nodded, then pointed down a hall. After a few more turns, they arrived at a set of stairs. They descended three flights. It was dark. Only a few crystals worked here. Many bricks were missing from the walls, exposing gigastone. It felt like the interrogation room in the Castle. They turned onto a dead-end blocked by a wall of solid black rock, but there was an old metal door set into a side wall near it. Dre opened a low metal box next to it.

"I hear something down the stairs," a faint voice said. Soon, several more voices and boots echoed loudly.

There was a small click, then the gigastone wall shifted. Gears cranked open a new pathway, and Dre, Alaan, Lakree, and Hila entered the new hall of black rock.

Rye didn't cross the threshold. Entering this secret place meant more than finding somewhere to hide until nightfall. This whole network of tunnels was swarming with guards. They wouldn't turn around and leave after they reached this dead-end. They would search all through the night and the next day. Each passing sunrise would be an additional mark against Rye because the Guard would know he didn't trust them. Going any further along with Juli's conspiracy or the twins' suspicion of Slithlor meant that Rye wasn't only helping his friends escape the draft, he was helping them escape a corrupt Guard. Rye couldn't ask for forgiveness or explain that he technically didn't do anything wrong other than run. He was shaking.

"How could you still want to join the Guard?" Lakree asked. He grabbed Rye and yanked, but Rye didn't budge. "No, come on."

"Let him go," Hila said, grasping Lakree's other hand. "He can join if he wants to." There was no hostility in her voice. It was a statement of understanding.

"Get in here," Alaan said. He pointed at the ground like Rye was a disobedient child.

"Juli knew your father," Lakree said in a quick breath. He clenched his hands. "The Guard thinks she is dead too, but she's not. She knows an important secret and your father knows it, too.

They were both elites. She could help you find him."

"What?" Rye said. He had accepted that his father had fled Lynit, hopefully for a good reason, but he didn't think he would see him again. He was an elite animalist. He wouldn't leave a trail. But, if he were in contact with an ally, he was reachable, findable, and huggable. Talking to his father once more was more important than any training in the Guard. He could learn instinct stacking from the best. The dizziness that had been building since he sipped his first beer returned in a wave. He tripped and fell as Lakree yanked him a second time. He banged his chin against the ground. He didn't bother to break his fall. Physical pain didn't matter anymore. He was going to find his father. The gears started up again and the wall sealed back up.

Chapter 15 - Dre

The gigastone tunnel looked like an escape route dug by a large spoon. The roof's height fluctuated, the ground was uneven, and the path curved needlessly. Glowing rocks provided light. Rye hunched, clutching his stomach with one hand. He was one of the rare few who wanted to be drafted. He didn't misinterpret the twins' choice to stop performing as fear of the Guard. Dre didn't initially make the connection of Rye's last name, but this boy was the son of Barin Ternitu, the first non-noble elite. Nothing would keep Rye from the Guard unless his father wasn't dead, as it had been reported after the Battle of Ki. For an elite to be in hiding was severe. And if this Juli person, a second elite, was also on the run, then Slithlor's general obsession with extraordinary children was only one of the problems. He could be up to something worse.

But Dre couldn't stop himself from smiling. When kids lost the ability to use more than one magic, there weren't alternating moments where they could use three magics and others when only one worked. The decline was gradual and unidirectional. Once strength in a secondary mage waned, it didn't come back. Dre's magic had joined perfectly with Alaan's. The illusions hadn't been weakened by sunlight and ran for a while before Dre lost track of them. The guards who chased after them would have a story to tell that no one would believe it. The Verbindous hadn't come for Dre after all.

"I hope your friend got away," Hila said. Alaan paused. Everyone stopped. Lakree silently reprimanded her. She mouthed, "Sorry."

"Alaan, you okay?" Dre said. He reached out a hand, but Alaan moved.

"I'm fine," he said, though he wasn't. He walked with his head down and steps heavy. He seemed upset about Tess. She was talented enough at protection to get drafted, but no ordinary child could outrun the Guard for long.

After a few minutes, the gigastone gave way to red rock and sheets of metal. The deeper they went, the more uniform the tunnel became until they were inside a compound. There were no doors, only differently colored pieces of metal and a turn every fifteen paces. It was like a nightmare school.

The hall finally ended at a rusty metal door. It squeaked as Alaan opened it. Inside was a small room. To the left, a long brown sofa and a neat white bed were tucked into a corner. On the right, there was a rough gray counter and stove. In the back, a bookcase full of scrolls was placed next to a closed black curtain. There were no windows.

"This is either an upscale prison or public housing," Hila said.

"How did you find this place?" Lakree said.

Alaan didn't respond.

"It's called the Medina," Dre said. "We didn't find it. It found us. Because of our wizardry ability, Alaan and I are at risk. There would come a point when the Guard decided our ability was more valuable to them than our freedom. We were offered a refuge before that day could happen, but we haven't used the shelter until now."

Lakree moved around the space, inspecting the walls, likely scanning with his sorcerer's eye. Rye lay down.

"Everyone, have a seat," Alaan said, his tone dry.

Lakree and Hila moved nervously next to Rye on the bed. They looked at Dre, but he guarded his face. He didn't know what was up with Alaan either. He shouldn't be this upset over Tess.

"Did we do something wrong?" Lakree said.

"I want the truth. What did you do?" Alaan said.

Lakree started to answer, but Alaan held up a hand. "I want to hear it from one of them."

"Lakree matter shifted into the throne room and through gigastone," Hila said softly. "Our magic is doing things it has never done before."

"Things we've never tried to do before," Lakree said.

"Quiet," Alaan said, then turned back to Hila. "Like what else?"

"We were trapped on a ledge in the Winder Plains. A quitol tried to grab Lakree and I couldn't let it get him. I pulled on every bit of energy I had. It's dangerous for elemental mages to pull more energy than we can control, but I didn't have a choice. It was that or death," she said. "Energy surged through me like I have never felt before. It was like my body was electricity and tired of being bottled up. I knew at that moment that the lightning wouldn't just hurt it. I knew it would kill it."

"Why did the guards attack in the bar?" Alaan said.

Hila shrugged. "Guards recognized us. I wasn't thinking, but I attacked them. I hurt one of them. I committed a crime. I'm a criminal."

"Hmm...but why the wanted signs?" Dre said. Alaan was on to something. Some of the facts in their story didn't add up.

Lakree raised a hand. "When I was being interrogated in the Castle, a guard asked me if one of my relatives sent me to assassinate Rigmen."

"The king regent?" Dre said.

Lakree nodded. "The Castle, but the throne room, in particular, is the most secure location in Lynit. It is warded against matter shifts and other displacement spells. They don't believe I arrived there by accident."

"The Guard wanted Lakree, and in the panic, he brought his friends along with him," Alaan said.

Dre shook his head. "This all reads too sloppy on the Guard's end. If they thought Lakree was an assassin, they would have put that on the news. They wouldn't have Rye and Hila on the wanted posters, too. They are children."

Rye sat up on the bed. "And there's more. When we arrived in the throne room. Slithlor was there talking to a woman. She was one of the psychics who escorted me to the MMA initiation. Those programs are separate. Why would they be talking?" he said.

"Lakree's aunt knew that the Guard would come for us. She told him before the draft even started," Hila said.

"Juli, the elite?" Dre said.

"Yes, Juli Pol," Lakree said.

"How is she a Pol? Your father is Yordin," Hila said.

"No, his father is Cast. His mother is Yordin," Rye said.

Lakree tapped his sorcery pin. "I wasn't the first one to pick a different magic."

"Of course. You're Yordin," Dre said, throwing his hands in the air. Nothing was ever random. This was likely the family opening Homin was trying to bargain off to the Poli Twins.

"What did Homin Yordin offer you?" Alaan asked.

Lakree hummed. "…short, bald. He is the civilian liaison to the Guard. I met him once, but he didn't offer me anything."

"Why did you follow us into the bar?" Alaan said.

"We didn't follow you," Lakree said.

"It was not an accident," Alaan said.

"I knew about that bar. I knew they served draftees. I figured it was a place we could hide," Lakree said.

"Homin sent you, didn't he?" Alaan said. He stepped next to

Lakree, towering over him. Lakree shrank back.

"Alaan, calm down. They are fifteen," Dre said. His brother was overreacting, but he was usually the more even-tempered one.

"But isn't it a wild coincidence that we met them today in that bar, of all the places in Poli and of all the days?" Alaan said.

"Even if they planned it, what would Homin's goal be?" Dre said.

"Your anger is not just about them. You've been acting weird lately. You were unfazed when our energies didn't join and similarly mute when it worked again."

"These kids aren't just running from the draft. I want to know if Tess sacrificed herself for some elite or Yordin political scandal," Alaan said, shaking a finger.

"I believe that is true, but I don't believe that is the whole truth," Dre said. He was tired of dancing around Alaan's odd behavior. From now on, he was going to call it out. Dre owed that to himself.

Alaan stepped into the kitchen. He gripped the countertop as if it were a tether. A heavy silence settled over the room.

A knock pounded the door, rattling the frame. Dre touched at his wizardry. Lakree and Hila screamed. Alaan stomped over to the door. Three women stood in the hall. One was short and wide with a round face. She had an oval-shaped red birthmark on her forehead. She carried a blue and black orb in one hand. She was a sorcerer. The orb enhanced her sorcerer's eye, allowing her to zoom in on the category of rules represented by the orb's colors. "The Poli Twins," she said.

"I don't believe it. They are identical," the woman next to her said. She wore a thin chain-linked metal shawl over thick leather armor. A strange glowing weapon hung from her waist. It was a spiked ball attached to a rod. It hummed with a white energy that wasn't wizardry.

"That isn't a shadow?" The third woman with dark eyes said. A red and white creature blinked into his periphery. Dre screamed and jumped back. When he checked the corner, it was gone. A few seconds later, the others had similar responses.

"What was that?" Dre said. He spun around.

When he turned back around to face her, the creature reappeared. Dre zipped his eyes over to catch it, but each time, it disappeared before he could focus on it. With his eyes steadily on her, the monster slid more and more into view until it was right beside her. It was a humanoid beast covered with long red and white hair that covered its body like a robe. Its hands were curled into thick fists as big as its head. It stood at the same height as her. Every time his eyes left the woman's eyes, the monster disappeared instantly. It was too quick. It wasn't an illusion. Dre had never seen foreign magic before, but this had to be it.

Then, the creature turned black. Its features flattened, melted like ice cream. It pooled on the ground before stretching out behind her and along the wall like a shadow.

"What kind of magic was that?" Alaan said.

"It's shadow magic," Hila said. "She's from Ries."

"But why did I have to look at her to see it," Dre said.

"I changed the focal point of—"

"Are you serious?" The sorcerer said. "First week on the job and you are telling people about your magic?"

"But this isn't a secret. You can ask anyone in Ries, and they will give you the basics. Learning shadow magic is a personal journey," she retorted.

"They can travel to Ries and ask someone. We don't share any magic knowledge in the Medina across nations. These boys are Lynitian," the sorcerer said. The Ries woman apologized. "Besides, I thought it was supposed to be just the twins. Who are these other kids?"

"They are in danger like us," Dre said.

"Alaan and Dre will go speak to Urura. The rest of you will stay in this room with me. Any use of magic will be considered an attack," she said, then blinked.

"Not again," Hila said.

"Are we prisoners here now?" Lakree said. "Why did you bring us here?"

"Calm down, calm down," Dre said. "You are surprise guests. We aren't supposed to bring other people here, but we believe they will let you stay. Relax and wait for us to come back. The Medina was made to protect kids like us."

Dre and Alaan followed the two women out of the room. They backtracked the twists and turns of the one hall. The escort stopped at a random wall. It was comprised of five different shades of metal. The woman with the shadow creature opened a panel, revealing levers. She flipped several, then closed the lid. The entire wall slid to the side.

There was a new room behind it. A strip of mirror wrapped around the walls. There were three desks: two with a stack of metal papers and a third covered in a board game. Three chairs were around the game table. A fat door covered in golden gears with a thick metal crank in the center was in the back. The armored woman ignored the crank and twisted three gears with her hand. The door swung open soundlessly.

It opened into a massive cave. The black ceiling stretched more than fifty feet above the red floor. The only place with this much black stone was Co Park. They were underneath it. It was the perfect place to hide. No magic could pass through it, well, except for Lakree's matter shift.

Buildings covered most of the cave floor, some nearly reaching the ceiling. A hundred or so people moved along the three levels of bridges that connected everything. Some were Lynitian, wearing recognizable robe styles and others wore clothing as strange as the one woman's metallic armor. A man wore only tight pants and a headpiece made of feathers. Lynit was a mix of magic and cultures of desert people, but the Medina was a small cross-section of the world—each of its inhabitants had a story of someone trying to kill or capture them.

The adults stared as the twins moved through the maze of walkways. The children watched for a bit, then moved on. It was the same above ground. Children saw new things all the time. Seeing human twins was no stranger than learning how magic worked. Adults were the ones clinging to what they already knew and were bothered by anything that challenged it. The other Lynitians called out to Dre and Alaan by name.

The escort stopped outside a seemingly random door. The handle was worn and the floor in front of it was scratched. Alaan knocked softly before opening it. Bookcases lined the entire perimeter of the room, each stuffed with volumes of various sizes and made of various materials. Most were made of metal, but the bigger ones were paper or parchment. Freestanding piles of hand-length thick tomes outlined a crooked path to an oversized desk smothered in metallic folders. The three seats around it were surprisingly book-free. Either it was an office covered in books or stacks of books in the shape of office furniture.

"Wait here until Urura returns," the sorcerer said as she closed the door.

The room didn't just smell of paper. The air tasted of it. It was like a noble's home but less organized. Libraries had more books than this but weren't so unprotected. A spark of magic would set this room aflame, maybe even melt down the whole building.

"Let me see the orb," Alaan said.

Dre patted his pocket. It was still there. He pulled it out. Alaan touched it and closed his eyes. The orb pulsed twice, then dulled. It couldn't find the other orb.

"It doesn't mean anything," Dre said, placing a hand atop his brother's. "We're surrounded by gigastone. No magic would make it out or in."

"She didn't escape," Alaan said. "I'm not stupid. I'm just mad." He walked to a chair and sat down.

Alaan was too hard on himself. Tess getting caught was more her fault than his. She should have turned herself into the Guard in the first place. A luxurious difference between hiding underground and living in the Castle was that the Guard had soap.

"I decided I am going to do the Verbindous," Dre said. Alaan sat up straight. "Of the Sass family. It will be the first public Verbindous. The Sass have trained in secrecy long enough."

Alaan shook his head. "That is not a thing, Dre."

"Imagine it. You have a sass off with a current member of the family. If you defeat them, they are kicked out and you are let in. That way, everyone stays on their toes. They are the seventh noble family, more powerful than the Kertics."

"That's a noble family I would join," Alaan said.

"Sass is something you are born with, unfortunately, but maybe there is an eighth family out there for you. I hear the Basics are always looking for new members."

Alaan punched him in the arm, then hugged him. "Thanks. I needed that. I know that I have been a little annoying lately."

Instead of saying, "More than a little," Dre hugged him back. "I am here to talk when you are ready."

Alaan pulled a book from a stack. It was titled *Lynit Post Ki: A Leader Knows No Bounds*. He flipped to the first page and read aloud, "'After the Battle of Ki, for the first time in Lynitian history, there was no Kertic of ruling age. The law states that a temporary king must be chosen for the intervening years, in this case, for five and a half years until young Lerrest Kertic turned nineteen. As the population mourned the loss of a beloved king, the nobles descended into chaos. They argued over who should lead, which was always someone from their family. These disagreements often ended in insults and duels. By the end of a week, the debates had trickled to the general public. Then, Rigmen campaigned. He wasn't noble, but no one could deny his experiences as head of defense and, therefore, his many years of working closely with King Kertic.'"

Dre picked up an unmarked metal book on the table. It was light. The pages were cut thin.

Inside, cramped handwriting covered the page. It was a sheet of black ink with little grey holes. He turned several pages that seemed to discuss different nations and different types of magic, but most of the writing was too small and sloppy to read. It was written like a journal. It mentioned new people who joined the Medina. On one page, a list stood out. It was written in a different handwriting, a neater script. It listed nine things. The first seven were crossed out. The last two were written on the same line with question marks next to them.

Slithlor, Juli, it read. Above, *Sewit* was crossed out. He read over the list twice. The other crossed-out items were unreadable.

Footsteps thumped outside. Dre slammed the book shut and put it back. The steps continued past the room. It wasn't Urura. There was still more time to snoop. Dre grabbed another book.

Uniformity - The New Child
By Andor Vous

He flipped to a random page.

Some of these individuals, extraordinarily brilliant and born with a unique magical capacity, defined generation after generation. They have become a marker for time. Every few decades, one stepped forward and produced a new spell or political ideology that launched Lynit ahead of the other nations.

Merely two months after the initiation of the draft—an involuntary Guard training program targeted at promising children —student performance significantly dropped nationwide because uniqueness was now a curse. This was not a planned side effect. Nevertheless, it has become an unavoidable one. However, this new fear hovering over our youth only outlines a more significant trend that started over twenty years ago. Even before the draft, there were other noticeable decreases in magic usage.

No golden rule specifies how many persons per capita are expected to have abnormal abilities. A short fifty years ago, eleven people, on record, out of the two million inhabitants of Virt, Poli, Wrisnt, and Nintur, had abnormal abilities. Now, in the year 1309, there are only three. This may not seem like an alarming decline, but when one takes into account the fact that the reason two of them are special is because they are twins and only have an abnormal ability together and the other person is nowhere to be found, we begin to see causes for concern.

"Alaan," Dre said, tilting the book, underlining the passage.

Alaan read along. "How many do you think were taken by Slithlor?" he said.

"I hope they all made it to the Medina," Dre said.

Urura arrived a few minutes later. She was in her seventies but weaved around her books with the grace of an acrobat. She wore a gold choker and two gold bracelets on each wrist. Her hair was wrapped in a white scarf.

"I hope you two know how to cook," she said. She closed the door and pulled off her scarf. Fluffy black hair fell to her shoulders. She then unfastened her necklace. "Once a month, we have a large feast, and any newcomers are expected to help with the cooking. There is no better way to know someone than to see them at work in a kitchen. I hope that your culinary technique matches your skills in the gigasphere."

"We can cook," Dre said, standing up. "Our father wouldn't let us hire a chef."

"Cooking and eating as a family are his only rules," Alaan said.

"Smart man," Urura said. She moved to her desk and sat down.

"The dinner is next week, which will give you plenty of time to contemplate your dish," she said. "Now, who are these three additional children you brought with you?"

"Do you want the long story or the short?" Alaan said.

"Long," she said. Alaan told her about the performance, Homin, and everything that happened at Daramis bar. He even mentioned Tess.

Urura pulled off the rest of her jewelry, then kicked off her shoes. "They sound like spies."

"Spies?" Dre said, laughing. He recalled a panicked Lakree trying to use wizardry. He shifted in his seat. "They're not spies. We approached them. They didn't even want to talk to us. We practically forced them to follow us."

"Spies have been sent after us before and the best ones are the ones you suspect the least. Fortunately, I suspect everyone. I invited a man and a woman into the Medina a few years back. They had known each other for a year beforehand. The woman was the one who needed protection and he was her partner. He was the spy, however. A psychic had walled off part of his mind so that he would believe the role he played. The best actors don't realize they are acting."

"You can be a spy and not know it?" Dre said. That was a new reason why psychics were the worst.

"What happened next?" Alaan said.

"The effect wore off and he remembered that he was supposed to report back to his superiors. He tried to sneak out in the middle of the night, but he didn't get far," she said. Though her voice was light, her eyes glinted with a hard edge.

"Did you kill him?" Alaan said.

"Fortunately, we have our own psychics. Let's say he is never telling anyone anything ever again."

Dre swallowed and it rang in his ear. He still didn't believe Lakree, Hila, and Rye were spies, but he hadn't considered the danger that entering the Medina could pose to them.

Urura searched through the drawers on her desk. "The Medina isn't a place. It is an idea. Certain people are worth protecting and that protection's reach is independent of the world around it. It is not conditioned on political ties, Lynitian laws, nor foreign ideals. It is provided to those who need it.

"The definition of need is easily subjective, but we define it to mean that if your existence puts you at risk of harm from your peers, you are in need. For most here, their ideas are what put them at risk. For others, like yourself, it's their magic. When it comes to ideas, we never know in advance which ones will cause a culture to turn against someone; however, with magic, it is the same every time. A unique magical ability either ends in praise or violent envy. That's why we gave you an open invitation before a material threat existed. We will help anyone from any nation, city-state, or village, but the danger must be from those who would otherwise protect them or from an entity their people cannot shield them against."

Dre and Alaan were unique from birth, but it wasn't until they showed unique power that the Medina considered they were at risk. Urura said that Slithlor's method for studying magic involved capturing, torturing, and experimenting on his test subjects. He hunted people with rare magical affinities, making him an enemy of the Medina.

"Has Slithlor kidnapped a Lynitian before?" Alaan said.

"A required service of some kind or death befalls anyone with special. The fact that it is the law of certain nations is meaningless," she said.

"That's why he told us to join the Guard ourselves. It wasn't a threat. It was a promise of what would happen," Alaan said.

"The Medina has a promise, too—two of them, actually," she continued. "The first is the promise of information boundaries. No one will ever be asked to and should not reveal anything about their magic or home place to someone not from that place. In your case, that means not speaking of Lynitian magic or politics to non-Lynitians.

"The second and most important promise is the dedication to transforming the world such that the Medina is no longer needed. With every additional member, we progress the world one step forward."

Dre leaned back in his chair, tapping his fingers together. All he wanted to do was end the draft and return to his old life. Changing the world was a lot more complicated than that.

"This place isn't for refugees. It is for people who have decided something is wrong with the world and want to do something about it," Alaan said.

"Exactly," she said.

"I am glad we never told our parents about this place. Our mother would have never let us agree to something like that," Alaan said.

"Think long and hard about that promise before you commit to it. The Medina is an idea you must accept in your heart," she said.

"Would ending the draft fall under that idea?" Dre said. Not only would it help his peers, but it would limit Slithlor's ability to collect more children. It was the only legal tool that he had.

"The law isn't the problem," Urura said.

"If you don't change laws, do you change people?" Dre said. She nodded. He hummed. In Lynit, it meant that they would have to change nobles because they were the ones who ran everything. And good luck with that.

Urura's office door flung open. The gust of wind wrestled papers.

"The city is on lockdown," a man with bushy eyebrows and dressed in a guard sorcerer's uniform said in a hurried breath. His face went blank momentarily as he noticed Dre and Alaan, but he quickly recovered. "Guards are patrolling the perimeter of the dome and the Easton Tunnels. They are looking for three children who broke into the throne room. They were last seen in Poli, in the Easton Tunnels with the Poli Twins."

Urura frowned, tapping her desk. "We have several important movements today, but now no one can leave." She hummed, then stood up, picking up her metal notebook. "If we return the three children, it will stop the search."

Dre stood up. "You can't kick them out, at least not now. They are special, too. Slithlor has the law on his side and will get them. He tried to get us, but we are protected by a court case for now."

"I will do my research on these children. I am curious why Slithlor tried to draft you simultaneously as the others. This situation feels sloppy, but Slithlor isn't a sloppy person. It means that there is some alternative that he is more afraid of and I want to know what has him so scared," she said. "Go back to your room and wait for me. If I don't like what I find, I'll deal with our extra guests accordingly."

Chapter 16 - Dre

Dre sprinkled flecks of tilly leaf, salt, and pepper on a long cut of jir. He dipped the pink meat into a bowl of amber seed flower, then carefully placed it in a sizzling pan. Alaan tossed green and orange vegetables in a black bowl, coating them in dressing. Fried jir with a wild squash salad was a simple meal, one of the first recipes they learned.

"That's not how it happened," Alaan said.

"Yes, they placed a wall between us. You charged at them instead of clearing away enough dark energy so that I could see you," Dre said.

"But she flung light energy at me. I had to explode it first," Alaan said.

"Meanwhile her sister attacked me with light and dark," Dre said. "I couldn't keep up, so I closed the distance and knocked her down with a hit to the sternum."

"Ah, yes, then her sister hit you with dark energy and knocked you off the stage," Alaan said. "Then I got the whooping of my life." Alaan laughed.

"If I can't see you or the person you are fighting, I don't know how you are adapting and you don't know what I am doing. Staying in sync is more important than whatever else is going on. The moment we aren't working as one, we lose."

"If you had used light energy to open a slit in the wall yourself, do you think we would have won?"

"If we had normal magic levels, of course. Otherwise, no," Dre said. "If at any point we find proof that being mediocre at both is better, then we can change it up. You are reaching for something that isn't there."

"If we put a little effort in, we can make great strides with the weaker energy. You saw what I did at the MMA exam after a few weeks of practice," Alaan said.

"It would take us years to pass the fourth round of the MMA exam with both magics. And we would have to relearn our fighting strategy. We have clear divisions of duty now. We would be like every other wizard if we used dark and light energy."

Alaan put down the salad bowl and turned to Dre. In a calm tone, he said, "That's exactly it, isn't it?"

"There is nothing wrong with incorporating new skills into our arsenal, but we don't need to break what already works." Dre finished cooking the meat, then cut it up into smaller pieces.

Alaan didn't say anything else because Dre was right.

"In any case, whether we stay in the Medina or leave Lynit, we have to find people to fight," Dre said. "Simply training isn't enough anymore. That could be why our magic hasn't been joining consistently lately. When we first discovered the ability, it was inconsistent, too."

Rye sat up on the bed. His face was heavy, his eyes red. It was the fourth time he had woken up that morning. Lakree rolled over next to him, burying his face into his sheets. He, however, had no trouble resting. He was asleep by the time Dre and Alaan returned the night before. Hila lay curled up on the couch, snoring softly.

"Right on time," Dre said as he slid a plate across the counter to Rye.

"I am never drinking again," Rye said.

"Sorry for pressuring you," Dre said.

"It's fine. It was all worth it," Rye said. "At first, I wanted to know why my father ran, but now I just want to see him again. I hope we find him."

They ate. The vegetables were too stringy, but the meat was fresh. It was similar to food above ground. Only on trips to see his mother's family did Dre have fresh fruit and vegetables. In Wrisnt, he could pick and eat an apple turnip from the ground. It was the magic of soil, water, and sunlight. In all of the Winder Plains, vegetation grew in only four places.

Someone knocked on the door. Dre wiped his hands before opening it. Urura stared back with bloodshot eyes, dressed in the same clothes as the day before. She nodded at the sorcerer stationed in the hall, then entered the room with an excited spring in her step as if she hadn't been up all night.

Rye made to wake his friends, but they were already up. Hila and Lakree popped to their feet as Urura introduced herself.

"I am Lakree Oldenfoot, of the families Cast and Yordin," he said.

"Wow, an Oldenfoot. It's not often that I meet a noble, let alone someone of two families. I can only imagine the pressure to pick a family name before your Verbindous," she said.

"Things are changing," Lakree said. "More of us are choosing magics that don't align with our parents."

"Not many, though, from what I hear. Is that why you transitioned to a public school?" she asked.

Lakree sighed. "The Vous didn't identify me as having a strong affinity, but I wasn't ready to give up sorcery. I was just starting to understand it. My parents supported my transfer because they thought I wanted more time to pick between wizardry and elemental magic."

"And now, did the Vous accept you?"

"I was accepted into a Vous school, but the Verbindous will be the final decision."

"So you still have something to prove to the Vous," she said, moving her soft, unblinking gaze to Rye. "Both your parents served in the Guard until your father deserted during the Battle of Ki."

"My father's body wasn't recovered, but he wasn't a coward," Rye said. "He was, is, the bravest man I know. We think he fled for the same reason as Lakree's aunt. She was at the Battle of Ki, too, and no one found her body, either. Tell her Lakree," Rye said.

It was subtle, but Lakree's eye twitched. He was hiding something. "Thank you for letting us stay the night, but if we are no longer welcome, we'll leave."

Urura continued, "And Hila, the most interesting of them all. You were born in Ries and moved here when you were seven. Since you don't have a birth record here, if you lose the ability to do elemental magic before nineteen, you will be deported. However, you are one of the few who know foreign magic and are young enough to attempt mixing it with one of ours. Slithlor would be interested in you."

"A noble, a civilian, and a foreigner walked into a bar," Alaan said. It was the start of a joke that wasn't funny. It was similar to a statement made by the king regent after King Kertic died. Though magic separated those groups, physical features did not, which was dangerous. Without a magic test, Lynitians couldn't tell them apart. This was why the king regent banned all foreigners, well, all except Hila.

"I'm Lynitian now," she said. Her pin tinged from a flick.

"I know," Urura said, nodding. "I know a fair bit about all of you; however, yesterday's events are still a mystery. Please, walk me through what happened."

It took a few moments for Lakree to regain his composure before he spoke, but he dove smoothly into his story. "We came here looking for Juli Pol, my aunt. She warned my family that the Guard would come for me. She will protect us."

"Why do you think she is here?" Urura asked.

"She told us to come to Poli to contact her. We didn't get a chance, though. I expected guards. I didn't expect the posters at all," Lakree said. Then he pulled out a photo. "This is her." Dre leaned in. The ink was faded, but the "E" on her chest was clear.

"We need to find her and my father," Rye said. Lakree's eye twitched again and Rye noticed. "What? He has to be with her. Where else would he be?"

Lakree didn't answer.

"If you want to leave, you can, but you will not be able to return and most likely, you will be captured by the Guard," Urura said. She pulled out a slick metal rectangular board from her satchel. Thin lines were etched across the surfaces, some joining in six-point intersections and the rest darting off independently. It was a map of the Easton Tunnels.

She said a few words that sounded like protection magic and tapped the map. Black dots appeared, some in groups, others alone, all moving. "These are the guards patrolling the tunnels you used to get here."

Lakree, Hila, and Rye leaned in.

"If you decide to stay, I would love to get to the bottom of your story."

Dre sighed internally. She wasn't kicking them out. He hadn't made a mistake by bringing these children here.

"That's like fifteen guards," Hila said.

"If you are to stay here, I need to know why the Guard wants you so badly. Can you demonstrate for me the magic they want from you?" Urura said.

"I matter shifted into the throne room and through gigastone, so

218

that is likely it," Lakree said.

"I killed a quitol, but no one saw it. I didn't even know I could do it," Hila said.

"My morphing speed is slow. I don't know why they want me unless it is because of my father," Rye said.

"Then we are in a tough spot," she said. She opened the door. "Follow me."

They walked down the hall. Urura turned left at an intersection that wasn't there before. The new hallway stretched higher as they continued until it doubled in height and ended at stone doors. Urura pushed softly and the heavy doors swung open. A long stone table sat at the center of the room. It was big enough to seat at least forty people. The ceiling was gigastone and the ground was red dirt like the rest of the Medina.

"Test the extremes of your magic here. We don't require you to show us the full extent of what you are capable of, but you must show us enough to prove you deserve to be protected. I'll let you decide how much that is," she said.

Dre stepped in. Lakree's ability was on par with his ability to combine energy with Alaan, so he should be safe. As for Hila, killing a quitol wasn't enough. But Dre's money was on Rye for the most exciting ability. A father wouldn't abandon their child without a good reason.

Urura motioned for Dre and Alaan to join her outside the room.

"All the wanted signs have been taken down. The Guard has officially written off the throne room intrusion as an accident. However, a quiet team of three elites arrived from Virt last night. Officially, no one knows what they are doing here, but they are looking for those three," she said.

"If elites are involved in this, then they are not here because of the draft," Alaan said.

"Have you heard the names Crimson Siat, Pri Zan, Carsi Certi,

Stavender Il, Drime Hullo, or Rolin Nafin before?"

Dre hummed, looking at his brother. "Stavender, Short Stavender?" He knew someone by that name. He was short, not abnormally short, but the smallest in year four. Kids used to say, "What is Stavender short for?" Someone would respond, "No reason," then laugh. A few times, Alaan asked Dre, "How do you spell short?" Dre responded, "S-t-a-v-e-n-d-e-r." Stavender usually stormed off at that point. The jokes were stupid and mean, but Stavender used to call them "baby quitols" since the creatures were known for having twins and he was the one that gave Alaan the scar over his right eye.

"Slithlor escorted the six of them from the draft area of the Castle in Virt yesterday," she said.

"He was drafted? I don't remember anything extraordinary about him back then," Alaan said.

"Were they released? We were placed in the MMA program by mistake. For the lie to work, there have to be kids who were drafted by mistake," Dre said.

"They aren't free. There is no record of them ever being in the MMA program anymore," she said.

"He is seventeen. He didn't age out," Alaan said.

"Slithlor can't just disappear away children from the draft, right? Yes, he is creepy, but he has always stayed within the law. No one has tried to kidnap us before," Dre said.

"If the king regent ordered it, it would be technically legal. And I guess that he did. Otherwise, Slithlor would have done a better job of disappearing away those children. A few people saw him do it," she said.

"Then all of this is not just about Slithlor's obsession with studying people with unique abilities. The king regent wouldn't need to be sneaky," Alaan said.

"Lakree, Hila, and Rye are somehow at the center of this. They break into the Castle, the Guard attempts to draft the five of you, these other children go missing, then three elites arrive in Poli. The Guard knows that the Medina exists, but they don't understand how sophisticated it is. Most think it's a group of stay-at-home parents who meet once a week to discuss government reform. Slithlor, however, knows that we are organized. We have saved multiple foreign people from him, but he is not one to miss a pattern. Slithlor has tried to find us in the past.

"If Lakree is not a spy, the map will keep him from trying to leave until he realizes the pattern is too random to be people. If he is a spy, he'll stay to collect all the information he can," she said.

"So no matter what, you have time to study them," Alaan said.

"They aren't spies," Dre said. "They're sloppy."

"Probably not, but it doesn't mean Slithlor isn't using them," she said. "For now, we will test their magic. If there is nothing special about them, then we will wipe their memory of this place and send them on their way."

"What?" Dre said. "You could rip out their whole personality."

Memories weren't independent things that were neatly filed away in drawers. They were sticky and gummed up every neural pathway they could. The very first technique that any child learned in school was how to wall off their mind. It was easy to put up a basic defense strong enough to keep out ninety-five percent of psychics. Unfortunately, every guard psychic was in that five percent who could break through.

"We placed a marker when they arrived, a memory marker. At most, they will lose a week," she said.

"How did you get through their defenses?" Alaan said.

"They were asleep," she said.

Dre dropped his head into his hands. "They won't even remember that they are on the run."

"This is why we never liked psychics, psychics or sorcerers. They can do things to you and you would never know," Alaan said.

"Yeah, exploding energy in someone's face is so much nicer," Urura said. Alaan shrugged.

"It's not an obvious process to discover an ability you don't know you have, but we have experience with that. We'll help them." Dre said.

"And I'll send someone to help, too," she said.

Dre and Alaan went back to the large room. Snowflakes fluttered down in uneven waves. The chill hit Dre's face, then hands. His breath misted. He twirled, messing up the clean sheet on the ground. Elemental magic was his favorite once, before his wizardry ability. An elemental mage, a Kertic, invented the mechanical turbines that powered the city. She created a machine to imitate her magic. Now, it was possible to live in the Winder Plains magic-free.

The snow stopped and the temperature snapped back to normal. The water evaporated. Hila moved on to another spell, a wind-based one. Dust swirled in front of her. Her posture was soft, but her movements were deliberate. Streams of wind whipped out of focus, but she coaxed them back into harmony with a wave of her arm.

"She's not Lynitian," Alaan said. Elemental magic was about power and control, but she wielded it more like someone who was almost carefree. She hadn't learned to move like that in Lynit. She was still connected to Ries, no matter what story she told her friends.

"Would she betray Lynit for her father's people?" Dre said.

"Probably," Alaan said, then cupped a hand around his mouth. "Have you tried a lightning spell, like the one you killed the quitol with?"

She paused. Her small cyclone collapsed. "I put all my energy into each element," she said.

"Did you experience anything extraordinary with the other elements?" Alaan asked.

"No," she said.

"Then why aren't you testing the one element that showed something strange," he said.

Her eyes shifted to Lakree for a moment. "Lightning is dangerous."

"Wind and water are just as dangerous," Dre said. "All magic is dangerous."

"I didn't kill anything with those," she said.

"Direct it at the ceiling. You won't harm the gigastone," Alaan said. She glanced up. She was skeptical. "The goal isn't only about power. It is to determine how your magic differs from every other elemental mage's."

On the other side of the room, Lakree was almost a blur. His legs and arms moved like he was walking, but his body traveled too quickly, like sprinting in a tight circle. As bits of dust drifted over the ring around him, they zipped to the ground. Time passed more quickly there.

"Can you slow it down again?" Dre said.

Lakree had tried, but nothing happened, or as he put it, "Time only slowed down by one-tenth of a percent."

"What is different now?" Dre asked.

Lakree shrugged. Next, he matter shifted across the room in a cloud of black smoke. He stumbled but caught himself. "My strength comes in waves. I'll rest and then try to move through gigastone again. That will be all the proof she needs."

"Focus on slowing down time," Dre said, holding up a hand. If Lakree left the Medina, he would discover that the map was fake, destroying his trust in the place. The three elites would find him within the hour and there was no telling what he might bargain for his freedom. He could give them information on the entrance to the Medina or be forced to matter shift Slithlor inside.

Lakree nodded. Dre waited until he restarted with time

manipulation spells before checking on Rye.

Rye stood in the form of a brown bird with long wings and a curved beak, a tipit. It was the first creature Dre learned during his stint studying animalism. It was a simple bird. Rye's next morph was into another bird. That one was blue and white, with red dots around its eyes and on its tail. A bright haze of energy rose above him as he shrunk down to its tiny size. He was no bigger than a foot. He leaped into the air, then flew around the room, singing. He tried morphing directly into another bird without passing by human, but it failed.

"Try something other than birds," Dre said.

"Birds are what I am best at."

Next, Rye turned into a lizard, then a canine with a long tail. He morphed into something large and blue, maybe a spangot, but it failed. After that, he took a break. A ring of sweat darkened his collar. He pulled off his shirt. His chest and abs were solid. The deep and elusive "V" disappeared underneath his pants. Even Dre's body wasn't that defined.

"Lakree's and Hila's magic is growing, but mine is doing the opposite," Rye said. "I'm getting slower."

"Alaan and I have to be in perfect sync for our energies to join. At first, it was a slow process. Now, it is second nature. Speed isn't important. Speed is something that you learn with practice."

"In animalism, speed equals strength. Everything else is skill," Rye said.

Dre's tongue buzzed. Thin lines of electricity zipped across the air to Hila. She spun two fingers around herself, pooling the magic together. Then she pointed up. A beam of lightning shot up. The light of the strike against the gigastone was muted, but the boom reverberated. Dust drifted from the ceiling.

"That's enough energy to kill a quitol," Alaan said, clapping.

"More than enough," Dre said. Knocking off gigastone dust

fragments wasn't easy. She wasn't likely in danger of getting kicked out.

Lakree held a thumb into the air but didn't stop casting his time spells. When Dre turned back around, Rye was pouting.

"Maybe I am losing magic altogether," Rye said. His head was tucked low.

"Did you stop practicing magic after the draft started?" Dre said. Rye shook his head. "Then you are just tired."

"Or there is nothing special about me," Rye said.

"I know it's hard. It is unfair to ask you to discover something so quickly, but you can't give up yet. You have to monitor your magic carefully. Alaan and I discovered our ability by accident, but the odd behavior of our magic was always there. We just didn't know where to look."

"With wizardry, I am sure you can stumble onto something, but animalism doesn't work like that. There are no accidental morphs. I must purposely control every aspect of a transformation. If I am also monitoring or testing for some supposed irregular behavior I don't have, it becomes too much to track."

Dre crossed his arms. "You think I haven't heard that before? All the other magics think wizardry is easy. Yes, it is easy to summon energy and form into simple shapes, but to compete against the other magics requires tremendous work."

"What if I was just born an ordinary animalist? Maybe I didn't inherit whatever made my dad an elite," Rye said.

"No one is born ordinary. Ordinary is something that you become when you decide to do nothing. It's a choice, just like picking your magic."

"I didn't pick animalism," Rye said, his face suddenly serious. "I was born with an affinity for it like you were for wizardry. School is designed to help us discover that."

Dre shook his head. "That sounds like noble propaganda to me.

This is exactly how they convinced people that they are ordinary by design. It's why everyone prefers to think of Alaan and me as noble. It's easier to accept that the others are special than to accept that you didn't try hard enough or didn't have access to the right education." Dre pointed at Lakree, who leaned over a small, dome-shaped field. He dropped a small brown object, wood possibly, and the sound of the tap on the ground was delayed. He had slowed down time.

"He didn't learn to matter shift because he is special. He learned it because he had gone to a noble school for most of his life. Matter shifting isn't taught in public schools. The only other way to learn it is in the Guard. Nobles have many secret techniques that they don't share with us. They are special because they get special training. Magic doesn't pass through blood."

"I don't have special training either. I failed the draft exam when I tried my hardest to pass."

"There's a book called *Uniformity: the New Child*. It says that in the absence of a challenge, we become uniform. Everyone becomes exactly like their magic, exactly like what you described, exactly like the nobles. You can become good at your magic but won't become more than that. All of its flaws will be your flaws. You become special by being more than just another animalist. What you are trying to test is hard. There is no script or set of known tricks to help you discover a unique ability. If you were trying animalist approaches to solve a problem, mix it up. How would a protector do it, or maybe a sorcerer? It takes persistence and luck to discover anything."

"I agree. You can't reach your best unless you work for it. But when it comes to extraordinary talents, you have to be born with them and I don't have any reason to believe I was," Rye said.

"If you don't have an ability, why did your father flee?" Dre said.

Rye froze, then closed his mouth.

Dre moved next to him. He summoned dark energy and condensed it in front of them. A black triangle rotated smoothly in the air, then twisted it, revealing that it was a pyramid. "This is how you've used magic all your life. You explored your energy down the two common dimensions everyone else used, shaping your opinion of animalism. You believe you have seen it all. But..."

Dre flipped the pyramid over, revealing the square bottom. "I need you to look for this. No one considered that light and dark energy could join. And it can't, for everyone except the two of us. We didn't know we could do it until we did it. There was no playbook. Even the original inventors of magic were seemingly ordinary people until they weren't."

"I'll keep trying, but my father wouldn't have feared the Guard taking me in because of my magic. Something more sinister has to be going on and it likely has to do with the Battle of Ki," Rye said, then stood up.

Dre agreed. Rye's father was one of five elites who were involved in this conspiracy, which was dangerous. Elites weren't low-level guards likely to bend the rules for a favor from Slithlor. They had proven themselves beyond reproach. There was no reason for them to flee, hide, or sneak around town unless they believed Lynit's safety was at stake. Somehow, a random group of kids threatened Lynit.

"We need to understand why all of this is coming to a head now. That will be key to unraveling all of this," Dre said. The varying success rate of joining his energy with his brother was new and coincidentally on the same timeline as Lakree, Hila, and Rye discovering their magical changes.

Later, a girl entered the room. Her hair was gray, potentially fake, but so were her eyes. Her skin was so dark that it was almost blue. Dark welts stretched up her arms and across her neck. Either she had been to war or was born with something protectors couldn't cure.

"I always wondered if the Poli Twins would come here. I didn't think you were at risk since you are famous, but here you are. Slithlor can't kidnap you if everyone is watching you, but using the law is a clever workaround," she said. Her eyes jumped back and forth between Dre and Alaan. She extended a hand. "I'm Chirchi Davenest. I am Lynitian, too."

"Davenest?" Lakree said, nodding. "I'm an Oldenfoot."

"Is that a noble name, too?" Hila said.

"Yeah, Davenast is Palow and Cast. There is a specific name for each combination of noble families," Lakree said.

"In Ries, they don't have family names. You are given a name at birth; when you become an adult, you pick a second name for yourself. I like that better," Hila said.

"Me too," Alaan said.

"I like our names, though my parents critiqued the political and social control nobles maintained in Lynit. Just because our ancestors invented magic does not mean they know how to write better sanitation policies," Chirchi said.

"Oh, the anti-noble Davenasts," Lakree said.

"I wouldn't call that anti-noble," Hila said. "That is simply fair."

"Anything that doesn't sing noble praise is anti-noble, especially coming from another noble," Dre said. It was something Dre and Alaan stood away from. Though their brand was strong, it wouldn't survive a direct rebuke of the nobility. The main problem wasn't the nobles, but the people like Rye who believed so desperately in the hierarchy of bloodlines that they would fight any who challenged it.

"The only lineage that matters to us is the magical one," Lakree said. "We are biological descendants of the inventors of magic, but that doesn't mean much. Magic doesn't pass through blood. In death, magic returns to the spirit realm, then redistributes to new people. The ancestors you inherited magic from are the only ones that matter. That is why we have the Verbindous. I will have to prove that I am Vous. It doesn't matter that there was a Vous somewhere in my family tree. If we go back far enough, we are all related to a noble."

"Any of us could be noble?" Rye said.

"...could become noble," Lakree corrected.

"Your best friend is noble. How is this news to you?" Alaan said. Dre didn't get it either. Rye had completely ignored when Dre and Lakree said magic didn't pass through blood. Maybe nobles weren't a conspiring group that fought to keep themselves above everyone else. Instead, they were placed on a pedestal and didn't shy away from the limelight. In a way, that was kind of what it was like to be a twin. Dre shuddered.

"Speaking of the spirit realm," Chirchi said. "That's why I am in the Medina. I can travel to the spirit realm on command. If you haven't discovered anything odd with your magic yet, I can take you there to observe your source. This is why Urura sent me."

Dre rubbed the back of his head. He recalled the tickling he felt in Sepotine. It felt like the spirit realm itself was calling him. Dre and Alaan spent their lives trying to understand the inner workings of their magical capabilities, but it was possible that more was still undiscovered. Chirchi should be able to give the final answer on what has been happening with Dre and Alaan's magic and its connection to Lakree, Hila, and Rye.

"Can you take us too?" Dre and Alaan said. Normally, Dre would have assumed that he and Alaan wanted to go for the same reasons, but now he wasn't sure.

"Yeah," Chirchi said.

"No thanks," Lakree said, throwing up his hands. "Why would we go to the place where spirit fiends live?"

"At first, I was scared of them, too, until I realized they weren't evil. The people from Sewit transported beings they didn't understand against their will. How could it have not been a disaster? In the spirit realm, some fiends are harmless, others are not, but that is no different than creatures in the real world. And there, you will see beings you couldn't even imagine, landscapes that can't exist in our world," Chirchi said. "I may have had to give up my old life because of my ability, but I wouldn't trade it for anything."

The blue sun didn't exist in the real world.

"We still aren't going?" Lakree said.

"My ability does not bring them here nor take you physically there. Your body will remain here. Only your mind will travel," she said.

"Lakree, what if my father knew something dangerous about spirit fiends? That would explain why he left and couldn't return. Everything related to the spirit fiends is banned at the international level and threatened with war," Rye said. He stepped forward.

"Rye, don't," Lakree said. "We don't know what's over there."

"I'm not making any progress on finding my ability either and I don't think I will on my own, not in the next few days at least," Rye said.

Hila stepped back. "I'm not."

"No, Rye, please," Lakree said. "We don't need to take any unnecessary risks. If we have to leave, we leave. I'll matter shift us somewhere safe."

"If you don't want to come, you don't have to. The four of us can go first. Have a seat everyone," Chirchi said. She sat down and Dre plopped down next to her.

"Rye, I lied about your father. He isn't on some secret mission with Juli," Lakree said.

Rye twisted around. "What do you mean?"

"I just said whatever came to mind to get you inside with us. I thought Juli was dead until she appeared during the Battle of Ki.

She had supposedly died on a mission when I was two. Whatever she knows has nothing to do with your father," Lakree said.

Hila covered her mouth with her hands. "No, Lakree, don't tell me you lied."

"My dad is not a coward," Rye said, his words strained.

"I wanted to believe that he didn't run, but they found the bodies of every other elite and King Kertic," Lakree said. "Maybe I made a mistake in pressuring you to come with us. Hila's and my magic are steadily growing, but I saw you. You are getting weaker."

Dre grimaced. Finding two out of three kids with extraordinary abilities was still good work, but poor Rye would be kicked out of the Medina. Though on the bright side, after a memory wipe, Rye would go back to thinking his father was dead and that his best friend wasn't a liar.

Rye charged at Lakree.

Chapter 17 - Rye

Lakree tried to move out of the way, but Rye tackled him.

Fluidity and adaptation were powerful tools, but in the end, animalists became obedient followers. They did what they were told and if they didn't like it, they found a way to accept it. Rye found ways to accept Lakree's crazy conspiracy even when it didn't make sense. He wanted to believe it. It was easier to believe it. So he did. His father wasn't hiding because he knew a secret worth abandoning King Kertic and his family over. Lakree's aunt told her family about her secret. Rye's dad would have done the same unless he was ashamed.

"Why?" Rye said as he gripped Lakree's thin neck. Lakree pulled at Rye's wrists.

Last night, Rye had dreamed about seeing his father, and for the first time in years, it wasn't a sad one. Guards snide remarks about his father had been reduced to gossip in his memory, but now they shouted "Traitor."

Dre and Alaan pulled Rye off.

Lakree coughed. "This is bigger than the draft, bigger than the Guard. Slithlor is after us and Juli is the only one who can protect us. They used to work together years ago. She must know his secret," he said, alternating between gasping and crying. "Slithlor is behaving as if we are disrupting his plan and I don't want to be there when he corrects it. I don't need all the details to know something is wrong."

"Three elites are in Poli looking for you," Dre said.

"You see," Lakree said.

"They are looking for *you*," Rye said. His bogus draft notice was crumpled in his pocket. The Guard's interest in him wasn't genuine. It was a ploy to deflect attention from the fact that they were really after Lakree and Hila, the noble and foreigner.

"Maybe the Guard isn't after you because of your magic, but they could think your dad told you something important," Lakree said.

Rye charged again, but Dre and Alaan held him. Lakree was making up new theories on the fly.

"Calm down," Alaan said. "You are here. You are safe. That is all that matters."

"You let me believe I might see him again," Rye said.

"I panicked," Lakree said.

"You could have told me afterward," Rye said.

"You might have tried to leave before I contacted Juli," Lakree said.

"Can you hear yourself? Just like a sorcerer, you don't care who you hurt as long as you get the results you want," Rye said. Each magic had its positive attributes, such as sorcerers being great strategists and abstract thinkers. But, there were also dark attributes, the negative ones that adults didn't mention on career day.

"Let's take a deep breath and calm down," Alaan said. "Lakree did what sorcerers do, what they are trained to do. He made sense of the wacky world around him and changed the facts to help everyone he could."

"How did you matter shift into the throne room?" Hila's voice was calm.

"What?" Lakree said softly, wiping his face. "I don't know."

Michael Green Jr.

"Tell the truth, for once. How did you do it?" Rye said.

Lakree swallowed. "The spell works by bending space such that the destination is bent to me, then when the universe corrects itself, it sends me and the destination space back to its original location. I didn't select the throne room as a destination. I tried to pick somewhere near the museum, but I made a mistake when I created the disruption. However, several location rules were still disrupted, so I figured I'd try anyway. The negative density field formed properly, but the p-band responses were off. At that point, the rules thrashed so much that I was surprised the spell worked. The Correction Factor sent us there."

The Guard had been nasty to Rye yesterday because of a broken system they had put in place. That was why they didn't want children dependent on it. If Rye were to repeat what Lakree explained, maybe they would forgive him, at least a little. He hadn't done anything wrong other than run.

He shook his head. He was already adapting to what Lakree said. But Rye didn't need to accept the nobles' suggestion that his father ran. They didn't have any real clue. The Guard didn't have one, either. Since he couldn't ask someone from Sewit, it was equally valid not to accept any narrative until there was concrete evidence. If Chirchi found something strange with his magic, it could lead him to an answer. "Are we still going to the spirit realm?" he said.

"Yeah, sure," Chirchi said. She stood a few feet off. Her arms were crossed.

"Rye," Hila said softly, "I don't want you to go either, but I won't tell you what to do. You sacrificed to get us this far. You could have stayed behind at Lakree's house but didn't. Just be careful."

Rye nodded, then sat down. Dre and Alaan sat beside him.

"Open your minds and hold hands," Chirchi said.

Rye closed his eyes. He imagined the room. Chirchi's hair glowed and a purple cloud hung above her. Then, the psychic energy slammed into her body, making her shine. The light pulsed inside her once, then passed to Dre, then Alaan. When it hit Rye, his hand clenched. The energy burned as it flowed through him. When it spread to his head, a voice called him.

The energy spun through each of them again. After each pass, it sped up and intensified. Dre's nails dug into Rye's hand, but Rye couldn't let go. He didn't have control over his body anymore. He was sinking, not into the floor, but into himself, until everything went blue.

Rye's body remained cross-legged on the floor, but it was distant. He wasn't in that room anymore. His mind traveled, pushing against a current toward the voice. It guided him, but his fury propelled him. The faster he could get away from Lakree, the liar, his oldest friend, the better.

"Pick an important idea or memory. Think about it. Connect it to other ideas and memories. Focus," the voice said. It belonged to the girl, the psychic.

Rye picked a moment, the day he left Lakree's house. A feeling —an instinct, human instinct, the animalist flaw—controlled him. He bit the hand of a guard instead of Hila's. If only he had done the right thing, he wouldn't be a fugitive now. He would be in the Castle training with an instructor who would teach him instinct stacking.

If his magic were special, different, then he expected that he would be drafted. The purpose of the draft was to find him and others like him. But a different logic played in his head while he sat on that couch. He thought he could have it both ways: help his friends and obey the guard. He was scared and stupid. Free from his body, he felt the particular area of his mind that computed the decision to flee. He concentrated on the flawed place. Something foreign nested there between his baser thoughts and desires. It was the MMA material.

It was how the flashcards knew what was happening to him and suggested something on the fly. It reacted off his instincts. It was flawed, too. He directed his full attention to that space. A tightness, a gravity responded, pulling him inward onto himself. It was like falling, collapsing.

In a burst, his vision returned and he was in a place that looked like the Winder Plains, dry and barren, except for the patches of pebbles rising as if they were reverse raining from ground to sky. Some pieces joined to form a large boulder positioned amongst the clouds. A single white moon lighted the sky, but the ground glowed like broad daylight. This was the spirit realm.

Chirchi stood next to him. Her scars were gone and her hair was black. She almost looked like a different person. Before her, a large blue cloud of dust hovered a foot above the ground. The specks shifted, some joining into clumps.

"Where are the twins?" Rye said.

"That's them. They came over as one somehow," she said. She moved around the cloud, inspecting it. "Try concentrating on different memories. Pick one the other doesn't know."

It was slow, but two points in the blue mist stopped moving. The rest of the cloud concentrated around them. Two growing balls collapsed into two people, Alaan and Dre.

"That was weird," Dre said.

Alaan patted his body. "My memories were doubled as if they came from two perspectives."

"Everything you see here is spirit energy, those rocks, the air, the sun. It is the matter of this place. Normally, our connection to this place flows one way, from here to our world, allowing us to manipulate magic. My ability reverses that direction," Chirchi said. "Your minds were drawn to the single source of spirit energy you share."

"I remember something, a memory, your memory," Dre said.

"You were in your room. It was late, but you couldn't sleep. You took down all of your livit posters and stuffed the trophies that Dad made us into a drawer. You were sad. Then, you started morphing. Your body shrank into a bird's. Maybe it was a tipit. I'm not sure. But I have my memory of the day. It was a few days after we selected wizardry. I thought you were celebrating with a fresh start, but you were mourning."

Alaan lowered his eyes. "It was a last farewell to the magic. I would have chosen animalism if things were different, but wizardry worked too well for us. Animalism is singular. It is the only magic where two people can't work a spell together."

"Not only do you two share an energy source, but you are also connected to something else in another realm," Chirchi said. "The magic you use is through a contract with the spirit realm. It provides us with energy and we transform it according to the rules that make up our specific magic. When someone can do extraordinary things, they have a slightly different contract with the spirit realm. And your contract is not like the other wizards. That much is clear. This connection, however, is to another spirit energy source that is not yours," Chirchi said. "This could be why Slithlor is after you."

"What does that mean?" Alaan said.

"I don't know yet. I have never seen anything like that before," Chirchi said.

"And is my animalism contract different?" Rye said.

She turned to him, "Oh, sorry. I was distracted by the twins. I didn't watch your transition, but I will on the way back."

"Wait, we can't just leave right away," Dre said. He held out a hand. "I want to see more."

"Is that okay with you?" Chirchi said.

Rye did want to know about his contract, but it would mean making a tough decision. If he were ordinary, he would leave Hila with a liar and turn himself in, confident that his father had died during the Battle of Ki. But if he weren't, he would only have more questions. He would need to stay a fugitive until he spoke to Juli.

He shrugged. "I'm in no rush to see Lakree's face again." He could use a break before he had to deal with reality.

Her eyes softened like the guards who escorted him from his classroom. "It'll be worth it," she said. "Follow me."

She led them up an incline and around boulders the size of buildings.

Rye caught a small pebble floating in his path. He held it for a few seconds before releasing it. It resumed rising. "How does gravity work here?"

"There is no gravity, no matter. Spirit energy doesn't weigh anything. We are on this ground because it makes sense to be here. When most of the ground is in the sky, it will make sense for us to walk up there. We will leave before the switch happens, though. Each realm has a personality," she said.

"How many realms are there?" Rye said.

"Eight that I know of…" she said.

"Wizardry doesn't work here," Dre said, holding out his hand.

"Pure spirit energy is hard to interact with directly. When we use magic in the real world, the spirit energy is tainted and we get used to manipulating that. It's like if you only drank tea your whole life, then someone offered you water. You wouldn't even recognize that you had been drinking water all the while."

Around a hill, water gushed down the face of a cliff. Before it reached the lake below, it fell up into the sky. It created an almost "U" shape surrounded by mist. Two rainbows played in the air, flowing in irregular patterns in the rising water.

"I've never seen a waterfall before, but I am sure this is the best one ever," Alaan said.

"It is," Chirchi said.

"Can we get in the water?" Dre said.

238

"Sure," she said.

The twins stripped down to their underwear. Even their bodies were identical, every muscle, every bulge. A patch of curly hair covered their chests and trailed down their waists. The public didn't get to see this view of the Poli Twins. Dre winked at Rye, then dove in. Rye fluttered his eyes away, though it was too late. He had been caught staring. He waited a moment before undressing, just in case, then jumped in.

He swam to the cliff face and back. It was like moving through real water and even tasted like it. Dre and Alaan splashed each other, but sometimes, droplets floated up into the sky. Rye dunked his head under. The water was clear. The lake bottom was bright. After two minutes, his lungs did not burn, so he paddled deeper. He experimented with breathing in water and the liquid filled his nostrils. His lungs swelled and he blew it out like air. He was like a fish. He swam and swam until he circled the lake ten times. The effort felt the same as in the natural world, but the fatigue didn't stack.

When he climbed out of the lake, everyone else was lying on the ground. The twins were dressed and somehow, Rye was too. He tugged on his shirt, rubbing it between his fingers. It felt like cloth, but everything here was a spirit energy replica. He lay down. The sky was cluttered with debris. It was like the moment after an explosion was frozen in time.

"Lakree and Hila are going to regret missing out," Alaan said, elbowing him.

Rye huffed. "Lakree can stay paranoid and afraid." Lakree didn't deserve the truth of this place or any truths.

"What happened exactly with your father?" Chirchi said.

Rye pressed his palms into his eyes, then told them about his father's missing body and Lakree's mysterious Aunt Juli.

"Oh," she said.

"Lakree must have panicked," Alaan said. "He wasn't thinking."
"Telling someone their father might be alive and part of a conspiracy doesn't just roll off the tongue by accident," Rye said. Lakree was noble. He knew what the Guard suspected, and he used it against Rye.

"What did he gain by lying?" Alaan said.

"I entered the Medina, didn't I?"

"But a personal benefit?" Alaan pushed.

"Nothing," Rye said.

"So he did it because he thought it would benefit you, even though it was still a bad way to go about it," Alaan said.

"No, there is no excuse for lying about something like that," Dre said.

"That's why I tackled him," Rye said.

"Lakree is a sorcerer," Chirchi said. "The rules of the universe aren't organized for simplicity or logic. They are chained together as if by whim and they learn not to question the connection, only to remember it. The more complex the conspiracy, the more real it feels to him. A lie to make the madness work...I could understand it. He was acting on instinct."

"Instincts are the universal threat," Rye told the boulders floating above him. Lakree wasn't free of his instincts either. It was possible that all Vous were liars when it suited them. "If being a Vous meant that Lakree inherited the spirit energy of a distant relative, does that mean he inherited their memories, too?" Alaan and Dre shared memories, at least here, because of their shared spirit energy.

"Nobles like to believe so, but that's neither here nor there," Chirchi said.

"Lakree said that people's magic returned to the spirit realm after they died. Is that true?" Dre said.

"Yes," Chirchi said.

Rye sat up. "So, could you find a person's memories by finding

240

their energy here," Rye said. It was a wild concept, but it meant that dead or alive, his father's spirit energy was possibly one of the floating rocks. If he could find and merge with it, he would get answers. His father knew the truth. Most of Rye's anger wasn't at Lakree but at returning to the big question he had posed to his mother. Not knowing whether his father was a coward was worse than whatever the truth could be.

"A person's spirit energy could be a pebble here and a blade of grass in another spirit realm. I can't look at something and know who it belongs to. It isn't just Lynitian people here. Everyone in the world, even those who don't know how to use magic, has a presence here. I would need a way to identify them and reach out to all those individual pieces. When you travel here, you pull all of your pieces together. I don't know how to force that on someone else."

Rye sucked his teeth.

"Talking to Lakree's aunt will probably be your best bet for answers. She is the only other person that was there," Alaan said.

"That's not true," Dre said. "There was another party at the Battle of Ki, spirit fiends. If they are powerful enough to kill a Kertic, they may be smart enough to remember what happened."

"They can talk?" Rye said. Not much was known about them. There were drawings of the four that attacked Nintur, but that was it. They didn't use magic because they *were* magic. Their presence caused metal to melt and stone to crumble. People exploded from a single touch.

"I avoid the ones that can. Their presence alone could pull your mind apart," she said. "Answers from them wouldn't be worth the risk. But if you are interested in seeing safer spirit fiends, I can take you to meet them."

"Yes," Dre, Alaan, and Rye said in unison. If animalism had taught Rye anything, it was that communication wasn't always verbal. There may still be something he could learn here.

Chirchi led the way. Parts of the route were gone, replaced with holes in the ground that led to blackness. Rye and Dre jumped a gap while Chirchi and Alaan shimmied along a ledge. They were on an adventure.

"Do you think Tess got away?" Rye said.

"I doubt it," Alaan said, frowning.

"She is better off there. She is fed, has a place to bathe, and they are training her. I doubt she saw her family anyway while she was hiding. This is what I wanted Lakree and Hila to understand. Running is worse," Rye said.

"The problem isn't simply the Guard or the draft. For Tess and most kids, they are being properly trained. But Alaan and I wouldn't be safe in that program because Slithlor runs it," Dre said.

"Even Slithlor reports to the king regent and the council," Rye said.

"I trust the council, but they can't oversee everything that every guard does. There is always one game or another between the nobles. They know better than to let it make it to the council's ears. Slithlor knows that, too," Chirchi said.

"Nobles have been after us, one way or another since we were born," Alaan said.

"If the Yordin could figure out how to make more twins, they would. It's the perfect representation of their magic and the best part is that you can join energies," Chirchi said.

"The best part of being a twin is having a twin," Alaan said.

"Aw," Dre said, squeezing his brother's shoulder.

"What about the fame?" Chirchi said.

"I like the fame we have earned but not the fascination with our birth. Otherwise, we are treated like nobles," Alaan said.

"What do you think your lives would have been like if you were just brothers?" she said.

"Boring," Dre said.

As Rye rounded a large boulder, he heard someone calling him. He didn't turn back to the lake but looked up instead. A soft tingle rippled through him, moving from his crown to his toes. It was like a summoning. His body, his energy, wanted to leave, float beyond the sky and out of this realm. The call wasn't coming from his physical body. It came from another spirit realm. Chirchi said there were eight. He should visit them all. And he still needed to explore his world. There was so much to see.

Rye rubbed the back of his head. "When this is over, I want to visit Flador Forest. A creature called the spangot lives there. It's a blind wolf with the best tracking skills in the world."

"There's a map of their known dens in your room here. We all actively avoid them," Chirchi said.

"You've been outside of Lynit?" Rye said.

"Yeah, many times, with my parents," Chirchi said.

"Where?" Rye said

"None of the other nations, but I've been as far east as Flador Forest, as far north as the Arvinit Mountains, as far south as the Grimnor Sand River, and as far west as the ocean," Chirchi said.

Rye's mother had once sailed the ocean. She had described a fish as big as a house that tried to gobble her boat whole.

"Dre and I have only been to Lynitian cities," Alaan said.

"We would have visited somewhere new if we hadn't come here," Dre said.

"Why do you stay in the Medina?" Rye asked Chirchi. He'd stayed in Virt all his life because he couldn't leave. His parents only traveled for work and weren't crazy enough to bring him along for missions. When he was younger, before Felix was born, he tried to stow away in his father's suitcase. Rye didn't make it halfway down the street before his father stopped and opened his bag. He had known that Rye was in there the whole time. Then he held Rye's hand as they walked to the dome wall. Once there, his father pointed to the red desert outside and said, "If you want to see the world, you have to get there yourself."

"Traveling is fun, but you can't live out there," Chirchi said. "The world is like the Winder Plains. You can survive in it, but you are never really safe. However, the creatures and elements are the easiest to avoid. The other humans are the real threat."

"But outside of the nations, magic is scarce," Rye said.

"Do you know what a sword is? Our magic is powerful, but we can't use it while we sleep. Someone always has to stand watch. Once, we stayed in an inn not too far from Lynit. In the middle of the night, thieves snuck in. They went from room to room, picking the locks. They robbed those who didn't fight back and mugged those who did.

"When they opened my door, we could have killed them on the spot. My mother was an elemental mage, and my father was a psychic. We could have leveled the entire building, but we didn't. We were in hiding. Lynitian magic is powerful, but it is flamboyant. If any thief survived, the story of us would make it back to the Guard."

"What did you do?" Alaan said.

"People outside of nations don't learn how to shield their minds. My father was able to convince them that they had already robbed us."

"That's living," Rye said evenly. Lynit was so sophisticated that most used magic only for entertainment. "If I had a reason to use magic daily, that would be bliss."

"Living isn't what you do with your life. It's who you spend it with," Chirchi said.

"Living is exploring. I could spend my life discovering new creatures. I could live as a creature," Rye said.

"Is that why you want to join the Guard?" Dre said.

"Yes," Rye said.

He followed Chirchi and the twins into a cave. It was eerily similar to the one in the Winder Plains. The entrance was wide, though the cave didn't dim the deeper they went. The sunlight was uniform. He didn't even have a shadow.

"Over here," Chirchi said, pointing at a back wall. Like the other walls, it was brown and red.

"Did we scare them away?" Alaan said.

Rye leaned forward. "I don't see anything."

"Close your eyes," Chirchi said.

Rye closed them. Tiny white dots resolved. Thousands of white insects crawled on the wall. A curved shell protected their tiny bodies and many legs. He heard them now, too. Their feet clicked softly against the rock.

"I thought nothing could top that waterfall," Dre said.

"Touch the wall," Chirchi said.

Rye extended a finger. A few bugs noticed. One approached, then rubbed him with an antenna. It tickled. The beetle crawled up his arm. The others noticed, then rushed to join. They spread across his body, making a glowing outline of his form.

"Do these exist in the real world?" Rye asked, waving his arm in the air.

"They shouldn't," Chirchi said.

"What controls them?" Rye said.

"What controls us here?" Chirchi said.

"Our minds," Alaan said.

"Insects don't have minds," Rye said. At least, that was what Mr. P said in class. Most creatures were on a spectrum. The simplest ones were entirely driven by instincts and the most advanced could learn new information to trump their instincts. But psychics couldn't speak to them and animalists couldn't teach them to speak.

"These aren't real insects in the biological sense," Chirchi said.

"They are like the idea of insects. All spirit energy is sentient on some level. The ground, the rocks, the moon, everything. Each realm looks and behaves the way it does because every piece of it wants to."

The white bugs crawled over each other, searching for an open surface area of Rye. They didn't stick to one another like they stuck to him. Some fell off if he moved too quickly. But they landed unharmed and ran up his leg.

They behaved like insects.

"Could I learn to morph into them?" Rye said. He raised his hand to his face. He pinched down and caught one bug between his fingers. Its shell was hard, but it bent with pressure. "What happens if I kill one and open it?"

"I wouldn't do that," Chirchi said. Her glowing-bug-covered body backed away. She yelped. As her arms flailed, she tilted back, falling. Then, she completely disappeared and her voice cut off.

Rye opened his eyes. The cave had changed. Much of the floor, walls, and ceiling were gone, up in the sky. There was a large hole where Chirchi should have been. The rate of reverse gravity had increased.

"Where did she go?" Alaan said.

Rye leaned over the hole. There was only blackness. Sunlight did not reach down there. "Chirchi had only said that the spirit realm wasn't more dangerous than the real world. At home, falling into a pit is pretty dangerous. Is she dead?"

Alaan stepped back.

Then everything blurred as Rye floated, leaving the spirit realm. A familiar force pulled him. It was Chirchi.

He snapped back to the real world. Alaan, Dre, and Chirchi were crumpled on the floor beside him. Rye squeezed Chirchi's limp hand.

"Ouch," she squealed as she pulled it back.

"I thought you were...I don't know," Rye said.

"That was scary," Alaan said.

"I'm okay, though my magic will likely be finicky the next couple of days," Chirchi said. Rye struggled to his feet. His legs were sore. He must have been sitting for hours, but it only felt like he had been there for thirty minutes.

"Did you miss studying Rye's magic contract again?" Dre said.

"No, I saw it. Instead of a single connection to another source, he has many connections that plug into his spirit energy. They are thin ones that appear to dissolve and reform on a whim. Small amounts of your spirit energy flow out on these connections. There are two that are significantly stronger and thicker and consume a fair amount of his energy," she said.

"That's the opposite of a special ability. I am losing energy," Rye said. It was why his morphs were so slow. This was a magical deficiency. It wasn't common, but some people's access to magic was stunted and, in some cases, non-existent. These people never left the domes.

"Yes, but there is a final connection, bigger than all the others combined. The only reason I recognized it as something different than the other big two is that the Poli Twins have a similar one. In this connection, energy flows in. The connection is to a source in another spirit realm," she said.

"We've found what we have in common," Alaan said. "Since our magic is increasing, it does make sense for us to practice both wizardry energies."

"Oh boy," Dre said.

Not only was this at odds with his hopes of returning to the Guard, but it was also counter to what he knew of the world. He shouldn't have a special ability. Magic, especially unique magic, came from the nobles, from birth. His parents were captains and his dad became an elite, but not because they had any intuitive connection to magic. They worked hard for their titles. If there was anything strange about Rye's magic, it meant it was something he wasn't supposed to have. It meant that something had been done to him.

"I can't believe I am the one who needs to apologize," Rye said. He scanned the room. His friends weren't there.

"I won't be able to return to the spirit realm right away. I need time to recover," Chirchi said. "I, at least, pinpointed the realm the twins have their special connection to. We can go there next time."

Rye left. When he flung open the door to his room, Lakree and Hila were on the couch. Their faces were close. It was like Lakree was telling a secret to Hila's mouth with his mouth. No, they were kissing.

Rye froze. His instincts had never warned him about this possibility because Lakree and Hila had never shown the slightest romantic interest in each other. The two weren't even compatible. Lakree loved to flex all of his wisdom and Hila loved to ignore it without question. He didn't recognize any of the signs and they didn't bother to tell him. Everybody kept secrets from him.

Lakree flew away from her, panic, then embarrassment on his face. Hila crossed her arms as if daring Rye to say something.

"Sorry for lying about your father," Lakree said, eyes everywhere but on Rye.

"Uh huh," Rye said slowly as his brain caught fire.

Chapter 18 - Dre

Dre lay on the ground. Pressure held him there. It was like every muscle and bone was shackled. Black energy churned above. He clenched and unclenched his hand, creating a sphere and a point of pressure on his body. He repeated it until seven balls floated above him. He still couldn't go past that amount of dark energy without it hurting. If he wanted to test his energy limits, he still needed his brother to summon light energy.

Alaan stood only a few paces away, brow set low in pointless concentration. Three small balls of dark energy were under his control and ten blobs of light circled above his palms. He only moved one type of energy at a time because having more power didn't translate to suddenly being magically ambidextrous. There were still too many skills he didn't have and didn't need to have because Dre had them. Eventually, he would snap out of this phase. Dre picked seven spots on the ceiling and hit every one of them.

He closed his eyes and MMA flashcards sprung into his mind. He skimmed over texts on weight distribution patterns, topology, and crystallography. One book was titled "Theoretical Approaches to Wizardry Energy: Breaking the Dichotomy." He pushed it aside. He grabbed a random moving image titled "Hallow Shapes and Hidden Energy." A woman solidified a dark cloud into a large sphere. She fired it. A wall of light appeared in its path and she snapped. The sphere faded away, revealing a smaller cloud of energy inside. She created a new sphere from that, fired the energy above the wall, released it, revealed that it was hollow too, then fired the last of the energy at a target behind the wall. This was different. There was an element of deception that wasn't common in dark energy. It was a sloppy condensing. Instead of pulling all of the energy tightly together, some of it was left unmanaged.

Dre reached out his senses. Wizardry pushed and pulled on his skin. He pulled out a slow stream of energy, mostly for effect. A black line of smoke danced above his head, spreading an even pressure across his body. He watched the flashcard one more time, then clenched his fist. Half of the cloud jerked down as a black sphere formed above his hand and the pressure on the upper half of his body concentrated to a single point. The remaining free energy stayed above him and its pressure redistributed across his body.

Dre sucked his teeth. The shape didn't work. It was still solid. The point of pressure on his palm was proof. He snapped away the energy. This time, he took a moment to visualize a hollow sphere. It was the root of condensing energy after all. If he couldn't visualize the structure, he couldn't create it. Instead of thinking about the outside of the shape, he imagined the inside. Curved walls surrounded him in all directions. It was a new angle, a new reference point for a shape. And he was at the center for once.

He clenched his fist again and a ring of pressure formed on his palm. The sphere looked the same, but it was hollow. There was nothing inside. He practiced that structure several more times, covering his body in rings. Each time he snapped away the condensed energy, there was nothing inside. The technique was more like an illusion with light energy than a dark energy shape. In an illusion, adjusting each fleck of light into the right hue for an image was impossible. The mass of energy was a system with the single goal of creating whatever visual the wizard had in mind. Everything changed together. Dre needed to manipulate the energy as one instead of trying to compartmentalize it as a shell and lose energy since that wasn't working. He considered asking Alaan for help but didn't want to get his brother started up again on the value of learning both energies.

Rye arrived in the training room without Lakree and Hila. There was a lingering tension between the three. It wasn't the open hostility from when Lakree admitted to lying. It was more awkward than that. Lakree and Rye wouldn't meet eyes and Hila acted as if nothing was wrong.

"Did Urura say that you can stay?" Dre said.

"Yes, but Lakree and Hila can only stay if they go to the spirit realm. She is giving them a week to decide," Rye said.

"Have the guards stopped their search?" Dre said.

"They patrolled through the night," Rye said. "This is just like with the wanted signs. The Guard is serious about catching us. It all makes me want to talk to Lakree's aunt even more. She has to know something about my father. It's too much of a coincidence that two former elites disappeared after the Battle of Ki and their relatives now have abnormal magic."

Urura hadn't fully absolved them of her spy suspicion or she would have taken back that fake map. Dre still didn't believe that they were spies, but he wouldn't share any more information about the Medina just in case. "How are you going to contact her?" he said.

"We will wait for the guards to leave. After four days of no new developments, the Guard switches from a narrow search to a wide one. They might leave one to two guards in the Easton Tunnels, but that should be it," Rye said.

Dre nodded. In two more days, when the map continued as usual, this son of guards would know something was wrong.

Rye continued, "Though, I hope there is an opportunity to go back to the spirit realm again before we go. I dreamed about it last night and woke up feeling like I need to see all the realms I can."

"Me too," Dre said. He dreamed he was on a green hill, like the place he saw at Sepotine through the portal. The call, the feeling was there. Alaan was there, too, staring off in the same direction. A brown thing, a creature maybe, ran down a hill towards them. Its head and shoulders were small and narrow. It stood upright with its weight squished into its hips. Thick, short legs scurried underneath it. The whisper came from it. It didn't just call him. It called Alaandre.

During the journey to the spirit realm, Dre's thoughts, concerns, and memories blended with Alaan's. They were Alaandre for a moment. Then it was all gone. The world was small again, split in two. Alaan's memories, his perspective, were out of reach, like a dream he couldn't quite remember. But one moment from the experience stayed with Dre. There was one place in Alaan's mind that Dre couldn't connect with. It was a memory stored differently than the rest. It was blocked off from Alaan's usual thought patterns. It was a secret locked deep down, so deep he sensed that even Alaan didn't remember it was there, or maybe he didn't want to. If Dre were intentional on his next trip to the spirit realm, he could pierce the veil to uncover what was there. There shouldn't be any areas of Alaan that Dre didn't know. Discovering that place could fix the inconsistency with their wizardry energy joining and might explain Alaan's stupid fixation with learning dark energy. They must regain their perfect alignment.

Alaan snapped away his energy and hurried over. "I dreamed about the spirit realm last night."

"But you never dream. Or at least you never remember them," Dre said, then cocked his head to the said. "Or, you told me that you never remember them."

"I don't usually, but this one is clear," he said. "I was on a hill, like the one we saw in Sepotine. Each blade of grass stood straight up. I decided to roll down the hill. It was steep, but I didn't care. I had never seen so much grass before."

"I dreamed of that place," Dre said, then giggled. "And you were there rolling down a hill. I still know you well."

Alaan didn't laugh. "Did you kick me?"

"Yes," Dre said slowly. At least Alaan understood that Dre was annoyed with his continued practice of dark energy. If Alaan kept it up, Dre might kick him in the waking world.

"We dreamed the same dream," Alaan said.

"But dream travel is a psychic ability," Dre said. The twins had tried it a few times when they were younger and could use a little mental magic, but it never worked. They even tried sleeping with their heads touching. According to Dad, it was complex magic.

"Were you there too, Rye?" Alaan said.

"No, I dreamed I was in a city made of clouds. Most of the streets and buildings were empty. There was no sound, but one area was full of strange creatures. They were all doing something or going somewhere. I couldn't tell. And somehow, I knew that I was in the spirit realm. But dreams are always weird like that. You probably dreamed of the same place because of your mental link."

"We don't have one," Dre said. "Or at least we didn't." He touched Alaan's shoulder. In a shared dream, they could practice routines and Dre could continually unseal any new secrets Alaan dared to keep. There would be no gap between them.

"It must be a side effect of our minds syncing for that moment," Alaan said, his face a knot of worry. "We have to talk to Chirchi."

Dre and Alaan left the training room, telling Rye to wait behind. Alaan opened the panel hidden in one of the walls. He flipped the switches in the order Urura had shown them. The wall slid open. There were people in the mirror room. The three women on guard duty this week sat at their game table, playing a different game involving dice and cups.

Two other women dressed in red robes cinched tight at the neck and feet observed the game. They were prepared for desert travel. "No, we aren't planning to return," one of them said. All of her vowels were shortened, but consonants were extended. She would have to make it out of the city with her mouth shut. She wouldn't make it two words without being discovered as foreign. "We can safely go back to Omber now. It won't be perfect there, but at least our lives aren't in danger anymore."

"Of course, of course. We are all excited about the change," the sorcerer said. She placed dice in a cup, shook them, then slammed it down. "I can only imagine your eagerness to go home. In Lynit, this has been normal since our founding. Racial and sexual minorities never had any problems here. But the issue with leaving isn't about coming back to Lynit. It's about getting out," the sorcerer said.

"The underground route wasn't a problem before. We are small. We will fit through the hole," the other woman said.

"That will get you out of Poli, but not Lynit. There is an elite animalist watching the desert. If you don't need to leave this exact moment, we don't recommend it," the sorcerer said.

"What's going on?" the first woman said.

Dre winced. Lakree, Hila, and Rye were likely the reason. "Can we go through?"

"Of course," the woman from Ries said. Her shadow creature wasn't present. She opened the golden door.

When they were alone again, Alaan said. "What's a racial or sexual minority?"

"Everyone in Lynit is a racial minority since there is an even split of the six peoples who moved to the desert. No one has a majority. But I'm a sexual minority and you aren't," Dre said.

"So, because fewer boys like boys than boys who like girls in

Omber, you wouldn't have been safe there?" Alaan said. "Are they like math people who have rules about percentages?"

Dre shook his head. "I don't know. The world outside the domes is a crazy place."

They meandered through the camp. There weren't many people moving about. Dre climbed up to the top floor. Most of the top floor spanned the center of the cave, where the buildings were smaller. A man stood above a crowd on a metal container. His voice resolved over the mechanical hum of the Medina.

"I am not sure we can even say that our influence was the direct cause, but we did help. This is proof that information is a tool. Given to the right people, they will use it. This is a case where a political change will create the opportunity for the people to change instead of the other way around. Toppling a monarchy is symbolic. It will force the people of Omber to think why they have their laws instead of simply accepting them because someone powerful created them."

Alaan tugged Dre. He pointed at Chirchi, who was seated atop a rail on the crowd's edge. She waved them over.

"We had a dream together," Alaan said. "Is that a side effect of going to the spirit realm?"

She shushed him, then slid to the ground. "Let's talk over there." They moved away from the crowd. Alaan explained the dream. "At first, I was going to say that your brains had simply synced up, which caused you to dream the same thing, but you described another real realm that exists."

"Well, we did see that place before. Students at Sepotine University opened a window into that realm yesterday. A lot of people saw it."

"That's not good," Chirchi said, shaking her head. "What if we had been there?"

"The Guard shut down the school afterward. There shouldn't be any more of that for a while," Dre said.

"I need to know what they are saying on the news," Chirchi said.

"So that dream was just a fluke?" Alaan said.

"Rye dreamed of the spirit realm but of a different place," Dre said.

"The spirit energy you are connected to is in that blue sun realm. I think our trip might have strengthened your connection," she said.

"How much longer until we can go again?" Dre said.

"I don't pick which realm I go to. I go wherever my energy happens to be and pull the rest of you there. It's a waiting game," she said. "But let's tell Urura. I am curious to hear what she thinks."

Dre and Alaan followed her to Urura's office, which was messier than before. The book towers were crooked and a new scent of old sweat was in the air. Urura sat at her desk, arms crossed and face hard. She wasn't alone. A pale old man with wispy hair leaned over a map, struggling to hold his jittery finger still. She introduced him as Qin, another leader in the Medina.

"Perfect timing. We were talking about you," Urura said. "I didn't mention before that the elite animalist tracked you to the spot where you entered the Medina. Until a few hours ago, the elite sorcerer had been stationed in the tunnel with his orb."

Dre reached for his suspenders. "They know we are in here."

"Not quite. There is no magic for the sorcerer to see. The entrance is mechanical and surrounded by black rock. The animalist is patrolling outside the city and the third elite is interviewing everyone from Daramis bar," she said. "They don't seem to know for sure where their target is. They are covering all the bases. The reason we were talking about you was because we believe that you could help here."

"How?" Alaan said.

"We need to distract the elites' attention from the Easton Tunnels. Your body left behind two traces that the animalist followed. The first is your scent, which is extremely difficult to track in such a large city, even for a spangot. The second is the residue you give off when using magic, which is difficult to track by anything other than a spangot.

"However, this residue fades with time and even faster in the Easton Tunnel because of the gigastone. To confuse them, we need you to return home. They aren't familiar enough with the tunnels to understand the speed at which magical energy traces degrade. They will think your trail only ended at the dead-end because it faded, not because you went through the wall. They believe you are with Lakree, Hila, and Rye. You have to show them otherwise."

"The elites are likely after them too," Chirchi said. "The twins and Rye had dreams about areas of the spirit realm that I didn't take them to."

"The elites are, but so is the whole city. When the twins first disappeared, their parents led thousands to the Castle, demanding the boys be released. Now, it is a full-on protest," Urura said. "The Guard insists they can't be sure of the last time they saw you because when they had cornered you in the Easton Tunnel, they realized they had been chasing an illusion, one that didn't fade in the sunlight. They don't know if you made the illusion or if it was someone else. They aren't even sure you were in the bar."

"It *was* us," Dre said. The combined illusion was a new trick they hadn't shown the world before.

"The public thinks that the Guard kidnapped you, but the Guard thinks Lakree, Hila, and Rye did it. If you say you were never in Daramis bar, the Guard can't charge you with anything. They will question you but nothing more. If you don't return, they could easily charge Lakree, Hila, and Rye with your abduction. Then, all of Lynit would turn against them. They will never be able to return if you don't return first," she said.

Alaan placed a hand on Dre's shoulder. "But we have a strange link to Rye and likely to Lakree and Hila. We need Chirchi to help us understand what it means."

"If you want to help Lakree, Hila, and Rye, leaving is the best way," she said. "Slithlor's draft attempt on all of you has been revoked. He won't be able to touch you without causing another uproar. But, the elites haven't stopped their search."

Dre opened his mouth, but the words escaped him. Kalin Pol had followed through on her support. Slithlor no longer had a legal way to get to Dre and Alaan, and so far, he has stayed within the law. However, Dre wasn't ready to leave the Medina. He wanted to merge his mind with Alaan's again, but that was selfish, so it was better not to speak.

"And most importantly, this request is about Slithlor," Qin said, his voice soft. He straightened his posture and his light green eyes stared past Dre. "I met him once at a meeting between the six nations and Sewit. We were on course to become the seventh nation, but some nations didn't like our methods.

"For the nations, their conquests happened hundreds of years ago, but for Sewit, it was in the present day. They feared that as we absorbed more magics into our empire, we would amass a power they couldn't match. Lynit and Ries agreed to go to war with us if we did not stop our expansion. We had planned to agree to the terms but with a few caveats. We wanted to be a part of their trade agreements. I was sent to communicate that sentiment. When it came time for me to speak, I thought I said that, but everyone else heard the opposite. So Lynit and Ries attacked us.

"Your Battle of Ki was our retaliation after we were attacked when we thought we had already agreed to peace terms. After we learned what I really had said, my people attempted to kill me for treason. I fled. Later, I learned about a man who was smart and powerful enough to cause a war with a sliver of his magic. I have no proof he did it, but I believe that if Slithlor is after you or the other kids, it is not for something simple. If you stay here, Slithlor never has to reveal himself. He can operate under the pretense of looking for a pair of missing children and the three who abducted the pair. He already has six children in his custody. We don't know how many more he is after."

"So we are bait," Dre said. He sat down.

"No. If you tell the Guard you weren't in Daramis bar, they can't prove it wasn't an illusion sitting in there the whole time. You wouldn't even be in trouble for attacking them. You will be able to return to your life. You can continue ending the draft and cut off Slithlor's pipeline for collecting children. Even Slithlor won't be able to touch you because the elites will be watching you," Urura said.

"Once we go home, our parents will make us leave Lynit. So we have to give a public speech first," Alaan said as he sat in Dre's lap. "Not only do we need a clever way to explain away our disappearance, but we have to redirect the public's anger at our disappearance. Dad is the best at PR, but Dre is second. We could spin this to help end the draft."

If Slithlor was plotting something, even within the law, it meant they weren't one hundred percent safe. This situation felt like the letter from the dead sorcerer that convinced him to perform in public. It was the right thing to do, but it still backfired. Dre wrinkled up his face. "Fine."

"We will continue studying Rye, Lakree, and Hila to find out what the connection to the other source in the spirit realm means and why Slithlor is interested in it," Urura said. "The Medina is spread all over the continent. Wherever your parents take you, we can reach you."

Chapter 19 - Dre

The Easton Tunnels were dark until a small light fluttered out from Alaan. The twins walked a circuitous route, doubling back multiple times. On the west side of the Poli, they rose above ground. The neighborhood was full of multicolored stone buildings, some covered in thin green vines. The orange sun sat low in the sky, light slipping between the metal towers to the east. It was late evening. A new mural stretched across the side of three gray buildings. It was Poli's outline, but two towers weren't towers; they were people, they were Alaan and Dre.

Dre rubbed his suspenders. "Are you ready to get murdered?"

Alaan grunted. "She'll cry for a moment before it turns into a blind rage. We'll have to explain then."

"What if we say that it isn't safe to leave Lynit? Out there, Slithlor could kidnap us and we wouldn't be able to do much about it."

"That could work," Alaan said. "Though, she wouldn't let us leave the house again."

"We can only handle one problem at a time," Dre said. "We would be able to stay in easier contact with Homin. Nobles could visit us."

"But no performances in our gym," Alaan said.

"Agreed," Dre said. If they were going to return home, they would return to the business of ending the draft.

A faint pulse of light flickered twice through Dre's shirt. It was the notification of a communication orb connecting to a network. Alaan reached into Dre's pocket and pulled out Tess' orb. The flashing meant she saw a similar response since her orb was a closed network of two. Dre touched it. He let in the buzz of energy on his finger.

"Alaan? Dre? Are you there?" Tess' sweet voice sang in Dre's head.

"Yes!" he said.

"Calm down, I didn't get away," she said. The excitement left him as quickly as it had come. "They captured me. I am in the draft."

The network was supposed to be private, but Tess could have been forced to open it. He needed to test her. "How did Alaan get the scar above his left eye?" Dre said.

"Stavender hit him in the face with a bolt of lightning. And the scar is on his right side," she said. It was the only permanent physical difference between the two. Fans assumed it was a birthmark, but it was a mistake that Dre could have avoided. He had seen the bully approach but assumed that Alaan had noticed him, too. Alaan paid for it with a hit to the face.

"It is you," Dre said.

"The Guard doesn't know I have this orb. I am hiding in the bathroom right now. They haven't asked me anything about you."

"I'm sorry, Tess," Alaan said.

"What are you sorry for? I was supposed to be here, and now I don't smell," she said.

Alaan said, "We could have escaped with us. It was my fault. If I had—"

"I don't have a lot of time," Tess interrupted. "Tell me about you.

I assume you got away since you aren't here with me. What happened with those kids? Is there something going on with the Magic and Martial Arts program?"

"We got separated. I have no idea what they are doing," Dre said. Alaan elbowed him. Dre glared back. Friend or not, Tess was in the Castle. There was no need to share anything she didn't need to know.

"What is the training like?" Alaan said.

"I haven't even started training yet. I've just been in orientation. On the first day, they talked about why there was a draft. They showed us a list of all the guards who died in the Battle of Ki and their roles. Even if we aren't fully fledged guards during the next war, we can still support them. There's something called quitol warfare that I don't fully understand, but I think it means that we hide in buildings and surprise attack invaders," she said.

"Are they experimenting on you by any chance?" Dre said.

"No, not that I know of," she said. "I have only seen Slithlor once. He came by to pick up six kids and they haven't returned."

"If he takes any more kids, let us know," Alaan said.

Dre wondered whether he should ask Homin to look for those missing children.

"Sure," she said. "Have you given any thought to my proposition?" she said.

"What proposition?" Alaan said.

"Helping the other runaways," she said.

"Girl," Dre said and rolled his eyes. "We've been busy."

"Found them!" someone shouted. Dre dropped his connection to the orb and spun around. A couple stood arm in arm, one of them pointing. One woman had Alaan's haircut but was much longer and perfectly straight. The other woman was dressed like Dre, wearing almost the same shirt and she had suspenders. Many imitated their style, but these two might have done it the best.

"Hi," Dre said. Alaan didn't take his attention off the orb. "We are back. Sorry for the scare. We needed some time alone."

"I can't believe we found them," the Alaan lookalike said. "Shamir will never believe this."

"Can we have your autograph?" the other one said.

"Sure," Dre said. The women patted themselves but frowned when they realized they had nothing to sign. "Come here." Dre hugged them and they squealed.

"Thank you, thank you," they said. One of them pulled out a communication orb.

Dre turned back to Alaan. "We have to move. We need to get home before all of Poli shows up." He pulled on Alaan's arm, but he didn't budge.

"She left," Alaan said.

"Ok. Let's get going," Dre said. Alaan looked south, the opposite direction of their house.

"Let's go to Co Park first," Alaan said.

"No," Dre said. "What did Tess say?"

"We won't get a second chance," Alaan said.

"To do what?" Dre said.

"We got away because Tess sacrificed herself for us. The least we can do is pay it forward," Alaan said.

"That's what we were doing," Dre said.

"I will give the speech at Co Park," Alaan said.

"That is not the plan you asked me to come up with," Dre said. They were supposed to show up in front of their house where even respectable reporters would likely be sprinkled in with the paparazzi. They could explain their fake story the moment before their parents burst from the house at the sound of their voices and dragged them out of the city.

"Do you want to give the speech?" Alaan said.

"No," Dre said.

"Then stop complaining. Let's go," Alaan said. Dre followed him. The girls followed, too.

A thick cloud sat over Co Park like a cap. Black, white, purple, blue, and red sparkles danced within. Mist flowed from the edges, filling the streets. Voices, grunts, and laughter rose out.

"What is that?" Dre said. In the dome-covered city, the weather was manufactured.

"Protestors have taken over Co Park," one of the girls said.

The mist tickled Dre's face as he groped down a side railing into the park. Two flights down, he was below the cloud. There were a thousand bodies spread out across the park. Above them, the flashing colors were spells clashing with each other. Fireballs hit blue shields. Blobs of purple energy dodged balls of bright white light. On one side of the park, several children were building a large structure made of dark energy. There were a few adults in the park, too. Three were civilian protectors guarding the tree and the rest were reporters.

"This looks more like a celebration," Dre said.

"It's been like this for two days," the other girl said. "For once, we can practice magic without the gaze of the Guard."

Dre grabbed Alaan's shoulder. "In and out."

"We'll be quick. The speech should be to the people and not the band of reporters waiting outside our house," Alaan said. "It is as much for them as for the Guard."

It took only ten seconds for someone to recognize Dre and Alaan and shout their names. Groups splintered from their practice to surround them. Dre smiled and nodded but did not slow. After a minute, "Poli Twins" echoed off everyone's lips.

Zalora was on the center gigasphere, walking in the opposite direction of the two blue shields spinning around her. The shields' movements weren't smooth. They jerked about and mostly only moved one at a time. Her concentration dropped when she spotted

Alaan and Dre. The blue lights faded. Gron leaped off the stage, yelling. He nearly tackled Alaan as he hugged him. The crowd celebrated the reunion.

"It's good to see you, too," Alaan said.

"I knew they didn't catch you," Zalora said as she approached.

"We are still the Poli Twins, after all," Dre said. She smirked.

"Let's talk on stage," Alaan said. They climbed onto the nearest gigasphere.

"Have you been home yet?" Zalora said. "Your mother tried to break into the Castle to find you."

"I wouldn't have expected anything less," Dre said. "But I am surprised that your parents let you be here."

"They yelled at me for going to Co Park. I didn't dare tell them that the Guard tried to draft us," Zalora said. "Then the news about your mother at the Castle broke. She protested alone for hours until the parents of other drafted children joined her. Then, more and more people joined them. My parents went too. When they came back hours later, they said that I couldn't let the work that the Poli Twins started go to waste. The MMA is our only shot at ending the draft. We have to keep at it."

"We believe other kids and adults believe each other," Alaan said.

"We believe adults, too," Gron said.

"Yes," Alaan said and patted him on the shoulder.

"I found three other MMA cohorts, two in Virt and one in Wrinst," Zalora said. "They haven't been drafted. We are planning a big practice with everyone in Poli."

"That's good news, no great news," Alaan said.

"Hopefully, they are further along in the program than we are. We could use a sneak peek at what to expect during the next rounds," Dre said.

"Are you going to tell us where you were?" Zalora said.

"Yes, we are going to tell everyone," Alaan said. He raised a hand. The crowd roared, then quieted. Sorcerers cast amplification spells. They knew the drill. "The sounds and colors of magic are back. It reminds me of when I was little. I couldn't walk for more than five minutes without seeing some young psychic floating by on a bed of purple energy or hearing the squawks and barks of animalists."

The animalists howled. Bright light boomed and flashed in the sky. Someone traced "Poli Twins" in the air with purple energy. Dre kept his face neutral, as he had trained himself to do. Alaan gave speeches like a seventy-year-old man reflecting on his long life. He repeated himself and spoke in roundabout phrases, but the people loved it.

"Since the founding of Lynit, we have enjoyed magic, food, and shelter. We were at peace with ourselves and the rest of the world. Then, the Battle of Ki delivered fear to Lynit. We learned that our six mighty magics were not the only might in the world and that our shelter was not safe. That fear changed us, but we must not let it define us. We must deny it a place in our hearts. We are sorcerers, animalists, protectors, elemental mages, psychics, and wizards. We are not afraid of anything, anyone, or any draft."

"End the draft," someone shouted. Others repeated it and it grew into a chant.

"Some believe the Guard kidnapped us. Others believe we were kidnapped by the three children who broke into the Castle. But we are here to say that neither is true. What is true is that the Guard attacked us in Daramis Bar."

The chants died. Voices shouted and complained. Communication orbs twinkled across the park.

"What are you doing?" Dre said while barely moving his lips. They were supposed to convince the Guard that they were never in the bar, not confirm that they committed a crime. If the Guard didn't arrest them, the elites would come after them. Alaan admitted to being Lakree's, Hila's, and Rye's last point of contact.

Alaan turned back. His face was stiff with anger, but his eyes were still sad. "Do you trust me?"

"Not right now," Dre said. He couldn't quite interpret Alaan's expression. He understood the emotion, but the meaning eluded him. The only explanation Dre could guess was that it was related to Alaan's secret. This small splinter between them wasn't a cute challenge anymore. When they got home, Dre would make him talk.

"We did not know who Lakree, Hila, and Rye were when we met them, but they showed us their draft orders, and in that moment, we were united," Alaan continued to the crowd. "We were in the bar saying goodbye to our friend who had been drafted as well. When guards attacked, fear blinded us. It wasn't a fear of harm. It was a deeper fear that had been with Dre and me our entire lives. Fifty years ago, there used to be eleven people with special abilities; now, it's only us. We feared that whatever happened to them was about to happen to us. We didn't know who was responsible for that danger, but in that moment, we mistakenly believed it was the Guard."

Curses filtered into the crowd's shouts. Alaan held up a hand to silence them.

"The draft is like our reaction in that bar. Lynit was afraid and, in a panic, made a bad program. Did you know that noble children aren't drafted? The nobles made a law to solve a problem for all of Lynit but did not include themselves in the solution. We have opened a challenge to the draft because of that. We will prove its implementation is flawed, not the desire to protect Lynit."

Dre clasped his hands behind his back. Nobles weren't drafted because they didn't need to be. Those children received the best education and had access to tips and tricks passed down from the original inventors of magic.

"But changing the law is not enough. To truly defeat the draft, we must defeat the fear and the only way to defeat the fear is to make ourselves stronger," Alaan said.

He pounded his chest. The ring of fans around the stage pounded their chest. Moving a crowd was a skill Alaan had in abundance. Their fame boiled down to Dre's snaps and Alaan's speeches, another reason for the unused S and S Twins name.

Alaan continued, "To all the runaways who fled the draft, do not lose hope. Too much was asked of you too quickly. Let us fight for you. If you need food, clothes, or a place to practice magic, contact us. We will help as best as we can. To all the parents of children in the Magic and Martial Arts program, you must let your children train. That program is our future. It is the only alternative to the draft. We must train to protect Lynit, but we do not have to lose our freedom."

Dre nodded slowly. This was what Tess said to him. As usual, she got her way. The runaways would be helped. Alaan turned back to Dre, a slight smile on his face.

Dre squinted. "It was a good speech. I give you that."

"It was the best speech," Alaan said.

"Don't push it," Dre said. "Let's get out of here before we get arrested."

The other MMA students stood behind Dre with stunned eyes. "I want to be stronger," Gron said.

"Then keep practicing," Alaan said. He walked to the edge of the stage and hopped off.

"Thanks for sticking to this," Dre said. "You are the ones that will end the draft. Alaan and I won't make it past the next test."

A reporter floated up, standing on purple energy. "Is it true that you are suing the Guard to end both the draft and MMA?" she said.

All eyes focused on Dre. He was the Poli Twin on stage. "No, we are not trying to end them. We only want them to be voluntary," he

said.

"The king regent suggested that draftees should be allowed to leave the Castle twice a week to visit their families. Do you think that could work as a compromise?" the reporter said.

"Only if going into the Castle in the first place is a choice," he said.

"Was Lakree's matter shift into the Castle his choice or someone else's?" she asked.

"We don't know and we don't know where he is," he said carefully. This reporter was sneaky.

"Is it true that you can make an illusion that doesn't fade in sunlight?"

Dre paused. They had already admitted to fighting with the guards. He was unsure whether to continue with their prepared lie.

Alaan shouted from off stage, "We are almost eighteen. Our wizardry no longer joins together. We are now simply two brothers born on the same day." The last sentence was not part of the script.

"You will always be the Poli Twins," someone said.

"Poli Twins! Poli Twins!" the crowd chanted in support.

"Train with us," Gron said. "You will always be the best pair of wizards."

But they weren't the best pair of wizards. The Balison sisters beat them.

"Dre, let's go," Alaan said. He slapped the stage. "I thought you said we needed to be quick."

Dre tapped his foot. "Who wants to see a show?" he said. Alaan had avoided sparring in the Medina, but Dre could force him in public. Dre wouldn't allow them to be reduced to just two brothers. Even without joining their wizardry energies, they could still perform.

"Yeeessss," some girl screamed while jumping and waving her arms.

Dre turned to Alaan. "I will use dark energy and you will use both energies. Let's see if the crowd thinks your extra practice has paid off. We won't spar. We will just demonstrate what we can do. We won't even share balance." Dre couldn't pull out his maximum energy without Alaan, but this demonstration wasn't about power. It was about technique. Alaan would embarrass himself with dark energy, hopefully reminding him that two energies weren't always better than one.

Dre moved to the far side of the gigasphere and extended a hand, an invitation. Alaan contemplated it for a moment before climbing on stage. The other MMA students jumped off.

Dre breathed deeply, then reached out his senses. The pushes and pulls of wizardry were strong. His senses were acute. He stopped himself from reaching out, feeling for his brother, attempting to share his balance. He waited for the push on his skin to be at its strongest, then he pulled with his mind.

Dark energy responded, flowing into existence like water. It pooled above him. It was so dense that it seemed to suck the color out of the air around it. The world looked like a muted picture in a newspaper. Then, the pressure hit him. His legs buckled. He slammed into the floor.

He tried to warn Alaan, but it was too late. A brilliant light sparked. Dre shut his eyes, but the red light was still there. The heat hit him with its own punch as the dense light energy exploded in a boom. Alaan yelped.

Something cracked. Black dust pattered on the ground. Dre snapped away his energy. A chunk of the gigasphere above Alaan was gone, blown away. It sailed over the park. People screamed as they dove out of the way. Dre crawled to Alaan. He was stunned but alive.

Dre looked back up at the broken gigasphere. Lakree matter shifted through gigastone and now Alaan shattered some. He and his brother weren't receiving a little bit of spirit energy from their connection to another spirit realm. Their magic was pushing further into the impossible.

"Get up. Time to go," Dre said. Not only would people not believe their energy no longer joined, but they publicly told Slithlor that he should redouble his efforts to capture them.

Chapter 20 - Dre

Dre and Alaan ran home. The tunnels were quiet, but several people spotted them when they resurfaced. They pointed. They shouted. One man chased them. Dre turned down the alley behind his house. He threw up a black wall behind them. Alaan opened the back door to their gym. They slipped inside before the man reached them. Dre flicked the lock shut. He braced his back against the door and panted.

The mannequins were scattered about. One was broken in half and another rested on a large printing machine in the back. The matted floors were dusted with footprints. This wasn't how Dre and Alaan had left the gym. It looked like their parents had their workout session, but it focused more on destruction.

Alaan paused before entering the rest of the house. Dre grabbed his hand and they walked in together. Dad stood in the kitchen, holding a tray. He stacked it with two plates of fruit slices and a tea kettle. He glanced over his shoulder, then the tray slipped from his hands. The metal banged against the floor. The steaming liquid spilled down his clothes, but he didn't flinch.

"Alaandre," he said, arms stretched out.

Mommy dashed into the kitchen. She pushed past Dad and gripped Alaan and Dre.

"My babies," she sobbed.

Four other people entered the kitchen, strangers: a tall woman with neatly cropped blond hair held the arm of a short, dark-skinned man with cornrows. They weren't wearing the colors of their families, but the scent of nobility wafted off them. It was in their posture, their calmness despite everyone else celebrating or being shocked. A curly-haired woman with a round face and blank eyes surveyed them. Her vibe was the opposite of the nobles, with her worn t-shirt and a tattoo on her left wrist.

"Where is Rye?" the last stranger asked. She wasn't in uniform but stood like a guard—square shoulders and hard-faced. Right before Rye tackled Lakree, he'd looked just like her.

Lakree's father pulled out a photograph. Lakree and Rye beamed into the camera, arms wrapped around each other. They were in the Castle in Virt during the tour put on by the king regent. Alaan and Dre were in the background of the photo.

"Are they with my sister Juli?" he said.

Dre shook his head. It was more than a coincidence that Lakree, Hila, and Rye were on the Castle tour. That day was the only day Slithlor had access to a large group of children with no other adults around except for the king regent. Slithlor was a skilled psychic. He could have discovered the magical anomalies Chirchi saw in the spirit realm. While the children played, he studied them. He identified the special ones, then started the draft.

"Then where are they?" Hila's mother had tears in her eyes.

"We got separated," Alaan said.

Mommy cupped Dre's face, pulling his gaze up to meet hers. Her eyes were big and imploring. "These parents are looking for their children. They are terrified like we were until a few seconds ago. Now is not the time to hide anything. This is very serious. What do you know?"

Alaan started to speak, but she shushed him.

"I am talking to Dre," she said.

"We were just with them. They are in the city. The Guard won't find them unless they are kicked from their hiding place. If they are, they may have some of their memory wiped," Dre said.

"What? Where are they?" Rye's mother stepped forward.

Dre flinched. Mommy turned his face back to her.

"We can't tell. It is also our hiding place. The Guard could decide to come back after us. This place was built to protect people like us, people with special abilities," Dre said.

"How long have you known about this place?" Dad said.

"Since before the draft," Dre answered.

"So you had a backup plan," Mommy said with a nod. "Good."

"Do you know why the Guard is after your children?" Alaan said. "We know that something is different with their magic."

"The Guard is after Hila. She wasn't born in Lynit. She grew up using magic from Ries. As part of becoming a citizen, she gave it up, but the Guard didn't stop asking her about it. She doesn't want to talk about it, but they could force her in the draft," Hila's mother said.

"No. The Guard is after Rye. Many noble guards never liked that my husband was assigned to King Kertic's personal guard during the Battle of Ki. They blame him for the King's death. They tried to send me away on a three-year reconnaissance mission to El, which forced me to quit. I couldn't leave Rye and Felix for that long," Rye's mother said. "Now they are taking their revenge out on my son."

Lakree's father shook her head. "This is all bigger than us and our children," he said. "More than ten years ago, Juli faked her death as part of some secret work for King Kertic. Before she did it, she told me and gave me a way to contact her in an emergency. I didn't hear from her again until the Battle of Ki. She gave me a memory crystal and asked me to keep it safe.

"A few hours after the children fled, Slithlor visited us. He asked about Juli, which was strange. He wanted to know the last time I had seen her. I panicked and told him the truth, but something told me not to mention the memory crystal she had left. Slithlor's face changed, though he doesn't usually show emotion. He is terrified of my sister."

"What's on the memory crystal?" Dre said.

"I don't know. She told me not to open it unless I and the protector that opened it for me were prepared to go into hiding. Slithlor would notice our behavior change once we knew his secret. Lakree has the crystal now," he said.

Mommy turned around. "I still don't understand exactly what is happening, but my boys have told you what they can. I don't know what you should or can do with that information, but I will have to ask you to leave. I wish you the best of luck with your children."

The Virtian parents were silent as they collected their things.

"If we hear anything, we will let you know," Mommy said.

"Tell Rye that his father wasn't a coward. Make sure he knows that," Rye's mother said. Then they left.

Mommy held up her hand. No one made a sound for a full minute. "Go pack your things. We will walk to Nintur, then buy ground transportation to Wrinst. We can disappear from Lynit from there. Bring only what you can carry. We can't buy a matter shift out of Poli," she said.

Originally, Dre wanted to scare his parents into staying in Lynit, but he didn't know what the best option was anymore. "There's more," he said. He told them about the spirit realm, their magic joining inconsistencies, and the flare-up of power they both had. The twins weren't born with enough power to break gigastone. This was new.

"I read in the news that your energies stopped joining before you left," Dad said.

"No, that part was me," Alaan said.

"What do you mean?" Dre said.

"I'm sorry, Dre. After our energy had an issue joining during the MMA test, I figured out that I could trigger the Correction Factor to *correct* our magic and stop the joining. However, the power surge is something else. Lakree and Hila described similar power surges, too."

Alaan had been so calm after their energy didn't join during the Co Park performance but so confident that they could create combined illusions in the Easton Tunnels. Then, he didn't want to practice joining magic while in the Medina. This was the secret Alaan had buried underneath layers of guilt. It was more than a lie or a trick; it was a betrayal that backfired. The pieces finally fell together.

"Tess' capture was your fault," Dre said, with all the ire he could muster, which was a lot. It was the only emotion he had at the moment. It filled him to the brim. Alaan squirmed. If they had used the illusions as a distraction earlier, Tess could have gone with them to the Medina or at least made it back to her hiding place. Alaan was angry when they arrived in the Medina because he blamed himself for her capture. "And this is why you were defending Lakree so hard. You said lying for a good reason was okay, but what's the good reason here?"

"Work this out on the road," Dad said.

"Oh, did you tell Dad you would do this too?" Dre said.

"Go pack," Dad said.

Dre stomped into his room. The children's league Gigasphere Tournament trophies mocked him. Something had changed since those days. When they were in the ring, the world was shut out. The vibrations of wizardry and anticipating each other's movements were all that mattered. The Alaan in the other room and the Alaan who fought alongside Dre were two different people.

He slapped several trophies off the dresser. One cracked on the floor.

"Dre. Pack," Mommy shouted.

He took off his suspenders. He folded them carefully and placed them in a grey sack. He was like that spangot. Despite all he knew about his brother, he was blindsided. He hadn't seen all sides of Alaan after all. There was another angle. Alaan didn't just dislike the term "twins." He didn't want to be one. Dre stuffed three changes of clothes, sunglasses, and a picture of him and Alaan when they were eight. Maybe Dre would have to sustain himself on his memories. Back then, there were no secrets between them. They used to share every wacky thought, desire, and fear. And now, Dre wanted to know why Alaan didn't like that anymore, but if recent history were any indicator, Alaan wouldn't tell him until something else went wrong.

A loud bang echoed outside his room. Dre opened his door. Alaan's door was across the hall and shut. He carried his bag into the living room. His parents wordlessly mouthed things to each other. Mommy pointed at the front door.

Someone knocked. "It's me, Homin. I know they are in there." His words were breathy.

Dad slapped his head. "I told security they could always let him in."

Homin banged again. Dad looked at Dre, then passed him towards the gym.

"Someone saw us come in the back way. It's compromised," Dre said.

"I am here to help. I have a plan," Homin shouted through the door.

"Let him in," Dre said. "Maybe we can do one last good thing before we go."

Dad checked with Mommy. She nodded, then he opened the door.

Homin burst into the room in a mountain of fluffy black and white fabric. He looked like he had stepped out of a fashion magazine, except he was panting and sweating.

"I don't remember running being this hard. Water, please," he said.

Dad brought him a glass full. Homin gulped it down, then slumped into a chair.

"Why did you make that comment about nobles not being drafted? It's not true technically, we aren't legally exempt," he said. "You made us sound like the enemy and the Cast and Palow didn't particularly like that. They sided with keeping the mandatory Guard programs. They want to force you to take back your statements and turn you into brand ambassadors for the Guard's youth programs."

"That's all Alaan's fault. He's the one who went rogue," Dre said. He felt guilty about Tess's capture and tried to make it up to her. Now, he owed Dre and all the other children in Lynit.

"But it is not all bad news. I don't know how you turned assaulting a couple of guards and escaping arrest into a positive publicity stunt, but it worked. Both the Vous and Pol have sided with us. That leaves the Finrar as the final family to convince. Otherwise, we must go before the council and the king regent, which would not be good for us since the king regent is determined to keep the draft going."

The Finrar dedication to adaptation was closely related to Yordin's focus on balance. The Lynitian environment was changing and they were open to changing with it. "There's a mob at Co Park demanding the end of the draft. I've never seen people this railed up. It has to have some sway," Dre said.

"Lynit doesn't function on mob rule," Homin said. "We have tried that before and it doesn't work. Long before Kertic, we had magic and war. In the storybooks, it sounds like magic was invented, we fought, and Kertic brought us together on the same day. But it took years. There were more deaths than ten Battle of Kis. That was when mob mentality ruled. It was like six different small nations fighting over resources. If four families agreed on something, they forced it on the other two. But relying on being a majority wasn't dependable. On one subject, one family was a part of the majority; on another, they were in the minority. In the end, everyone was a minority in one way or another and had their land stolen or relatives murdered.

"The Kertic family's power is that they are a minority, but it takes not just the majority but all the noble families to stop them. Kertic established that every law is for the benefit of all, not just the majority of the moment. Because if all of these minorities got together, they could decide they didn't need a ruler. The Kertics protect themselves by making sure we are all served."

"By we, you mean the nobles," Alaan said. He stood on the edge of the room, arms crossed, leaning against the wall.

"Not at all. When he made us share our magic with everyone, he put us in the same position. If the nobles did anything to anger the general population, we could not stand against the public. So we, too, make laws that benefit all because you could decide that you don't need the nobles. Every other nation in the world is based on one magic. Every time a second magic developed somewhere, it ended in one of the magics wiping out or subjugating the other. Lynit has thrived since its inception without a civil war or genocide. We won't do anything stupid enough to jeopardize that. We didn't make the draft. Slithlor's program was supported by the king regent, who also isn't noble."

"And it was supported by the Yordin council member during the first court case," Alaan said. "Haven't you changed your mind to support us now?"

Homin adjusted his puffy robes. He didn't seem to like that the twins discovered the little fact he had failed to mention. "The family, yes, but the council is different. If a council member decided for the sole benefit of their family, the other five would have them removed. And by removed, I mean killed," Homin said. "We can only guess what the council members will do based on their family's guiding principles. This is why no one likes sending decisions to them. With the king regent suggesting new ways to reduce the fear of the draft, depending on all six council members to vote against him is too risky."

"So what's the final play?" Dre said.

"I got us a meeting with Victoria Finrar. She's the only Finrar who doesn't think that this case has to be decided by the council. She is the most non-noble seeming noble and you two are the most noble-like non-nobles. There is a potential beautiful balance that you can create together," he said.

"You mean that we can bridge the gap between nobles and the general population to quell the protests?" Alaan said.

Homin nodded. "Finrar's support is conditional on you walking back the statements you made against the nobility. And so is the Yordin's continued support. Lynit is headed towards an unbalanced state."

"When is the meeting?" Dre said. He had thought that he wouldn't get to meet her unless his suspenders clothing line were well received. Only in Poli could a fashion designer be the deciding factor in a military and political court case.

"In a few days," Homin said.

Dre pouted at his mother, though he didn't expect her to care.

"Can you give us a moment?" she said. Homin leaned back in his seat and drank more water.

"And we need to talk about your magic," he said. "The Yordin had guessed at the possibility of an illusion made from combined energies being able to resist sunlight, but we didn't expect your strength to increase. I know you won't let us study you, but I think there is still much we can help you discover about your magic if you haven't already. It comes down to different ways of applying your unique balance."

"Whatever Dre and I achieve, it will be on our own," Alaan said.

"I meant, wait outside," Mommy said. She helped Homin up, then led him out the door. When she turned back around, she said "We were supposed to leave a week ago. I'm not waiting another day."

The four of them awkwardly climbed out the side bathroom window. A few people saw them, but after a look from Mommy, they didn't follow. Alaan led them into the tunnels. Dad produced purple light, then squealed at a group of voroborous that darted past. Though he was from Poli, he was squeamish.

They resurfaced a few streets away from the dome wall. This close to the edge, the buildings were low and wide. The curvature of the dome was shallow, only a few stories high. Wanted signs for Lakree, Hila, and Rye were still posted here.

A white rectangular outline traced the permeable section of the dome. Two lines of guards extended from the wall, at least ten on each side. Crowds exited the city, but a small trickle of people entered.

"Please make sure you have your ID. They are not required for exit but are required for re-entry," a guard said, her voice loud but not strained. She repeated herself every few seconds.

The four of them joined the line heading out. Dre pulled his hood up, but everyone recognized him anyway. Most whispered, but no one pointed. Mommy was more famous than him at this point. They knew not to annoy her.

However, a guard stepped in their path. "Hi, good afternoon. If you don't mind, could I speak with you for a moment?" He motioned for them to step out of the line.

"Nope," Mommy said. "We have our IDs. We are good to go."

"Actually, I have to make a call before I let these two exit the city," he said.

"We are their parents. We are taking them on a much-needed vacation," Dad said.

"When a child is reported missing, all of the dome patrols are alerted and we do our best to make sure those children are not taken out of our city. I must verify with the Castle that we can remove the 'Missing' status," he said and smiled.

Another guard stepped beside him. "The Castle will want to speak to them after the incident," he said, not smiling.

"There were no charges filed," Mommy said.

"Ma'am, I am just doing my job," he said.

"Don't ma'am me," she said.

Dad put a hand on Mommy's shoulder. "How long will this take?"

"Just a moment."

They followed the two to a small post about the size of a bedroom. It was a metal box with glassless windows. The two guards stepped inside, taking the IDs with them.

"Run. I'll cause a distraction," Mommy said out the side of her mouth.

"No, Mira," Dad said. "Didn't you just spend the night in jail?"

"They can have me, but Slithlor can't have them," she said.

"Mira, we thought the Guard had them, but the Guard thought they were kidnapped. They are making sure the boys are safe," Dad said.

Mommy fidgeted. "If they try something, I am killing everybody."

Dre looked at Dad, then at Alaan. The two looked at each other. He glanced at strangers who were exchanging their own glances between them. The cycle repeated. They had all heard what Mommy said. Dre hoped that, for the guards' sake, they would be allowed to leave the city. Through the window, both men picked up communication orbs. They were contacting different people within the Castle. If one of them was Slithlor, then the escape plan was over. Slithlor wouldn't let them leave.

Dre's breath caught in his throat when the guard station door banged open. The nicer guard apologized, then handed Mommy back the IDs.

"You're all set," he said. He escorted them to the dome wall as the second guard watched from inside the station.

The heat and shine outside Poli hit Dre's face like a blast of light energy. The red ground glowed. He put on his sunglasses. Two lines of people waited outside to get into the city. One line moved quickly, with guards checking their IDs. The second line was of angry foreigners who were told they weren't allowed in Lynitian cities anymore.

The king regent and Slithlor were slowly destroying the nation. The Kertics were the royal family for a reason. They knew how to bring people together. There could have been only one guard left after the Battle of Ki and King Kertic wouldn't have started a mandatory draft. He would have improved the public education system instead. If the nobles were trained enough to easily join the Guard at nineteen, then so should everyone.

Two blue lines stretched across the desert. The shields on the safe roads were activated by travelers from other cities. One led to Virt and the other to Nintur. They walked in silence for a long while. It was a two-day walk to Nintur, but Mommy was a protector and they had food and water. They would make it.

Tiny black dots clouded Dre's vision a few hours into the march. He blinked a few times, removing the sunglasses. The dots didn't go away. They increased in size and number. Mommy extended a hand and they stopped. Then, in a swoosh, the blackness twisted in on itself and faded, revealing three elites, a protector, an animalist, and a sorcerer, their faces covered by their high collars.

The sorcerer unfastened his collar first. The hair on the sides of his head was clipped short in an urban style, but on top, his long black hair was in a braid that extended down his back. He was short and his hair nearly reached the ground. He was a Vous but from Poli. He was the youngest elite, only four years older than Dre. He was famous. He held a sorcerer's orb filled with dark red and gold liquids that did not mix.

The animalist was a Finrar. His hair and skin were the same shade of light brown. He was tall, broad-shouldered, and had a mustache. His green and white robe was neat, the creases on the shoulders and sides sharp.

"I am Ser," the protector said, forgoing her formal title and noble name, but with a large "E" on her chest, a title was redundant. "This is Grintinari and Rish." She was as dark as Dre, but her hair was shoulder-length and dropped to one side of her head. Her gold rings clanked as she pulled her collar away from her face. Her lips were painted a faint shade of red that matched her eyes.

"How can we help you?" Mommy said. They had only a slim hope of getting out of Lynit before the elites caught up to them anyway.

"We are looking for information on the whereabouts of Sorcerer Lakree Oldenfoot, Elemental Mage Hila Kolit, and Animalist Rye Turnitu. You met them in Daramis bar two days ago," Ser said, her tone casual.

"We don't know where they are," Alaan said.

"Do you mind if we sit?" Ser created a small sphere and sat before waiting for an answer. "This may take some time." Everyone turned to Dre. They expected him to create dark energy chairs for everyone.

His mind flashed to the broken gigastone at Co Park. He couldn't trust his magic at the moment. "I'm not feeling well," he said.

Ser created six more shields. Dre sat down carefully. The physical shield supported his weight.

"I read the file on these three missing children. It was mostly empty. Hila's grades were average, though Rye did win Best Tipit Morpher seven years ago in Ms. Carvin's second-period class and Lakree had the best grades in all his classes after he switched to public school. Then, I looked at what the three accomplished in one day.

"First, a fifteen-year-old matter shifted three people outside the Virt dome, which was impressive but not extraordinary since they only moved a few feet. Then, a couple of hours later, they matter shifted over a mile into the throne room, the most protected place in all of Lynit. Then, an hour later, they matter shifted through gigastone and traveled halfway across the city. The final matter shift moved them over twelve miles," Ser said.

"I'm sorry, but what does this have to do with us?" Dad said.

"It will make sense in a second. I promise." Ser raised her hand. "These three children then traveled miles, on foot, through the desert, but not on the path and killed a quitol in the process. They sneak into Poli and then run into the Poli Twins the same day they return to the public after two years. You meet up with Tess, who had been hiding from the Guard for three weeks and she helps the five of you escape into the Easton Tunnel, where your trail disappears abruptly at a wall. Today is your first time leaving that place, but Lakree, Hila, and Rye didn't leave with you."

"We don't know where Lakree, Hila, and Rye are. We got separated in the Easton Tunnel," Alaan said.

Dad's eyes darted down to Dre, then to Mommy. Mommy didn't even blink. Grintinari pressed his lips tight. Rish's attention was on the desert horizon. Dre clenched his teeth. The elites could arrest them for lying.

"I will tell you how I see this situation. Whenever I face a problem, I make sense of the scenario by thinking about the boundaries. It's like protection magic. If I understand the boundaries of something, then I understand its nature. Unfortunately, in this case, none of my boundary conditions make sense. The smallest and simplest boundary was that these children were ordinary, and everything was a huge misunderstanding, but the first and second matter shifts were beyond that. No one sent these children; they willed those spells into reality.

"The second boundary frames these children as simply panicked teens fleeing the draft, but matter shifts three and four don't fit that scenario. Lakree, Hila, and Rye left Virt to find Lakree's aunt, Juli Pol, and the problem with including her in any boundary condition is that she is supposed to be dead. She was an elite who reportedly died many years ago. I've researched her. She's a protector. Her research into negative spaces and reverse boundaries is still a subject of interesting debate in universities. What stood out the most in her record was a list of twelve counts of treason."

"Treason?" Dre rocked on the shield chair as he leaned forward.

Ser held up another hand. "We were tasked to find and kill Lakree, Rye, and Hila because they stole something that could start a war if it fell into Juli's hands. So now you see that when I ask you 'where are these children,' I do not care about your attempt to protect them from the draft," she said, rising to her feet, a smooth heat in her eyes.

"What was stolen?" Mommy grabbed Dad's hand.

"The device Sewit used to summon spirit fiends," Ser said, eyes still on Dre and Alaan. Grintinari's eyes were on Dre, too, but not directly. His gaze was slightly off as he likely scanned him with his sorcerer's eye. Dre wished that there was a mental block that he could put up for sorcerers like he could for psychics.

"There is no way three children would do that alone. They are being manipulated. You can't kill them for that. They might not even know what they stole," Dad said.

"Is Slithlor the one who gave you this mission? Is he the only one that knows what those three took?" Alaan said.

"Why would you say that?" Grintinari asked.

"And did Slithlor conveniently remove six children from the draft right after Lakree, Hila, and Rye disappeared?" Alaan said.

"How did you hear about that?" Ser said.

"The people hiding Lakree, Hila, and Rye are conflicted about them. On the one hand, they recognize that Slithlor's interest in them started only after they proved to have extraordinary magic, which is his pattern. On the other hand, Slithlor wants them killed in secret. Slithlor has tortured and killed people from other nations to learn more about magic. As head of the draft, he's turned his focus inward," Alaan said.

"Is the Medina protecting them?" Rish said.

Dre looked away.

"We, too, believe something is wrong with this scenario. Grintinari specializes in chaos and decay. He can identify the age of matter. Juli's treason files were dated more than ten years ago but were produced two days ago."

"By Slithlor?" Dre said.

"We don't know yet. He assigned Grintinari to this case, knowing that he could discover this discrepancy. He sent me, a protector who doesn't use battle magic, and Rish, the best tracker but not an assassin. There is a final boundary that I construct around a problem when all else fails. This boundary is reserved for issues that are above my pay grade. This boundary is for the council and king regent.

"To involve them, I will need more information than I have now, which is very little. The conspirators will know what we are doing if I go through formal channels. But I still must not allow Lakree, Hila, and Rye to meet Juli if they haven't already done so.

"This is where the Poli Twins come in. You have a case to end the draft. If the government and Guard disagree, it will go to the council and king regent. Then, they will look into everything related, including the fugitives and Slithlor. Therefore, you will return to Poli to ensure your case makes it to them."

Dad and Mommy jumped to their feet, protesting. Ser waited patiently. She wasn't rude, but her posture said the decision was already made.

"Slithlor has the law on his side, so we have to use the law against him," Alaan said.

Dre wasn't ready to accept the Medina's requirement to dedicate himself to changing the world, but exposing Slithlor to the council was a first step. He looked towards Poli. "We must make the nobles feel even more threatened by us. That guarantees the Finrar will vote against us, giving us a tie."

"But if we are too direct, then all the nobles might turn against us," Alaan said.

"Then we'll just have to be clever," Dre said.

"Is the chance of war real?" Dad said.

"I hope not," Ser said.

"Whatever this is, it's Slithlor's doing," Mommy said.

Chapter 21 - Rye

One minute twenty seconds. Rye turned his small head to the other side to confirm the time on the sandglass with his other eye. He scrapped his clawed feet against the ground. His wings itched to fly up and away, but the black rock ceiling denied the request. The gigastone hid the Medina from the Guard but was also a cage. He dropped his gaze. He guided the return to human. He stretched out on the ground, breathing heavily.

This had been his slowest morph into a tipit all day, but his fastest was only five seconds less. The sub-minute morph was still out of reach. The problem wasn't his technique. He was weak and getting weaker. Energy flowed out more quickly than was replenished by the source feeding him. And now, it was too late for Chirchi to take him back to the spirit realm. He couldn't delay returning to his room for much longer. The Guard's presence in the tunnels should have cleared up and Lakree and Hila were eager to contact Juli. She'd have answers about Rye's spirit realm connection.

A memory from his recurring dream of the spirit realm played in the back of his mind. He was in a city in the sky where the roads and buildings were plump clouds. Large hideous creatures with tiny wings floated by carrying briefcases. They rushed down streets, entered buildings, and exited them. Two stood at a table signing papers. A third one flung the completed stack into the air every few seconds. The city was the trap of adulthood. The allure of magic was distant and settling for a job behind a desk was the only option. Spells that people spent years perfecting faded from memory. And something similar was happening to Rye. His life had been so serious the past years that he had forgotten why he liked magic in the first place. It was fun and didn't need to serve a purpose at all. Even if it took him an hour to morph into a tipit, the ability to use magic was gift enough.

The dream was like a warning to never stop training. Magic was the most abundant and wonderful resource in the world, but like a muscle, if he didn't use it, he would lose it. The dream also gave him an idea.

In the spirit realm, thoughts and magic were the same. Chirchi had said that the insects there were the idea of the insects in the real world. When Rye morphed here, his spirit energy had to respond to the idea of transformation. Maybe it changed shape over there. His magic might make it so if he believed he was a bird. It was a stretch, but he didn't see any other options.

He pressed himself into a handstand. When his body was still, he closed his eyes. He imagined he was in the sky, soaring above the Winder Plains. The air cooled the higher he went. Up there, the only rule was the rule of wind currents and all wind blew away from Lynit. There was no place he couldn't go, no danger he couldn't escape. He leaned into the feeling as he morphed.

When the last of his feathers whitened at the tips, he checked the time—fifty-eight seconds had passed. He squawked, then flew several laps around the room. It had worked. He had learned something valuable in the spirit realm. He landed and returned to human. "I'd find my way to the forest with this," he said. He went back to the room. He took a deep breath and knocked before entering.

Lakree hovered over the map Urura gave them. After over six years, he had cut his hair for the first time to even out what had been burned off. There was a new freshness about him. Rye wouldn't have recognized him if it wasn't for the still-present stern look on his face.

Hila lay on the couch reading a book. She was dressed in a dark green dress that the Medina provided. It was the first time Rye had seen her in one. It was as strange on her as short hair on Lakree. His friends looked like new people, but the pairing still made no sense. Lakree was noble and Hila was the furthest thing possible from that.

"I had a breakthrough with my morphing. I am under a minute now," Rye said.

"Did Chirchi take you back to the spirit realm?" Hila said.

Rye shook his head.

"You still have time," Lakree said. "The guards haven't stopped searching."

"But four days have passed as of this morning," Rye said. He had started counting from the moment they arrived in the Medina and added a few hours for good measure. Having so many guards looking for three children was a waste of resources. Extending the search beyond protocol was obsessive and stupid. Some noble who didn't like Rye's father must have made that command. Maybe it was that sorcerer captain from the throne room.

"And I still can't find any flaw in their patrol," Lakree said.

"They aren't following procedure anymore. There's no telling how long they will stay there," Rye said. There were a couple of ways he could sneak out alone, however. He could turn into a voroborous and blend in with the other rodents. There was also a camouflaging creature that could blend in with stone, but it wouldn't help Lakree and Hila make it to Juli. "They have to be lured away then. I could do that." A torist running through the halls would grab everyone's attention and they wouldn't know it was

Rye.

"It's not worth the risk," Lakree said. He drew another set of lines on his paper.

"What do you think we are connected to?" Hila said.

"I don't know. Spirit fiends? It would explain the Guard's behavior. Juli will know," Lakree said.

Rye tilted his head to the side. Lakree's entire plan was based on paranoia.

"What if we can't reach her?" Hila said. "She may have all the answers, but we don't know if she is still alive. It's been five years since you last heard from her."

Lakree gripped the edges of the counter. "We leave Lynit."

"We could go to my Dad," Hila said.

"That'll be the first place they'll check," Rye said.

"Then we pick another place," Lakree said.

"You want to run forever?" Rye said. "At some point, we have to turn ourselves in, spirit fiends or not. Our families are worried about us."

Rye was putting his family through a terrible cycle. After the Battle of Ki, Rye, his mother, and his brother waited for news on whether his father would return home. It was several days of actively suppressing the mind's tendency to imagine the worst, only to discover that the worst had already happened. There was a terror in having a gut feeling even if it was only correct one in one thousand times. Hopefully, the Guard told his mother he safely made it to Poli.

Hila tapped the book in her lap. It was called *Uniformity: The New Child*. Dre dropped it off before he and Alaan left the Medina.

"Listen to this. 'At Lynit's founding, the Verbindous was for everyone. People challenged themselves and pushed boundaries. New spells were performed and cataloged. It was a way to gain respect and lift social status. Over the years, it waned in popularity until only the nobles still practiced it. Today, the draft seeks to start a new tradition.'"

"The draft is nothing like the Verbindous," Lakree said. "The Verbindous is how we prove our family connection. It's about respecting magic. The draft is about making soldiers."

"But I know you aren't simply afraid of becoming a soldier," Hila said.

"The Guard might not have tried to draft us if I hadn't matter shifted into the throne room. I somehow proved that I had an ability they had only suspected up until that point. Then, it was time to capture all the other people they suspected. They didn't know they wanted the Poli Twins, the most famous fighters in the country, until then, too. It feels like they experimented on us somehow," Lakree said.

"Did you know the twins would be in that bar?" Rye said.

Lakree rubbed his chin. "That part was a coincidence."

"They must have done something to us during the MMA program introduction. Psychics were in our minds," Hila said.

"I watched with my sorcerer's eye when they implanted the material. There were no other spells active. I even check when I access the material in my head, but nothing strange happens," Lakree said. "But it doesn't mean they didn't cause that spirit energy connection that Rye and the twins have. Chirchi said that it was giving them energy, which would be something that the Guard wanted. The only other time we were somewhere together was during the Castle tour. Drime and the Poli Twins were there."

Rye laughed. "You can't be serious. Not only are you accusing Slithlor, but also the king regent. He was there, too." Though Rye had been to the Castle many times, the tour was the first time he was inside the throne room. It was when he first met Hila. She was there alone. She stood out because she could only use one Lynitian magic. Her mother was an elemental mage, so it was all she saw before she moved to Lynit. Rye didn't notice her accent because he was still learning what proper magic looked like.

"Slithlor isn't good simply because he has a high title or knows others with higher titles," Lakree said. "I've heard some terrifying stories about him. They were about things he did to foreigners to learn about their magic, but it shows what he is capable of. There are honorable people in the Guard, but the Guard itself isn't completely honorable in the way it wants you to believe."

Rye shook his head. "No. There are dishonorable people in the Guard, but the entire organization isn't corrupt." His father didn't speak much about Slithlor, but he spoke highly of the king regent when he was head of defense under King Kertic. Even all the council members thought he was trustworthy. If the king regent was plotting with Slithlor, it was to protect Lynit.

"See Hila. I told you. He worships the Guard," Lakree said.

"So? I told you to leave him be until you have proof that we are in more danger than simply being drafted," Hila said. "He isn't trying to leave."

They didn't care that his father was a coward because they wanted Rye to be one. He crossed his arms. "Not only have you been dating behind my back, but you have planned ways to keep me here. Are there any more secrets you want to tell me while you are at it?"

Hila shut her book. She squinted and raised a finger slowly. "I knew it."

"Knew what?" Rye said, adding extra bass to his voice.

Lakree's smile dropped.

"You've been acting weird. You're mad and it's not just at Lakree. You're mad at me, too. We aren't together if that's what you think," she said as she stood up.

Lakree's eyes widened.

"I don't care," Rye said, though it wasn't entirely true.

"Well, it's time we talked about it," she said, stepping closer to him. "We can't pretend it didn't happen. And I get it. You felt left out."

Rye chuckled. "Left out?"

He should have been left out of Lakree's escape plan. There were wanted signs with his face on them all over Lynit. He was a fugitive. He was invested in helping them get what they wanted, but what about his desire to explore the world or find his father? No one else was invested in him.

Hila leaned in as if for a hug but kissed him on the lips. He stared down at her, frozen. This was his first kiss. He never would have guessed that it would have been with Hila, or any girl for that matter. His eyes moved over to Lakree, whose mouth gapped open. She pulled his hand to her chest. It was soft.

She pulled back. "There, now you didn't miss anything." She smirked, then twisted around. "Lakree, get over here. It's your turn."

"My turn?" he said, his surprise turned to confusion.

"His turn?" Rye said, his voice shot up. The thought of his lips touching Lakree's made his knees weak.

"Rye is not going to stop being mad until you make out with him," she said.

"Hila, that's not it," Rye said. "I was mad at Lakree for lying about my dad, but I let it go. He was trying to help me in his twisted way. I was annoyed about the kiss, but mostly because it surprised me."

"Mm-hm," she said with a pleasant smile as she pulled Lakree over.

"Sorry," Lakree said, then dove in. Rye giggled at first as Lakree's stubble tickled his face, but he held the kiss for a little longer.

Lakree smelled a little of funk, but his odor flared Rye's nostrils.

He inhaled the same scent when they were together in the cart. Heat moved down his body. Time passed in slow motion, like when he tried stabbing himself with the rod.

He had imagined this moment many times, long ago. The fantasy had hinged on Rye becoming a captain or an elite, the only titles that could bring him close enough to be considered by a noble. And with the recent changes happening to his magic, Rye might be closer. However, Lakree didn't even like boys. But then again, three days ago, Rye would have sworn that Lakree didn't like Hila. So for right now, he enjoyed this kiss.

Hila clapped him on the side. "See, boys? Isn't this much better than fighting?"

A tingling jolt shot through Rye when Lakree grabbed his crotch. His eyes flapped open and he jerked back.

"I forgive you, I forgive you," Rye said.

Lakree shrugged. "I never kissed a boy before. I just assumed that was the first thing you went for."

"It's not," Rye said, but honestly, he didn't know either. Lakree was the first boy he'd kissed, too.

"You live and you learn," Lakree said. He touched his lips. "And you were pretty good at it, Rye."

"He touched my chest, so I touched his crotch. A fair exchange in my book," Hila said.

Lakree grabbed Rye's hand and pulled it towards him, but Rye snapped it back. He couldn't be greedy. It was better not to know.

"What are we doing?" Rye said, taking a step away.

"I was mad at him, too," she said, poking Lakree on the side of the head. "It took all of my energy not to punch him. But regardless of what Lakree's aunt might know and whether he did the right thing by lying to us, we are in a mess. The wanted signs, the draft orders, the Poli Twins, and the changes to our magic don't add up. It's why we haven't left the Medina yet. I was terrified when you went to the spirit realm. When you slumped over, I had a panic attack. I couldn't breathe. He brought me back to calm me down. Then, I don't know what happened. Our faces were close for a second and we kissed. That was it."

"Oh," Rye said. This made a lot more sense. The mental somersaults it took to imagine Lakree and Hila going on a date were more challenging than picturing his father in hiding.

"I don't know what we need to do next, but I know we will need each other to do it. We would have been caught if each of us didn't do our part. Every moment until this is over, we have to trust each other completely. We have to become like the Poli Twins—one unit," she said.

"The Poli Twins don't make out," Rye said.

"I wouldn't put it past them. I caught Dre wistfully watching Alaan a few times. Every time I turn around, they're holding hands. They cuddle. That's weird. They're weird," she said.

"They are brothers, Hila," Lakree said.

"They are like the same person in two bodies. It's basically mas —"

"Hila," Rye interrupted. He was even hotter now. He sat down. He fanned himself. He had considered everything she had said many times before. Everybody considered it at least once.

She rolled her eyes. "They are amazing fighters because they don't have to talk out strategies. They've had their whole lifetime to learn each other's habits. They react in sync. We need to speed that up."

"Well, Rye and I already basically cuddle on that cramped bed, so we are halfway there," Lakree said.

"The bottom line is that the next time we get in a fight, I am grabbing everyone's crotch and not in a fun way," she said.

"Are we good, Rye?" Lakree said.

Rye pulled a piece of blond hair off the bed. He wouldn't be able to roll over and fall asleep like before. It would be like when they were kids and he laid awake during sleepovers, waiting for Lakree to confess his secret love. Rye had become so good at pretending he only wanted Lakree as a friend that it became true. But in an instant, all of that had been undone. With his connection in the spirit realm, he was on a path that drew him closer to nobility than the Guard ever could. "More than good."

"Rye, you are the only one who hasn't studied the map. It's your time to wreak your brain," Hila said.

He joined Lakree next to the map. The dots marched through eight different halls. It was almost random, but there was a structure somewhere, even if he didn't see it yet. "All forms of security are based on repeated processes."

His mother had said something similar to him once. She had a book called "Fight or Fight." It chronicled moments in history when people had two choices: fight to survive or fight to thrive. After the six magics were invented, Lynitians no longer struggled to survive. Vital resources were accessible. However, the battle for a better life continued.

There was only one story in the book that confused him. It was about a Finrar who killed a Cast after Queen Kertic married a Finrar because of an old grudge from fifty years prior. His mother explained it away by saying, "All forms of violence are based on repeated processes."

Lakree slid over a sheet of metal paper. Straight, squiggly, and angled lines were drawn in various sets.

"What is this?" Rye said.

"It's a shorthand for describing sequences. We use it in sorcery. It is useful for notating what happens during a disruption and the order in which rules are corrected."

"So what is this?" Rye said, pointing at six lines of different lengths ending in swirls.

"These patterns overlap perfectly for various stretches, then break off into one of the six different endings. So when I see the common part, it's hard to guess which ending it will have. It all looks random. There's no way we can get past these guards unseen," Lakree said.

"The soldiers have to follow a predefined routine that they have memorized. To one person, their route has to be the same or they would get confused," Rye said.

"What if we can't find a pattern because there isn't one?" Hila said. "Couldn't chaos be its a form of security?"

"Not unless they know we are watching them," Rye said.

"What if all of this is to scare us? The Guard knows that we are down here but don't know where. They are likely trying to keep us from leaving," Hila said.

"If that is the case, then they will never stop," Rye said. In hindsight, he should have known that the Guard would have broken from their usual four-day search pattern. As he told Hila in the desert, they were in the storm.

"It means they aren't looking for us because I broke into the Castle. They are afraid of us," Lakree said.

Rye backed away from the map, shaking his head. The Guard didn't fear him, but they feared his father. When Rye was in the Castle, they asked questions about the missing elite. They didn't ask Rye about his particular contract to the spirit realm. The Guard didn't know about that. He needed to speak to Juli as soon as possible.

A MMA card brightened in his mind. It was of a small white creature that sprayed a gas that caused visions. "Let's use that fear against them. I can learn to produce a hallucinogen that will cause a waking nightmare of us or whatever scares them the most. If we ran past, they wouldn't be sure we were ever there. I'll just need help spreading the gas through the tunnels."

"I could do that with wind," Hila said. "But what if Juli doesn't show up?"

"Then we turn ourselves in," Rye said.

"I'll matter shift us back here," Lakree said.

"You couldn't do it the last time you tried," Rye said.

"We have a few days before we have to leave the Medina. I'll figure it out by then," Lakree said.

"And if you don't?" Rye said.

"Then I will go to the spirit realm," Lakree said. "That'll buy us all the time we need."

"Sounds good to me," Rye said.

"Rye, if Juli told us to leave Lynit forever, would you do it?" Hila said.

"If she knows what happened to my father, I'd do whatever she asked," he said.

"Good, now we have a real plan," Hila said.

Chapter 22 - Rye

Rye stood in Lakree's palm. He was in the form of a hinlin, the small white creature that produced a hallucinogen. Lakree sniffed him. Theoretically, the best way to morph into a creature was to reproduce its DNA but Rye wasn't anywhere near that skill level. Therefore, he settled for replicating the shapes and behaviors of larger structures like organs and blood. However, the internal shape of the glands that produced the odorless gas was chemically sensitive. An imbalance of pH caused the compound to break down into inactive molecules that smelled of sugar. Either hinlin produced it perfectly or they died, as the sweet smell alerted predators to a tasty meal.

"It's working," Lakree said.

Rye stopped the spray, then bounced. He slept only a few hours last night, but it paid off. It was the first time he'd lost sleep over a morph. In school, new morphs were about grades or a distant future of joining the Guard. For once, he had an immediate need. Though he had considered sabotaging their escape plan to force a trip to the spirit realm, he didn't want to risk not being able to contact Juli. Potentially learning more about his magic would be nice, but the chance, even if small, that Juli knew any information about his father was too good to risk. When Urura's ultimatum time limit ran out in four days, Rye wanted to be ready to sneak out of the tunnels. He couldn't bank on Lakree and Hila wanting to stay after a spirit realm visit since they'd have haunting dreams like Rye.

There was a name that he couldn't quite remember, but the creature it belonged to was clear in his mind. Its claws, beak, and wings were all white. Each of its feathers was longer than his arm. It wasn't anything taught in school or the MMA material. But it was the one thing that made the sky creatures stop their nonsense. A swift shadow rippled over the streets and everyone dropped their work. They shouted its name and flapped, but their feeble wings couldn't lift them that high. The white bird could take Rye far away from Lynit.

Lakree clenched his eyes shut. "I see Juli dead."

Rye paused his celebration. He had assumed that Lakree would hallucinate a guard chasing him. That was the fear that came up when Lakree preached his conspiracy. Each day, he reiterated and dissected all the facts of the MMA program, their magic, the Castle tour, and his aunt. He never reached any conclusion other than a rock-solid belief that Slithlor was up to no good. But now it was clear that Lakree was more afraid he would never find answers. Talking to Juli was his last hope.

Rye crawled up Lakree's arm, nestling in the crux of his neck and shoulder. When Lakree petted him, Rye purred, which surprised him. He didn't know that hinlins could do that. Lakree rubbed his chin on Rye's soft fur. They snuggled until the hallucinations were gone. Rye returned to his human body.

"Despite everything, I am glad I came with you. This is sort of what I imagined it would be like if we had joined the Guard together. We would go on long missions to foreign lands. I would hunt for food while you strategized ways to cripple the enemy. And if ever there was a moment when we were in danger or scared, I would be there to comfort you."

Lakree squeezed Rye's shoulder. "You are a great friend," he said.

He stared back into Lakree's brown eyes, trying to imagine what more than friendship could be like: cuddling, seeing Lakree naked, getting married someday. After the kiss, Rye's imagination traipsed eagerly down impossible futures. "I'll tell Hila the good news and let you get back to concentrating on your matter shift," he said as he backed away. But the truth was that Lakree still only saw Rye as a friend.

A tang grew in his mouth the closer he got. At the giant stone doors, his jaw tingled like it did after eating an unripe lemon beet. The air tasted like magic. He cracked the door open and a deep, almost growl spilled out. It sounded like a storm. In the center of the room, a fat funnel of wind cycled red dirt around and around. The top of it reached the ceiling, sanding the arches. Inside the tornado, the thick stone table bobbled off the ground. But the best part of everything was Hila. The wind wanted to break apart, pan out, but she wouldn't let it. While her arms flew about in swirls, her feet remained planted for support. She gracefully maneuvered it, keeping it contained. Her accent was beautiful.

Soon, the spell weakened and the arc of her movements shallowed. She compensated by taking sharp steps. Gusts escaped her grasp. Then, the spell failed in a puff, spiraling out red dust. The table banged into the ground.

"It's harder than I thought," she said, brushing herself off.

"When I said that we needed wind, I meant that we needed a soft breeze," he said. If a hurricane blew through the Easton Tunnels, no one would have a chance to breathe in the gas. He should have remembered that subtlety wasn't her instinct.

She wiped the sweat from her forehead. "I have power, but I don't have control. Elemental magic spell words are a blueprint. They describe the element to convert my energy into; however, once it gets there, it takes on a life of its own. Wind is powered by heat. Too much and I make a fire. Too little and I can't control the little spurts it produces. It might blow the gas back at us."

He pictured Hila in the multicolored elemental mage guard robes. Someday, she would become the woman who chased them in the tunnels, full of care and precision. "There has to be a chapter in the MMA material that could help."

She shook her head. "It's more like holding mud that's dripping through my fingers. If I shift my hands back and forth, I can stop most of it from falling to the ground. When there is only a little energy in the spell, losing one drop can mean losing all of it. So I have to work even harder, but it dries if I move too fast. And my power fluctuates. I can't always predict how much energy will come out when I start the spell. I am connected to something in the spirit realm. I can feel it."

He hummed. Her explanation was complex, but she wasn't casting sorcery. It sounded like the reasoning that prevented him from stabbing his hand. It was a fear-based instinct. The tiniest doubts could expand into an essay in a fraction of a second. He grabbed her hands. "What are you really worried about?"

"I have this recurring dream. We are in the Winder Plains and the quitol's head dips from above. I attack it with lightning, but the face that is blackened is Lakree's."

"You saved our lives that day. You should be proud of that," Rye said.

"I also burned off half of Lakree's hair. What if I panic cast a spell that hurts you?" she said.

"We only have three options: You cast a breeze, we turn ourselves in, or we go to the spirit realm," Rye said.

"Turning myself in is out of the question. My mother would kill me. I am willing to go to the spirit realm, but if Lakree doesn't go too, he will be kicked out alone," Hila said, then stood up and sighed. "I'll keep at it."

She simulated elemental mage drills, but instead of switching between elements in rapid succession, she shifted between varying levels of magical strength in wind spells. After a couple of hours, she managed to slide the table instead of lifting it but couldn't produce anything small enough that didn't blow Rye across the room. After two days, she managed to rustle Rye's clothes consistently without knocking him off his feet.

"Now, Lakree has two days to get his act together or we go to the spirit realm," Hila said.

"But at least we will be able to contact Juli no matter what," Rye said.

The next day, when Rye woke, Hila and Lakree were gone. He found Lakree grunting as he pressed his hands against the front door to the Medina. The door was primarily gigastone, but there were a few spots of silver. Inside the rock were metal gears that controlled it. After a few seconds, he relaxed his tensed arms and kicked the door. "I hate magic," he said.

"No, you don't," Hila said. She sat cross-legged on the ground, reading a book. It was about the king regent before he was put on the throne. He had directed the construction of safe paths between the cities, which notified the Guard when wanted criminals used them. Luckily, Rye had guessed the danger of those roads. "Welcome to what it feels like to fail at something."

"Maybe if my life depended on it, I could push through gigastone again," Lakree said.

Hila nodded. "Yeah, we were in danger when you matter shifted into the Castle."

Intention was a part of magic. Spell words were just syllables strung together without it. The mindset of the caster shaped the spell. "But the second time through gigastone?" Rye said.

Lakree scratched his head. "Slithlor signed our draft orders. I would not bet my life on him."

"There is no higher intention than survival," Rye said. It was a reflex, free of thought. The body reacted in ways the mind didn't want to consider. Survival was too primal and selfish for the mind to handle those decisions gracefully. But Lakree's instincts were still misplaced. The draft didn't equal death.

Hila reached underneath her shirt and pulled out a green stone necklace from Drime. "Matter shift this."

"No," Lakree said, shaking a hand. "That's all you have from him. I might destroy it. The Correction Factor wouldn't protect an object."

Hila extended her hand again. "Your life will be in danger if you do."

"I am struggling to recreate what I did before," he said. "I know to target the Calif region on purpose this time, but I don't know which sections exactly nor how to reproduce the p-band responses."

"If you went to the spirit realm, you might discover how to do it," Rye said. "My morphs improved after my trip."

"Sorcery is about rules. I have to change the correct ones in the correct order," Lakree said.

Rye smirked. He had said the same thing to Dre about animalism. It was true, but it wasn't the whole truth. Once, his father stayed in the form of a feline for several weeks. When he had said it helped to think about how he was a cat versus running through a list of details that described a cat, Rye hadn't understood, but now he did. It was a counter-intuitive approach to magic, but it helped Rye morph into a tipit in under a minute. This likely explained why people outside Lynit couldn't guess their way through Lynitian magic. They didn't know what it felt like. First, there was the technical foundation of the rules and methodologies, but afterward, it was a form of magical memory.

"Think of this as your Verbindous. If you show the Vous this, you will be a Vous," Hila said.

Lakree rubbed the back of his head, then took the necklace. He pressed it against the door, back tensed. He braced himself against the wall as if he were trying to physically press the necklace through the stone and metal. "Scard pert invid craimum ordum sansi frasit vidid manpri crip." A black dust flickered around his hand. The flecks thickened into beads and blended his hand with the black wall. Then, the mist pulsed. There was a rhythm to it, like a heartbeat. But each pulse contracted more than it expanded. It reminded Rye of when he landed in the Winder Plains and it seemed like a hand might burst through the mist to grab him. He could almost taste the man's hand he bit.

It took a day, but Lakree transported the necklace through the door.

"Initially, I tried complex variations of the spell and watched for subspace movements, but in the end, I didn't need any of that. I tapped into a burst of energy and used it as fuel. I pushed until the universe obeyed, but that isn't the Vous' way," he said as he wrung his hands. He wasn't as ecstatic as Rye.

"This is only the beginning," Rye said. "Let Chirchi take you to the spirit realm. Trust me."

"I need to think," Lakree said. "Casting a spell through gigastone with brute force is something only a spirit fiend could cause."

That night, Chirchi and the sorcerer showed up. Chirchi was dressed in clean clothes. Her hair was braided with beads mixed in. Either there was a hair shop in the Medina or she went above ground. The sorcerer wasn't in a Guard uniform but wore oversized clothes similar to what Urura wore; only the colors differed.

"Did you find out why Slithlor is after us?" Rye said. "The guards still haven't left." He handed the map to Chirchi, but she didn't take it.

"Is this yours?" The sorcerer said as she lifted Hila's necklace.

"Urura told you that if you left the Medina, you wouldn't be able to return."

"We didn't leave. I matter shifted that outside to test my magic," Lakree said.

Hila slapped her forehead. "Oh no, this means that if we did need to come back after contacting Juli, we couldn't anyway."

Lakree shook his head, mumbling something under his breath.

"Or were you leaving a clue for Slithlor?" the sorcerer said as she tossed the necklace at Lakree, though Hila was the one to snatch it out of the air.

"A clue to what?" Lakree said.

"There are only two options forward: either Lakree and Hila go to the spirit realm or leave the Medina now," the sorcerer said.

"Why is going to the spirit realm so important? You aren't simply trying to prove if I have a special ability because you know I do," Lakree said.

"In the spirit realm, Chirchi will check if your minds' were split," the sorcerer said. Rye's father had described the procedure before. A spy would be trained in the local customs and history of the target society, then have their Lynit memories suppressed so that they could play their part to perfection. It was a great way to infiltrate foreign cities.

"You think they are spies," Rye said. The Medina knew he was trustworthy since he had already been to the spirit realm.

"Your minds won't be able to condense if you have two completely different personalities," Chirchi said.

"You would let us leave even if you think we are spies?" Hila asked.

"We placed a marker in your memories the day you arrived. We would wipe memories from those days," Chirchi said.

"But then we wouldn't remember that the Guard is after us," Lakree said.

Chirchi didn't respond.

Rye bit his lip. Lakree could matter shift them out of the Medina to keep his memories intact, but that should be after they went to the spirit realm. He wasn't interested in understanding his magic flare-ups. His only weakness left was Juli. "Juli is the crux of your plan, but so far, she did the bare minimum to protect you," Rye said. "We don't know if she is alive or in Poli. But we don't need her if we figure out why the Guard is after us,"

Lakree tried to push a phantom dreadlock behind an ear. He stood quiet for what felt like minutes. "Chirchi, could you break a connection to a spirit fiend?"

"If there is a way, I'll find it in the spirit realm," Chirchi said.

"I was hoping that Juli could do it, but I realize now that I had based that on nothing," Lakree said. "We'll go. We need to know for sure what we are connected to."

"Good choice," the sorcerer said. She blinked. She likely had been prepared to counterspell Lakree.

"Have a seat," Chirchi said.

"I'm going too," Rye said.

Chirchi's voice guided Rye to the spirit realm. He arrived on a green hilly landscape that stretched to the horizon in all directions. There were a few large parks in Virt, but there was always a container or boundary for anything green. Real grass was wild and uneven; however, here, it was manicured. Each blade was the same length. A heatless dark blue sun floated in the sky. This realm was almost like a painting.

Two clouds, minds, floated next to Rye. One of them looked like a nexus of competing ideas. Its edges were jagged. The energy twisted and pulled itself apart. Other portions moved in different patterns. One side shrank and expanded in bursts. A stream of energy raced around the cloud, treading between the gaps in other areas. The center of it all was calm, however, as if oblivious to the chaos around it. It was like a hurricane.

The other cloud was almost the opposite. Each idea moved independently of the others in clean, straight lines, forming a grid. However, one glob floated around the periphery, looking for a way in. Now and then, it timed a jump and blended in with another process until it was detected and spit back out on the other side.

"That's Hila and Lakree," Chirchi said. Her hair was black again. Rye wondered if that was what her hair used to look like or if it was how she imagined herself. "And you are connected to them."

Two strings anchored to his chest connected Rye to the strange clouds. He touched one and Lakree's thoughts bombarded his mind. *The only time we were all in the same place as Slithlor was during the Castle tour. He must have used the device on us then, but how did Juli know that? Something doesn't add up.*

"Organize your mind," Chirchi said. "Think of a memory that makes you happy. When was the last time you experienced it? Remember that, concentrate on it."

The two clouds picked spots to condense around. Rye felt the memories through his connection. For Hila, it was the day she declared elemental magic. The deportation fear lifted off her when the blue, green, red, and white pin was fastened to her shirt. For Lakree, it was the day he met Rye. He was the first non-noble kid he'd ever had a conversation with. He was curious why they weren't as strong at magic. Instead of finding something wrong with Rye, he found a friend.

However, a spark of panic disrupted both clouds' condensation. Though Hila enjoyed being Lynitian, it was at the cost of her Ries' heritage. She already lost the ability to use shadow magic. She would forget the language next. Lakree's cousins were in noble schools training for their Verbindous and he would never make it to his. He would never be a Vous.

"Rye, you are feeding them spirit energy. They don't know how to handle it," Chirchi said.

The first time Lakree matter shifted, Rye was there. Hila killed the quitol because Rye needed her to. None of his friends' extraordinary moments happened when he wasn't around. "Did I send us to the throne room?" Rye said. It wasn't Lakree's determination alone.

"Relax or they won't be able to condense," Chirchi said. "You are sending them your thoughts, too."

"It's been me all along," he said. Their fear of dishonoring their families originated with Rye. He couldn't find anything extraordinary about his magic all this time because he had passed his strength on to his friends. The clouds pulsed with the revelation. He took a few steps back.

"What is fourteen divided by two plus one?" Chirchi said as he shook Rye. She yanked his face to hers. Her eyes weren't solid grey but had specks of black.

"Eight," Rye responded as his eyes drifted down to her lips, which were only a finger's width away. He hoped she wasn't going to kiss him.

"What shape has that many sides?"

"An octagon."

"What color do you imagine that shape to be?"

"Brown," Rye said, then shook his head. Her lips were brown. "Yellow, I mean."

She snapped three times. "What is the opposite of yellow?"

"Purple?"

She asked random questions until the clouds were calm. "They need to condense to confirm that they aren't spies. Guide them," she said.

"Think about the day Drime left for the draft," Rye said. It was the first shared memory that came to mind. "He had received his orders two weeks before, but we were still in disbelief. We walked him to the Castle. Some bystanders cheered him on, others protested. Drime didn't cry because he wasn't scared. He was excited. He wanted to join the Guard. When it was all over and everyone left, we stayed for a while longer on the bridge. That's when we made our pact. We said we would protect each other because we couldn't depend on the adults anymore. We are forever bound by that."

The clouds froze. Slowly, piece by piece, the energies condensed around the memory. Lakree and Hila still wanted Rye's help, even if he was the reason they were on the run.

"Whoa," Hila said once her mind had solid form. The blue string attached to her chest pulsed, sending ripples throughout her body.

Lakree condensed. "Did we pass your spy test?" he said.

Chirchi nodded but was looking off into the distance. "Yes, let's go. We've attracted unwanted attention," she said.

A moment later, pressure hit Rye. It covered the side of his head to his calves. A brown spirit fiend stood at the top of another hill. Its round head sat on a long, thin neck and wide bottom—like an uneven hourglass. Its black eyes took up most of its face. Then, it tilted forward and rolled down the hill.

"What is that?" Hila said.

The thing bumped and bounced like a ball.

"When I said that I run from the spirit fiends that talk, I was referring to that one. It was at the Battle of Ki. It's dangerous."

The creature stopped, then pushed itself back on its fat legs. Its steps were too slow to be frightening by real-world standards. But the pressure increased as it approached. It wasn't a physical force but a direct affront on Rye's mind. This creature represented an idea that threatened to rip Rye apart, but it held him with its gaze. Rye's instincts warned him to flee. This must have been what his father felt during the Battle of Ki. And the thought was enough reason for Rye not to run. He had to master his instincts. This was an opportunity to get some answers.

"Leave, Rye." Chirchi's body struggled against the force. She flickered, warped. Lakree and Hila were already gone. "This trip over, I measured the energy you are receiving. It has to be from a spirit fiend, but this one isn't it. Yours is in another realm." Then she evaporated away.

When the creature was an arm's length away, Rye said, "Did you kill my father?" It placed a slender hand on his head, waiting for permission to enter his mind. He imagined an opened door.

Rye's life played back like a moving picture, focusing on his father. Their moments together were a collection of game nights, conversations around the dinner table, and strolls through the city. His father was playful, strong, and funny. The stories of his adventures as a guard were only a fraction of him, but they took up the most space in Rye's mind.

His father's funeral was dim. Rye didn't revisit that memory often. There was sadness and confusion there. An elite with nearly fifteen years of service had died, but only Slithlor, the king regent, and a handful of guards came to say goodbye.

"We don't have death here, but I understand what it means now," it said.

Scenes of Nintur and the Battle of Ki flashed. Buildings burned. Screams filled the air. Uniformed men and women flung colorful lines of magic, but a brown hand knocked the spells away. The spirit fiend called itself Rombinanandi and this was its memory. It strolled down crumbling streets. It tried to speak to the people it met, but the ones it touched burst as energy flooded their bodies. Civilians fled, and guards did, too. The terror in their eyes was all the same. Their magic couldn't save them, which was something that Lynitians didn't understand. The impossible roamed.

Then Rye's father came into view. He was below on the ground amid broken slabs of stone and bent metal rebar that looked like twisted fingers. He was dressed in his green and white Guard uniform. His brown hair was matted with blood and debris. He was crying, gripping the sides of his head. And the terror was in his eyes, too.

It was the opposite of his serene smile when he left for work that morning. Rye wasn't even dressed yet and his mother and brother were already gone. It was the first time Rye got himself ready for school. He practically pushed his father out the door because he was excited about the responsibility. Rye did manage to get to school on time that day, but when he came home, his father wasn't there to congratulate him.

"Be strong, Barin," Slithlor said. He stepped around a corner, a shiny orb floating beside him on a puff of purple energy. His robes were drenched in red. "You are the first non-noble elite. You must be part of Lynit's future and sticking with me, though you are scared, is what it takes."

Then Rye's father turned and ran. Slithlor chased after him. Rigmen trailed after them with his head lowered. The scene ended as Rombinanandi moved away.

"We did kill in your world, but none of us killed your father," it said.

Rye dropped to his knees. "He fled." He had hoped his father was killed by the same spirit fiend that killed King Kertic or was on an honorable mission with Juli, but the Guard was right. He didn't die defending the king. And he likely didn't die at the hands of a stray Sewitian soldier. Sewit released the spirit fiends as a last resort. Most of their army had been defeated or captured already.

"Is Alaandre coming here?" Rombinanandi said.

Rye didn't shrug until the spirit fiend asked again.

Rombinanandi turned around, beginning an awkward climb back up the hill. It had no idea the type of news it dropped on Rye. They didn't have families in the spirit realm and didn't know what it was like to be happy, ashamed, and disappointed all at once. Rye's father was possibly still alive and hiding from his family and there was oddly a last lesson in that fact. It was what Rye had said to Hila when they were hiding in the bar: Don't do anything you can't apologize for later. His father couldn't apologize for abandoning his post or his family. No words were enough.

At the top, the spirit fiend paused. "To find Tenaju, you must go to the sky." Then, it slipped out of view.

Chapter 23 - Dre

Streaks of purple and white moved across the night sky. A group of psychics and wizards traversed the city from above. Dre hadn't seen that since before the draft. Adults had reduced their magic usage in public either in solidarity with children or not to tempt them. The Co Park protest still raged as a faint hum in the distance, even at this late hour. The Castle was dark, save for a few windows that shined light from the inside and the illuminated Lynitian symbol at the top.

The stone bridge over the waterless moat was quiet. No one crossed. Only two guards stood watch at the bridge's edge. The Castle almost looked like an ordinary fortress behind them but for the faint shimmer of a shield that covered the entire structure. In daylight, this spell that detected magic was invisible.

"You will only have three minutes to get to the bridge as the guards walk back to the Castle's entrance," Ser said. She wasn't in her uniform anymore. She wore a matching black and grey shirt and pants, the same as Grintinari and Rish. Their outfits seemed to be Guard stealth-wear, but with Rish's large size, Dre doubted that he was the least bit stealthy unless he was in creature form. Even in the dimly lit alleyway they hid in, his figure loomed.

Dre, Alaan, and their parents wore their regular clothes. They hadn't returned home after their thwarted escape because the paparazzi had discovered the alley behind their house. Once they did return, they wouldn't be able to leave again without being followed.

"That's not enough time?" Alaan said. The bridge was about fifty feet away and they had to reach it without making any noise on this quiet street. If they were caught, the guards would likely only ask for autographs, but this chance run-in with the Poli Twins would make the news. They wouldn't get in trouble, but the mission would be a failure.

"You don't have to cross the bridge in that time. You just have to get underneath it and out of sight. Then you'll have forty minutes to scale the Castle and paint the eclipse while your parents spread out, dropping piles of the pins," Ser said.

Dre adjusted one of the straps on his bag. Earlier that day, he had carried essentials for an escape out of Lynit; now, he carried a bucket of paint and brushes. The Castle was at least one hundred feet tall. He was confident in his ability to climb, but he assumed he would have more time. "If the guard catches us up there, we could get arrested. Even if people still find the pins, they won't know what they are for," he said.

Dre and Alaan landed on the eclipse as their new brand logo years ago because it emphasized what they could do instead of their birth. But Dre liked the astronomical meaning even more. An eclipse only existed because of perspective; otherwise, it was just a star and moon in space. Painting it over the Lynitian symbol was the statement to give the pins significance beyond the Poli Twin brand. There was a saying in the tournament fighting circuit, "For every combatant, there were one hundred who weren't good enough to qualify." Dre bet that the pins would lower the barrier of entry into protesting. It was a way to visibly support the twins' cause without having to skip work or say a word.

"It will be seen as Yordin merchandise, which would still work in our favor," Rish said.

"No, only to nobles is everything black and white Yordin," Alaan said. "However, if we are caught painting it, Homin will think we are working against him by impersonating the Yordin. He will pull their support and we would likely lose the Finrar, which is one noble family down too many."

To force the court case on the right to practice magic before the council and king regent, Homin and the other nobles needed to believe that someone else painted the eclipse. The families who already supported the twins wouldn't retract it because of some vandal, but it could be enough to scare Victoria Finrar from joining their side.

"If we caused a distraction, would that give us more time?" Dre said.

"To get Castle guards to break from their routine, there would have to be an attack on Lynit. And in that case, every guard would be on alert," Ser said.

"So that's a no," Dre said. Ser nodded.

"And I still don't like splitting up," Dad said.

"This isn't espionage, but we must take similar care," Rish said. "The more of us who move together, the more likely we will get caught."

"And I don't have confidence in your ability to scale the Castle without using magic," Ser said, looking down at his round stomach.

Dad crossed his arms.

"I won't let the boys out of my sight," Grintinari said, placing a hand on Dre and Alaan.

"Why can't you do this without us?" Mommy said.

"You are attempting to aggravate social unrest. We are elites. We can't take part in that. But, we can protect a family that is critical to our investigation," Ser said.

Mommy shifted her sack of pins to the other shoulder, causing them to ting softly against each other. She massaged her neck. "After this court case, will you leave us alone?"

Ser sighed. "At that point, this situation will be in the council's and king regent's hands," she said, turning over a palm for each entity. "And we will follow whatever orders they give us."

"So that's a no," Mommy said. Ser responded with a shrug.

Dad pressed his lips tight. "And if you don't get the court case?"

"You won't be able to leave Poli until we find Lakree, Hila, and Rye," Ser said, which meant that the elites would likely force Dre and Alaan to take them to the Medina.

"We'll get the court case," Alaan said. "Victoria Finrar won't want to work with us after a million people show that they blame nobles for the mandatory service programs."

It only took the twins staying in the house to tank the draft and running from guards to start a riot. Painting an eclipse over the symbol of Lynit, which was really the symbol of nobility, would push tensions to the next level.

"Our former PR team will recognize the eclipse pins as ours, but they are loyal. The public won't know we did it, but they will know that it represents us. We saw a new mural of us as towers in Poli's skyline. This could be viewed as a response, a call to rally behind our fight for the right to practice magic," Dre said.

Dad hugged Alaan, then Dre. "Be careful," he said. Mommy repeated it.

Ser, Rish, and Dre's parents left.

Dre, Alaan, and Grintinari approached the bridge while sticking to the shadows. One guard was a sorcerer in black and gold, and the other a protector in red and blue. The sorcerer's eyes roamed as she recounted her night at a bar in Virt.

"You would have thought it was a noble bar. No one knows how to have any fun in that city," she said.

"I've only been to Virt for work, but that was enough. The guards there are so proper. It was like every conversation was a Verbindous test. To make it to captain in Virt, you have to be noble or sound like one," the protector said. They both shuddered. The protector tossed his head towards the Castle, then they both headed towards it.

After Grintinari's signal, he, Dre, and Alaan crept the last twenty feet to the bridge. Dre imagined what his life could have been like as a thief. Most, if not all, of Lynitian security was based on magic. He could take whatever he wanted if he scaled museums or noble homes. All he would have to do was trip the alarms with magic on his way out. The victims would focus on improving their spells instead of locking their balcony windows. Infamy was fame's evil twin. And it was all that Dre could have if Alaan continued on his destructive path of stopping their energies from joining.

A thin ladder ran down the side of the bridge to a grated platform underneath. Carefully, he followed Grintinari down. Dre's paint cans bounced, hitting him in the ribs, but he clenched his teeth to suppress a noise. He then stepped on Grintinari's hand and received a glare. However, the three made it to the platform without alerting anyone. The walkway was almost pitch black, save for the glow of the protection shield around the Castle that looked like a ghostly wall. Dre held onto the safety rails until he reached the Castle's white stone outer wall. Grintinari pointed at a ledge around the perimeter of the building. The three climbed over the railings.

The stone slabs up the side of the Castle were like a ladder. There was enough space between slabs for a hand or foot. He climbed with ease thanks to training under the pressure of dark energy. His legs were strong. Alaan managed without much trouble. Grintinari, however, struggled. His hands slipped a few times, but he didn't fall and no one was alerted by his grunts.

When Dre reached the top, the shape of the Castle was more pronounced. The building was six-sided. The Guard didn't waste an opportunity to pay homage to the six noble families. Dre figured that if he looked hard enough, he would find some structural element representing the Kertics. Maybe it was the waterless moat, the seventh ring to contain nobility.

"Have you ever climbed up the Castle before?" Alaan said.

"Without magic? No, but a few of my friends from my Verbindous year have," Grintinari said.

"Rebellious teens," Dre said, laughing.

The three of them crossed to the front of the Castle. Dre leaned over the edge. The giant Lynitian symbol was below and as tall as him. About five feet further down was the throne room skylight, which illuminated it and was the only place to stand.

"Uhh..." Dre said as he took off his sack. "You'll have to pass the bags down to us."

"Stand on the beams between the windows. The glass isn't sturdy enough to support your weight," Grintinari said. Dre imagined a noble teen crashing down on King Kertic during a meeting.

Alaan pulled a rope out of his bag and looped it around his waist. Dre tied the other end around himself. He hopped up on the edge of the building. When Alaan was ready, he leaned back. He walked backward down the wall. He carefully balanced his feet in a wide stance across the two beams the skylight windows were anchored two.

Dre lifted his hands. Alaan crawled over the edge. He stretched down until his feet touched Dre. Dre's feet wanted to spread onto the glass as he took on Alaan's weight, but Dre held his position.

"Instead of me coming down all the way and then lifting you to paint, I should just paint," Alaan said.

"I am not sure if I can hold you that long. You're the best base," Dre said.

"Supporting your weight on your hands is the same as supporting me and your legs are stronger than mine," Alaan said.

"Fine," Dre said.

Grintinari passed the paint bag down to Alaan.

Dre watched as his brother smeared black over the carved circles until a splash hit his face. He dropped his head, which caused him to wobble a bit. More paint splattered on his head.

"Stay still," Alaan said.

"Just hurry up," Dre said.

Below, the throne chair was visible on the back wall of the throne room. Though the Castles in the other cities were replicas of the one in Virt, the throne chairs weren't the same. The replica chairs were made of materials that represented the city. The Poli one was made of gigastone, the only material more expensive than wood.

A long shadow moved across the throne room floor, followed by the bald figure in purple robes that caused it. Behind them, six smaller people, children most likely, scurried to keep up. These children weren't dressed in uniform; they wore varied colors and styles. This was an odd vantage point, but the guard looked like Slithlor. He led the children to a side wall. A narrow slit opened as he approached. It was a hidden passage, likely an emergency escape for the royal family. Each child turned sideways to fit in.

From the little Dre learned about the inner workings of the draft from Tess, he knew that this wasn't it. There wasn't a lesson on sneaking around the Castle in the dead of night. Children in that program weren't even allowed in the main areas. They were relegated to barracks. "Those are the kids Slithlor kidnapped," Dre said. Urura had mentioned six names and there were six with Slithlor. If anyone was connected to spirit fiends, it was those children. But the question in the back of Dre's mind was whether Slithlor was after him because of his wizardry ability or because he was potentially connected to a spirit fiend.

"What?" Alaan said as his weight shifted, causing the paint can to rattle. Dre's arms wobbled. He tried to reassert his balance, but it was too late. The paint can fell. It hit Dre on the shoulder, covering his arm in black, before banging against the window. One of the panes was blotted out. Slithlor looked up.

It was like when Dre was younger and Slithlor threatened him. Even though Dre was nearly two years older and a foot taller since then, he felt just as small and exposed. He narrowed his eyes to slits, hoping his dark skin and grey clothes would blend him in with the night sky. It was possible that travelers passing overhead accidentally dropped things all the time and that Slithlor was only startled. In a few seconds, he would return to his devious work.

The last kid through the hidden passage looked up too. His eyebrows were thin, almost invisible on his face. At that distance, Dre couldn't spot much else about the boy's face, but Dre did recognize a quick hand signal from him. It was three fingers on one hand sitting on top of four fingers pointing down. It represented a quitol and was one of Stavender's favorite taunts when they were classmates.

"They recognized me," Dre said.

Alaan scrambled to reach and climb back up, but Dre lowered him instead. There was no point in running now. Dre had seen something he wasn't supposed to see and Slithlor would not let that slide. Even a matter shift from Grintinari wouldn't save them. Slithlor could force all of the Guard to hunt them.

Purple energy sprouted around Slithlor, first as a halo before expanding into a tempest. He shot up to the window, his stern face growing bigger. Two slivers of purple streamed around the edges of the window frame, one touching Dre and the other Alaan. Slithlor's voice echoed in Dre's mind, *Why are you working for Juli?*

The window rattled. Dust sifted onto Slithlor when a latch clicked and the window swung open. Slithlor floated up to eye level. He wasn't smiling. Dre caught himself before thinking back at Slithlor. He didn't know if he could mask his intentions that way. Instead, he imagined a door on his forehead and shut it.

"We aren't working for anyone," Alaan said.

Slithlor's mental energy spread across stone, brushed over the paint buckets, then finally skimmed the Lynitian symbol. Dre hoped that Grintinari had backed away.

I don't believe you met Lakree, Hila, and Rye by accident, Slithlor said, his voice penetrating through Dre's defenses. An image popped into Dre's mind. It was a woman with dreads in protector robes with an "E" on her chest. A slight smirk crept up the side of her face. *Have you seen this woman?*

Dre didn't recognize her face but knew that Lakree's aunt was a previous elite protector. She predicted that the Guard would go after her nephew before the draft started.

"No," Dre and Alaan answered. Dre made sure not to look at his brother. He didn't want Slithlor to read anything in their exchange.

But, you know who she is. This woman is wanted for treason. If you don't tell me everything you know about her, I will arrest you and force the information out.

Though Slithlor continued to push words into Dre's mind, he didn't attempt to pull anything out, which would have caused Dre to collapse in pain. This must be the legal line Slithlor didn't want to cross. Dre and Alaan were minors, after all. But, if they were connected to the treason charge, Dre's secrets wouldn't be safe. For treason, he would be executed. The Guard wouldn't hesitate to bust open his mind for information beforehand.

"Lakree said that he was looking for her. She predicted that the Guard would come for him," Dre said before Alaan could speak. This wasn't a time to lie. Psychics were trained to detect deception even without using magic. Navigating the truth was safer.

How?

"We don't know," Alaan said.

Does he know?

"I don't think so," Alaan said

Good. She isn't in the city yet, which means that the three are still in Poli, protected by the Medina, I assume.

Dre wrinkled his forehead. Slithlor was only one step away from deducing that the twins had been in the Medina and Dre couldn't deflect a direct question. "What's Midani?" he said. It wasn't lying to ask a question.

Slithlor squinted and didn't speak for a long pause. Dre flinched under his gaze because trying to project confidence would have been an obvious tell. Slithlor had all the power and Dre had to behave as such. Slithlor looked up at the partially covered Lynitian symbol. He hummed as if carefully constructing his question. *Who put you up to this?*

"This was our idea," Dre said, puffing up his chest, letting a smidge of pride slip into his voice. "We will rally enough support to end mandatory service for all children."

My little anarchists, Slithlor said. *You helped Lakree, Hila, and Rye escape. You blamed nobles for something that wasn't their fault. Now, you deface their symbol. You are working for someone even if you don't know it.*

"We are not working for Homin Yordin either. He is the civilian liaison to the Guard. He is working for us," Dre said. Technically, they worked for the elites to expose Slithlor, though Dre wouldn't mention that. "There are kids who are losing their magic because they are afraid of being drafted and we are trying to stop that."

Slithlor's posture relaxed.

I don't want children to lose their magic. I created the draft so more children would be weaned off the Correction Factor. That dependence is why most don't make it into the Guard. Nobles could have addressed this before. I don't believe they invented a new education system in response to a failing draft. They might have been loading their children with years of knowledge for centuries.

They won't let us grow unless we force them.
"What do you want with us?" Dre said, adding some boyish innocence to his voice. On one level, it was the general question of why Slithlor had practically stalked the boys their whole lives. But at the moment, the answer would explain why Slithlor didn't reach for the glinting silver whistle around his neck. He hadn't called for help or alerted anyone to the irregularity. He didn't consider the twins a threat anymore.

If you join the draft willingly, that would improve morale. You aren't the only one with extraordinary magic. Two children died recently in magical accidents. If you are with me, I can help you. I have long hoped for great things from you and you continually surprise me. Together, we can shape Lynit for the better. You are the future.

This was likely the same sales pitch he gave to the children he was sneaking through the Castle. But if Slithlor's intentions were wholesome, he wouldn't have tried synchronized draft attempts on the twins, Lakree, Hila, and Rye. However, it was more apparent now that Slithlor was using the draft to further a goal beyond rebuilding the Guard.

"Give us some time to think about it," Alaan said.

Boots scuffed below in the throne room, but thick purple energy blocked the view. "Slithlor, is that you? We detected mental energy outside the Castle?"

I could report what you are doing here, which would cause you trouble. But we are on the same side. We both want what's best for Lynit and I am worried that your next power surge could be your last.

Dre's first thought was that Slithlor believed that Lakree, Hila, Rye, Alaan, and he were connected to spirit fiends. However, it didn't explain why Slithlor charged Lakree, Hila, and Rye with treason but made the twins an offer for partnership. Slithlor's actions were driven by more than his general interest in extraordinary magic. He was reacting to Juli, who was thought to be dead until recently. Slithlor asked about her when he first saw the boys as if she was his primary concern. And if the boys had said they were working with her to paint over the Lynitian symbol, they might have been arrested. He was scared of her, as Lakree's father had said.

Slithlor lowered through the cloud that supported him. "Yes, it is me. You may return to your posts."

"Understood," the guard said, then boots stopped away.

I'll give you a day to decide, Slithlor said in Dre's mind as his lingering mental energy closed the window shut. Slithlor landed on the ground, then walked out of sight.

Dre and Alaan didn't speak as they finished painting the eclipse. They climbed back to the roof and Grintinari signaled for them to remain quiet as they crept back home. In the house, Grintinari warded the place against eavesdroppers. Then the twins told him everything that Slithlor said.

"We were searching for the children that Slithlor took out of the draft and now we know where to look. If they are connected to spirit fiends, that will be all the evidence we need," Grintinari said.

That night, Dre dreamed of a panel of judges sitting in a raised booth. They each wore the same puffy white robe that obscured the shapes of their bodies. Their faces were hidden behind colored metal masks representing the noble families they came from: black and gold for Vous, purple for Palow, blue and red for Pol, green and white for Finrar, red, white, blue, and green for Cast, and black and white for Yordin. The council, old and frail nobles, were the most powerful people in Lynit. Had they so chosen, they could have defeated King Kertic when he was alive.

Across from them on a small platform, Alaan hunched. Thick purple chains bound to his wrists and ankles. He was on trial.

Dre scanned the room for escape routes, but there were no doors. He was seated in the audience with people who didn't hide their grins. He shifted in his chair and rubbed his suspenders.

"Alaan Word, you have been charged with treason," Council Member Vous said. "The bodies have been buried, the buildings rebuilt, but the memory of the Battle of Ki is alive in the minds of all Lynitians. The draft was created to prepare a new army to defend Lynit from foreign invaders, but you disrupted that. You left us ill-equipped and now I am dead. The Vous find you guilty." He carefully lifted his gloved hand to his black and gold mask. It split down the middle and fell away. The hard-faced person peering down at Alaan with scorn wasn't the woman who sat on the council. He was a copy of Dre.

Alaan wrestled with his chains and the sound echoed in the chamber. "I'm sorry. I'm sorry."

The audience cheered.

Dre checked his hands and body. He was still in the audience, still himself. The faces of the people next to him weren't as clear anymore. They had eyes and mouths, but they were more like quick sketches. Dre stuck his hand out in front of a snarling woman, but she didn't react. She didn't notice him. She wouldn't look away. Dre sighed. He wasn't dreaming alone. Alaan was dreaming with him.

"Our bond was stronger than stone, but you introduced a crack, a flaw. Now, there is a chasm. When I needed you most, you were distracted and now I am dead. The Cast find you guilty," Council Member Cast said, removing her multicolored mask and revealing another Dre.

Alaan shook his head. "I didn't mean for this to happen."

"We were each other's protection. When you were weak, I was your shield. When you were too tired to speak, I spoke for you. But you cannot speak for me anymore. You don't know how to speak for me because you do not know me. You did not care for me and now I am dead. The Pol find you guilty of treason," the judge said. He removed the mask. He was a third copy of Dre.

The real Dre leaned back in his seat, crossing his arm. It was true. The imbalance between Alaan and him was wrong. He didn't know Alaan like he used to. Over the years, Alaan changed from shy to social, from compromising to argumentative. Dre adapted, but Alaan didn't adapt to Dre, who was changing in his own ways, and Alaan knew it.

"The world survives on change. It is how we grow, learn, and become more. But, underneath it all, there was a constant connection between us. Its form bent and stretched but never broke. We were free to be who we wanted to be. For that, the Finrar find you innocent," the judge said, then removed the green and white mask. However, this time, it wasn't Dre. It was Tess. Her purple hair puffed out around her.

The crowd booed. They stood on their seats and shouted. A few leaped to the floor and charged at Alaan. They surrounded him, clawing at his feet.

"Now that's too far," Dre said as he jumped down. He pushed his way to the front. He climbed onto the platform with Alaan, then kicked back anyone who got too close. This made them angrier.

A whack pierced through the noise. The dream people screamed. Dark cracks stretched across the white ceiling. They grew like veins, pulsating. Then the ceiling broke. Chucks of stone fell. The screams didn't fade as people were hit. They grew louder, building in pitch into a cacophony. Dre tugged at Alaan's chains, but they didn't budge.

A voice clear over the terror said, "From birth, I studied you. You are my greatest creation. You cannot hide from me. I will capture you, and together, we will complete our mission, the destruction of Lynit. I find your mission of treason complete." Council Member

Palow spoke directly into their minds. Purple energy surrounded their face and lifted the mask. Slithlor smiled the same smile he gave when he'd threatened Alaan and Dre in the Castle.

"It's a dream, Alaan," Dre said. "We are dreaming."

Alaan's gaze was slow, but he looked at Dre for the first time. Then, the world froze and fell silent. "Dre? Is that you?"

"The real me," Dre said. He hugged him.

Alaan sighed and his chains fell away. "Thank you." He jumped to the ground. He stepped over rumble and ducked around frozen outstretched limbs. "This is a weird dream. You, Tess, and Slithlor, as the council, would make for wild laws." Alaan laughed.

Dre didn't laugh. He marked that Alaan avoided the obvious. "Why did you stop our magic from joining?"

Alaan paused for several seconds. "I wanted you to say no when I offered to help Tess."

"I said no."

"But then you agreed with me anyway."

"It was important to you. I accepted it."

"You didn't have to. We didn't have to agree."

"We are barely surviving a conspiracy. We can't afford to be physically separated, let alone magically and mentally."

"Dre, I like that we are in sync and work well together, but sometimes I feel like that is all you want us to be. You want us to be one person, like when we were kids and pretended to be. But I am not half a person and you aren't either."

Dre hopped down from the pedestal. "We are twins. We were one once. Our magic comes from one source in the spirit realm. We aren't one anymore, but that means working hard to compensate. Sometimes, I have to concede on things that I don't like, but I am okay with that. You just have to be ready to reciprocate. You are the one having a nightmare about betraying me. Don't pretend you don't know that you did something wrong."

A tingle surged through Dre. It was a soft pull that grew into a yank. He squared his feet and braced against it. Alaan's face changed. He felt it, too. One judge was left out of the six, but their mask was different. It wasn't the Yordin colors. It was brown, and there were deep black pools where the eyes should have been. Fur lined the edges, and slender lips were painted on the surface.

"That's not a mask," Alaan said.

It smiled and the pull on Dre intensified. It called to him like it did at Sepotine and in the spirit realm.

"I, Rombinanandi, find Alaandre guilty of capturing my interest," it said, its voice airy. It was the brown dot moving across the landscape in the portal at Sepotine. It was the brown creature from their first dream together, but now it was as clear as Dre and Alaan.

"What are you?" Dre said.

"I am a lot of things. Once, I was Fury, then later Mischief. I traveled to all the spirit realms as Explorer. Sometimes, I return to old things, back to passions I had millennia ago, and sometimes, I come across something new and follow it. You have been calling me for a while and I initially ignored it. I didn't know where you were and didn't believe it was worth the effort.

"But you persisted, bombarded me with your thoughts until I found something I liked. I scoured my realm looking for you, but no one knew the way. However, you found me. Once, I saw you in the sky. Later, I felt you closer. Then you brought me here to this new place, an interesting place made by your combined minds," Rombinanandi said as its gaze moved across the courtroom. It leaned forward and licked the rail of the judge's box and the box vanished.

"Are you from the spirit realm?" Alaan asked.

It tilted its head until its eyes and mouth were inverted. "Of course," it said.

"Alaan, wake up now," Dre said. He closed his eyes and pulled on his mind, pulled up and away.

"Do not go," it said.

When Dre opened his eyes again, he was in his bed in his room. Sunlight washed the room in a soft orange glow. He sprung from his bed and flung open his door. He reached across the hall for Alaan's door, but it swung inward. Alaan stood in his room, eyes wide.

"We are connected to a spirit fiend," they said in unison, then covered their mouths. It was the source of their new strength and the destination of the connection Chirchi saw in the spirit realm. Going there must have strengthened the link.

Alaan looked towards the front of the house. Grintinari was stationed outside. "Slithlor knows, but he is keeping it a secret," he whispered. If another nation found out, it would plunge Lynit into war. "It said that we brought it to a place made of our combined minds. We can't sleep at the same time anymore."

Dre braced himself against his doorframe. The court case against Slithlor wouldn't matter if the elites found out. Dre and Alaan were a threat to Lynit's safety on their own. The Guard wouldn't hesitate to kill them. And, it was odd that Stavender made the insulting hand gesture when the twins hadn't seen him in years. But if Slithlor were talking about the boys' similar connection to spirit fiends, they would have been at the top of Stavender's mind. "Slithlor has plans for us and I don't like it."

Chapter 24 - Dre

"The protests have devolved into a riot," Victoria Finrar said when she arrived at Dre's house. She wore thin sunglasses, a simple white crop top with a low neckline and a white fur coat. She was flanked by two assistants who were also in white. They were likely nobles, too, but didn't have on identifying colors.

Instead of jumping up to greet her, Dre checked the clock. He slumped in his chair. His eyes burned, but he kept them open. Alaan was supposed to be awake by now. If he didn't come out of his room in the next ten minutes, Dre would throw water on him. Resting in alternating shifts sucked. However, Dre wouldn't be able to relax enough to sleep anyway. Slithlor's vague threat still played in his mind. Slithlor might only leak to the press who drew the eclipse or he might redouble his efforts to kidnap the twins. Ser was in the Castle snooping around for the missing draftees, but if she didn't find them in the next sixteen hours, Slithlor would attack, one way or another, because Dre and Alaan would not join the draft voluntarily.

"They think that we run the place. I can't tell if they are blaming the Yordin for the draft or if wearing the pins is a way to persuade us to end it," Homin said.

"Neither," Victoria said. "Nobles have tried many times to

introduce family colors into civilian styles, but it never worked. People actively refused to wear them. Though they respect us, they know they are not one of us. However, they wear black and white pins to represent the Poli Twins."

Homin shook his head. "People have been trained since birth to recognize six color combinations. Whether consciously or not, everyone will see Yordin in that symbol."

Dre's parents brought out the pastries they had been baking all night. They invited Grintinari in for a snack. He was the only one who was sleep-deprived but didn't look haggard. He explained his presence as added security for the twins. Homin and Victoria accepted it without comment. Grintinari went into the kitchen.

"It's not about the colors," Dre said. "It is an eclipse. It's a symbol of our magic joining."

"Ohhhhhhhh," Homin said.

"People are showing their support for the Poli Twins to end the draft," Victoria said.

"So the ransacked homes of guards who work in the draft are because of the Poli Twins?" Homin said, turning to Dre.

"I wasn't the one that gave the impromptu speech yesterday," Dre said, shrinking deeper into his seat.

"The eclipse itself seems simple on the surface, but painted over Lynit's symbol, it becomes a statement. It implies that the Poli Twins are so famous or powerful that they eclipse nobility. They are saying that our time is over and my concern is that people have accepted this too easily. It means that an underlying distrust of, or at best, an indifference towards the nobility has always been present. We won't be able to stop the riots as easily as we thought," she said.

"You don't think the pins were printed overnight?" Homin said.

Victoria shrugged. "Only three manufacturers in the city could produce them so quickly. I have sent people to investigate."

All Poli Twins' merchandise was produced by the same

manufacturer and the owner promoted that in their advertising. Fortunately, that shop wasn't one of the big three. However, Victoria would still have her answer about the pins being created in advance. And now, Dre wasn't sure he didn't need her help. The elites' plan to expose Slithlor hinged on finding evidence against him. The council could interrogate every guard, but if Slithlor were the only one who knew his plot, it wouldn't help. Therefore, the council would need those children.

In addition, Slithlor wasn't concerned that the twins saw Stavender, which meant that he might not be afraid of getting caught. If Slithlor weren't found guilty of anything illegal, then the draft would continue. And when another kid used an extraordinary spell, Slithlor had a legal right to collect him.

"What if we were the ones who put up the symbol?" Dre said as he sat up in his chair. Ceramics clattered in the kitchen. Grintinari stepped back into the room. Usually, his gaze danced around the room as he reviewed invisible rules, but now, it was locked onto Dre.

"What do you mean?" Homin said. His hand on the table was now a fist.

"I mean, let's not deny responsibility. That way, we control the narrative."

"That's exactly why I still came," Victoria said. "People see you as a bridge to the nobility, which means you are also our bridge to them. You should wear the pins and walk back your statements blaming us. Show that you are working *with* us to end the draft. And you can wear *this* for all of your public magic practices." Her assistants pulled out two leather armor suits. The helmets were a dark turquoise and the rest of the suit darkened with a gradient. The hands and feet were completely black. The only thing distinguishing the two suits was a white "V" on the left breastplate of one and an "F" on the other. "This is our newest line of protective training gear.

The quitol hide dampens any magical attacks. The jaspin and spangot hairs identify your attunement to magic and allow you to access your magic without any distorted effects from the quitol hide."

"That's a little close to Finrar colors," Homin said.

"My brand color is white and green happens to be in this season. Everyone knows that I use all colors equally in my work. Though my name is Finrar, VF is not a Finrar brand," she said. "VF recognizes that magic is part of life but isn't life. Defining yourself by your magic or its colors only defines an imitation of yourself."

"The average person outside of Poli is not that enlightened. The rioting is all over Lynit. And the Yordin won't support any confusion about the twins' relationship to nobility," Homin said. Under different circumstances, Dre would have said, "And what relationship was that?" but kept quiet instead. Once the elites got what they wanted, Dre would leave Lynit. It wouldn't matter what people thought about him.

"We need to show that there is respect between the twins and the nobility," she said. "I am the best brand for that. VF is the only brand created by a noble that non-nobles will wear and it is exactly because I don't use color to represent a family. Besides, Finrar can't support your case if we don't stop the riots first."

Homin crossed his arms and leaned back. Dre pulled on the suit with an "F" on the breastplate, then reached out his awareness. The waves of wizardry pulsing against his skin were soft. The itch behind his ear, the call from the spirit fiend, was gone. He pulled a little energy. A stream of darkness floated above him. He stopped when his gear started to sizzle from holding back the additional energy that didn't belong to him.

"I like it," Dre said. Maybe this suit would block Rombinanandi from finding the twins when they dreamed together. If he and Alaan had worn this during the magic display at Co Park, they wouldn't have exploded off a chuck of gigastone in front of the whole city. He clamped his blue suspenders to the sides of his pants, then twirled around. "Now everyone will know it's me under this."

"It's going to look like Finrar's support was bought. The Pol and Vous are going to ask for favors too or possibly switch sides," Grintinari said as he stepped into the room. His hand was in his pocket, which faintly glowed. He was on a communication orb. "Wouldn't it be best to go before the council?"

"Nobles are the ones that need to adapt and this is our one chance to. These riots won't stop until that fear and anger are directed towards the right problem. It's an honor for the Finrar to be part of that redirection, but this is for the benefit of all. The other families will thank us," Victoria said.

"But if the case doesn't go before the council, people will think the mob forced the decision. The people will adapt, but it will be to believe that change comes from destruction," Grintinari said.

"We already know that the king regent supports keeping the draft. We would need all council members to overrule him. I don't like those odds." Homin said.

"If the Poli Twins wear this gear, but we still have a council vote and lose, then that will destroy my gear sales if not my brand. There's no need for me to take that risk. The rest of my family believes we must send this decision to the council on principle. If I can say nothing, we go to the council," Victoria said.

"Could we petition the Prince to get involved? We need a Kertic for this situation, not the Regent, who has been a close ally of Slithlor for years," Alaan said as he entered the room. He was dressed in pajamas and his fin hairstyle looked more like a strip of kinky twists. The bags underneath his eyes completed the too-exhausted-to-bathe-before-showing-up-to-a-meeting look.

Homin laughed. "He is training for his Verbindous. He probably doesn't even know there is a draft, let alone a riot."

"We can make him care," Alaan said. He took a seat at the table and grabbed a pastry. "Next year, when the Prince becomes king, Dre marries and convinces him to change the law."

Homin's eyes went wild. "The Kertics will marry into the Yordin this generation." He paused for a moment before looking back at Dre and Alaan.

"Try on the gear," Dre said, not bothering to tell Homin that Alaan was joking.

Alaan put on the "V" suit. He struggled with the helmet. His hair prevented it from sinking into place, but everything else fit him. He looked like a warrior supermodel.

"We should sleep in these," Alaan said.

"It is comfort and protection from unwanted energies," Dre said. If the sorcerer who disintegrated herself had access to quality gear like this, she might have been alive. There was no telling how many other children were connected to spirit fiends and teemed with excess energy. If Slithlor didn't catch them and did whatever he planned to do with them, they could die.

Alaan pulled a bit of energy. His eyes locked onto Dre's when his gear sizzled.

"What was that?" Victoria said. "Is the gear disrupting your connection to each other?"

"Oh, that's what that is," Alaan said but didn't look away from Dre.

"What if all the MMA participants wore this?" Dre said. Slithlor wouldn't know who to target with his draft mixups if the rest of the MMA kids didn't have accidents.

Alaan nodded his head slowly. He didn't seem to fully understand Dre's point but agreed anyway.

Homin hummed. "That way, it doesn't look purely like a Poli Twin endorsement. That could work."

Grintinari fidgeted. Dre's parents served more tea. They made eye contact to ask Dre what he was thinking, but he didn't answer.

"And we could have a noble kid assist each magic with their practice. That would show some solitary among the children," Victoria said.

"Only if the twins are the only ones to help the wizards," Homin said. Dre didn't bother to object.

Victoria instructed one of her assistants to get the measurements of the MMA participants.

"So we have the Finrar's support?" Homin said.

"It all depends on being able to stop the riots before we make a policy change," she said. "We have to change the people, not the environment."

"It has to work," Dre said. "We'll start spreading the rumor that we drew the eclipse. With that settled, I'll take my nap."

"Not yet. We have to design a Poli Twin invitation flyer for the MMA participants. It needs to look like your brand," Homin said.

"It is quite alright," Victoria said. "When I was young and starting VF, I had many sleepless nights. Sometimes, it was because I worked late; other times, it was because I was afraid I would fail. The consistent cost of building anything of value is sleep."

"Alaan can review that without me," Dre said.

"But Dre, if you are going to do this, you need it to happen tonight," Alaan said. He was right. The next day could be too late. If Slithlor announced that the twins drew the symbol, Victoria would take her armor back.

"Wait, why so soon? It will take time to do the tailoring," Victoria said.

"We won't have time to print flyers," Homin said.

"Okay, set the event for tonight then," Dre said as he rubbed his eyes. "Homin, go borrow that broadcast orb again."

Chapter 25 - Dre

Dre, Alaan, and Grintinari moved through a crowd of thousands along the edge of Co Park. Many had on eclipse pins and the ones who didn't had the symbol painted on their shirts or hats. "If you were going to arrest us, you would have done it already, right?" Dre said as he yawned. He received looks for his VF gear, but interest always returned to the park. The strobing magic cloud had doubled in just a day. Below, bodies nearly blotted out the black ground. Music echoed through the city. Everyone seemed to be dancing, even the ones using magic. It was not a riot as Victoria and Finrar had described. It was simply a party that nobles weren't invited to.

"If he did that, this would become a real mob," Alaan said.

"You're our best information source. We'll find new leads if I spend another day with you. Slithlor's interest in your wizardry ability causes him to be sloppy," Grintinari said as they approached the stairs down to the park. Grintinari hadn't questioned how the twins broke the gigastone, but if he spent a few more days around them, he would notice if they lived in magic-blocking gear. It wouldn't be long before he realized the children he sought were right next to him.

A man with puffy cheeks and a bald spot stepped before them. "Only children are allowed in until after the MMA practice," he said. With four noble families supporting this event, it wasn't hard to spread the word to all MMA children across the country and gather a crowd to witness the unity of nobles and the Poli Twins.

Dre pulled off his helmet, followed by his brother, which caused a ruckus.

"They're wearing eclipses too," someone shouted. A roar of encouragements and affirmations boomed.

"How did you get up there?" someone else said. Dre waved but didn't respond. He didn't fully admit to doing it because he could be charged with vandalism, but the crowd already knew.

"Oh, sorry, go ahead," the man yelled against the voices. He stepped aside.

"I'm with them," Grintinari said, not removing his helmet. If a reporter broadcasted that he followed the twins around, Slithlor would discover that the elites weren't following his orders. They would lose their only advantage.

Children parted for the boys and a synchronous chant of "No More nobles" sounded over the music. Many shook their pins to a solidifying beat.

Alaan held up a hand, which quieted people enough for him to start a new chant, "End the Draft," which picked up more steam. Instead of waving, Dre nodded at people, tilting his chin up. They were co-conspirators in ending the draft and thwarting Slithlor's plot. They deserved more than a wave.

Zalora, Gron, and the fourteen other kids from Dre's MMA cohort waited on a single gigasphere. Metal crates stamped "VF X Poli Twins" were stacked behind it. Dre and Alaan hopped onto the stage while Grintinari stayed behind.

"How have you been?" Dre said. Seven responses were blurted out at once, describing the riot or the eclipse symbol. "I mean your magic. Has it behaved oddly in any way?"

"Like how you were so weak that you didn't qualify for the draft, but now you can break gigastone?" Zalora said. "Or like the sorcerer who disintegrated herself."

That was precisely what Dre meant, and the clarification dampened the excitement of the others.

"Preferably neither," Alaan said.

"Well, I didn't matter shift into the throne room or anything," Gron said with a slight laugh.

"Is that why you are wearing this protective gear? Are we in danger?" Zalora said.

"No, no, no. Everything is fine. We have new noble friends who want to help end the draft. They want us to practice without fear of accidentally hurting ourselves," Alaan said, pointing to the crates.

"How can you be Finrar now if you are Yordin?" Gron said, flicking his eclipse pin. A few other kids nodded in agreement. Fortunately, Homin wasn't there since he would have passed out or said, "I told you."

"We aren't noble, Gron," Alaan said. "Dre and I invented our style of combat to become famous. Nobles are born into fame."

"But despite that difference, we are working together," Dre said, eying Alaan. The time for the old hard line on the difference between the twins and the nobility was over. Victoria made it clear that Finrar's support was contingent on improving public attitudes towards nobles.

"But everyone knew who you were the day you were born," Gron said.

"No, that's not the same thing," Alaan said. "I'll rephrase it. Nobles are born into respect. We had to earn ours."

Dre scratched his forehead. Alaan still cared about their fame, though he risked it by blocking their energies from joining. It didn't add up. Their skills of working together were strong, but if there wasn't magic to back it up, they were just carnival performers. His goal was the same as during the MMA exam: he wanted to prove that their fame wasn't only from their ability. If it were, then they were no different than the nobles. Then, they would be perpetuating the lie that magic and skill came from blood.

"How close are we to ending the draft?" The boy who was losing his magic said.

"Very close, Finrar is the last family we have left to convince," Dre said.

"So we have to promote their merchandise?" Zalora said.

"Basically," He cracked open a crate. "Now get suited up." Gron squealed.

Each kid pulled on the gear tailored to them and tested their magic. Dre listened for a sizzle. None of them had one.

"I bet that no one else in Lakree's, Hila's, and Rye's cohort is connected," Alaan said.

"Or what if the connection is too weak or faded away for everyone else?" Dre said.

"If so, do you think we could reverse our connection?"

"Chirchi might know," Dre said.

A mass of windblown children approached the stage. Most of them were shivering. Red dirt covered their thin clothing. They represented four cohorts, one from Virt and three from Wrisnt. All of them wore eclipse pins. Some kids thanked the twins for their first trip to Poli, others for the chance to meet celebrities.

"Thank you for protecting us from the draft mixup," a boy from Virt said. He was part of Lakree's, Hila's, and Rye's cohort.

"Now, let's protect all children from the draft," Alaan said as he directed them to the crates.

The last to arrive were five nobles, four kids and Jamil, who was nineteen. They were dressed in their family's colors, which the crowd noticed and heckled them for.

"We don't want you here," someone said. Everything after that was a threat.

The young nobles stood in power poses, but their eyes flitted about. They were uneasy.

"Before you ask, I couldn't let Tess one-up me, so I had to weasel my way into this," Jamil said. "This babyface got me past security to this hip teen club."

Dre hugged him, which paused the crowd's harassment.

"Who are they?" someone said.

The four noble kids representing animalism, protection, elemental magic, and psychic magic introduced themselves with elaborate descriptions of their skills. Dre hugged them, which extended the crowd's pause.

"There are nobles in the MMA?" Zalora said as she adjusted her helmet.

"They have tested out of both the draft and MMA, so they have the skills we need to pick up," Dre said.

"If they are here to train us, then where is the Yordin?" Zalora said.

Gron laughed as he patted her on the back. "Now, who's the naive one?"

About half of the MMA participants were dressed and separated into groups based on magic. Alaan shook his head when his eyes connected with Dre's. None of the kids tested so far were connected to spirit fiends.

Jamil leaned next to Dre's ear. "I have some good news that should alleviate at least one of your concerns," he said. "Your Verbindous hasn't happened yet. If it had, you would lose magic in one direction, but you broke gigastone. Though, it is odd that you are suddenly getting stronger."

"Is it reversible?" Dre said.

"Yeah, I initially worried that if you could break gigastone, you would overpower the Correction Factor. But you two already don't depend on that. You should be fine," Jamil said.

"But if we still wanted to reverse it?"

"Magical oddities are caused by energies in the spirit realm. There's no way to observe them directly," Jamil said.

"That's not true," Dre said. Chirchi could go to the spirit realm. Chirchi had identified the twins' altered contract. If she took them back again, maybe she could figure out how to break Rombinanandi's link. All he had to do was get away from Grintinari, who stood on the other side of the stage with his hand in his glowing pocket. He was likely reporting back that to Ser.

"No legal way," Jamil said. "Sepotine is still shut down because of the window."

"But nobles should know something extra about the spirit realm. Isn't that the basis of how you check for who belongs to which family?" Dre said.

"We only observe the manifestations of the spirit realm here," Jamil said.

Dre yawned and rubbed his eyes.

"Are you sleeping okay?" Jamil said.

Dre sighed. For half a second, he considered telling Jamil the whole truth but instead landed on sharing a truth. "I already knew that the Verbindous hadn't happened yet since Alaan admitted that he was blocking our energy from joining."

"Ooooh, I see," Jamil said, nodding. "Did he say why?"

"Sort of." Between sleeping in alternating shifts and Grintinari's constant supervision, Dre and Alaan didn't have much time alone.

"If you need someone to talk to, you know I am always here."

This was exactly what he said the day they broke up. He wanted to remain friends, but Lynit was attacked, and neither followed up. Dre still didn't know why Jamil had ended it. It was apparent now that Jamil still cared for Dre. Therefore, there was another reason why he wanted his distance. Possibly, it was the same reason why Alaan did what he did. It was like they both waited for Dre to discover his big flaw.

"Why did we break up?" Dre said.

Jamil's eyes widened. He fumbled with his hair, retying a knot. "You were twelve and I was fourteen, so there's that. I was the one who said the words, but I felt like you broke up with me. After Alaan ended it with Tess, we rarely spent time alone. We went to see the Poli Silvercats and you brought Alaan, who doesn't care about livit. You were only okay with us spending time alone when Alaan was with Tess."

"You sound just like Alaan, annoyed that we're twins," Dre said, rolling his eyes.

Jamil pressed his lips tight. "That's not fair."

Dre walked away. The last of the MMA suited up, but no gear sizzled when they used magic. None of them were connected to spirit fiends. Dre didn't have an exact number of other children he expected to find, but it was more than zero. He would have been less shocked if it had been all the MMA participants. At least once they end the draft, Slithlor won't be able to hide any other kids connected to spirit fiends. Dre could get them all to the Medina.

Dre joined the wizards, who grouped in a gigasphere with the animalists.

"Are we going to learn how to break gigastone?" the youngest wizard said.

Someone elbowed her. "No, and they aren't going to teach us how to join energies either."

Dre didn't want to teach them anything. Teaching meant showing and showing meant Grintinari would get curious about the sizzling. "Let's work on physical strength. Strong legs make for a strong wizard."

"Umm...can we work on theory instead?" one of the older boys from Wrinst said. His cohort was the oldest at six months old. Several wizards groaned. "Maybe theory is a bad word. It's more of an understanding shift. There's a document in the MMA material called 'Theoretical Approaches to Wizardry Energy: Breaking the Dichotomy.' The other wizards in my cohort failed the fourth exam because they didn't take this subject seriously."

"It has 'theoretical' in the title," a girl with auburn pigtails said.

"Theory sounds great," Dre said. He sat down and crossed his legs before anyone else could complain.

"I'll list three examples and you think about which relationships are most like the relationship between light and dark energy. Number one, we have water and seed. When they are put together, the seed grows and becomes a plant. This plant then produces more seeds. If you extract the water already in the plant, it dies. If you stop providing the plant with more water, it dies. Once the seed becomes a plant, it can never be a seed again.

"Number two, we have iron and carbon. They have different properties that make them useful in different scenarios. If the two are mixed in the correct conditions, they make steel, a stronger material. It is difficult to separate them, but it is possible to retrieve the original substances.

"And finally, we have the council and the Guard. The council is a panel of old nobles and the Guard is a deadly weapon. With only one, Lynit wouldn't survive."

"Light and dark are most like the third example," a girl with a heavy Wrinstian accent said. "The Kertics are like the wizard and the Guard and council are their energies."

Alaan said, "Wizardry isn't like any of them."

"Hmm?" Dre said, scratching his head. Theory was never a strength of his. He felt his way through wizardry. It was the only way he could react so fluidly in battle. If, in the middle of fights, he pondered whether an opponent's attack was a plant or steel, he wouldn't have won many fights. "Is it because none of the examples are opposites?"

"Light and dark energy aren't opposites," Alaan said.

"Yes, they are," Dre said. Opposition was the foundation of balance. One energy pulled the wizard into the sky while the other crushed them into the ground. Dark energy didn't run cold, but it was as solid as ice. To say that the two weren't opposites was to say that they didn't balance each other.

"Alaan is right. They aren't," the makeshift theory teacher said.

Dre closed his eyes. He didn't need to search for long. The MMA textbook presented itself, opening to the chapter "A New Dichotomy."

The moment before a wizard uses any magic, they have what we call Potential Energy. They are at their most flexible. They haven't made any decisions yet. The wizard can respond to a scenario without wasting energy. The first bits of energy summoned are the easiest and quickest, which makes them the most valuable. Once summoned, the energy transitions to Active Energy, which can be solidified or exploded as needed.

The more time energy spends in its Active form, the more likely it will be wasted as the wizard adjusts their plan. This energy requires balance, which constrains the wizard's actions. A wizard will release or attack with energy to recapture the benefits of weight or lift. Active form forces an endless cycle of rebalancing. By these definitions, Potential and Active energy are opposites.

"No, light and dark energy cancel each other out. That is the definition of 'opposite'. It's like positive five and negative five," Dre said.

"I had the same confusion, too. Your example isn't the same as light and dark energy. The definitions of those numbers are opposites. Light and dark energy don't technically cancel each other. They join and become inert. They become potential energy," he said

"Everyone talks about light and dark energy with predefined roles, but that is limiting," Alaan added, then hummed. "We never investigate the uses or value of one magic in certain situations because we were taught that the other magic was better in that scenario. For example, dark energy is said to be best for controlling what a person can see by creating walls that physically block their view and that an illusion has no practical applications in battle. But I have learned that with light energy alone, you can cause blind spots by causing your opponent to focus on that energy. People are afraid of a burn from light energy. They rarely let it out of their sight."

"Don't pretend this is the first time you considered this," Dre said. There were small comments over the past years as they practiced new routines. Sometimes, Dre agreed to include these counter-intuitive wizardry use cases because the goal was to surprise. They didn't add value on their own merits. Light energy couldn't replicate dark energy. Alaan couldn't snap his fingers like Dre and was sour about it. "The energies may not be opposites by definition, but they are still halves of something whole and the energies should accept that."

Alaan huffed. "Whenever there are two of something, people position them as incomplete or dependent on the other. Dark energy is happy being confined to half a bottle, but if you condense light energy, it explodes."

"You wouldn't have to pressure light energy if it didn't sneak around like a coward," Dre said.

"You lost me," someone said.

"Or is it that dark energy knows that it is nothing without light," Alaan said.

"What is that supposed to mean?" Dre said.

"It is not obvious, Poli Twin?" Alaan said.

It wasn't obvious. Without Alaan to share his balance, Dre couldn't even access his full strength, but the same was true for Alaan. But Dre brought a hand to his chest at the venom in Alaan's tone. Despite Alaan's life being in danger for his connection to a spirit fiend that sent him enough power to break gigastone, he still felt stunted because he couldn't use dark energy. And, worst of all, he was throwing a tantrum in public. This was not the venue for real emotions. Dre wasn't the one who needed to grow up. "Alaan, stop talking and let these kids practice their magic. This is a performance."

"It's always a performance," Alaan said, then paused. "Correction, you're always a performance."

Dre was the one who wanted more training, more truth, more togetherness, not less. Too much distance had grown between them and Dre would not adapt to Alaan's selfishness. His quitol leather crinkled as he balled up his fists. He bucked and Alaan jerked back; some other kids did, too. "Who do you think you are talking to?"

Alaan cocked his head to the side. He started some retort but was interrupted by Grintinari. "Alaan, Dre, come here." The sorcerer's voice was amplified by magic. He slapped the stage and beckoned. Dre turned back to his brother. He slid his right foot into a more stable placement. If Alaan wanted to spar right now, Dre was game. Sometimes, words couldn't explain what had to be proven. "Now. We need to leave."

Alaan's stance broke. He grunted, then moved first. He hopped off the stage. "What is it?"

Dre closed his eyes and took a deep breath. He would forgive Alaan because he chose to be the smart one today. That was a form of compromise. Dre joined them. "Why? What happened?"

"Just follow me," Grintinari said.

Alaan grabbed him. "Did Ser find them?"

While still holding the communication orb in one hand, the

Grintinari twisted Alaan's arm and flipped him over. He pressed a knee into Alaan's chest. "Don't think that because I look like your peer, I am," he said.

Dre almost swung at Grintinari on reflex, but he stopped before he likely found himself sprawled out on the ground next to Alaan. Dre crossed his arms and said, "We still need to make our statement about working with nobles."

"We have bigger problems," Grintinari said.

They walked home. When they arrived, Alaan kicked off his shoes and tried to stomp away, but Grintinari held his arm. Alaan pouted like a spoiled brat.

"Anyone else still here?" Grintinari said.

Dre's parents sat at a table holding a communication orb. "Victoria and Homin left," Dad said.

Grintinari cast a spell that dampened the house's sounds to absolute silence. "Ser found the six children Slithlor took out of the draft program. They were lying unconscious around Sewit's spirit fiend device. They were in the spirit realm. Ser had studied a girl who could go to the spirit realm years ago and these kids' vitals matched hers."

"That's great," Dad said.

"We finally got him," Mommy said.

"When the children woke up, they said that they needed our help to stop Juli from reaching Lakree, Hila, and Rye because they are connected to spirit fiends," Grintinari said.

The draftees likely knew about the twins' connection, but Slithlor didn't want them to reveal that information to Ser. Slithlor wasn't worried about spirit fiends crossing over. Again, he was more concerned about Juli.

"It's misdirection. They are the proof you need to show the council. They have the device," Dad said.

"The orb can be used to sever a connection to a spirit fiend as well. Slithlor was the only one who knew how to use it, though he may have trained these children. We don't know if they are still connected or telling the truth," Grintinari said. He moved across the room and peered out a window. "Either Juli is to blame and Slithlor is trying to stop her, or vice versa."

Qin, the other leader of the Medina, believed that Slithlor started the Battle of Ki, which meant that Slithlor was fully capable of anything. Though, Juli wasn't particularly innocent either. She didn't warn the council or the Guard of Slithlor's supposed deeds. "Slithlor wouldn't keep the danger of spirit fiends secret unless he was part of the problem, right?" Dre said.

"Where are they now?" Alaan said.

Grintinari leaned against the windowsill. "Ser tried to detain them, but they escaped. She had surrounded them in magic-blocking and matter-blocking shields, but they still disappeared. We don't know what these kids are capable of."

The draftees didn't go to the spirit realm to sever their connection. They went to strengthen it. Rombinanandi couldn't find Alaan and Dre until their trip to the spirit realm.

"Why did you make us leave Co Park?" Dre said.

"Do either of you remember if Slithlor carried a head-sized metal device during the Castle tour in Virt? It's not a perfect sphere; it has a divot with several nobs and buttons," Grintinari said. "We have a theory that Slithlor used the device on children then. It was the only time he had access to all the children in question and those who died in magical accidents since the tour."

Hundreds of children competed in various magical activities that day. Slithlor wasn't studying them; he was experimenting on them. Though Dre's memory of the event was hazy, he hadn't forgotten when Slithlor cornered him and Alaan. At that moment, at least, he wasn't holding anything. Dre shook his head.

"We don't remember anything suspicious," Alaan said. "Do you know if any other MMA participants were there?"

"They all were, but I don't think the connection to spirit fiends took for everyone," Grintinari said.

So much of Slithlor's twisted plan fell into place. He started the draft to capture children whose magic responded to the spirit fiend. After the draft caused kids to hide their magic, he needed a new way. He worked with someone in the MMA to select the groups of children based on who went to that event. Rye had mentioned that the psychic who entered his mind to plant the MMA material spoke to Slithlor just before he was drafted. Spirit fiends could enter dreams, meaning they had some link to the mind. If a psychic knew where to look, they might be able to spot the connection.

Grintinari pulled out an orb, but it wasn't a communication orb. It was a dark red and gold sorcerer's orb. He aimed it at Alaan. "Can you take off that gear? I want to study your magic."

The connection to a spirit fiend would start a war if another nation learned about it and Lynit couldn't survive another so soon. Once the Guard knew about Rombinanandi, they wouldn't let the twins go on their merry little way. Dre's parents blocked Grintinari's view.

"The Guard has been trying to study Alaandre since they were born and the answer is still no," Mommy said.

Grintinari took a deep breath. "We have to help every child connected to a spirit fiend."

"You would have murdered Lakree, Hila, and Rye on day one if you could have. Now get out," Dad said.

Mommy repeated the command.

"I was ordered to kill three children because they could start a war. Do not think that I am not risking my career and Lynit's safety by disobeying that order. You think three elites can't get into a hideout underneath Co Park?" Grintinari said with a smirk. "We like them there because Juli can't get to them either, but we need to know if a spirit fiend will spring out during a MMA practice and plunge Lynit into war."

"Magic privacy is a right," Mommy said.

"Slithlor has authorized the public release of the accusations against Lakree, Hila, Rye, and Juli. With Alaan and Dre as the only ones who can reach them, the Guard will interrogate them."

"We had our memories altered to protect them," Alaan said, which wasn't true. But even if they were arrested, they wouldn't talk about the Medina. That place stood for something bigger than them. Dre moved next to Alaan.

"If the treason charge falls to you, a psychic will extract what they need. Memories can't be erased. They can be buried or dismantled but are always there in some form. Putting them back together is complex and dangerous but not impossible. And the memories of your magic will be mixed in there," Grintinari said.

Dre shuddered as he recalled the week-long safety lesson on mind shielding that every kid had. If a powerful psychic pushed through the defense, fighting back would only cause more harm.

"The device is in Slithlor's possession. If he uses it for good, he will eagerly break the connections. If he's the one who created them, then we need proof so that we can force him to break them. We can protect you from any prosecution if we know you are a victim," Grintinari said as he approached the door.

The elites meant well, but there was another angle. They didn't follow through on their orders because they were suspicious of Slithlor. The man ordered the secret death of three children he had tried to draft even though they were exempt. It was obvious that he lied, which opened the possibility that there was no real threat. Revealing Rombinanandi might be the best way to stop Slithlor, but Dre preferred any other option that involved not becoming a verified threat to Lynit. If Slithlor fled or refused to break the connection, the Guard would be forced to protect Lynit by killing the boys. And Dre wouldn't count on Slithlor to do the right thing before or after he was caught.

"I'll give you a moment to think it over. I'll cover your home in more spells to stop anyone from entering or leaving," Grintinari said, then stepped outside.

Mom led them to the gym. Dad turned on one of the old sewing machines. It sputtered, cranked, and shot dust into the air. Mommy covered them in a magic-blocking shield.

"We need to get that thing out of you," Dad said.

"The best chance is to go back to the Medina, but we have to get away from Grintinari first," Dre said.

Alaan rubbed a hand along his arm. "What if we broke the link ourselves? In the spirit realm, our thoughts took us to our spirit energy. Our mind is the link to Rombinanandi."

"But it doesn't exist in our separate minds. It only shows up when we dream together," Dre said.

"What if I went with you into a dream? I would be able to look around and see what we could do. I took a course in grad school on dream spaces," Dad said.

"But that thing is there," Mommy said.

"If it shows up, then we can question it. If it means harm, it is better to know sooner than later," Dre said. "We can't wear this gear forever."

"How could Slithlor do this to me, to us?" she said as she leaned on a machine.

"He was always a monster," Dad said.

"We need to make him pay," she said.

"If we break the connection, then we won't have any evidence ourselves that he did anything," Dre said.

"What about the Castle tour and the other children he connected?" Mommy said.

"We tested the two MMA cohorts he tried to draft and three

others, but no one else had it," Alaan said, then explained how the gear sizzling was an indicator. "And even though he is creepy and obsessed with us, Juli could have done it. We don't know for sure if it was him."

"Someone else might have seen the device?" Mommy said.

"I know you said that you don't remember anything odd individually, but there could be small details like smells or sounds that Dre knows that could spark Alaan to recall other details and vice versa," Dad said. "If you combine your memories in a dream, you might be able to build a clearer picture of what happened."

Mommy kissed Dad. "If we know when, where, and what Slithlor did, we can use that against him. I want to be on the offensive for once."

"I just want my old life back," Dre said. He pulled off his gloves, then unfastened his vest. His skin buzzed.

Alaan took off his pants. "Will all of our memories be joined or just the ones related to the Castle tour?"

"No idea. This is new territory," Dad said.

Alaan winced, then paused with his vest half unbuttoned. "Can we try separately first? I don't particularly want to merge my mind with Dre's."

"Why not?" Dre said.

"My whole life is with you, which I enjoy, but at least my thoughts are private, my own," he said.

Dre rolled his eyes. "Stop being dramatic. I'm supposed to be the dramatic one."

"There it is, even in your jokes. You have this image in your mind of who we should be together and you divide the pieces between us. I'm not who you think I should be. I want to be Alaan, not one-half of the Poli Twins."

"In our day-to-day life, we can be whoever we want to be, but in the ring, when handling fans, when navigating this ridiculous predicament we are in, we have to move together. If there is any space between us, people will dig in their greedy fingers and rip us apart. Everyone wants a piece, you know that. If we give them a chance, they will take it," Dre said.

"Tess never got her piece," Alaan said. "She wanted a piece of me only for her, but I couldn't give her that. I didn't know how to give it to her."

"You stopped our magic from joining over Tess?" Dre said. His gloves and helmet fell to the floor.

"No. I did it for me. I needed to break the public image of us as the Poli Twins, which would break your image of us. It's like a box we've folded ourselves inside. We fit, but we are trapped. I want to be distinguishable from you by more than my hair and light energy."

"Too bad." Dre pulled off the rest of his armor. He reached out his senses and the pulses of wizardry thudded against his skin. The pushes and pulls were not only stronger but flipped back and forth sporadically. The spirit fiend caused this new rhythm. Maybe by changing their magic, it was changing them.

"I figured that if I proved we weren't magically dependent, you would realize that we didn't need to be mentally dependent either."

Dre huffed. "But we are magically dependent, Alaan. Can you create eclipses alone?"

Mommy raised a hand. "I, nor anyone, can tell you what works for the two of you, but hear me out as your mother. You've been sharing everything since you were born. When you were toddlers, we would sometimes dress you differently. You were content with the clothing until you saw your brother. Then, you would both cry until you were dressed the same.

"As you grew older, you wanted your own rooms and own things. Dad and I may still call you Alaandre and the rest of the world knows you as the Poli Twins, but you are two young men with different personalities, preferences, and interests. However, there is a special connection that the two of you have that no one else does.

"You two are just so in tune with each other. As you get older and move out of the house and live separate lives, your bond will always be there. It's for the two of you to figure out what that means to you. I'm very close with my sister, who is only one year older, but it is nothing like the two of you. You must cherish the gifts you are given."

Alaan rubbed his palms into his eyes. "But I know Dre. If he knows my thoughts, he will change himself to better align with me. I don't want that either. I want Dre to be Dre and me to be me."

Dre pointed at the ground. "Lie down. The spirit fiend is bigger than both our feelings. Our lives are on the line."

"That's fair," Alaan said, nodding. "Dre, focus only on the Castle tour. No traipsing through any other memories."

"That's fair," Dre said.

Dad stepped forward. "I'll induce sleep."

Chapter 26 - Dre

Hundreds of feet slapped against marble floors. Laughter echoed off the throne's high ceilings. A song played from a music box. The king regent sat in the throne chair, nodding and tapping to the beat. For many years as the head of defense, he oversaw the creation of new protocols to keep Lynitians safe. Not being noble himself, he was supposed to understand the challenges facing the average Lynitian and do his best to address what he could in the short years until the Prince was of age. Slithlor stood silently to his side with his hands clasped behind his back.

The king regent introduced two structures in the middle of the room. One was like a gigasphere, but instead of keeping energy from spilling out, it directed attacks at whoever was inside.

The second one was a six-versus-six strategy game. It was a series of blocks connected by twisting metal rods. The blocks slid along the paths to various intersections worth varying points or blocked opponents from reaching other nodes. Dre and Alaan had tried the game once, but coordinating four other people who couldn't think more than one step ahead was too frustrating.

Slithlor lurked on the other side of the game, his arms still behind his back. He didn't speak to any of the children. Halfway through the event, Dre and Alaan slipped away to find a restroom. When they returned to the throne room, Slithlor cornered them by the door. His candy-scented breath filled Dre's mind.

"You are the future of Lynit. When you turn nineteen, come find me or I will find you," he said. He backed away slowly. He returned to lurking, but he wouldn't turn around. His hands stayed hidden.

"I can't remember him ever turning his back to us," Alaan said.

Dre followed Slithlor. As he meandered through the crowds, he continued to move backward. Dre darted behind him, but Slithlor's gaze followed him like a picture. "I can't see behind him," he said.

Alaan moved to the opposite side. Slithlor was between them. "I see his front, too," Alaan said.

"This is creepy," Dre said.

"Your memories were tampered with," Dad said. He circled Slithlor. "He doesn't want you to remember what he had behind his back."

"I saw something that I thought was a deep secret in Dre's mind when we joined in the spirit realm, but maybe it was this," Alaan said.

"You should have said something," Dre said. "I didn't say anything because I thought the secret was that you blocked our energies from joining."

"Yeah, I made some mistakes," Alaan said.

"You mean you made bad decisions," Dre said. Alaan still didn't understand why what he did was wrong. It wasn't about the outcome. It was about the input. If they had separate agendas, then they weren't working together. They wouldn't be able to beat the Balison sisters and they wouldn't really be twins anymore. They would be celebrity siblings. "You weren't trying to do the right thing for me. You were only trying to get what you wanted."

"Not now, boys," Dad said. He poked at Slithlor a few times, then pulled on his robes. "He didn't remove your memory of him. That would be noticeable and traceable. It looks like he distorted your perception when you stored the memory. But he didn't count on that together, you can recreate the full picture. Circle him in opposite directions."

Dre moved clockwise, and Alaan walked counterclockwise. The rest of the scene froze as his attention honed in on every detail he could define of the tall, bald man with gapped teeth. It was dizzying to have the room move in his periphery and the psychic's image remained fixed, but Dre pressed on, speeding up. With each rotation, Slithlor tracked him a little less. Soon, he saw the side of his shoulder, the profile of his nose, and finally something silver cupped in his hands. It was a shiny metal ball with a divot of buttons. And there was something else behind Slithlor: Rombinanandi.

"It's here," Dre and Alaan said. Dre stopped moving and Slithlor snapped back to face him.

A round head with black saucer eyes peered out from behind Slithlor. It looked around, then hopped out. It turned to the music box, which was still playing. It tapped it a few times. Nothing happened. It pushed the box tentatively until it tipped over and the music cut out.

Rombinanandi jumped back, eyes larger than usual. "What was that sound?"

"Did you come from that orb?" Dad said. A stream of purple energy peeled off him. It stretched towards the creature.

As soon as the energy touched Rombinanandi, it swatted it away. The energy evaporated in a wave that hit Dad. He blinked and dimmed like a dying light bulb. His body destabilized. He screamed, clutching his head. The pitch increased by half steps up several octaves. Dre covered his ears, but the sound didn't dampen. He screamed, too, but his voice was lost under Dad's siren.

Dre grabbed and tried to hold him fixed, but it didn't help. Dad shot off into the sky, then the screams stopped. "What happened? Is he okay?"

"We have to go," Alaan said. Dre closed his eyes and turned away. His physical body was distant, laying on his uncomfortable quitol armor.

"Stay," Rombinanandi said, his words thick. They clung to Dre somehow, like sap. He pulled harder, trying to yank himself awake, but he was weighed down.

"I can't wake up. I can't wake up," Dre shouted. His vision was reduced to the spirit fiend. The groves in its face were as fine as wood.

"We can't make a deal here. You must come to me," it said as it stepped closer.

"Stay back," Dre said. He tried to lift his arms but couldn't. He was trapped.

It walked up beside Dre, brushing its body against him, sniffing him. A surge passed through Dre. It rushed up to his ear and rang. But the sound didn't hurt. It was more like the fast beat of a drum. It was the oscillations of light and dark energy. It was power.

Rombinanandi stretched to its full height, rising to eye level. Its eyes were black pools. Dre fell into them.

The scenery changed. Lumps of grass bubbled up, forming hills. The sky darkened to midnight blue. A wild breeze swept across the landscape. Fluffy balls of cotton tumbled about. Something brown - Rombinanandi - sat at the top of a hill. Its gaze was turned to the sky, to Alaandre.

"Let me in and I will give you power," it said.

"What do you want?"

"I want to split myself the way that you do. There are many versions of me and I want to be them all at once," it said.

"And if I say no?"

A loud boom shook the world, snapping Dre back to the dream space with Alaan. The children, the music, and the walls wavered like an illusion in sunlight. Then another sound, a name, Dre's name, lifted him free of the spirit fiend's hold. It was his mother's voice.

He awoke on his side. Alaan sat up next to him. Mommy stood over Dad, who was bleeding from his nose and covered in a red shield.

"Don't worry about him. Worry about that," she said, pointing up —a large magical shield covered all four of them. A thick nexus of light and dark wizardry energy floated beyond it. The energies were combined and formless like a dense gas in water.

Dre checked the room. No one else was there. "Whose energy is that?" A magic shield surrounded him. Any energy of his outside of it should have evaporated.

The black and white cloud moved like a living organism exploring a space. It stretched in some directions and recoiled in others but was constantly expanding. Dre and Alaan's ability to combine energy worked through the connection between them, but there were no pulses coming from Alaan. There weren't even pushes or pulls on Dre's skin. The energies were able to join without him.

"The energy has its own balance," Alaan said.

"No, it doesn't," Mommy said. "Over there."

One side of the energy cloud separated and broke down, sparking. Then, a larger chunk of dark energy evaporated. The leftover light energy exploded, sending a ripple through the rest.

"If all of that explodes, the building will collapse," Mommy said.

"We have to release it in pieces. You release the light energy, then I'll snap away the dark. Mommy, take Dad and go," Dre said.

"Either we all go or no one goes," she said.

Dre and Alaan stood up. Alaan extended a hand, which Dre grasped tight. "We're ready."

The thin film of blue protection dissolved and a force socked into

Dre. He absorbed the initial shock with his stance, but his skin stung with the sense of Alaan. The energy responded, increasing in volatility. It splashed and popped. The wizardry was more stable without them. Alaan's breaths were too rapid, unbalancing the pushes and pulls. The torsion burned.

Dre gritted his teeth. The energy was theirs, but it wasn't divided the usual way. All of the dark energy didn't belong to him. Half was Alaan's. And half of the light energy was Dre's.

"We have to both release light and dark simultaneously," Alaan said.

"The light energy is shifting around too quickly. I can't pinpoint which energy is mine," Dre said.

"Follow my lead."

Dre leaned into his connection with Alaan. The pulses were rough, but there was a pattern to them. A soft mumble, a voice, was encoded in the cycles of pushes and pulls. It coached Dre to an exact framework. It was Alaan's voice. He spoke through the connection. The psychic link in their dream had crossed over to the waking world. Their breathing matched and the cloud stabilized. Lifting their arms in sync, they teased off the first chunk cleanly. It evaporated safely.

"That's it," Mommy said.

By the time they cleared away half of the cloud, Dre's skin was raw and purple with bruises. A thin cut ran up the inside of his leg, and his feet throbbed. Guard wizards spoke about wizardry's physical toll, but this was the first time Dre felt it, the first time his magic was stronger than his skin.

A bit of energy was released incorrectly, sputtering sparks on the matted floor and starting a small fire. Alaan's stance broke, a knee dropping to the ground. He grunted. In response, a patch on Dre's chest was pulled in a different direction, ripping open a gash.

Dre screamed as more energy broke off from the main body of

the cloud. It bubbled before exploding. The force knocked Dre back. He stumbled into a mannequin, tumbling over it. Pain arced through his back. Above, all the remaining energy started to bubble.

"Mommy," Dre said.

In a blink, a magic shield sealed into place as the energy exploded. The boom hit, warping the shape with a dent. The blast also reached up, blowing a hole in the ceiling. A physical shield formed as bricks dropped. Alaan scrambled to Dre as the entire roof caved in. The shields protected them, but the mannequins were crushed. The gym was destroyed.

Mommy coughed through the smoke. "Contact the hospital. Dad still won't wake up."

Chapter 27 - Rye

When Rye's mind returned to his body from the spirit realm, the first word out of his mouth was "Tenaju." It was foreign to his lips, but it clicked in his mind as the name of the great white bird from his dreams. It had to be the spirit fiend he was connected to.

Lakree, Hila, and Chirchi crowded over him, but they were purple and so was the ceiling behind them. Everything was purple. It was the tint of mental energy.

"He's up. He's up," Hila said, tapping his face.

"Rye, look at me. Are you okay? Where are you right now?" Chirchi said.

Rombinanandi's presence felt like it had followed Rye into the real world, pressing him to the ground. He tried to sit up but couldn't. "I'm here," he said.

"What's the name of this place?" Chirchi said.

Rye's legs and arms didn't move either. There was only enough leeway to wiggle his head. "What's going on?"

"He's okay. Let him go," Hila said.

"He was there too long. The spirit fiend could have taken over his mind," Chirchi said. Warm energy tapped Rye's forehead.

"I knew we shouldn't have gone," Lakree said. His eyes were teary. He was scared. So was Rye. He fidgeted.

"Let me in Rye. I need to confirm that it's you," Chirchi said. Rye created a door on his head and opened it. A few images flashed. "He's okay."

The purple energy dissipated. Hila helped Rye up. "Now we know why there are elites after you," Chirchi said.

Rye thought of the crumpled draft order he carried. He wanted to become powerful enough to survive in the wild, but not at the cost of Lynit's safety. He was more dangerous than the Nightmare Killer, but he was just a boy who wanted one last hug from his father. "If Juli knew this, why didn't she do more?" Rye said through clenched teeth. Maybe everything was her fault.

"That's my question, too," Lakree said. He tried to push a nonexistent dread behind his ear.

"Then that is what we ask her," Hila said. She started towards the door. "Let's contact her now. We can come back if needed."

"The elites will kill you if you leave," Chirchi said.

Hila turned around slowly. "Why? We didn't do anything. This was done to us."

"What proof do you have on who did it?" Chirchi said. "And why would it matter if you did? Will the law be less broken or will there be less of a threat of war if you are victims?"

Lakree and Hila believed that Slithlor was to blame, but Rye still didn't. Slithlor was the one who stopped the spirit fiends during the Battle of Ki. He wouldn't turn around and destroy Lynit years later. However, he must have recognized the signs that Rye shouldn't have been allowed to leave the Castle. "What if we aren't the only ones this was done to?" Rye said.

"The Poli Twins for sure…" Chirchi said. "They broke gigastone and yesterday they blew up their home. The sorcerer who disintegrated herself must have been connected to a spirit fiend."

Rye's instincts didn't panic at the prospect. Unlike the other magics, animalism didn't have any external energy. It couldn't accidentally harm him or others. The worst case would be that he morphed faster and faster, but then again, instincts weren't reliable.

"Is that going to happen to Rye?" Hila said.

"If we can find the spirit fiend, then it should be possible to break the connection," she said. "From this trip, I could tell that traveling to the spirit realm strengthens your connection to the spirit fiend. The power will keep flowing into you and you will keep passing it on to the Lakree and Hila. It would kill them before it finally consumed you," Chirchi said.

"No," Rye said. He followed his friends to Poli to help them, but he was the danger.

Hila rubbed his back. "It's not your fault," she said.

Lakree wiped a hot tear from Rye's face. "We'll get through this. We'll go back to the spirit realm."

"Trying to break the connection still has its risks. Traveling to the spirit realm again would increase the energy flowing into him and his spirit fiend could still take over his mind," Chirchi said.

"There has to be another way," Hila said. "Could we find the device and use it to reverse everything?"

"Even if it did work, the Guard wouldn't know the difference. They would still see you as a threat. It will never be safe for you to return to your old life," Chirchi said. "After the Poli Twins' explosion, they and their parents have gone missing."

"Are they alive?" Hila said. "The Guard is helping them, right?"

"The Guard would put Lynit's safety first, not the lives of a few kids," Lakree said. "After a spirit fiend destroys another city, the other nations will send their armies. Lynit won't survive that."

"How can we make sure no spirit fiends are released?" Rye said. It wasn't just about saving himself. They needed to help anyone else who was connected.

"Our only hope is that Juli spent the last five years preparing for this. Let's contact her now," Hila said.

"Or we leave Lynit before we accidentally start the war," Lakree said.

"You still want to run?" Rye said. Running was never the solution. It only led to regret.

"Either we run or die," Lakree said. "I've only ever expected that Juli would help us run."

"I'll talk to Urura. You're not alone. The Medina will help. But if you choose to leave, you can," Chirchi said. She explained how to open the front door, then left.

"So when I said that this place looked like an upscale prison, I was right," Hila said.

Rye cried himself to sleep that night.

He dreamed of a black chasm with a thin bone bridge. Children walked across in single file to meet Rye's father on the other side. He was dressed in the green and white robes of an animalist. A letter was stitched onto his chest, but it was blurry. He smiled as he beckoned. Rye took his first step forward. The bridge moaned.

Below, darkness swirled, flickered, and stretched like it was alive and calling him. A thin string connected Rye to it. It was attached to his chest as a black letter "D." He tried to scratch it off but couldn't. He pulled off his shirt, but the "D" was on his skin. It weighed him down.

The bridge warped and shook as he took more steps. He braced himself against the rails. Bones split and shattered, pieces of femurs and ulnas disappearing into the darkness. But the letter on his father's chest came into focus with each step. The left edge of the letter was a straight line. By the time he got three-quarters across, the letter resolved. It was a "D" like Rye's. His father wasn't guiding the children to the Guard; he was leading them away from the Castle. A line of children was behind him, all smiling with "D" on their chests. The bridge shattered and he dropped like a meteor, propelled into the depths by the truth.

Voices sang, "We are deserters."

Every test he had failed and every morph he purposefully interrupted prepared him for desertion. He tried to grasp at the voices, wring their mouths shut, but they were him. He was just like his father. The traits he admired and feared were inseparable. It was in their blood. While the nobles invented magic to protect Lynit, the Ternitus hid, chucking their responsibilities onto someone else's back.

A twinkle of light sparked, giving form to the things in the darkness. They were shadows, remnants of the doubts and instincts Rye failed to smother. They reached for him. He swatted and kicked, but they stuck to him like sap. The light grew until he squinted against it. The shadows didn't like it. They screamed, but the rushing wind drowned out the voices. The light started to take the shape of wings, a beak, and talons. It wasn't a light. It was Tenaju. Rye should have been more afraid, but he welcomed it.

The majestic beast swooped under him. With one flap, it stopped the descent and with another, they soared upward. Rye latched onto its large feathers. He and Tenaju sprung from the canyon. Rye's father reached for him, but Rye didn't reach back and Tenaju kept taking him higher and higher. The Castle soon faded into the distance.

They approached the dome over Virt. "Stop, stop, stop," Rye said, clenching Tenaju's sides. He tried to steer the bird away.

"Boundaries are meant to be crossed," it said.

Rye braced, but there wasn't a crash. He passed through to a different sky. Instead of scattered clouds, scattered islands formed in the air from rising dirt. Below, loud water tumbled down a cliff into a lake. It was the spirit realm.

They continued rising. This time, Rye didn't say anything as he passed through a floating island like it was a cloud. The moisture tickled his face. He breathed it in and his ear tingled.

He arrived in another realm—the cloud city. The wind whistled down busy streets, knocking the strange workers into each other. They were bloated fish in formal robes carrying briefcases. Lights flickered on and off in the windows of empty buildings. In the center square, lightning danced in a black storm tower.

"I have traveled to every spirit realm. I've seen the beginning, how the realms were created, and their end. Unburdened by attachments, my wings fly swiftly. But this place is my favorite. I have always been interested in your realm, the realm of matter, and this is the closest to it. The boundary between these realms is the only one I haven't been able to cross. The world of matter is about conditions and contracts. This is strange to me. I am not tied to anything. I fly where I wish when I wish.

"But through our connection, I could cross. You carry the weight of others, which burdens you and makes you sluggish. If I lend you my wings, there will be no chain that can hold you. We can tour your world together. All you have to do is come to me. I am here. I am waiting."

When Rye awoke, he was sticky with sweat. Dim crystals in the kitchen flickered, casting jagged lines on the front door. He rubbed at his chest, but there was nothing there.

"I'm not a deserter," he said. He didn't have the skill of a guard yet, but he did have the resolve. He ran once, but not away from his duty. He ran towards safety for Lakree and Hila. He did his part. They made it to Poli and were safely in the Medina. It was time for Rye to return to his own story. It was time to return to the Guard.

He had to warn the king regent of the threat of spirit fiends. If he was lucky, Slithlor could use the device to break his connection to Tenaju. If he wasn't and had to die, at least the energy would stop flowing to Lakree and Hila. In either case, Lynit and his friends would be safe.

"Huh," Lakree said softly as he moaned. He shifted in the bed. He tugged on the sheets. "Is it morning already? I miss the sun."

Rye swallowed. "Can I see Juli's note?"

"Why?" Lakree said quickly, his voice rising.

"I haven't read it yet." And it was mostly true. He cut himself short from reading all of it the first time. All he knew was that Co Park was significant. After Lakree and Hila were no longer in danger from his magic, the Medina wouldn't protect them. They would be kicked out to the elites who were waiting for them. If Juli was alive, she still could help.

"Oh." Lakree turned to face him. The light from the kitchen cut across his face, illuminating the grey edge around his brown irises. They were face to face, less than a handspan apart on the small bed. Lakree was beautiful even when most of his features were in shadow. It was the intensity in his eyes. All Vous had it, but with him, there was a softness behind it that suggested adventure over rules. It was why Lakree wasn't quite like the other nobles. He wanted something more out of life than adding more titles to his name, which made Rye a little jealous. The title he was born with was enough. Rye, on the other hand, had to earn one.

Lakree propped himself on his elbows, creating a little distance between them. "You didn't want to know anything that could hurt us."

If Rye touched Lakree's face, the reaction was predictable. Lakree would welcome it because he liked being comforted, but it wouldn't register as anything more than that for him. No matter how Rye felt in the deep corners of his heart that he failed to snuff out or how progressive Lakree was, Lakree was still noble. That would forever separate them until Rye received a title. If Rye survived and became a captain, he could try again in earnest. Both Rye's parents were captains. They didn't just love each other, they respected each other's skill with magic.

But Rye couldn't stop his reflex. He brushed a hand against

Lakree's cheek. He rubbed the soft hairs that grew in patches. Lakree licked his lips, then leaned forward. He kissed Rye once, then twice, and on the third time, their tongues connected. He placed a hand on Rye's chest and it felt like Lakree was sending energy into Rye instead of the other way around. This kiss wasn't like the one that Hila had initiated. Lakree wasn't pressured into this moment. He wanted to kiss Rye, which was almost more unbelievable than being connected to a spirit fiend.

Lakree pulled back. "Sorry, I couldn't help myself. I know you don't see me that way."

"Wha…?" Rye said. Since they first met, Rye wanted Lakree to see him as more than a friend, but it was a dream Rye knew he couldn't have. It would have been like hoping to maintain two magics after nineteen. Maybe a Kertic or a noble could reasonably wish for that, but not Rye. He wasn't worthy.

Lakree leaned off the bed and fumbled with his pants. He handed Rye a crinkled paper.

Rye lifted the note into the dim light, his heart still thumping. He couldn't let himself think further about what Lakree just said.

Lin,

The Yordin won't be able to protect you. Prepare your affairs, then find me. I will be hiding, but you can contact me in Poli at Co Park. Near the tree are two things: a public communication orb box and a water main control box. One of the communication orbs is permanently dull with an "M" etched into it. This orb is not connected to the public news network. You can leave a message explaining where you will be in one hour. Then, place it in the water main control box. In one hour, I will meet you.

Think of Lakree.

Keep the crystal safe.

- Juli

"I wanted to join the Guard, too," Lakree said. "I would have done it as a wizard or elemental mage because I was content with following the norm. When Juli visited during the Battle of Ki, there was a panic in her eyes that I'd never seen in any noble, let alone a protector. It scared me. It made me fear the Guard. I accepted that if I wasn't going to be part of it, I might as well pursue the magic I wanted. I switched my focus to sorcery. Then, I dropped this conspiracy on you with no time to process and no silver lining to enjoy. You didn't run with us because you believed me. You came with us because we asked."

Rye folded up the note. It would have been easy to reach over and pull Lakree closer. This was his chance to evolve their friendship into something more, but it would only make his choice more difficult. He had made a promise to the guards during his draft exam. He would be stronger than his father and this was what it meant. It wasn't about being good at magic. It was about making the hard decisions. "Can I see the stone?"

Lakree breathed heavily through his nose. His eyes weren't on Rye's anymore. He was looking at Rye's chest. Then his feet touched Rye's. "Focusing on sorcery has limited me in a way. We learn to study the details of things, understand how they respond to events, and trace the rippling effects. This helped me navigate being a noble in a civilian school and passing exams, but it didn't prepare me for the real world, where nothing went as planned. Out here, I need to rely on you because you shine in the unknown."

"All animalists adapt in the wild," Rye said as he pulled back. He didn't deserve praise for doing what was expected of him, though he congratulated himself for identifying his life's true challenge. Defeating his human instincts would be a life-long journey.

Lakree scratched his head. "What I'm trying to say is that I'm sorry for lying about your dad and ignoring your dream of joining

the Guard. I care about you a lot and it makes me crazy sometimes."
He bent off the side of the bed again and handed Rye the red stone.

"Thank you," Rye said softly, clenching his teeth against the water welling in his eyes. In under a minute, he went from kissing his long-time crush to hurting his feelings. It was Rye's fastest morph. Now, he was a monster.

He laid on his back, holding the stone up to the light. Tiny beads of smoke floated inside. He pressed it tight until it hurt.

"It's a memory crystal," Lakree said. "Something important that my aunt witnessed is on it. It takes a protector or a psychic to access it."

Rye stared at it for a long while, imagining how his life would have been if spirit fiends had never attacked Lynit. King Kertic and all six elites would be alive. Rye's Dad would have taught Rye how to do instinct stacking. His mother would still be in the Guard and children would practice magic carelessly in the streets and parks. Hila would have her father in her life as well. And when Lakree kissed Rye, Rye would have grabbed his crotch.

But when Lakree's breathing eventually deepened and his slight snore returned, Rye slipped out of bed. He wrote a note reminding his friends to blame Sewit and not him, then left.

As Rye tiptoed down the Medina hallway, the voices in his head could have filled a stadium. He was abandoning his friends. He would never be a guard. He was running to his death. His instincts writhed, but a faint image kept him placing one foot in front of the other. It was a room packed with captains, elites, the council, the king regent, the Prince, and the Princess. They all had come to Rye's funeral to pay their respects.

At the gigastone entrance, he pressed against a small panel on the side of the wall and it opened, revealing four levers. He reached into his MMA material and pulled up a flashcard. It was of an orange hairless mole. It crawled across a grey boulder in a moving image.

A black figure entered the scene and the creature's skin changed. Both its color and texture shifted to match the gray rock. The black figure rubbed a hand over the boulder. It glided over the creature without noticing it. The backside of the card described the creature's chromatophoric and electroactive skin.

He morphed. He gritted his teeth as the tickling of compression intensified. He was twenty times the weight and ten times the creature's length. It was like the burn of many hands squeezing and twisting his skin and bones. The hallway grew. His sticky paws formed. He released the excess mass as a flare of heat.

He crawled up the wall. The levers were difficult to maneuver with his small limbs, but he flipped all of them. Something clicked. Gears churned. The door cranked open. He could see a few feet into the tunnel, but beyond it was solid blackness. The crystals lining the tunnel weren't activated. Shadows shifted like in his dream. Lakree was too afraid to consider it, but Rye was the only one who could contact Juli undetected. This would be his final favor to them.

He crawled out cautiously, sticking to a corner of the ceiling. He took two lefts, a right, and another left, arriving at a hall where three guards were supposed to be. But no one was there. The only sound was of other rodents scurrying about. He felt his way down another hall, which was empty. Lakree couldn't crack the Guard's patrol pattern because there wasn't one.

Rye pounded his tail against the wall. It was the hinlin's reflex when it was scared. Steady vibrations warned other lizards in the same tree. Eggs responded to the call by hatching early and running. Lakree and Hila could flee the Medina to contact Juli. But the tunnel stone was too dense for Rye's tiny slaps. No one would feel his warning. After a moment, Rye suppressed the hinlin's instincts and calmed himself.

The Medina wasn't the enemy. They could have poisoned him or never took him to the spirit realm. The Medina was only trying to protect itself. Urura simultaneously wanted to uncover the conspiracy surrounding Lakree, Hila, and Rye but wasn't sure until last night if Lakree and Hila were spies. She couldn't stop Lakree from matter shifting through gigastone, but she could scare him. The map was a trick to make them stay. His friends weren't in danger. He didn't need to warn them about anything. Contacting Juli was still the best way to help them. Even if the tunnels were clear, it didn't mean it was safe for Lakree and Hila to walk around the city. He exited the tunnel.

The sun was low in the sky, bathing everything it touched in red and orange. The tall metal buildings were dark, like sleeping guardians watching over the city. Co Park, however, was wide awake. Clouds of multicolored energy twisted in the air. The tree was hidden underneath. Laughter and music echoed down empty streets.

Rye crawled down the steps leading into the park. He couldn't see more than a few feet at a time. Different types of flyers littered the ground. Most were about the Poli Twins and others complained about the Guard. None were wanted signs for Rye. At the bottom, there were too many people to count. Some were sleeping on makeshift beds of cloth. Others played instruments. They all wore white and black Yordin pins. There were animalists in creature form wagging their tails to the beat, so Rye did the same to blend in. Poli was the party city that he had read about.

He approached the metal bin next to the tree. The chilly air greeted him when he released his morph. He checked over his shoulder, but no one watched him. He opened the lid. Less than ten communication orbs were inside. He rummaged until he found one that didn't light up to his touch, one with a small "M" on its side. He clutched it tightly.

The energy in the orb pressed into his fingers. He let it in. There were no voices like the usual public communication orb. Instead, he focused his thoughts into it. He told it about the matter shift into the Castle and draft orders. He described the Medina and where to find it. Everything that happened in the past two weeks spilled out of him, including his connection to the spirit realm. He was morphing faster and a threat to his friends. He offered her a deal. He would protect Lynit from himself and she would protect Lakree and Hila from Lynit.

When he finished, the orb flickered. The message was sent. He placed it in the service box. He backed away carefully, as if a sudden movement would break the moment. He left the park. The Castle was to the east. The tall buildings eventually gave way to smaller brick and stone ones. He passed shops selling designer telephones and cookware. Strangers brushed past him but otherwise paid him no attention. Many wore black and white pins.

Several people gathered in front of a storefront covered with a large-print newspaper. "Treason," it read in thick black font with a sketch of a familiar woman underneath. Rye stopped.

Juli wasn't depicted as the refined guard Lakree carried in his pocket. A loose bonnet was wrapped around her head. Strains of frizzy hair poked out at her ears and hairline. The collar of her guard uniform was wrinkled. She stared down her nose as if threatening all who saw her. She looked like Slithlor.

She was accused of domestic terrorism and dealings with foreign powers. She faked her death years ago, but now they believed she was alive and had brainwashed a group of children, Lakree Oldenfoot, Hila Kolit, and Rye Ternitu, to steal a powerful device from the Castle. It could start a war if it fell into the wrong hands and Juli's hands were the wrong ones.

Someone said, "I didn't think the Pol would let the crimes of one of their own go public."

"It's to distract us from the attack on the Poli Twins," another person said. "Why don't we show them what it is like to have one of their own go missing?"

Rye imagined a trial of the six council members, each in white robes with masks representing their family colors. Juli, Lakree, and Hila were chained to a podium. Instead of the three being given the honor of dying by magic, a hooded guard approached them with a large blade to kill them like creatures.

Rye tiptoed away from the storefront, then doubled back to the Medina, nearly tripping a few times. Whether Juli was the one that connected Rye to Tenaju or not, it didn't matter. She couldn't protect Lakree and Hila because other elites would be trying to kill her. She would only put them in more danger from the Guard or spirit fiends. He activated the tunnel lights and made a few wrong turns but arrived back at the Median entrance. It looked like any other dead-end gigastone hall, but the rusted metal door and service box beside it were unique. He panted as he opened the service box. He flipped all the levers, but the door didn't open. He banged on the stone, but he only hurt his hand. He stumbled back, then balled up in the corner. His body shook as he hyperventilated. Juli was going to find Lakree and Hila because of him.

"What have I done?"

An hour later, the Medina door slid open. Rye scrambled to his feet. Hila stood on the other side, holding the tunnel map. Lakree carried a stuffed bedsheet slung over his shoulder. Lakree's face turned to stone. "You looked me in the eye and said nothing. You are a coward," he said.

The words hurt, but Rye didn't flinch. He was only a coward because of them. If Rye turned himself in, the Guard would believe that Lakree and Hila were working with Juli and connected to spirit fiends. He couldn't fulfill his duty to Lynit because it threatened Lakree and Hila. It wasn't the way the world was supposed to work. The Guard didn't protect everyone; instead, it protected most. So Rye had to make up the difference. Maybe someone else could shame him for it, but he wouldn't accept it from Lakree.

Hila waved him in as she stared at the tunnel map. She didn't look up again until the door closed. "We are good. The guards didn't hear us."

"The map is fake. There are no guards," Rye said.

Her mouth dropped.

"We have to contact Juli," Lakree said.

Rye pressed his lips tight. "She has been charged with treason. Every guard is looking for her with the order to kill on sight."

Lakree dropped his sack. "For what?"

Rye told them everything he read in the paper.

Lakree shook his head, "No, she would never."

"Lakree, you have only seen her once. You don't know her," Hila said.

"My father trusts her and I trust my father," Lakree said, his hand trembling as he rubbed his head. "And we didn't steal anything."

Urura stepped around the corner carrying a communication orb. Though her pace was quick, her eyes showed her fatigue. "We received your message for Juli," she said.

Rye pointed a finger. "You were working with her all this time." He took a step back.

"I contacted her the day you arrived. She had been away for several months but will arrive tonight," Urura said.

Rye flipped the levers. "We have to go now. We can't be associated with her." The door reopened.

"The guard didn't publicly say what she is accused of stealing, but it is a device called S-X. It was recovered from Sewit after the Battle of Ki. It is capable of connecting humans to spirit fiends," she said.

"She did this to me?" Rye said.

"She wouldn't have, right?" Lakree said. The sheet slipped from his fingers, spilling jars of food on the ground. He didn't attempt to pick up the mess.

"That's why you wanted us to go to the spirit realm," Hila said. "You wanted to know if she used it on us."

"She was holding us for Juli," Rye said.

"Juli wouldn't use magic to endanger anyone. She believed in the Medina," Urura said.

"But you thought it was okay not to tell us and keep us prisoner," Hila said.

"Young lady, we do not owe you anything. You broke into the throne room, bit a guard, attacked several more, and even punched a shopkeeper. On the other hand, we have given you refuge, food, clean clothing, and the freedom to practice magic. What have you given us? When we first met, I gave you the option to leave. You chose to stay in a place you knew nothing about. Don't blame me for your choice," she said.

Hila dropped the fake map and crossed her arms but said nothing.

"We need to leave Lynit," Rye said. It was the only way to escape Juli and the Guard. Finding a location with water would be easy since every region other than the Winder Plains had it in abundance. Food was everywhere and Rye knew how to hunt and skin. He would leave cooking to Lakree and Hila. "But first, I have to sever my connection to Tenaju. Tell Chirchi to take me to the cloud city. "

Chapter 28 - Dre

Dre rubbed a finger around the rim of a stone cup. The heat of the hot water inside warmed his hand. He stood before a table topped with twelve silver containers, each filled with a different tea. The two on the ends were the only ones he hadn't tried. He opened up the left one. It was a bright orange and smelled like a spicy flower. It stung his nose. He sneezed. A little tea flung out onto the table.

He gripped the other container but struggled with the lid. It was tight and switching hands didn't help. His fingers slipped off. He slammed it down and the clank rang in the quiet hospital common area.

"Do you need help? The valic tea gives everyone a hard time," a man behind him said.

"No," Dre said without turning around. He didn't want the stupid tea anyway.

Footsteps approached. "Let me help you." He pulled up beside Dre, grabbing the container. He was dressed in all white. He was a protector.

"Don't worry, I won't ask for an autograph." The man wiggled the sides of the lid until it popped off. "Here."

Dre sniffed the black tea. It smelled rotten. "Hmm, no thanks, I'll try the other one."

The man laughed. "That's why I opened it. The polite face of disgust is the same on everyone. Valic is an acquired taste." He wore an eclipse pin.

Dre averted his eyes and shook flakes of the orange tea into his hot water. He fumbled with the strainer.

"There are so many wild theories out there about why your house blew up and why you disappeared. I respect your privacy here, but you should make a public statement."

The hospital was in a wealthy area of the city, meaning there should be nobles milling out, but Dre didn't see any when he dared peek out the windows. He did, however, glimpse groups of roaming protesters, their numbers growing daily. His absence only exacerbated the protest, but his priority was his dad. "If someone wakes up my father, then I'll gladly do it," Dre said, then returned to Dad's room.

He lay in the bed. He looked like he was sleeping and, in a way, he was. His body still breathed and pumped blood, but he hadn't opened his eyes in a week. Each protector who failed to diagnose what was wrong was a small treat. At the least, no one thought that his mind was completely fried. So, no news was good news. There was still a chance to undo what Rombinanandi had done to him.

Grintinari stood over him with his sorcerer's orb. Mommy sat in a chair beside the bed with an open book in her lap but was asleep. Alaan slumped in the chair to the right of her. He picked at his quitol leather gear with a fingernail. The gear still numbed the tingle in Dre's ear. Two nights ago, he and Alaan fell asleep at the same time while in it, but Rombinanandi struggled to enter their dream. It was a thin wisp that blinked in and out of existence, but part of Dre still itched to remove the suit. Before the gym collapsed, not only did his energy exist when he was separated from it, but he had heard Alaan's thoughts. The spirit fiend wasn't only increasing their strength, it was improving their magic.

Dre sat next to Alaan and sipped his tea. Alaan stood up. "I'll have tea, too." He often moved when Dre stood near him, afraid of their thickening connection.

Dre stared at the steam rising from his cup. "Try a different floor. Someone out there is wearing an eclipse pin."

"Nevermind, then," Alaan said. He went over to Dad.

Dre sat in silence until Ser and Rish arrived. They were both in uniform and covered in desert dirt. Dre elbowed Mommy. She jerked awake and caught her book before it fell. She first looked at Dad, then at the new elites in the room. "Can you help him?"

"I'll try," Ser said. She was the elite protector. If she couldn't help him, then no protector could. She placed a red bubble around him and recited augmentations to her spell. Symbols concentrated over Dad's head. "He's in the same state as the draftees when I found them."

"He's in the spirit realm?" Dre said. She nodded.

Rombinanandi must have sent Dad there. Dre remembered the lake and floating rocks from his trip and the blue sun and grass from the experiment at Sepotine. If his father were stuck in one of those places, Chirchi could find him. Dre moved next to his father. He kissed his forehead. Next to his ear, he whispered, "We'll bring you home."

"How do we get him back?" Alaan said as he grabbed Dre's hand and squeezed, which meant that he was scared and, therefore, hadn't figured out the good news.

"We need to know how he got there," Ser said.

Alaan sighed, "When we said that he was in our dream, that part was true, but...ah," Dre clenched Alaan's hand so hard that he heard a knuckle crack. They didn't need to reveal the full story yet.

"It was actually a nightmare, but we left out something," Dre said. "He was there to help us unlock a memory that had been tampered with. Slithlor didn't want us to completely remember the

Castle tour. He was there with a metal orb."

"Tampered memories are a start, but they are not enough alone. We still need a child who has been connected to a spirit fiend," Ser said.

"It is enough to get the council to authorize a test of all children," Grintinari said.

Rish pointed at Dad. "If he is in the spirit realm, who used Sewit's device on him?"

"That's not the only way," Alaan said. Dre tapped the back of Alaan's hand with his thumb. Alaan needed to stop talking before he said too much.

"My guess is that your nightmare was a spirit fiend and it did this," Ser said. She created a light blue shield to repel magic, placing it around Dre and Alaan. "Let's find out the answer right now. Take off those magic-dampening suits." She nodded at Rish, who then started morphing. His body turned blue as he dropped down on all fours.

"No," Dre and Alaan said.

Mommy stepped in front of them. "We've been over this. They have rights."

"Ser, let's not do this here. We are in a hospital," Grintinari said. "I was waiting for their father to recover before I confronted them again."

"If they aren't connected to a spirit fiend, what are they afraid of? They are the Poli Twins. They are the definition of showing off magic," Ser said. "But if they are connected to one, this is the only proof we need to show the council. We could go now. We don't have to wait for the court case."

Rish continued turning into a spangot, the most magically sensitive creature on the planet. His growing frame knocked over a chair. He would be able to smell everything about their magic. Grintinari mouthed, "Sorry," as he turned his sorcerer's orb towards the boys. This wasn't good.

"It might help us understand how to help your father," Ser said.

"Stop, it's too dangerous. That was how they blew up our house," Mommy said.

"Then we can go somewhere safer. Sepotine University is still closed. The gigastone field will be empty," Ser said.

"We need more time."

"Time for what?"

Before Dre could run or consider turning himself in, he had to tell Chirchi to guide his father back to the real world. That was non-negotiable. He couldn't take a gamble on what the elites hoped they would discover. His eyes slid to his father, whose breathing was the only noise until voices sounded outside the door.

"Sir, Sir, you can't go in there. Sir."

Homin slipped inside the room. He shut the door quickly behind him. He sealed it shut with a black wall. He scanned the room. "What's going on?" He hunched over to catch his breath.

"Nothing. We were talking," Ser said and dropped her shields. Grintinari lowered his orb and Rish released his morph.

Dre sighed.

"Good, because if anything happens to the Poli Twins for real, we would remember the kidnappings as the good old days," Homin said.

"What do you mean?" Alaan said.

"You disappeared after being dragged out of Co Park by a man later identified as Grintinari. Three noble children have been kidnapped in response. Their ransom is the release of the Poli Twins," Homin said. "There is a treason charge against a former elite protector and that gets less coverage."

This reminded Dre of the letters from fans that he and Alaan ignored. The world interpreted his desire for privacy at his father's bedside as a battle cry for action. The Poli Twins were treated like seventeen-year-old celebrities until they didn't show their magic. Then, they transformed into symbols of everyone's fear. This was what Alaan usually complained about. Dre imagined the press conference they would have to do and the heightened security on them. He wouldn't be able to sneak anywhere. "Great," Dre said, plopping down into a seat.

"I imagine being drafted feels like a kidnapping, too," Mommy said.

"I am sure it does," Homin said.

"What did the Finrar decide?" Grintinari said. He slipped his orb into his pocket.

"They aren't supporting us," Homin said.

"So the court case is still on," Ser said.

"Technically, but what happens to the twins today is the new challenge," Homin said.

"What is it?" Mommy said.

"The Correction Factor's breakdown is accelerating. Another four kids died in magical accidents. Reducing the fear of training under proper guidance is the new priority. Slithlor allowed some draftees to leave the Castle and talk to reporters about their wonderful experiences, then challenged whether Dre and Alaan should still be in the MMA program since they passed the test together when every other child took it separately. Elite Palow acquiesced and is having you retested separately."

If they failed the test, then Slithlor would disappear them away like the other missing draftees. If Rombinanandi's power overflowed, the elites would shove them before the council and they would likely disappear afterward. This was worse than before. Refusing to show their magic wouldn't help. Dre gritted his teeth.

"So they will have to show their magic or Slithlor will draft them after they are kicked out of the MMA," Grintinari said. The elites turned to Dre and Alaan.

"When is the test?" Dre said. The suits would sizzle when he used magic, but now he could pull enough light energy to meet the needs of the exam.

"In an hour. The Guard wants to quell the civil unrest. They think the easiest way will be to have you become the spokesman for the draft. The Yordin, however, would rather you perform the same role but as the civilian liaison to the MMA. You would get full oversight of the MMA and be the government's representative of the program. The draft will be suspended as long as the MMA program is running. All the noble families support this. However, since the MMA is distinctly a noble-created program, only a noble could run it. And the only family you could be part of is Yordin."

Dre pinched the bridge of his nose. Right when he was starting to hope that Homin was a decent human being, he pulled a Yordin.

"We can't become Yordin without a Verbindous," Alaan said.

"What are you talking about?" Mommy said. She put a hand on Alaan. "Wait, they want you to become Yordin? Not Cast?" She tapped her arm.

Dre resisted a smile. It was his same reaction at the first MMA test. A family photo of ninety-eight pale, tall Yordins crowded around Dre and Alaan would look ridiculous.

"The usual Verbindous isn't until nineteen, but an earlier substitute has been arranged," Homin said.

"Was it the MMA exam the other Yordin sat in on?" Alaan said.

"No. What you displayed was interesting, but not enough. However, we recognize that you didn't want to show your best. The Gigasphere Tournament tomorrow will be your chance to showcase your individual balance to all the noble families. You'll need to compete in individual matches," Homin said.

Alaan wasn't alone in wanting them to use both wizardry energies. The Yordin didn't care for the Poli Twins' balance either. "Passing the MMA exam separately is enough challenge," Dre said.

"If you fail, then we have to do things our way," Ser said, which was true. It would be worse to be drafted and under Slithlor's control.

"Why can't my boys just be?" Mommy said. She paced across the cramped room.

"Only if you promise to heal our dad," Alaan said.

"We will do our best," Ser said.

Grintinari matter shifted Dre, Alaan, Homin, and himself to the Castle. They arrived in a marble room. Two sorcerers sat behind a desk. Both flipped quickly through papers on their clipboard. They complained about the unauthorized matter shift until Grintinari stepped out in front. Homin led the way to the MMA training room.

"We did kidnap them," one woman they passed in the hall said. This threw everyone else into a frenzy. There was a clear divide in the Castle. Two-thirds complained about the Poli Twins being the cause of the riots and kidnappings. The other third didn't say anything but nodded, tilting their chins up.

Dre entered the exam room, which was quiet. There were only two people there, both in purple robes. Slithlor stood in the center of the room in a power pose with his arms behind his back, but his sunken eyes undercut the image. He looked as sleep-deprived as Alaan.

The old elite who ran the MMA opened the door to the gigastone inner chamber. "If either Dre or Alaan passes, the entire cohort continues to the next round. If they both fail, their whole cohort will be out of the MMA program," he said in a deep raspy voice.

Alaan started towards the inner door to the gigastone room, but Dre pulled him back. "I'll go first." His first use of wizardry would be unpredictable, but his light energy was inherently weaker and less likely to explode. If Dre passed, Alaan wouldn't need to risk pulling his much stronger, more dangerous light energy that could destroy gigastone.

Alaan gripped him tight, then released. "Okay."

Before Dre stepped inside the room, Slithlor spoke. "He will need to remove the magic dampening gear. We wouldn't want it to interfere with his examination."

"Of course," the old man said.

Dre balled a fist, then released it. He turned to catch Slithlor's eye. The man wasn't afraid of people seeing what he had done to Dre, which was odd. Unless Slithlor hoped that this test could kill Dre. Funk wafted as he removed his vest and pants. He hadn't bathed in a few days. All he had on was his underwear, blue suspenders, and boots. The look was iconic. Victoria Finrar would be proud.

Slithlor tried to follow him into the exam room, but a fluffy arm blocked his path. "We want the exam to be fair. Having the head of the draft in the room will add unneeded pressure," Homin said.

"I need to confirm that the exam is administered fairly. We have already seen inconsistencies," Slithlor said.

"I'll go then. I'll observe on your behalf," Grintinari said.

"That's acceptable," the old man said.

"Homin is a government official, not a member of the Guard. He shouldn't be in here," Slithlor said. His death stare would have been scary under other circumstances, but right now, it was hilarious. The man who had hunted and threatened Dre his whole life was petty.

Homin quoted his title as civilian liaison to the Guard several times as he was escorted from the room. Then Dre, the old man, and Grintinari entered the gigastone room. Two sorcerers were already in the back corners with their gold paddles. Instead of two wizards, a single one sat in a chair. Long auburn hair spilled around her like a throne. It was Oran Yordin, the elite wizard.

"What is she doing here?" Dre said. The Yordin will always find a way to keep their eyes on the twins.

"She's going to administer your test," the old man said. "Which energy do you prefer to start with?"

Dre lay on the ground. "Dark," he said. He would be able to better support the pressure while on his back.

"We will start with light then," the old man said. "It's better to start with the weaker skill first; get the hard part out of the way."

Dre sucked his teeth. Now, he would have to test his magic's new behavior on the energy he had the least control over. He absentmindedly reached out for Alaan but couldn't feel him through the gigastone. The Guard always forced Dre to be alone at the worst times.

He stood up, extended his senses, and his skin lit up with heat like an exposed wire. The pressure of potential dark energy intensified to a squeeze. The waves were both deep and long. A crater of energy rested within him, every contour clear in his mind. It defined a topology of sorts.

As the force reversed, swooping up and away, it pulled on him. It was like ascending a mountain into a storm. It was powerful, but it was dangerous. Summoning energy at the peaks released the most. The problem was that he couldn't sense precisely where he was within the light energy zone. It was murky.

He felt his way carefully through several more oscillations. The timing of pulls and pushes were the same, but the passages along their gradients were different. Dark was slow and even, but light was jittery.

Four energy disks solidified in the air, two above Dre and two above the elite wizard. She didn't even twitch with the effort. She was known for her ability to use wizardry without movement.

Dre waited until the pressure on his skin flipped into a pull, then pushed. Light glittered around him, forming a cloud. The heat warmed his body and tugged on him. He rose onto his toes, then his feet lifted off the ground. For the first time, he was weightless from his own might. Maybe he would practice light energy, even if he never used it in battle.

The round started with the wizard firing a ball of dark energy and a puff of light energy. Dre swung his arm through the air like Alaan usually did. Half of his cloud moved into the path of the fast dark energy. The black sphere entered the cloud, but nothing exited. Less energy pulled on him. Dre's slow ascension stopped.

He split his remaining energy in two and directed it at the Yordin. It soared past her, ignoring the light energy that approached him. She destroyed one of his disks, but then he destroyed both of hers.

"Round one complete," the old man said.

"I did it," Dre said. He finally had enough light energy to use for something. He searched the viewing slits for Alaan, but they were empty.

The disks were reset. Dre reached out his senses again. This time, he waited a fraction of a second longer after the pressure flipped to a pull. Light energy blazed around him. A cloud as big as the last round formed in a blimp, but more energy continued to come. His feet were yanked off the ground. He fell up.

The energy didn't stop pouring out, increasing his speed. He rushed to the ceiling. In a sharp burst, everything went white as a second surge of light energy snapped free of its balance with dark energy. He shut his eyes against the new heat. He tried snapping, but new energy cropped up to replace it.

Below, his light energy flashed. He didn't need to condense it. It was concentrated on its own. A black blur darted out in front of him a moment before it exploded. It was the wizard. Dark energy pooled around her. Booms rocked the chamber. The other guards in the room shouted. Shards of stone scattered.

"I got you," she said. She pressed a hand on his chest, pinning him against the ceiling as his light energy winked out. The smoke cleared. Grintinari, the old man, and the sorcerers were safe, protected by dissolving dark energy walls.

"Thank you," Dre said as she lowered him.

"I heard about what you did to a gigasphere and the explosion at your home," she said. "I'm here to keep you safe."

Dre's two disks were gone. "Does this mean I failed?" he asked.

The old man nodded, then held out a hand towards the door. "It isn't safe for you to practice magic alone. Sorry to say this, but the draft program is best for you."

Dre shook his head. Slithlor wasn't the answer. "I will remember that you tricked me."

"Dre failed," the old man announced when they exited the gigastone room.

"Oh, what a surprise," Slithlor said.

Alaan approached. He wasn't smiling.

Dre hugged him as he passed. "Don't pick light energy."

"He knows that we know. Find out how to undo the connection," Alaan said, then released the embrace.

Dre spun around to watch him slip behind the gigastone door. Either he was eager to get away or focused on passing the exam. Everything depended on him.

When they were alone, the psychic said, "Bring me Rye and in exchange, I'll end the draft." He hadn't moved from his spot at the center of the room.

The shock of Slithlor's desperation took a moment to run its course, but Dre kept his face even. He noted that Slithlor only mentioned Rye and put his hands behind his back. "Tell me how to break our connection to a spirit fiend, then maybe."

"Bring me Rye first, then I'll do it."

"Tell me now or I will let the Guard study my magic more closely," Dre said as he stepped closer.

"Since birth, you have been an anomaly. Anything they saw would be attributed to that. But my offer to help you gain control over your connection to a spirit fiend still stands. You are already familiar with how unpredictable your magic has become. It will only worsen until it kills you unless you bring me Rye," Slithlor said.

Slithlor attempted to draft Dre and Alaan but didn't order their deaths because he wasn't afraid of them being discovered. Juli couldn't leverage the twins like she could Rye, the son of a former elite. Maybe Lakree wasn't as big of a threat since any extraordinary magic would be attributed to nobility and Hila was a foreigner who, in theory, still had access to non-Lynitian magic. But Slithlor should be afraid of Dre and Alaan.

"Did you know that we can combine our memories?" Dre said as he circled Slithlor. Unlike in the dream, Slithlor didn't follow Dre. He stayed in place like a statue. "Even though you tampered with how they were stored, we could correct the angles. We remember that you carried Sewit's device behind your back during the Castle tour. Elite Palow or Council Member Palow will be able to confirm that."

Dre stepped back in front of Slithlor, whose eyebrow twitched. "That's unexpected, but my answer remains the same. I don't want you harmed, but I need you to convince Rye to leave the Medina."

It was a bold response. If he were caught, Slithlor would be charged with treason, and oddly, he had a preference over who implicated him. "If you care about us, then why did you do it? You are the one who put us in danger."

"I am creating a seventh noble family and you will be the face of it."

"A seventh magic?" Dre said. This aligned with the Medina's perception of his obsession with magic. The stage after understanding was creation.

"Not necessarily, but a power that doesn't pass through blood."

"Magic doesn't pass through blood. The nobles already know that."

"Before Lynit was formed, it did; nobles only taught magic to their offspring. When Kertic required that magic be shared, it was, but the nobles didn't share everything. They kept knowledge for themselves and used it to build up their image as superior. The power that passes down isn't magic. It is nobility itself. But, a seventh family will disrupt the historical balance between them and the Kertics. There will be chaos, but something new will emerge, a stronger Lynit where anyone powerful enough can become noble."

"The nobles will stop you."

"Not if we become powerful enough to topple a family or two. And maybe the others will help us. They have grudges that date back to the founding of this nation."

This would be a civil war. Dre shook his head. "You're a monster."

"I'm no different than you. You are destroying the nobility, too, with your clever little eclipse. People are fed up with being excluded from their power and respect. We can work together. All we need to do is keep Rye away from Juli. I'll even help you get away from Grintinari."

"We are nothing alike," Dre said through gritted teeth. He wanted to break the idea of nobility because it didn't value hard work. It simply expected performance from those who had it. But Lynit needed the nobility in some form. The other nations with multiple magics fought until there was only one. The nobility maintained respect between magics because they needed each other. Lynit's growth was through transforming nobility into something that benefited everyone, not by destroying it. "If another nation finds out, it would be an even worse war."

"Give us a few years and Lynit will be even more powerful than before," Slithlor said.

"Why are you telling me this when you know I could show what you did to us?"

"You know what would happen if you did. It would inconvenience me, but Lynit would deal with you first. Though you love fame, I don't see you as the martyr type."

It was true that Dre was afraid to share the evidence with the Guard, but he had hoped that he could at least use it as leverage. Slithlor had started his scheme years ago, so he had plenty of time to think through the risks, but he couldn't mitigate all of them. There had to be an angle other than Juli where he was weak.

"We've turned the public against the nobility. We can turn them against you," Dre said.

"No matter what you do, you are forwarding my goals. The fame you've enjoyed your whole life isn't by mistake."

"What does that mean?"

"You were one of my first attempts at a seventh family. I meant for you to be a single person with twice as much magic, not two people. But it was still a success. Your magic unites the people more than the nobles'. "

"Huh?" Dre leaned closer. He heard him but didn't know what to make of it. The idea that he was made was too crazy. What he valued most in the world was the experiment of a psychopath. Everything felt like it was spinning. His hands pressed against the side of his head. His fingers scrapped his scalp. "You're lying."

"Don't insult me. I planned to tell you once you were nineteen, but I didn't expect Sewit's device to work on you because your magic was so weak," Slithlor said. "Stabilize your connection to the spirit fiend, then choose to use it however you wish. Just help me give Rye the same choice. I know that you have been to the Medina."

The exam room door screeched open and Dre snapped around. He noticed that his heart was pounding but wasn't sure when it had started. Alaan walked towards him with the three elites and two sorcerers in tow.

"Alaan passed," the old man said. "Their cohort will remain in the MMA. All future exams will be taken separately."

Dre turned back to Slithlor. "You're just like the nobles. All you see in us is our magic and you will regret that," he said, trembling.

Slithlor winked, then turned around. "Grintinari, we need to talk."

Dre pulled Alaan out of the room.

Chapter 29 - Rye

Rye arrived in the spirit realm on a bed of delicate and whimsical clouds. They stretched in all directions, forming buildings and mountains alike. Creatures with tiny wings moved about the city with their briefcases. Up close, they were even uglier than in his dreams. Their fish-like faces and bloated bodies were slick with an oily glob that oozed off them. One floated past him. It was shoulder height. It dipped its head and motioned as if removing a hat that wasn't there.

"If you are connected to one of these, you should be safe. They are harmless. At worst, they'll strengthen your work ethic," Chirchi said.

Rye reached behind his ear. His fingers grasped a thin string and his vision changed. He was falling; no, he was diving. Wind split around his sharp beak. His wings pressed flat against his body. He descended a black tower. Rye released the string. In the city's center, a dark storm in the shape of a column stretched to infinity. Streams of silent lightning zigzagged from top to bottom. Rye's ear warmed with each step closer. Tenaju's voice rumbled within him. "We will explore all worlds," it said.

"No," Rye said to Chirchi, shaking his head. "These spirit fiends envy what I'm connected to."

His dreams of this place didn't start after his first trip to the spirit realm; that was only when he started remembering them. He had dreamed of this place many times over the years because he understood what it was like to be trapped like the worker fishbirds. Since his father disappeared, he held his head high when guards glared at him, but deep down, he wanted to escape it all. Joining the Guard was about proving himself, but it was also a means of getting out of Lynit. Becoming stronger than his father, the most skilled non-noble animalist, was next to impossible. It was easier to go where no one would recognize him. In the wild, there was no judgment, no shame. He would survive until he didn't.

Tenaju's pressure dug into him as he stepped into the dim tower. Small lights flashed on a pedestal at the center. Hundreds of floating colored disks bumped into each other, sometimes interlocking. There was a brief moment when six of them touched each other and it looked like Lynit's symbol, but then it was gone. Shadows flickered from behind. A soft-faced boy, no, girl with spiky hair, leaned out. The reflection of the colorful lights looked like dancing make-up. Behind her ear, a blue string connected her to one of the rings. She wasn't alone. Four other people stepped from behind the pedestal. Not only did Rye not expect to see other people in the spirit realm, but he didn't expect to recognize one of them.

One boy was skinny with buzzed black hair and wispy fuzz on his chin and jawline. He didn't look like the nerdy sorcerer who used to like math problems. His gaze was stern. A lot had happened in a few years, but he was still Drime. The only reason Rye didn't run across the room was because Drime was supposed to be in the Castle.

"Is this part of your training?" Rye said.

"It's good to see you, Rye," Drime said. He hopped off the pedestal and crossed the room. He stuck out a hand. Rye pushed it aside and hugged him. It was the first time they hugged. Drime had bonded more with Lakree and dated Hila, but that feeling of closeness flowed through Rye. His connection to Lakree and Hila went both ways.

"Finally, the big reunion. So cute," a tall girl said and clapped. She smirked.

A boy in a sleeveless shirt rolled his eyes. "He must be in the Medina with her."

"You must have Sewit's device," Chirchi said.

"What do you know about this?" Drime said. He tapped his ear. A faint blue string rested there. All of the other children had a similar one. Rye reached for his ear but stopped short of touching it. It was hot, but no heat radiated off it. Tenaju was fast approaching. Above, a white dot grew from the center of the swirling black clouds. "We all feel the pressure of the approaching spirit fiend. Is it yours?"

Rye nodded. "Who did this to us?" he said, then paused. "And why?" The dangers of spirit fiends were clear. Not only did they destroy Nintur, but the beings also killed Sewit's soldiers. They weren't weapons because they had agendas of their own.

"Have you made contact with Juli?" Drime said.

Rye's mind flashed to the front-page newspaper article on her. She was the type of person children ran from. "I've never met her. How could she have done this?" He flicked the string and winced. It vibrated. The force rippled up and away until it pinged with Tenaju. His vision blinked to a different perspective. The seven children in the room were dots against the white ground.

"You need to come with us," Drime said. "If another nation finds you, it will start a war."

"You are the draftees who went missing," Chirchi said as she stepped forward. "You are working for Slithlor."

Another boy jumped from the pedestal. His dark brown eyes matched his skin. "Hi. We have been looking for you. We are here to help." Rye shook his hand. When Rye released his grip, the boy didn't let go. "The spirit fiend that you have been dreaming about is giving you power. If you ignore it, it will kill you. I am sure you heard of the girl who disintegrated."

Rye shuddered, then his eyes dropped to the strings on his chest. The spirit fiend's power didn't stay in him. It passed through to Lakree and Hila. Lakree's next matter shift could be his last and Hila's next lightning spell could kill everyone around her. "How do you break the connection?"

"Why would you when you can control it? This is a once-in-a-lifetime opportunity," Drime said. "Merge with the spirit fiend and in exchange, it will give you power to rival any noble, maybe even the Kertics. It will change your magic based on the idea that it represents."

Rye shook his head. Tenaju offered him power but with a condition. It wanted to travel to the real world and discover all there was to discover, but that meant war for Lynit. If another nation spotted the great white bird soaring across their skies from the west, they would prepare their troops.

Rye tried to pull away, but the boy held him. "Lynit can't survive another war."

"True, it does add a risk, but Slithlor has a plan for that," Drime said. He placed a hand on Rye's shoulder.

"Quiet, he could still repeat everything to Juli," the boy said, snapping at Drime.

"It will be too late if we wait and we can't force him to do anything here," Drime said.

Rye's gaze shifted to Chirchi, the only one he trusted here. If he had met these kids in person, they might have kidnapped him.

Crimson turned to the others in his group, who either shrugged or agreed. "Be quick. We need to go." He looked up. The pressure of the spirit fiend's presence pressed down like a mountain.

"A few hours after you matter shifted out of the Castle, the king regent charged you with treason and ordered your death," Drime said. Rye would have called him a liar, but it made sense. Slithlor tried to draft him, guards broke into Lakree's house, and wanted signs were plastered all over Poli. The king regent and Slithlor were trying to protect Lynit. "He knows that you are connected to a spirit fiend and plans to have you killed before anyone finds out. But Slithlor wants to keep us alive. He wants us to start our own noble family, a new legacy of power."

nobles set the rules, expectations, and the thread of blood that defined their lines. A new noble family meant that Rye wouldn't be bound by the Finrar's and animalism's instincts control mandate. His father's fear of spirit fiends wouldn't have been cowardice. It would have been respected as intelligence. And all of the Ternitu descendants would be proud of their history.

Chirchi pushed Crimson away from Rye. "This is all so stupid. Why would Slithlor do this?"

"What will happen to Lakree and Hila? They are charged with treason but aren't connected to a spirit fiend. They are connected to me," Rye said. Two of the kids burst into clouds and floated away. "And what about the ban on spirit fiends?" The other nations wouldn't sit idly by as Lynit celebrated doing the one thing that was illegal. Nor would the Guard. The entire world would want Rye dead.

Drime pouted for a moment. "No one will find out about you if you join us. The charges against Large and Hila will be dropped," he said.

"Where can I find you?" Rye asked.

"We'll be in the Easton Tunnels. Just leave the Medina," Drime said as he evaporated along with the remaining draftees.

"Don't trust him, Rye. There will be nothing secret about a noble family in Lynit. I think I can break your connection here. Your contract is one of those disks on the pedestal," Chirchi said. She pointed, but her arm distorted, folded back on itself. Then, she disappeared.

Rye's ear spiked hotter. Above, snow-white feathers rustled. Before colliding with the ground, Tenaju spread its wings, spanning the room. There was no burst of air or sound. Its feet touched down with grace.

What is your answer? Tenaju spoke, though its beak didn't move. The voice traveled down the string attached to Rye, filling his entire body. Its black eyes were the only non-white part of its body. They didn't reflect Rye's image but reflected other spirit realms.

How can I stop my magic from passing into my friends?

You will be able to do more than that. Once I discover a place, I can always find my way back to it. You are anchored to people and I can teach you the power of that.

Either Rye could return to his old life where his mother stressed over him being drafted, where guards looked down on his family, and where Lakree would forever be beyond him. Or, Rye could create a new path for himself. With Tenaju's strength, he could protect Lakree and Hila no matter what the Guard decided. He could protect the next king in the next war, even if he were the cause of that war. Since these other children were keeping their spirit fiends, Rye was no additional threat to Lynit.

I accept.

Tenaju burst into a thick cloud of energy. Rough currents twisted and bent the energy into a torrent. But the energy wasn't wild. Many threads wove together, linking many thoughts and realms to a single purpose. Rye spun around. The tempest blotted out everything. Then, in a wave, it pinned Rye in place. The stab of a knife probed his mind, searching for a weak point. He formed a wide door on his forehead.

Tenaju cracked the frame as it pressed in. Rye screamed into the blinding void. It filled his mind with a new light that eclipsed the dull flash of the MMA material. Memories of hundreds of different realms poured in. There were deserts, oceans, grasslands, but also strange, dream places. The spirit realms were the thoughts of humans solidified, then that space, in turn, gave power to the person. Rye's fantasy of marrying Lakree and becoming a noble by proxy was full of spirit energy. It wasn't his alone; many others pined over someone who was close but out of reach. It was almost a property of the universe. Tenaju traveled between all of these places, learning and growing.

But Tenaju's hunger craved more. The doorframe split in half. The crack ran up the wall of the mental construct, then sliced Rye's mind completely open. At the core of Tenaju was the single concept of discovery.

Rye's goal of becoming a guard was squished into a silly afterthought and he didn't miss it. It was like a morph, a reorganization of the brain. Tenaju wasn't a foreign presence. It was familiar. Rye, too, had a hunger inside him to explore the world and its beautiful creatures. Tenaju latched onto that.

It wasn't just changing Rye. It was consuming him, absorbing his life. Tenaju pressed until only a tight knot of Rye remained. It was his instincts, the last stubborn part of him. Packed tight with his MMA material were Rye's anchors. He felt the energies of his mother, his brother, Lakree, and Hila.

In the spirit realm, distance didn't matter. A shared idea was enough to link them. These were the connections that he needed, not Lynit, not the respect of the Guard. He mistakenly thought these instincts were the enemy, the barrier to his goals. Instead, they protected a truth he needed to accept. There was a duty to Lynit, but a more important duty was to his family and friends. He didn't need the Guard to prove he was capable or brave. Protecting those he cared about was proof enough. Human instinct was a warning that his deepest connections were at risk.

Another energy scattered across countless realms vibrated in harmony with Rye. It knew him. It was his father. In death, spirit energy was unchanged. The ideas they represented remained forever. His father's dedication to his instincts was within Rye. There was a message there, a lingering memory. His father wasn't a coward when he fled. He knew of a danger far more critical than his duty to the king. He not only ran to protect his family but also all of Lynit. Now that he was dead, that responsibility was passed down to Rye.

A wave of serenity flowed out from that small space surrounded by the mind and power of Tenaju. Rye expanded out. His mind grew, remembering his strength, but not by rejecting Tenaju. He absorbed it into him. The spirit fiends connections to places were just like his connection to people. They were both connections built on respect.

The tower snapped back into view, but his vision was different. Hundreds of lines of energy stretched from his body. They were all of his connections. Tiny ones linked him to the MMA students from initiation. There was a thickening connection to Chirchi. Lakree and Hila were blazing beams of light. He would always find his way back to all of them.

Now for your end of the deal, Tenaju said. His voice spoke from within.

Chapter 30 - Dre

Dre and Alaan ran out of the Castle. Several lines of guards blocked off the bridge, holding back a mob. Homin waited for them."Did you pass?" he asked. Dre nodded but continued past him. Homin darted in front. "We found the manufacturer who made the eclipse pins and he was more than happy to share that he made them for you years ago. Now, together, we will craft that into a Yordin symbol."

Dre stopped. The Yordin had given him an idea. He beckoned a nearby sorcerer over. "Amplify my voice." Her lips moved quickly as she rattled off the spell. The crowd quieted. "We are safe and sound. However, if we don't show up at the Gigasphere Tournament tomorrow, it will not be because of the Guard as a whole or the nobility. It will be because Slithlor kidnapped or killed us."

Homin swiped his hand across his neck in panic. The sorcerer ended his spell, but it was much too late. The crowd broke out in a chant of "End the Draft."

"What was that for?" Homin said.

Dre didn't answer. Instead, he ran towards the edge of the bridge. He jumped and reached out his senses. He didn't want to warn Alaan or lay out a plan. He just wanted his brother to move with him. And Alaan did. Dre shared his balance with Alaan, who trailed after him with light energy. Dre glided over the waterless moat. Once their feet touched the ground, they darted through the city and dipped underground.

After a few turns, Alaan stopped. "What did Slithlor say?"

Dre stared into his beautiful and innocent eyes. Alaan didn't know. Slithlor didn't admit his master plan to him. He didn't tell Alaan that his existence was an accident. Thinking about it made Dre want to vomit, so he pushed it aside. "First wake up Dad, stop Slithlor, and then we talk," he said.

Alaan nodded, then sprinted towards the Medina.

The only illumination in the tunnel was from light energy controlled by Alaan until the crystals in the wall turned on. At an intersection with another tunnel, a boy stepped into the path. He had straight black hair and brown skin and wore shorts. Instead of politely sticking to the tunnel's edge, he moved down the middle. Judging from his light clothing, he wasn't from Poli. And he didn't behave like a fan.

"Something is wrong," Dre said. They doubled back to the nearest hub and took a different tunnel. There was more than one path through the Easton Tunnels. Halfway down the next tunnel, a girl stepped into view. She was appropriately dressed in a sweater with a growling quitol stitched on the front, but her intense grin was maniacal. She laughed as she blocked the tunnel with her arms stretched to her sides.

"…missing draftees," Alaan said in a quick whisper.

Dre and Alaan turned around. Back at the hub, a different kid approached from each tunnel except the one that led back to the Castle. They had to have been sent by Slithlor.

"We don't have time for this," Dre said. He summoned dark energy, causing his gear to sizzle. A spark of light flickered in front of Alaan. It spread around them, creating a halo-shaped cloud. Dre eased into Alaan's balance as he condensed twenty-five spikes, five for each kid. "Move."

Another source of wizardry disturbed the air. Stavender canceled Dre's and Alaan's energy in a quick flurry of his arms. "Calm down, Poli Twins. I thought you would be happy to see me," he said. He was short, muscular, and grinning.

"I meet so many fans that I forget faces easily," Dre said. "We know each other?"

Stavender frowned.

"But you know who we are, don't you?" The first boy said. He revealed a shiny metal orb that he had been hiding behind his back.

"What do you want?" Alaan said.

"...to talk. I'm Crimson, a psychic," he said. He was likely their leader. The other kids introduced themselves as if they were at a party.

Dre tuned his senses to the pushes and pulls of wizardry. A deep abyss waited for him. "What do you want?"

"A better question is: What do you want?" Crimson said.

"To get by," Dre said.

"We are in the same predicament as you." Crimson held the device directly in front of him. It was the same ball Slithlor hid behind his back in Dre's memory. It was what connected Dre to Rombinanandi. "Let's get by together."

"What did Slithlor promise you?" Alaan said.

"Our lives."

"Our father is sick. We have to help him first, then we can talk," Alaan said.

"There is only one option, but there are two paths: the easy way or we make you," Carsi said. "I hope you don't think Slithlor told you all that information for no reason. He knew you would come here where no one would see us."

"Stavender, please," Dre begged as he mustered all the sadness and exhaustion he could. If he could have dropped a tear on command, he would have. He wasn't above looking pitiful anymore. "Give us until tomorrow."

"So you do remember me," Stavender said, stepping closer. "We won't let you go to the Medina nor let Juli find you."

Dre sucked his teeth. They weren't particularly old friends anyway.

"Why are you so sure you can trust Slithlor?" Alaan said. "He used a dangerous foreign device on us. We could have all died."

"You trust Juli? What do you know about her?" Crimson said.

Dre pretended to think about it as he recalled a map of the Easton Tunnels. There were a few paths to the Medina. Dre and Alaan were powerful together, but maybe not against five, and likely not against five who each had a spirit fiend feeding him extra magic. But the twins didn't need to win a fight. They only needed to escape and Dre and Alaan had planned many versions of this scenario before.

Dre reached a hand into his pocket. "If we go with you, first, we have to get rid of this. We are being tracked with this."

"No," Alaan said as Dre flung Tess' communication orb into the air. Dre covered his face and clenched his eyes, but there was no flash. Instead, Alaan tried pulling away. The communication orb banged against the glass ceiling, then hit the floor. It broke and faded away.

"Was that from Ser?" Crimson said.

He had done his part of the distract and flash combo, but Alaan didn't do his. Now Dre had to compensate. He squeezed Alaan's hand tight.

"What's that?" Dre said, pointing at the ceiling. He shut his eyes and slapped his hands over Alaan's as he pushed out light energy. A sharp jolt lifted him off his feet. He clung to his brother's head as an anchor, but Alaan rose. They were still sharing balance. The draftees screamed, but the explosion drowned out their voices. The blast scattered stone and smoke. Dre fell on top of his brother.

Dre scrambled to his feet. As he ran past Stavender, he tried to punch him, but Stavender dodged it. However, he wasn't prepared for the second punch from Alaan that hit him in the throat.

They darted around several corners, taking a few unnecessary turns to mask their destination. They entered another six-way hub. The stairwell to the lowest level of the tunnels was down the path directly ahead. As Dre crossed the center, his shoe caught on the ground like he had stepped in glue. His foot slipped out of his shoe as he fell forward. Alaan tripped next to him. He hit the ground. He didn't slide.

"What was that?" Dre said. The ground was relatively clean, save for dust and pellets of voroborous poop. He tried to drag his shoe, but it wouldn't budge.

Alaan tapped a finger on the ground. "It's a friction increase," he said as he stood up. He extended a foot, placed it on the ground, shifted his weight, then raised his back foot. Dre pushed himself to his feet. He hopped towards the next tunnel.

"Running won't help," Carsi said, though the sound didn't echo in the hallway; it echoed in Dre's mind. One by one, the tunnels smoothed over with brick, except for the one where the five draftees stood.

Alaan swirled a thin film of light energy around them. Purple energy in the air became visible. It touched Dre and Alaan and stretched back to Carsi. It evaporated, but the visual effect of the covered tunnels didn't fade. Above, sunlight shined down, which ruled the coverings out as normal illusions.

"I don't know what kind of spell that is," Dre said softly.

"Stavender used to defeat us in duels by himself," Alaan said. "Now he needs four more to help. What happened?"

"Bring Rye out," Drime said.

"If Shorty can't defeat us in a fair fight, then we will never accept what you have to offer," Alaan said.

"Shorty? Is that you?" Carsi chuckled, turning to Stavender, whose face squished in anger.

"Don't call me that." He summoned light and dark energy.

"Oh, maybe we do have a few minutes," Carsi said. "I would love to see this."

"They may dance around on a stage, but they only have the strength of one person," Stavender said. "Drop the friction spell Drime."

Crimson shook his head but then gave Drime permission. The draftees spread out around the edge of the hub.

"I've been waiting for this," Stavender said as he lunged forward. Dre cut to the left. He summoned dark energy in his wake. Since he still maintained balance with Alaan, his steps were quick. He fired spheres and Alaan exploded nuggets of light energy, but Stavender blocked all of them.

The twins circled the edges of the six-tunnel hub, firing attacks from different angles. Stavender spun around like a madman, ducking and dodging. Dre angled a few attacks off from Stavender, aimed at the draftees behind him, but Stavender blocked them too. His access to wizardry was heightened and his training was sharp. He didn't waste much energy.

Dre aimed his next volley of attacks at Stavender's feet, but it didn't help. He controlled his balance finely. His steps were delicate. However, he mistakenly lessened his attention on Alaan and didn't notice a swift ball of light. It exploded near him. He slid across the hub, disappearing through a tunnel covering.

Dre shared a look with Alaan. Some sort of visual spell was at play. Rombinanandi allowed Dre and Alaan to communicate when their energies were joined. The other spirit fiends would have changed the draftees in other ways.

"Don't lose, Shorty," Carsi said.

Dre condensed a quick sphere and shot it at where Stavender fell.

The energy passed through the covering without causing a ripple.

Dre touched his elbow and slid two fingers down to his wrist. Then he clinched his fist twice. The fake walls didn't trap Dre and Alaan, but the draftees who stood next to each tunnel did. Running away down the only open tunnel wasn't worth it. The only path was forward.

A flicker of panic blinked in Alaan's eyes. He repeated the gesture but without clinching his fists. Dre double-checked the size of the hub. Its radius was about thirty feet, but its height was only eight. A big explosion would collapse the roof. They might still escape, but they could kill these brainwashed children. To not be a murderer, Dre had to fight with some constraints.

Stavender stepped through the fake wall. He held a thin black sword and an oversized shield. Two balls of light circled above him.

As Dre summoned a giant cloud of dark energy, Alaan created one of light. Dre pressed his energy into Alaan's. The two joined into a cloud of tiny eclipses. Together, Dre and Alaan condensed it into six spheres.

"Oh, this is why the eclipses represent the Poli Twins," Crimson said.

"Let us pass or else," Alaan said.

They swooped their arms, lining a sphere up with each draftee and keeping the sixth one in reserve.

"Oh, I have tricks, too," Stavender said, snapping away his energy. He opened his mouth and a white light shined through.

"No, Stavender," Crimson said. "Are you stupid? You can't do that here."

"Oh, I guess we aren't the only ones who think you're stupid," Dre said in the ditziest voice he could manage. Even if Dre couldn't use his full magical power, he could flex his ability to push someone emotionally to their edge.

Carsi laughed. "I like him. We are going to get along just fine."

Stavender turned to her. "Shut up! You are so annoying."

Before he could turn back around, Dre and Alaan punched up their reserve ball of energy. It burst through one of the glass ceiling panels and shot into the air. Dre snapped, releasing the dark energy in the rising energy. The boom shook the tunnel. A few seconds later, whistles blew.

"That was the 'or else,'" Alaan said. "The whole city will be coming now."

"Enough of this," Crimson said. "We have to take them and go now." Purple energy flared from his head. The other draftees prepared spells.

Dre and Alaan punched again. Four of the five balls of energy hit the draftees in the chest, carrying them screaming through the covered tunnels. Stavender reacted by flinging himself into the air with a cloud of light energy. Dre swiped his left arm up in sync with Alaan, and the energy Stavender had dodged arced up to hit him. It pinned his chest to the ceiling. He cursed.

Dre ran underneath him. He steeled himself as he ran into what looked like a bricked wall. He passed through the other side, but a bright light was waiting for him. The energy retracted before exploding.

The boom hurt Dre's ears. His gear dampened the heat, but the force hit him like a boulder. His feet and hands trailed out in front as he bumped into Alaan and they both tumbled back into the hub. There were voices, whistles, and a constant buzz.

Stavender was still pinned to the ceiling. He launched more attacks, thrashing about like a wild quitol. The attacks thudded into Dre, pounding him into the ground, but they felt like punches and not magical burns. Victoria Finrar's gear was the best in the business.

"You will not get away from me," Stavender shouted.

Dre held up his arms to protect his head from the volleys.

"The Poli Twins are being attacked," someone said. Dre glanced over. A young girl's head dipped through the missing glass panel in the ceiling. Her jet-black hair hung two feet lower. She jerked back as a black ball of energy shot her way.

A quick anger twisted in Dre. He snapped. He released the dark energy in the ball that held Stavender. It exploded dust and debris. If Stavender screamed, Dre didn't hear it. But Dre heard his body hit the ground.

"What did you do?" Alaan said as he scrambled over to him.

"There's a line at attacking bystanders," Dre said as he pulled Alaan away. They took two turns and descended a set of stairs to the lowest level of the tunnels. Whistles filled the tunnels now. Voices called for the Poli Twins. Dre turned the last corner to arrive at the gigastone entrance to the Medina.

Alaan flipped open the metal box and twisted the water gauges in the correct pattern. It didn't work. He reset them and tried again, but the gigastone door didn't slide open.

"Let me try," Dre said as he pushed him aside. He took a deep breath. He turned the gauges carefully. The door still didn't budge.

Alaan banged on the stone with a fist. "Open up. Let us in."

"They changed the code," Dre said as he tried it again. He put it in backward, then rearranged the order. Still, nothing worked.

A heavy-footed hobble tromped down the hall. Dre created a black wall of energy, sealing him and Alaan in a small ten-square-foot space.

Alaan summoned light energy. "We'll break in."

"The door is a foot of gigasphere," Dre said.

"I broke it before. Stand back."

"No, then anyone could walk in after us."

A hole grew in Dre's wall as outside light energy ate into it. For a moment, Stavender was visible. The front of his shirt was burned away. His chest and face were scorched and blistered. Blood seeped through clenched teeth.

Something glinted in Stavender's hand. Then, a black ball shot forward. It was too late for Dre to condense a shield to deflect it, so he sidestepped and sealed up the hole. Alaan placed light in the path of the attack, then made a sound like he caught something heavy. He staggered back, hitting the wall and sliding down. There was something on his stomach. It was a metal hilt. It stuck to him as if it belonged there.

"Help me," Alaan said as he pulled at it.

"No, don't," Dre said. Dark red liquid covered a hand-length blade. Alaan spasmed as the knife clattered against stone.

"Run," Alaan said weakly. A shaking arm propped against the ground was the only thing stopping him from crumpling over. His eyes drooped.

Dre pulled up Alaan's shirt to see a red line just below his ribs that seeped blood. Dre didn't know enough about protection to gauge if this was healable, but it wasn't the worst injury he had ever seen. Nearly mangled bodies have been restored after tournament fights, but the thought didn't comfort him. This was the second time Alaan was hurt because of him. He had seen a flicker of metal. He didn't know what it was but should have deflected the attack or shouted. This was how Alaan got the scar above his right eye from Stavendar. When the bully attacked with the lightning spell, Dre dodged it. He had assumed that his brother saw it too but was wrong. Alaan was hit in the face. This was exactly what Alaan complained about. Dre pretended so much that Alaan should know what he thought that in a crunch, he communicated less, not more.

As Alaan slumped further, specks of energy rose off him. Two specks pressed together and sparked. His wizardry was escaping. The last time it happened was when they were asleep and Rombinanandi invaded their dream. Alaan was going to pass out.

"They're in there," Stavender said. "I've got them trapped."

Dre looked over his shoulder to see the four other draftees arrive. His dark energy wall was gone.

Pri covered Stavender in a red healing shield.

"We need to get out of here," Crimson said.

"Heal him," Dre said through gritted teeth as more energy flowed from Alaan. It stung Dre's hands and face as it hit him, but he didn't move. It also burned away the healing sphere Pri cast around Alaan. She tried another, but it only lasted a few seconds before the wizardry ate it up. Everyone knew that light energy evaporated mental energy, but Dre didn't know that healing energy was weak to it. If this energy didn't stop leaking out, no one would be able to heal Alaan. "Please, please stay awake," Dre said, kissing his forehead, slick with sweat.

"What do we do?" Drime said.

"I can't do anything until the light energy stops," Pri said.

"This is Stavender's fault," Carsi said. "He can't follow orders. We were told to bring them in unharmed."

Dre lifted Alaan's drooping head. The only option was to shock Alaan awake. "Slithlor said that he made us twins," he said.

Alaan's eyes twitched, then locked on to Dre's.

"He didn't mention that," Carsi said.

"Stay with me, please. I will do whatever you want. We can end the Poli Twins. We'll use both energies," Dre said.

The door to the Medina slid open, knocking Alaan on his side. He groaned. Rye, Lakree, Hila, and Chirchi stood at the entrance.

"They found us," Chirchi said.

"What happened?" Lakree said.

"Drime?" Hila said.

The sounds of the approaching whistles and footsteps ramped up a notch. Guards had found the stairs to the lower level.

"We have to go," Crimson said.

"Come with us, Rye," Drime said. He held out a hand.

"No," Rye said.

"Alaan needs help," Dre pleaded. Everyone acted as if they didn't see the blood.

Hila squatted next to him. "Put pressure on the wound."

"Get him inside," Lakree said.

"I see them," a guard said. The E.D.s all looked left, then vanished. Chirchi pulled Alaan into the Medina on a cushion of mental energy. The door slid closed behind them. The sounds from the Easton Tunnels were muted. Chirchi didn't pause and ran Alaan back to the room. She placed him on the bed, then left in search of Urura. Hila ripped the bedsheets and tied them around Alaan's stomach.

Alaan's gaze drifted lazily. His lips moved slowly. Dre dipped his ear to his brother's face but couldn't make out anything. Alaan groaned as a wave of sparks puffed off him. It hit the bedding and set it on fire. Dre lifted him.

"Anuni Cantirili Mintanora," Hila said. Two controlled streams of water rained on the bed, putting out the flames.

Dre placed him back on the wet mattress. Alaan's face was no longer tense. It was soft. His breathing was shallow but steady. More energy trickled out of him, creating steam. It pooled above into a dangerous cloud. Not only did Alaan's energy make healing him difficult, it would destroy the room.

"He can't contain the extra energy," Rye said, his voice calm.

"You have to cancel it before the whole room explodes," Lakree said.

Dre didn't know how. Only Alaan knew the secret to disrupting their energies from joining when they touched. Instead, Dre wiped his forehead and pushed dark energy into Alaan's light. As the energies combined, Alaan's voice entered Dre's mind. He repeated one sound, one word, one name. *Dre.*

When Dre answered, it broke the mantra.

We were an experiment? Alaan said.

We were a failed experiment, Dre said, his tears dropping on Alaan. A burst of light energy crackled in the air. Dre condensed a quick slab of dark energy above everyone. He supported it with three pillars right as Alaan's energy exploded. The blast shattered the glass in the kitchen. The coach caught fire and debris pattered against the temporary new roof. Smoke filled the room even as Hila put out the new flames.

We are the first and only twins. We can't fail because we are the standard, Alaan said.

But I failed you as your brother, Dre said. He had spent his life trying to convince himself and the world that they were one person across two bodies and that what one knew, so did the other.

Alaan's eyes remained narrow slits, but his gaze lulled in Dre's direction. *We failed each other. I thought pushing you away would give me space to find my balance, but I was wrong. No one other than me can affect my internal balance. I wasn't putting in the work. We weren't putting in the work.*

More energy flowed out of Alaan. As it hit the condensed dark energy above, it didn't join with it. It canceled it, eating small holes in the covering. Bits of dust and pebbles fell through. Alaan sneezed and a thunderous roar thrashed above. Everyone screamed as Dre's covering shattered and the entire room was set ablaze.

Chirchi returned with Urura and the three women who kept watch in the entrance chamber to the rest of the Medina. They scanned the room for a few seconds before entering. Urura cast a light blue shield around the combined wizardry and a red healing sphere over Dre and Alaan. Chirchi created a path by smothering the fires with mental energy.

"Move," Urura commanded.

Lakree, Hila, and Rye stepped back. As Dre tried to move, Alaan's hand reached for him. Their eclipse cloud shuddered and a portion exploded, bursting Urura's shields.

"We are connected to a spirit fiend. It's causing this," Dre said.

"Then you need to get control over it," Rye said, turning to Chirchi. "Take them to the realm with green hills and blue sky. Rombinanandi is waiting for them."

"Do it," Urura said.

Chirchi placed a hand on Dre and Alaan.

The pain of traveling to the spirit realm was soothing, a welcomed distraction. Dre could have stopped the attack if he hadn't been so selfish. Alaan traveled beside him with a similar guilt. The greatest gift in his life, in the world, was his brother and he had actively worked to push him away. It wasn't just selfish; it was stupid.

As their minds blended, they bathed in each other's misery. Dre floated through Alaan's memories of practicing magic alone. Alaan poorly imitated Dre's wide stances and snaps. He had struggled with the details. He'd continued tinkering with dark energy even after they made the deal to focus on separate energies. It started as a desire to maintain a surprising ability for an emergency but grew into resentment from never having enough time to become self-sufficient. After they began joining energies, there was a deep sadness that he lost his sparring partner and for the rest of his life, he would never really have anyone to compare himself against.

Meanwhile, Alaan visited Dre's memories from before they were famous. Guards and academics from all over Lynit traveled to meet and study them. At school, classmates teased them for their magical weakness once the fascination with their birth waned. They were both a spectacle and a freakshow. Dre was the one who pushed them to train four hours a day after school. He wanted praise and was willing to work for it.

Then, together, they relived the Castle tour. The memory was sharp. Slithlor moved through the groups of children who were distracted by the games on display. The metal device, the same one carried by Crimson, sat in his hands behind his back. Thin blue lines arced off the device, touching only certain children he passed. Their faces were clearer, too. Lakree, Hila, and Rye were there, as were all the MMA children and the draftees.

Chirchi's voice called out, "You must condense now. It's coming."

The memory of the Castle tour rippled and blurred, but Slithlor remained clear. Slithlor had created the terror of a generation so that he could capture and examine the small group of children who were changed by the device. Anger bubbled up within both of them.

Fleeing Lynit was out of the question. They had an opportunity to stop Slithlor and a responsibility to take it. To stop him, they would have to become the most powerful force in Lynit, more than the Poli Twins. They condensed around that agreement.

The spirit realm snapped into view. Grass stretched out in all directions. Blades swayed in an invisible breeze. A dark blue sun floated between two large hills. Its blue light radiated out, a gradient across the sky. Opposite the sun, the edge of the horizon was white.

"What happened? There's only one of you," Chirchi said.

"We are Alaandre," they said. Their minds were finally woven together into the perfect being they were always meant to be. They were one. All memories were reshaped with a broader perspective.

A tingle expanded from Alaandre's ear and flowed down their body until their toes burned. The spirit fiend's energy inside them responded to Rombinanandi rolling down a nearby hill.

A man ran down the hill after the creature. He flailed his arms until he tripped and tumbled down. At the base of the hill, he popped back up and continued sprinting.

"Alaandre," Dad called.

"I can't stay here," Chirchi said.

"Take our father with you," Alaandre said.

420

Chirchi's face squinted as if she were about to ask a question, but then she didn't. Rombinanandi hobbled slowly closer, but their father continued to run. He stopped before Alaandre and stared into their eyes. He rubbed their face. Chirchi touched him and they both evaporated.

"We will teach you how to divide if you teach us how to be more than two," Alaandre said.

It tilted its round head. The thin grooves in its skin were even clearer than in the dreams, almost like fingerprints. "Deal," Rombinanadi said, then dove into them.

Chapter 31 - Rye

Everything was covered in dust. Clouds of wizardry and mental energy hung in the air. It looked like white cocoons of black insects were being herded by a psychic. Alaan didn't stop leaking when he crossed into the spirit realm and Dre started leaking. Their energies joined. The eclipses floated through the red healing shield that surrounded them without causing a ripple. After moving the twins to the more spacious training hall, Chirchi divided the clouds into safer sizes. Still, a small piece of the wizardry exploded every few seconds, chipping away at the gigastone ceiling.

Rye sat beside the twins' heads, just outside their healing shield. The risk Drime had warned him about was very real. Tenaju almost smothered Rye out of existence. If the twins lost that battle, Rombinanandi would cross over with nothing to stop it from pursuing whatever it desired. It could kill everyone in the Medina or read all the books in the city. There was no way to guess. When Alaan twitched, Rye's hand clenched around the jagged piece of gigastone he held behind his back.

The large stone doors on the far side of the room swung open. The woman from Lakree's photograph entered. Her face was rounder, a few of her dreads were gray, and she was dressed in loose clothing, but she moved with the vigor of a guard. Urura greeted her first. They wrapped their arms tight around each other for a long moment as they asked each other a myriad of questions. They were more than acquaintances, more than allies.

"Aunt Juli," Lakree said; his voice was soft and hesitant, but it carried. He stood still, but the hand that held his water flask shook.

She took him in. "You have grown so much."

No one else moved until Hila stepped beside Lakree and carefully pried the water from him. He approached his aunt but stopped a pace away. She stepped closer to hug him, a warm smile lighting her face.

"What did you tell my father when you visited?" Lakree said. He didn't lift his arms to hug her back.

Rye stood up. Lakree's question was in the back of his mind as well. She was the reason they fled Virt. She warned her brother of a danger, but it couldn't have been about Rye's connection to Tenaju that happened years later.

Her face changed. She pulled back. "First, tell me why you have come looking for me."

Lakree told her everything that happened in the past two weeks. The strangeness started with matter shifting into the Castle and catching Slithlor talking to Rye's MMA psychic. Not only did the Guard try to draft them, but hours later, they also tried to draft the Poli Twins. Urura added her intel on the elites after them and Juli's treason charge.

A flash of light boomed, another explosion of the twins' energy. Three large shields sprang from Juli, surrounding the wizardry and mental energy. The purple energy faded, but the combined wizardry didn't.

"I've never seen that before," she said.

"We don't know if they always could do that or if it's the power of the spirit fiend," Urura said. Chirchi described what she witnessed in the spirit realm.

"What did it do to you?" Juli said. Everyone turned to Rye.

"I can share spirit energy with those I choose. The Poli Twins will be changed in a different way," Rye said.

"Do you have the S-X orb?" she said.

"A group of draftees connected to spirit fiends have it. Slithlor is creating a little army of them," Chirchi said.

"He is trying to make a new noble family," Rye said.

Juli took a deep breath. "Can I have some of that water?" She moved to the table. Lakree and Hila followed her. She tilted her head back as she drained the entire flask. She sighed heavily. "I never would have wanted to burden children with this knowledge, but you deserve to know why I need your help. You have a serious choice to make." She sat down and ran her hand through her hair like Lakree did. "During the Battle of Ki, I saw Slithlor use the S-X orb to kill King Kertic."

Rye's mind flashed to the scene that Rombinanandi showed him. Slithlor was covered in blood and carrying a metal ball. It had to have been the moment right after the murder. The king wasn't visible, and neither were the other elites. The gigastone shard slipped from Rye's hand. He shook as he stepped backward.

"I knew it was something like this," Lakree said. "You were so scared."

"So that's why Urura let you into the Medina," Chirchi said.

"Slithlor has been after this orb for years. He stole one from the Unts, the original inventors, but couldn't figure out how to use it without killing the subject. The device doesn't work on a person after the Verbindous. Eventually, it broke and by that time, the only other orbs were in Sewit's possession after they conquered the Unts. I believe that Slithlor started the war with them so he'd have the opportunity to steal one," she said.

"Why didn't you go to the council?" Lakree said.

"I was a dead woman, at least on paper," Juli said. Her eyes flicked over to Urura, then back to Lakree. "King Kertic asked me to root out any internal organizations that threatened Lynit. This meant investigating factions within nobles, the Guard, and civilian populations and sometimes, making deals to gain their trust. I faked my death to more freely mingle in the shadows. Only King Kertic, Rigmen, Slithlor, and my brother knew I was alive. If Slithlor had acted alone, my testimony might have been enough to present to the council, but with Rigmen and who knows who else on his side, I'm unsure whether I could win in court. They didn't have an obvious motive for working together until now. I stored my memory on a crystal to keep it fresh in case it was years before I shared it and as a backup in case something happened to me," she explained.

Lakree pulled the red crystal out of his pocket. "I have it."

She pressed her lips tight. "I told your mother to keep it with her, but I am glad it is here. You will want to watch it so that you can see for yourself who we are dealing with."

"Did Slithlor kill the elites, too?" Rye asked. The only way to the king was if the elites weren't there.

"Slithlor used the orb to direct several spirit fiends at the king. The elites fought hard and drove the beings away, but all were killed except the animalist. Then, when he and the king thought they were safe, Slithlor attacked," Juli said.

This was the danger Rye's father had seen. He didn't run because he was afraid of spirit fiends. He ran because of Slithlor. Far away across many realms, his father's energy pulsed. "What happened to the animalist?"

"He tried to flee after the king died, but Slithlor killed him, too. I would have attacked Slithlor, but I didn't know if I could defeat him with that orb. And Rigmen was there. Rigmen did sob for his king, but he did not avenge him. I don't trust him either," she said.

Slithlor had offered Rye's father a place in his new twisted world, but he refused and died for it. Rye should have never let anything make him doubt his father.

A new pain started in his chest. It wasn't like the other pains animalists learned about, reactions to nerve stimulation. In class, he once skinned a creature while it was alive. First, he studied its pain from the outside. There was blood, increased heart rate, screeches, whimpers, and thrashing, followed by shock, fatigue, and stillness.

Next, he studied that pain from the inside when he had the procedure done to him while in the form of a brist. The pain was blinding. It muffled his sense of hearing, smell, and taste. His mental processes ground to a halt. That day, he had learned how to counter the panic-driven instinct to scream and buck because if he lost himself, he wouldn't remember the path back to his human form.

Lakree and Hila wrapped their arms around him, but he barely felt it. This new pain numbed. His body was a hollow shell.

"It was a coup," Urura said. "No one could steal the throne in Lynit, not directly. But it could be given away temporarily. The nobles wouldn't trust each other enough with it, but the non-noble head of defense was a safe bet."

Rye cried out not only for his father but also for Lynit. It was in greater danger than he could have imagined. The most powerful people in the nation were sabotaging it. His knees gave out, but Lakree and Hila held him.

"We're here," they said in unison. No one spoke for a long while.

Two sharp gasps sounded. Dre and Alaan sat up. Their faces were calm as they scanned the room. Wordlessly, they snapped three times. Their blobs of energy hovering above evaporated.

"Slithlor is trying to create a seventh magic," the twins said, their words and intonation in sync.

Juli told them about King Kertic's murder. "We will let the council speak to Qin, who Slithlor used to start the war with Sewit, show them my crystal, and finally present the three of you. Slithlor

426

won't be able to slink his way out of that. I never had a motive that I could prove, but now I do."

"Even if Slithlor is guilty, whoever goes before the council will be a known threat to Lynit," Dre said. "Slithlor may know how to break the connection to spirit fiends, but he won't share it. Three elites already heavily suspect that Alaan and I are connected to a spirit fiend and want to use us as proof of Slithlor's experiments. We will let them. They don't need to know about Rye."

"The Guard will kill you," Lakree said.

"They won't. If we go missing, it would start its civil war, but it would be the Guard vs the people," Alaan said. "The council won't let that happen. It's time we flex the full might of our fame."

"Or I kill Slithlor," Rye said. He pulled on his connection to Tenaju. Instead of passing it along to his friends, he held it within. The MMA presented him with flashcards, but he didn't need to look at the details of the creatures. He felt their shapes. They were just different ideas that he could become. And this excited Tenaju. It didn't know death or the concept of taking a life, and it was eager to discover it. Before, Rye entertained Slithlor's quest to create a seventh family, but now, he would destroy everything Slithlor cared for.

"Don't underestimate him," Juli said. She was a dim light. A fast connection was growing between them because she knew his pain. She had witnessed the murder of her king and was helpless to stop it. Guilt, fear, and fury were within her, but they weren't knotted. They were tools for her to direct. "Slithlor can stop a spirit fiend, but he can't stop justice."

Rye huffed. Justice wouldn't bring back his father and revenge wouldn't either, but at least it would feel good.

"What about the other children who are connected to spirit fiends? What if one of them summons a spirit fiend by accident?" Hila said.

"In the tower in the cloud realm, I saw that all the draftees had a blue string that connected them to a disk on the pedestal," Chirchi said. "From there, I can break all the connections. I won't even need to know who it's attached to. All I need are a few more trips to the spirit realm with Rye or the twins and I'll figure out how it all works. I need a day or two."

Juli shook her head, then paced. "Guards saw me enter the city. They are preparing to drill through Co Park to find me. We don't have that much time," she said.

"Normally, righting the wrong of an assassination or magical experiment would be beyond the scope of what the Medina protects, but anything that would hinder Slithlor is for the benefit of all in the Medina and even those who haven't made it to us yet. We will fight to protect you as long as we can," Urura said.

Alaan and Dre shared a glance for a few seconds before Alaan spoke, "It's not worth it. If Slithlor knows Juli has left Poli, he will shift the Guard's focus. He is terrified of her."

Dre cracked his neck, then stretched his arms. "You will leave Lynit to stop Slithlor from potentially unleashing spirit fiends, but we don't know what else he has planned. He wants to destabilize the nobles by turning people against the families so that when a new power arrives, it is accepted. But no family will sit quietly if they lose a seat on the council. A war between the families will spill over into the public. Alaan and I need to stay in Lynit to repair the animosity we dredged up. That's how we stop Slithlor and anyone else who attempts anything similar with another magic for good. Besides, we have unfinished business with the draft."

Rye's father rejected Slithlor's ultimatum not only because he had witnessed King Kertic's death but because Slithlor promised more wars to come. "And how will we prove to the council that Slithlor killed my father, that my father wasn't a coward?" Rye said. It wasn't only about stopping Slithlor or even getting revenge.

Clearing the stain on the Ternitu name was as important. Rye could imagine his mother returning to the Guard. A former captain shouldn't be working in a restaurant. She should be leading soldiers.

"Once the twins prove that he is connecting children to spirit fiends, we will be able to link it to King Kertic's and your father's murder. My memories and testimony will be enough after that," Juli said.

Chapter 32 - Dre

The noise of Co Park reached Dre long before he stepped above ground. It sounded like all of Poli was there, and when he arrived, it looked like it. The gigastone ground was hidden underneath bodies standing shoulder to shoulder. It was like old times. On the back side of the park, just above the rim, was a pack of thirty to forty guards. They weren't interested in the Gigasphere Tournament that was about to start. They maneuvered three large machines, trying to get them down into the park. They weren't like the cranes that populated the city. A thick bar of twisted metal sat at the front of each one.

"We have an hour tops before the drilling starts," Dre said. Gigastone was the most precious material, more precious than wood, but Slithlor had convinced the Guard that catching Juli was worth its destruction.

"The tournament will stop once it does. We will be Yordin before then," Alaan said.

They entered the park. Some people cried, some cheered, some screamed their names. A small bubble formed around the twins as the crowd squished out of their way. It was a reminder that Dre was a different substance than his fans. They didn't mix. He headed for the raised metal bleachers. Despite almost everyone in the park wearing eclipse pins and cursing noble names, the nobility had shown up in force.

For once, Homin didn't stick out. A knuckle of Yordin in tasteful but dramatic black and white robes sat at the core of the stands. The five other color combinations of attire threaded around them. All the nobles watched as Homin descended to greet Dre and Alaan. "I knew you would come."

"Will the draft pause protect runaways, too?" Alaan said.

"Yes, Slithlor oddly lobbied for a language that says anyone not currently in the Castle," Homin said.

"We figured," Dre said. Stavender and the gang would be released from Guard. They'd hide their abilities until Slithlor was ready to unveil them.

Homin pulled out a parchment from under his robe. "This will be your announcement speech," he said. Dre reached for it, but Homin pulled it back. "Winning a trophy isn't important to us. We will be judging *why* you use wizardry. Yordin's don't choose to use wizardry; we are wizards. Either you both are Yordin, or neither of you are."

"Otherwise, you would have to explain how two people with the same blood didn't belong to the same family," Dre said as he inspected his fingernails. There was always a catch with Homin or the Yordin, or maybe that was a principle of balance. Any amount of aid given had to be balanced with selfish gains.

Homie shrugged. He wasn't even embarrassed. He pointed at an erected metal pane with sixty-four magnetic blocks. Dre and Alaan's names were on opposite sides of the bracket. "I already signed you up for individual matches."

"You were always my favorite person to fight, the only person I cared to compare myself against," Dre said. For once, the idea of using magic alone didn't frighten him.

A loud bang rang in the air. It caused a blimp in chatter as everyone turned to see dust rising from the drill that had dropped into the park.

Alaan snatched the speech. "Tell us as soon as we look Yordin enough. The tournament won't make it to the end."

Homin nodded.

When Dre walked on the stage of his first match, beaming faces chanted his one-syllable name. It was the first time he hadn't heard his brother's name or Poli Twins mixed in. These fans had picked Dre as their preferred one to watch. He twirled in the limelight, then did a back tuck, which energized the crowd further. Hopefully, Alaan heard the noise over the lame spectators who chose him.

An elemental mage with a square chin and a headband that pressed his long, curly hair out of his face stepped onto the stage. No one shouted his name. He vigorously shook Dre's hand, then stepped into a fighting pose. He wore the loaner protective gear given to combatants who didn't bring their own. It was painted black to look like gigastone.

Dre reached out his senses. Wizardry pushed on him, pressed against his skin and his bones. The descent into the cavern of energy was smooth, but a dark abyss waited at the bottom. Rombinanandi lived there and its power could crush Dre into oblivion. Dre was only a spectator in that place.

The pressure lightened as the polarity reversed, his ascension cleaner than before. The murky cloud at the top of the mountain was pushed further up. A lingering memory or two of Alaan's guided him. On the descent back into the safe zone, he pushed. The crowd gasped as white dots brightened around him. The stream was ragged, but it didn't blow up the stage.

"He can use light energy?" Several people in the crowd shouted.

"Of course, he can," Homin said. He was at the edge of the stage. His presence surprised Dre and the crowd. A noble had sneaked into their ranks. A group encircled him, throwing insults and threats. "I don't have children, so there is no one to kidnap."

"Leave him be. He's with me," Dre said. It wasn't only the nobles that Homin wanted to be convinced of the twins' Yordin-ness. All of Lynit needed to believe it. Dre and Alaan would be the first, publicly, to transition into nobles, or as the Yordin would likely phrase it, just more nobles to uncover their ancestry. The hecklers apologized.

Dre started the match by flinging the bar and running at an angle. He fired eight spheres. A gust of wind knocked everything off course. Some spheres were pushed back at him. He released them with a snap, pulling him off his feet. The light energy above unbalanced him. He snapped away an equal amount of light before firing more spheres. The burden of balance was his now and it didn't take him much to adjust. He added an extra snap after dark energy evaporated. The handicap he was born with was finally gone.

"Are you toying with me?" the elemental mage said after he dove near where light energy hung, but Dre didn't use it.

Simply having light energy out was enough for this warm-up. Dre responded by flaring his light as he fired spike after spike with a new smile, releasing or summoning energy as needed to keep his feet firmly on the ground. The elemental mage flung spells, but Dre didn't stop moving. He blocked fire and wind attacks with a shield. For lightning ones, he dodged. They exchanged several attacks, but neither landed anything. Dre directed attacks low, which kept the boy moving. Soon, sweat drenched the elemental mage's clothes and his sidesteps became sloppy. Dre still breathed through his nose.

Dre fired a low horizontal bar. As the boy jumped, Dre snapped. The energy shell faded away, releasing a black cloud. He condensed and fired the revealed energy, hitting the boy from below and the side. Then, a final attack hit the boy in the forehead and knocked him out. The depth of energy that Dre dared pull on was the same level as his opponents, but the extra thousands of hours he spent training delivered this easy victory. However, he didn't need to see Homin shake his head to know he hadn't reached the Yordin threshold. Dre was well aware that he still had more to give.

The second match was on a different gigasphere. His opponent was already on stage when he arrived. She was dressed in dark blue and red Guard robes with "Draftee" stitched on her chest. Her purple hair was dyed black and pulled into four thick cornrows. It was Tess.

"What are you doing here?" he asked, searching her face. She had been with Slithlor for a few days, but he couldn't believe she had joined his crazy mission. There had to be another reason. "You look so corporate."

"I didn't want to cut it." She patted her head. "And if the rumors are true, I am here thanks to you. The Guard is trying to show that the draft isn't so scary by having us compete in the tournament."

Dre nodded slowly. Homin mentioned that draftees had been interviewed. Showing off what they learned was the next logical step.

"I tried to avoid fighting you by doing individual matches, but you are the one who switched up the most," she said.

"A lot has happened," he said.

"I can throw the fight if you need me to," she said.

"No, I need the challenge." The only time that Dre had beaten her was when Alaan was fighting with him. To win, he would have to replicate fully his skill with Alaan. "I need to perform."

The bell rang. Dre used a single slow breath to steady himself before he jumped to the left and directly into a shield she made. The vibrations on his skin dampened. His access to wizardry was reduced to the volume of the magic shield. She had guessed his first move. He sucked his teeth as he pulled as much energy as he could access. As he continued moving, the shield followed, but he pulled more energy from the fresh areas he passed through.

When blackness crowded his vision, he created spikes in a tight ring around his body. They circled him, and as each one faced Tess, he fired it. The first four studded against her shield, but the fifth one broke through. She covered herself in a shield that blocked his subsequent six attacks.

He ran at her. She didn't move. Instead, she created a red shield between them. Small lines of electricity zipped through the interior. A few zaps from those and he would pass out. Anesthesia was a weapon. He pivoted, barely dodging it.

"I know all of your tricks," she said and it was true. She had attended every one of his performances. She knew his strategies, his maneuvers. She knew him. Well, technically, she knew the old him.

At first, she wasn't surprised when he summoned light energy since she knew he could use it, but her face changed as he continued pushing. As his feet started lifting off the ground, he pulled out dark energy.

Dre swirled his arms, forming a ring of light perpendicular to the ground, like a doorway to his old friend. He filled the empty space with spikes. He flashed the light as he fired each attack. He spiraled around her. The shield stopped the attacks, but the ripples grew larger. After several more attacks, it popped. A spike made it through, hitting Tess in the chest. Her feet flew up and she banged into one of the gigastone pillars. She replaced her shield. Dre replaced his spikes as he dashed forward. To defeat her, he couldn't give her a chance to think.

He summoned more light energy, which lifted him. He brightened it as he reached the apex of the gigasphere. A blinding light filled the stage. When he passed over her, he snapped, releasing his light energy. The pressure of gravity pulled him down hard. He fell through her magic barrier.

She wasn't inside with him, however. There was a small red bubble in her place. He twisted out of the way, but then her sphere moved. It hit his hand and within a few seconds, it fell limp. He summoned light energy to burn away the numbing spell.

"I know Alaan's tricks, too," she said.

But she didn't know any of their new maneuvers. Dre pushed bright light behind him and covered himself in dark energy. He separated the light into three, shifting a wispy form of dark energy in front of each. This was an alternative version of the trick Dre and Alaan used during the first MMA exam. Since he couldn't block out the sunlight to produce an illusion, he settled for indistinguishable humanoid shadows.

Her squinting gaze moved from figure to figure. She backed close to the edge of the stage, then covered herself in a physical shield and a larger magic shield. Dre placed himself directly in front of her and the two decoys at the one-hundred-and-twenty-degree mark. In her periphery, their delayed movements would be subtle.

He rushed her. She created three separate red bubbles. Instead of dodging the one placed in his path, Dre flipped the decoy to his left up and over its one. The other two red spheres dropped as Tess redirected her attention to the left decoy.

The energy surrounding him thudded against her outer magic shield as he passed through. Her head whipped over in surprise. He summoned a quick ball of energy and shot it. It broke her physical shield easily. She stumbled back, but he grabbed her. Now, he was too close for her to put any shield between them. With his other hand extended behind him, he condensed a sword and a hot ball of light.

"I surrender," she said, throwing her hands up.

"Yes!" Dre said. He had done it. As usual, he didn't win by strength but by skill. He was balanced.

Someone in the crowd started the "End the Draft" chant again, which drowned out the applause.

"You are different. What happened?" Tess said.

Part of him wanted to walk her through the ups and downs of the past weeks, but the rest of him reread the "Draftee" on her chest. She was his friend but still belonged to Slithlor's program, at least for now.

"The MMA material is really good," he said with his best fake smile. She leveled her eyes as he walked off stage. Of course, she didn't believe him, but he didn't care.

"Am I a kidnapping candidate yet?" Dre asked Homin. His shadow clones were peak creativity.

"It may have felt like a triumph to win your first two rounds solo, but it still wasn't to Yordin standards. You are in your comfort zone," he said. "We need to see you perform at your limit."

"In terms of power?" Dre said.

"Strength is a consequence of balance, not the cause. Your energies were balanced in a textbook sense, but not your style. This is the same issue Alaan had in his first two rounds. We know there is balance between you, but we need to see it within each of you."

"I haven't practiced light energy in so many years. I can use it, but I am best at dark energy," Dre said.

"The beauty of balance is that it doesn't mean fifty-fifty. It's the combination you require to be your best and you haven't shown that," Homin said. Dre had only known one form of balance with Alaan, but that didn't mean it was all there was. Homin's words reminded him of the three wizardry examples: water and seed, iron and carbon, and the council and the Guard. None of them were opposites. None of them balanced the other. Dre and Alaan were never opposites, either. Sass wasn't the opposite of sarcasm. They were just different flavors of the same humor. But if Dre wanted to use light energy well, Alaan was still his best reference. "Besides, a Verbindous is against peers. You'll face your first one in the next match."

Dre's third opponent wore a light green jacket over a thin white shirt and brown pants, all made of quitol hide. VF logos were stamped all over them. A small, beaded, dome-shaped hat was clipped atop his curly hair and his hands were covered in green and gold rings. The boy pulled off his jacket and handed it to someone who attended him on the side of the stage. He was a Finrar-in-waiting.

"I admit that initially, I was excited when I heard that the Poli Twins were participating in single matches, but your first rounds were so disappointing," he said.

"The grandson of Council Member Finrar participating in the Gigasphere Tournament? It will bring shame to your family when you lose." Dre shook his head in mock pity.

"It's not about winning. You should know that," he said, touching his chest as if shocked.

"If this is a performance. We play by performance rules," Dre said. He had never fought against a noble kid, nor had he seen them use magic as they trained in secret in their noble schools. This Finrar kid likely had trained as many hours as Dre but with expert tutors at his side. Dre didn't doubt that this would be his most challenging fight ever. "Morph into your best creature."

The Finrar grinned and bowed. "Summon all the energy you can."

The bell rang and the boy's body changed. It swelled and darkened. Thick hooves clanked against the ground. His back sparkled in the light of Dre's energy amassing above. His face squished into a snout and a thick horn grew. Then he bared his finger-length teeth. As a diamond-backed natsin a quarter the size of the stage, he growled.

The crowd shouted for Dre to surrender. The creature was more resistant to magic than a quitol and its jaw was strong enough to crush rock. Even the MMA material suggested retreat maneuvers. People have died in these matches before.

Dre took a deep breath. Quitting wasn't an option. Juli, Lakree, Hill, and Rye wouldn't be able to make it out of Poli if all of Lynit's attention wasn't pulled away. There had to be a way to defeat the creature. Someone must have if an animalist was able to study it. He only needed to find the best attack angle.

He nodded, and then the beast charged. The crowd quieted. Dre attacked with everything he had. Balls, spikes, blades, and explosions—none of them slowed the animalist. He leaped around the stage like an acrobat. Instead of quantity, he tried quality. From all his years of single practice with dark energy, he was an expert in crystalline and lattice structures. He created shards. These whizzed out, chipping bits of the creature's scales or the stage. But this only seemed to anger the Finrar. Dre tried condensing light energy as tightly as he could but hesitated. He remembered his second MMA exam. He couldn't risk knocking himself out.

After what felt like an hour, the creature was bloody, but Dre's dodges were slow and his skin was numb. With a misplaced landing, he twisted an ankle and fell. He tried to roll to avoid being trampled but was too slow. A hoof cracked his shin. The pain was sharp. It was hard to believe that his foot lay calmly on its side while his knee shook. Blood splattered everywhere. He screamed. The crowd gasped. The Finrar turned around for another charge.

There was an easy way out of this. A protector pressed close to the edge of the stage. A red bubble hung next to her. All Dre needed to do was surrender and the pain would stop. She would numb him as she repaired the damage. He wouldn't even finish with a scar. It had been naive to think he could use light energy well enough to defeat a Finrar kid who never depended on the Correction Factor. His family taught him a creature that wasn't learnable in any public school or university.

Dre gritted his teeth. Winning this tournament meant ending the draft and stopping Slithlor's plot. The pushes and pulls of wizardry were a distant vibration, but he reached out his senses for his safety net, his brother. With his twin, he was invincible. The gigasphere would have been a barrier, but Dre's connection to Alaan wasn't just in this world anymore; it was in the next. Dre found him quickly.

Alaan's crisp voice reached Dre on stage. "Dre, you don't need me. We can't be more than two if each of us is not at least one." There was a challenge in his tone. "Get up."

The hulking Finrar charged. The pounding shook the stage, chattering Dre's teeth and reminding him of the rhythm of pulses when he joined energies with Alaan. The external balance he struggled to build with his brother was a distraction.

Dre sucked in a ragged breath as he summoned light and dark energy. Wizardry's oscillations smoothed until they were a constant note and the equilibrium made him weightless. He floated. When he pressed his energies together, the specs didn't cancel each other out. They joined into eclipses. Muted light filled the air. Alaan and Dre shared a single magic source in the spirit realm, not a divided one. Anything they could do together could be done alone. His internal balance had been ignored all his life, but not anymore.

Dre shifted horizontally, narrowly dodging a swipe of the horn. The crowd shouted, but it wasn't louder than the hum inside him. The Finrar charged again. Dre formed a ring of energy. When the creature's head passed through, Dre clenched it around its neck and lifted. It reared up on its hind legs, exposing its fatty underbelly. This was the angle Dre needed. He punched an eclipse bead into that place, then snapped. Dark energy evaporated. Light flashed, then exploded. The Finrar fell back, the remaining shards on its back shattering under its weight.

The beast shrank. The morph was broken. Dre tightened the

choke. The boy blacked out before he made it back to human. The bell rang and a red shield enveloped both of them. Dre collapsed.

When he woke up, he wasn't on stage but inside a medical tent. Bruises ran up his entire leg. The pain was gone, but he was still in a healing sphere. A low chant of his name echoed from outside. Alaan swatted next to him while several Yordin surrounded them. One woman wore black and white earrings. Another woman's hat and shoes were black, while her dress was dark blue with white stripes. One of the men had come to Dre's first MMA exam. His oversized robe was black with four sets of white suspenders hanging down like tentacles.

"I did it?" Dre said as he propped up on his elbows. He had joined his energies. It was so Yordin of a move that it was more Yordin than the first Yordin. They had to admit him.

"You both did. Welcome to the family," Homin said. "The draft and MMA are now voluntary programs."

Dre reached out to hug Alaan. Slithlor won't be able to collect any more children in secret. All that was left was to cause the distraction and turn themselves into the elites. The council needed to see what Slithlor did to them.

Homin pointed at a set of black and white quitol suits hanging on a rack. On the back of each was an eclipse. "It's finally time to merge the Poli Twin brand with Yordin."

"I am not surprised," Dre said.

When his leg was healed, he exited the tent. The total volume of the thousands of fans hit him. However, underneath all the voices, there was a consistent whirl. It sounded like a turbine, but instead of chopping air, it grounded rock.

Dre pushed out light energy, rising a few feet off the ground. On the park's far side, a shield rose over the drills. Shards of gigastone flew into the air, thudding against it. Alaan and the other Yordin floated up next to him.

Alaan asked sorcerers to amplify his voice but didn't pull out Homin's scroll. He would never read a speech written by someone else. "Dre and I were born to two ordinary parents, but our lives have been a spectacle. Physically, we fascinated the world, but magically, we were pitied for many years. We were weak, possessing half the strength of children our age. Discovering the skill to join wizardry energies did not make up the difference, but hard work did. For eight years, Dre and I trained for four hours a day. This is what made people call us the Poli Twins. This made us famous. And today, I am here to announce that we have finally achieved something bigger than fame. We have passed our Verbindous and achieved nobility. We are finally Yordin. All of our efforts have paid off."

A silence stretched across the crowd. Many touched the pins on their chests and others laughed. They were confused because two dark kids said they belonged to the palest family.

"That's not...," Homin whispered between them, but his voice was still picked up by the sorcerer's spells and transmitted across the crowd. He tried to jerk back, but Dre pulled him close. If Homin wanted to disrupt this, he would have to do so publicly and Dre knew he wouldn't.

"Is this a joke?" a close-by boy said.

Homin fidgeted.

Alaan continued. "With this new title and the responsibilities that come with it, we realized that there was more we could do for Lynit. Thanks to the Yordin's efforts, we have made all mandatory Guard programs for children illegal. That means that no new children will be tested or given draft orders, and runaways can rip up any paperwork they have. Anyone currently not in the Castle is safe."

Someone shrieked. "The draft is over," a familiar voice shouted. It was Gron. He jumped up and down, arms flailing in the air. Zalora and other MMA participants in VF gear did the same. Across the park, wizards and psychics zipped into the air. They cheered. Dots of lights sparkled across the park as communication orbs were activated.

Dre lifted a hand to settle the crowd before they missed the essential part. He said, "Yordin is focused on being the best and building the best. We recognize that extraordinary talent is in all of us, but it needs to be nurtured. You can become noble, too, if you earn it, just like us. The Verbindous is a Lynitian tradition and is open to all. We are opening a public Yordin Academy, where all wizards are welcome. It will cover the MMA material and beyond. It is time for nobles to be more active in nurturing the best talent. We have the knowledge. We have the experience. It is time we shared it. Will all the wizards who want to be trained by the Yordin raise their hands?"

"Any wizard can become Yordin?" some kid said.

"Every wizard who passes the Verbindous becomes Yordin," Dre said. He doubted that even one percent of them would make the cut, but creating more Yordin wasn't the purpose. Slithlor's goal was to play on the discontent with the current nobles to push the public toward accepting a seventh family. As more and more kids displayed extraordinary magic, Slithlor would invite them into his gang. But if nobles absorbed these children into their families first, the division would be swashed before it could start.

Hundreds of hands shot into the sky. A low "Yordin" chant started. He pointed across the park to the raised metal bleacher. The nobles were huddled together, likely more shocked than the crowd. "Will another noble family accept the responsibility to train the next generation of Lynitians? It is the final stage of Kertic's rule that magic must be shared. Otherwise, there is nothing new for us to offer Lynit. We should be measured by how much we shared." The crowd turned. If the nobility wanted to use their names to get elected to office, they would have to work for it.

One woman raised her hand. Victoria Finrar wore a wide-sleeved dark orange robe and a wide-brim hat. She was the only one up there who was not in family colors. "Not only will Finrar train the best animalists, but they will be the best dressed," she said, her voice loud.

After a pause, a Palow raised a hand, followed by a Pol, a Vous, and a Cast. More sparks of magic flew in the air. Kids chanted all the noble names. Homin started clapping, his uncomfortableness gone. With all the families involved, the Yordin were still balanced; all of Lynit was balanced. He and the other Yordins headed towards the bleachers.

Dre and Alaan lowered to the ground. Rish, Ser, and Grintinari waited for them.

"Come with us," Ser said, her face stern. "We waited until you ended the draft out of courtesy, but things have escalated with Juli's arrival. We have an immediate audience with the council now."

"Leave them alone," a boy said.

"Are you mad the Poli Twins ended the draft?" a girl said, stepping before them.

"Move, this is a Guard matter," Ser said, then flung her out of the way. A few people gasped. They didn't understand that guards weren't polite when on a mission. People huddled together, but Rish and Ser pushed them aside one by one. Despite their anger, no one dared attack the elites.

"Grintinari, get us out of here," Ser said. Black specs fluttered around Dre as a blue sphere soared over the crowd. It was a protection shield. A person in brown robes glided inside, a teacher: Mommy.

"Uh oh," Dre said. He had stupidly forgotten all about her.

"Run, Alaandre. Your father is awake," she said.

A small dark blue shield flickered between Dre and Ser. It expanded quickly and knocked Dre away. Another physical shield surrounded him, then lifted him up and away. Alaan moved in the air with him. They floated over the crowd. The elites below weren't smiling.

"Mom, no," Alaan said.

A magic barrier flickered into place around Dre, larger than the shield his mother carried him in. The inner shield bumped into the outer shield and stopped. The shield itself was magic and couldn't pass the threshold. After a jolt from the outer shield, Dre was hurtling back to the ground.

Four new shields blinked into existence, one around each elite and then a larger one around all three. Ser's shield that pulled Dre down vanished.

"Run," Mommy said.

The elites jumped apart, casting spells. Rish morphed. Grintinari's sorcerer's orb was in hand as he rattled off a spell. The shield around him darkened, then crumpled away like rotten cloth.

"Run, Poli Twins," the crowd demanded.

Ser said a long spell and several layers of shield covered Mommy. Symbols raced across the surface. Ser yanked her hand down and Mommy slammed into the ground.

"No, don't hurt her," Dre pleaded. "She's just scared."

"The Guard will never let us be," someone in the crowd said.

"I said they can't have you," Mommy said, her voice cracking. "Don't take that power away from me."

The look in her eyes was anger and fear all in one. She pleaded and commanded. All of Dre's convictions left him. It was like a parental spell that stole his willpower to defy her. He didn't blink as dark and light energy flowed out of him. They combined and passed through the shield. The energies joined with Alaan's and flashed a rainbow of colors before settling on brown. High above the park, a fifty-foot unwavering illusion of Rombinanandi sneered. It mimed at grabbing someone.

"No!" Ser said a second before the screams started. Chaos rippled across the park.

"That should be enough proof for the council," Dre said.

Chapter 33 - Rye

The Medina rumbled. It sounded like a monsoon but with an unnatural ping. Streams of dust spilled from the ceiling. Rye pressed his palms over his ears, but it didn't help. Lakree shielded his face and mouthed something. His eyes roamed around. Hila moved next to Chirchi, who created a thin covering of purple energy that blocked the debris. Then, the sound dampened. It was Lakree's spell. Rye dropped his hands.

"Time to go," Juli said.

Rye's fingers fidgeted as he folded up the letter he had written to his mother and brother, then handed it to Urura. He didn't mention Slithlor or his father's murder because it could put them in danger, but he did tell them that he was leaving Lynit. He couldn't stop them from worrying, but at least they would know he was going to a place where trees and insects lived. When he returned home, his mother and brother would be on the edge of their seats, waiting to hear about his adventure.

The drilling noise returned when they left the room. It filled the dark tunnel. A purple glow from Chirchi provided light. Juli opened the rusted door next to the Medina's entrance. Inside was a dimly lit stone stairwell. It zigzagged down for several flights. As Rye descended, a sour odor filled his nostrils. It smelled like clothes that

447

took too long to dry. Every surface was slick with a grimy slush. Eventually, the grinding of the drills was replaced by the hiss of steam. The stairwell ended at a door with a foggy window.

"No matter what happens from here on out, you must make it to our transport outside the city. If you do exactly as I say, it will go smoothly," Juli said. Her gaze moved from child to child until they agreed. She opened the door and heat washed over him. There were more stairs, but they were made of metal. Each step clanked and a second sound accompanied the steam. It was the whirl of machinery. The next door was almost fused with the wall, but the bottom corner was warped, bent open.

Gross muck covered Rye as he shimmied through, but he didn't complain like Lakree did. He stood up in a cavern spanned by a grated bridge. Thirty feet below, turbines sloshed in a lake. The heat and steam wafted from there. It was the most water Rye had ever seen. Pipes snaked up from it into large vats on the bridge. Smaller pipes rose from the vat to boxy machines on another grated bridge twenty feet above. There were also people up there. They wheeled carts from container to container. Sometimes, they cranked it with a wrench; other times, they swapped out parts.

Juli lifted a hand to her lips as she led the way by sneaking from vat to vat. Each one had an overhang to hide under. They crossed to the other side of the cavern. A door was built into the red earth wall. Inside was a cramped closet. Boxes were stacked haphazardly. Juli rearranged a few to reveal a wide metal panel on a side wall. She grabbed the edges and pulled it off with ease. Behind it was red rock with a hole in it. They crawled through. Rye lifted the magnetized panel back into place behind him.

"We are out of Poli," she said, though she hadn't needed to. Rye felt the desert heat.

"This was the path Santi and Gamine told us about," Lakree said. He pointed at an "M" scratched into the cave wall.

"It's been so long since I've been fully outside," Chirchi said.

Rye held up a hand against the light as he exited the cave. The sky was as bright as his first time outside. He was at the bottom of a crater. Dusty wind swept up over a single bridge that spanned it. It was the bridge Rye and Hila argued over crossing. A picked-clean carcass lay mangled on the ground. It was a quitol, likely the one Hila killed. He moved in front to block her view, but she had already seen it.

She stepped past him. "Let's be quick before you get sunburned again."

Rye marched up the steep incline. The top was over a hundred feet high, but the path winded the side of the crater back and forth, creating ten stories of ramps. Before they crested the top, Virt rose above the lip of the crater in the distance. It was a silver blip on the horizon.

"Where are you going?" someone said. It was a boy's voice coming from above. He sat on the edge of the crater, waving. It was Crimson, the draftee who wouldn't stop shaking Rye's hand.

Drime was next to him. There was no small light beaming within him. There was no connection between them, at least not anymore. Slithlor had changed him. Warmth and sadness played across his face as his gaze moved from Hila to Rye. He held out a hand. "Come with us, Rye, and no one will get hurt."

The three other kids connected to spirit fiends stepped into view. "Where are the Poli Twins?" Stavender said, his eyes on the cave exit.

"Drime," Hila said. "Slithlor murdered King Kertic. He's the real threat." Drime opened and closed his mouth a few times but said nothing.

"Slithlor warned us not to believe anything you said," Crimson said.

"Just leave Drime. Don't make us fight you or you will regret it for the rest of your life," Hila continued.

A gust of wind swept through the crater. The draftees covered their faces.

"If you bring war to Lynit, you will regret it for the rest of your life," Crimson said.

"If that is truly what you are afraid of, then we will not leave Lynit if you are willing to testify about who gave you that orb," Juli said. Pri shifted the silver orb she held behind her back.

"It's too late for that," Drime said as Stavender shot a spear of dark energy.

"Mutilov Dobnin," Juli said, blinking a big blue shield to life above Rye and the others. The attack thumped into the shield and faded. Next, light energy exploded. Barely a ripple disturbed the shield. Crimson and Carsi's mental energy attacks didn't affect the shield either. Drime rattled off a spell.

"Only three more flights, let's go," Juli said. She didn't even flinch at each attack. It was the confidence of an elite. Five children with their spirit-fiend powers didn't scare her.

Progress up the ramp was slow but steady. As Rye reached the next level, a smaller shield sprung inside the outer shield. It was a physical shield. A rock passed through the magic shield and ricocheted off the inner one. Then, a spray of rocks rained down, bouncing off the shield like water off the dome.

Lakree and Chirchi yelped, each one grabbing one of Rye's arms. Then, light exploded above. Momentarily, it was brighter than the sun. The boom drowned out Rye's scream and dislodged a massive chuck of rock. It hit the inner shield with a thud that sent large ripples throughout. Rye ducked. The rock slid to the front of them, blocking their path.

"Step back. I will release the physical shield, then make another. If the rock slides, jump on top and I will catch us in the new one," Juli said.

"Uhh…" Hila said.

"I'm not athletic," Lakree said. "What if it tumbles towards us?"

Before anyone else could respond, Juli released the physical shield. The rock slammed into the ground but didn't slide. She covered them in a new shield only a few seconds before another rock ricocheted off it.

Juli turned around, a small fire in her eyes. "Do as I say. Keep your doubts to yourself."

Lakree nodded. "Sorry."

She climbed over the rock. Rye pulled Chirchi and Lakree along, both still clutching onto him. Ahead, a cloud of black energy solidified into a wall. The outer magical shield bumped into it. A moment later, a second wall sprung up behind them, trapping them.

A new bridge of dark energy formed, connecting to the other side of the crater. Stavender floated down to the bridge, the light energy above him slowly dissipating.

"We tried to give you a choice, but you chose treason," Crimson said as he landed next to Stavender, cushioning his fall with mental energy.

"And I give you a choice. Turn away or regret it," Juli said. Rye shivered at the tone in her voice. A warning from an elite, even if she was a former elite, was a threat.

"We may not be able to stop you, but we can stall you," Stavender said.

"And we can call for help," Carsi said. Purple rose from her head to form giant letters in the sky. It read, "Juli is here."

Juli released the magical shield around them, then blinked in five new shields, one around each draftee. The purple letters disappeared. The black walls and bridge dissipated. Stavender and Crimson dropped.

Carsi, Pri, and Drime dashed apart, but Juli tracked them. Light blinked close to Stavender inside his shield. He covered his face from the heat but floated back up. Crimson caught himself with the new mental energy he produced.

Stavender landed on the ramp several paces behind them. He snapped away all his energy and hunched over. A ball of light slinked from his mouth as if it were made of clay. Then, a black blob fell next to it. The blobs grew and elongated. Arms and legs separated. High-pitched voices laughed with glee from small mouths, sending vibrations through the forming entities. They looked like angry toddlers.

"This is why it is too late. The spirit fiends are already here," Lakree said.

The white thing touched the magic barrier around it. It shrieked as the shield rippled, then banged on it. Both things thrashed. Stavender remained still as the energy beings whipped around so quickly that they blurred. With an audible pop, they broke Juli's shield.

"Get Rye," Stavender said. The energies dashed forward. Juli shielded Stavender again, but the energies didn't disappear. She tried to surround them in separate shields, but they dodged her attempts.

"Go!" Juli shouted.

The white-energy creature popped the physical shield with a touch. Juli created a smaller magical shield. The creatures rammed it but didn't get through. They pressed their faces into the barrier as if trying to gnaw their way inside. The curves of their chins and cheeks matched Stavender's, but the eyes weren't of this realm.

"Lynit is already in danger," Lakree said.

Rye pulled Lakree up the second level as more mental energy attacks pounded against the shield. It was like pretty purple clouds were trying to kill them. The other draftees were all out of their shields now. Juli didn't re-shield them and instead focused on keeping the energy creatures back. She created another shield a second before they broke through the first one. She lifted her arms and the shield expanded. It hit the creatures at an angle and knocked them into the crater. They howled all the way down.

"No." Stavender reached a hand after his mini clones, but the energies did not fly back to him. He didn't seem to have control over them.

"They are writing in the sky again," Hila said. Carsi laughed as she wrote even more things in the air. Now it read, "Help! Juli is kidnapping me."

"This is what we want. The Guard needs to know that we left Poli," Juli said.

Rye's jaw dropped. Things were still going according to Juli's plan.

Before they reached the top of the crater, Juli's arms flailed. She lost her balance. Lakree steadied her. She picked up a rock and tossed it ahead. It slid back down like it was on ice.

"This is starting to get annoying," she said. "The sorcerer removed friction."

Drime slumped on the other side of the crater, supported by Pri. His head hung to the side. He looked like Lakree after a matter shift, but his lips still moved.

A shadow moved across Rye's arm. Above a large rock, no, a boulder plummeted.

"Watch out," Hila said as she dove into him.

He elbowed Chirchi in the face as he fell back. The rock banged into the ground as all three tumbled down the ramp. Rye banged his head. He scrapped his arms and hands as he protected his face. He stopped when he hit a wall.

"Are you okay?" Lakree shouted from the top of the ramp. He and Juli had dove uphill.

Rye checked his arms. They stung and were bloody, but it wasn't anything Juli couldn't heal in a minute.

"Now, Carsi," Crimson shouted.

Juli created a shield around Rye just as a cloud of purple energy pounded into it. Before she could create a second shield for her and Lakree, they vanished.

"Lakree," Hila called. No one answered.

Chirchi picked herself up with mental energy. "I twisted my ankle."

Rye squinted. Lakree was gone from his natural vision, but a light in his form still glowed in Rye's mind. It was panicked, but Rye's spirit energy still flowed to a spot at the top of the ramp. "We can't see them, but they are still there."

The draftees floated across the crater on a bed of purple energy. Drime was stretched out like he was asleep, and he likely was. Pri covered him in a red healing shield.

"Rye, this is your last chance to come with us peacefully," Crimson said. His voice was strained. He was tired. Carsi stood beside him, her gaze fixed on the top of the crater.

Stavender approached from the ramp below. "Capture Rye. Kill the rest." His energy creatures sped past him.

MMA images flashed into Rye's mind, but he ignored them. With a tingle growing in his ear, he sent energy to Hila.

She dashed out of the shield. Fire whipped around her like silk. She punched and a puff shot out. It hit the white-energy creature and sent it flying. She punched again and fire socked the dark-energy creature square in the chest. Flames enveloped it, but it didn't slow. Rye pushed out more energy until his ear burned.

Hila shot another fireball. This burst of fire hit the dark-energy creature hard. It slid down the ramp, narrowly missing Stavender as it slammed into the wall. The other draftees landed nearby.

"What do we do?" Chirchi said.

"Go up," Rye said. He backed up the hill. Chirchi followed, aided by her mental energy. She didn't put much weight on her left foot.

Hila sent several more attacks. Pri moved a shield to block a blast aimed at Carsi, who remained outside any shield. Hila switched to water. It gushed around Pri's shield and sprayed Carsi. Pri increased the size of her shield to protect the psychic further.

Then, a magic shield appeared around Carsi. "No," she screeched.

"There they go," Lakree said. He was exactly where he had been before he disappeared. Carsi must have been the one hiding them with her magic. Lakree started mumbling a spell. Rye switched his energy to Lakree. The sound of Hila's splashing water deepened. The draftees' movements slowed.

"Lakree, chant that spell until the birds land," Juli said.

Rye ran to the top of the ramp. To the East, high above the horizon, four brown and black beasts soared. They weren't birds. They were cantigriffs, furry, winged felines. They weren't from the Winder Plains. They would suffer in the heat once they landed.

A sound flapped from behind, clothing maybe. Chirchi gasped as a head rose from the edge of the crater. The corners of Slithlor's grin reached up to his eyes as he swiped a hand. His bald head wrinkled with glee. He was dressed as a guard, but he was a monster. He was worse than any foreign enemy. He didn't care about Lynit, any place, or any people. Rye flung himself out of the way. Chirchi tried to jump but pushed off her bad leg and fell. Slithlor grabbed her. Juli shielded everyone else.

Thick purple energy flowed from Slithlor. It surrounded Chirchi, smothering her attempt at a defense. A few seconds later, her body fell limp, but her breathing didn't stop. She was still alive. Slithlor held her up like a prize. "Rye, why is Juli here?"

Rye's instincts pricked at the loaded question. Slithlor wanted to know the evidence against him and believed that Rye still trusted him. A wrong answer and Slithlor would kill Chirchi, the only one who could unravel any attempt to connect more children to spirit fiends. Fear gripped Rye as much as his anger did, but he couldn't stop himself from saying, "You killed my father," as he picked himself up. He met Slithlor's unblinking stare. Slithlor should know that Rye saw him for the scum that he was.

"Leave the talking to me," Juli said as she stepped in front. "Slithlor, your concern is with me and what I saw during the Battle of Ki. Let these children go."

"Who was his father?" Stavender said.

"He was the first non-noble elite. I respected him despite his reluctance to follow Lynit into its new era," Slithlor said. "And Rye, you have the same difficult choice to make. Will you choose Lynit's future?"

"A clever statement, but I saw it all, Slithlor. I saw you kill King Kertic," she said.

Slithlor's face crunched into a knot. Purple energy twisted Chirchi's head at a disgusting angle.

"Are we the bad guys?" Pri said.

"No, no, she's lying," Crimson said. Slithlor told us not to trust anything she said.

"If you let her go, I'll go with you. I don't want any more death," Rye said.

"Do you think I don't know who this is?" Slithlor said as he shook Chirchi's body in the air. "She is the only one with the potential to break the spirit fiend connections and you have so graciously delivered her to me. I was only curious how Juli found out about Rye, but it sounds like it was a coincidence."

"We can break the connections?" Drime said.

"Not anymore," Slithlor said. The crack of Chirchi's neck sent a shutter through Rye. Chirchi's head limped to the side. Her breathing stopped. Rye babbled as the small light winked out. Slithlor flung the lifeless body into the crater.

"If anyone finds out about you, I won't be able to protect you,"

Slithlor said. "Capture Rye and kill the rest."

The E.D.s looked to Crimson, who frowned, then nodded. Stavender's black and white clones rammed Juli's shield. Large ripples warped the magic. Carsi and Crimson lifted large rocks overhead, but Drime and Pri didn't move.

"No matter what happens next, you must get on those birds," Juli said. She shifted her stance and rattled off the longest spell Rye had ever heard from a protector.

The shield around them pulsed as symbols moved across their surfaces. Her arms rotated around her like a wizard controlling light energy. The shields spun in response. They hummed as they whipped up dust.

The energy creature's tiny fists ricocheted off the shield, flinging them off their feet. The draftees dropped the rock. It hit the physical shield, causing it to bow inward. Before Rye could duck, it shifted and fell off the side. Slithlor and the draftees launched more attacks. Most were deflected, but some damaged the shield. Dark spots now whirled around the shield. Juli moved about, casting new spells that repaired the damaged areas, but new ones cropped up faster. After a few minutes, Juli's shields were such a deep blue that they were almost black and difficult to see through. Behind, the cantigriffs drew nearer.

"Rye, I will spare everyone's lives if you come with me. They didn't do anything wrong," Slithlor said.

Juli's magic shield popped. She created a new one, but the energy creatures dashed inside it. They sneered with glee as they reached for Lakree and Hila. Juli created an even smaller bubble, but the light energy creature blocked it from sealing. It was so close that Rye felt the heat radiating off its body.

Then, two fist-sized balls of dark energy thudded into the light-energy creature, puncturing holes in its body. It staggered and then collapsed. A moment later, balls of light exploded, knocking

Slithlor and Crimson out of the air. Rye kicked the temporarily stunned dark-energy creature.

Above the Poli dome, three figures soared on what looked like a rain cloud covering the sun. Two of them moved their arms in unison, wearing matching quitol leather suits. It was the Poli Twins. The third person was a girl with "Draftee" stamped on her chest. Dre, Alaan, and the girl leaped in the air. The cloud they rode on reshaped into a copy of the twins. All five landed inside Juli's shields.

"Sorry, we're late," Alaan and Dre said in unison.

Slithlor picked himself off the ground. He stood in the middle of his child gang like a stunted adult who never made friends his age. His face contorted in anger. "I'm going to take them too," he said as he shot into the air. "You will have no proof, Juli."

Dre swung his arms. Alaan did the same. Their copies ran forward. They dodged rocks and spells. The illusions didn't obey the laws of gravity. Dre's illusion double jumped. It abandoned a side flip midway to snap back in the opposite direction. There were even audible gasps from the draftees when Dre's illusion scooped up Stavender's hissing energy clones. It tossed one at Crimson and the other at Carsi. Pri created a magic shield that blocked the attack and pulled the draftees closer together.

Dre shifted his style and elongated his movements. As his copy circled the draftees, it stretched and thinned, leaving behind a wall of light and shadow. After a complete lap, the draftees were surrounded. Something metallic glinted in the sky as it soared over the wall. It was the S-X orb. Dre clapped his hands above him and the fence sealed into a dome, trapping the children. They shouted and thudded spells against their prison, but Dre's magic held.

"What did you do?" Slithlor snapped as he shot mental energy to intercept the device.

But Alaan's copy was already in the air, burning up the purple.

When it got close, Slithlor punched it, but the illusion softened into dough and crawled up his arm, eventually wrapping his entire body like a liquid coffin. Alaan pushed both arms out in front of him, which sent Slithlor soaring away.

"That felt good," Alaan said as he relaxed his posture.

Hila caught the device. "Thank you," she called out, then touched Drime's necklace.

Four cantigriffs landed. Their noses were black upside-down triangles and they squinted as if they did not like what they saw. They roared and flapped their large wings, whipping up more dust. One of them shrank and changed color. Its harness and saddle slipped to the ground. After a few more seconds, a man with a sprinkle of grey and tattoos covering his arms stood up. He emptied a satchel of raw meat on the ground. He walked from creature to creature, petting them, checking their harnesses, and giving them water as they ate. He was an animalist.

"Was that Slithlor I saw? Are you fighting him?" he said.

"Long story, we have to go now," Juli said.

"After I finish a safety check," he said. "And there are seven of you. There were supposed to be five. I can carry two, but the cantigriffs won't make the full trip with double the weight."

"Just get us out of the Winder Plains," Juli said.

"We can do that," he said. After a last pass around the creatures, he clapped twice. They responded by kneeling and extending their wings. "Get on." He stepped into his harness, then turned back into a cantigriff.

Dre and Alaan hopped onto the nearest one. Juli and Lakree climbed onto the animalist. Rye jumped on one, then helped Hila climb up.

"They're gone," Tess said.

Rye turned around. Dre's dome wasn't there. "It's Carsi. She can make things invisible without touching you with mental energy,"

Rye said.

"And make you see things," Alaan said.

"Forgive me," Juli said. She waved her arms as she cast the largest protection shield Rye had ever seen. It covered where Dre's dome was. However, it didn't reveal anything inside, but it did reveal Slithlor flying high above with a storm of rocks shifting around him. Tess put up a shield that blocked a spray of pebbles. She flung herself from her cantigriff only momentarily before a boulder broke her shield and crushed the creature. She barely scrambled onto the back of Rye's and Hila's cantigriff before all the creatures took flight while barking and howling.

"Go, go, go," Juli shouted as she slapped the animalist. Rye didn't dare hit his ride. He was just thankful to be airborne.

"Get back here," Slithlor screamed, his voice cracking. More purple energy rushed out around him. He was the eye of a purple hurricane raining stones.

In a moment, Rye was high above the Winder Plains. The twins put up a wall of dark energy that blocked Slithlor from view. Rocks pinged against it until it broke. Juli tried to create a new shield, but the blue boundary stretched oblong as they moved. It sealed too slowly. The spell failed. She covered Lakree with her body and took hits in the back and arm. Lakree screamed and grabbed his side. The animalist was hit, too. He dripped blood. He lilted up for a moment, then started returning to human. He was unconscious or dead. Juli and Lakree fell beside his body.

Before a thought could pass through Rye, he was falling, too. He clenched his arms at his side in a dive. Slithlor would not take anyone else from him. This connection would not be broken. His body burned as he thought of Tenaju's fluffy feathers and sharp claws. He didn't just pull in the spirit fiend's energy; he summoned its form. His skin, organs, and bones morphed into a new biology. He became the idea of the bird made flesh. He was Tenaju.

Juli pointed at Lakree, who flailed. Rye swooped underneath him and caught him. Something hit Rye and it hurt, but he didn't slow. Alaan, Dre, Hila, Lakree, and Tess cheered as Rye flapped harder. He outpaced the cantigriffs. His speed was unmatched by any natural creature. The rush of wind was like a massage on his face. He accelerated until he outran sound and the green line on the horizon grew into a forest. But his vision dimmed as each flap became harder than the previous one. The adrenaline made the pain in his side only seem like an annoying sting, but something was stuck there, something beginner than a splinter.

They sank until they crashed onto a mat of grass. Lakree said something, but Rye couldn't understand it. Warm blood matted his feathers. An inner voice, his animalism teacher, Mr. P, reminded him that there was no Correction Factor outside of Lynit. He forced his body back to human in reply. He crawled to rub the bark of the closest tree. It was cool or maybe he was cold, but he had made it. He was finally out of Lynit. The insects and tiny critters waited for him.

Lakree twisted him onto his back. Even with his face squished up, Lakree was still handsome. He cried as he pressed his hands on Rye's side. The falling tears were like rain pattering on Rye's face, or at least what he imagined it to feel like. His whole body was numb.

Rye reached up and touched Lakree's cheek.

"Kiss me one last time," he said just before his hand dropped.

Chapter 34 - Dre

Dre flew for a long while before the distant forest resolved into individual trees. He had imagined that there would be a slow gradient of grasslands between the desert and forest, but there wasn't. The tree line looked almost like a fortress wall or the many towers in Poli, but instead of being a marvel of science, it was of nature. Though the shift from red to brown and green was stark, the smell surprised him the most. The scent of pines and dew reminded him of the mornings after a scheduled rain in Wrinst. He had thought that the mile of vegetation on his grandparents's farm was extraordinary, but it was only a frail imitation of the world outside Lynit.

As he crossed the boundary of the Winder Plains, he leaned forward and rested his chin on Alaan. "Out here, no one will find us," he said.

"Even the Guard can't patrol the world," Alaan said.

Tess and Hila flew beside them. Tess grinned as she scanned the horizon. She was the only one who didn't need to be on the run for her life. She could have returned to her family, but instead, she chose to help the twins yet again. She was a protector through and through, whether she chose protection magic or not. When her eyes locked with Dre's, she shook her head slowly. She was still in disbelief at the adventure. Hila, on the other hand, gripped her cantigriffs' reigns tight as if willing the creature to fly faster.

"What if she's right and Lakree and Rye need help?" Dre said. She wasn't as optimistic that her friends were okay. Rye was hit by a rock and was bleeding. After he shot off as the white bird, he faded out of sight within seconds. The cantigriffs followed his general path, but Rye could have ended up anywhere.

"Juli gave them instructions on where to go. We have to assume that they will follow them," Alaan said.

Even if Rye were severely injured, they could do nothing until they found him. "Well, it's a good thing Hila is with us or we wouldn't know where to go," Dre said. Dre, Alaan, and Tess weren't part of Juli's original plan. She didn't prep them.

"We'd be fine no matter what," Alaan said. "Rye is the one who wouldn't have a protector on the way."

"And what will we do without Chirchi?" Dre said. She was their way back to the spirit realm to break the spirit fiend connections.

"As Ser had put it, this is above our pay grade now. We did our part," Alaan said. "Now it's the council's turn to save Lynit."

"True, true," Dre said. Dre thwarted an attempt to destroy nobility by becoming a Yordin when he only wanted to return to the life of a tournament fighter. Now, he would miss the next Gigasphere tournament, which would likely become the competition grounds for the new noble academies. This was the best time to be a kid and the worst time to be Slithlor.

Dre imagined the man on trial held in a tight gigastone cage. There were no rocks to throw or children to manipulate. His psychic energy thrashed uselessly as the council voted on his fate. Lynitians cheered as he was stripped of all his titles and sentenced to death for the murder of King Kertic, bringing spirit fiends to Lynit, and illegally making the Poli Twins. "I wonder if we will ever know all of Slithlor's atrocities."

"I am sure there are many city-states and villages that would want to execute him," Alaan said.

Dre nodded. "Though it is weird to say it, I am glad he made us twins, at least."

"We don't owe him credit for an accident. His experiment technically failed. He wanted one child twice as strong, not twins with half the power," Alaan said. "And, he didn't give us the ability to join our energies. We invented that."

Dre snuggled closer. "Yeah, I think so too." All magic came from the spirit realm, so no one could have altered their contract with wizardry before birth. Their hard work to compensate for their magic deficit made them who they were. "I wonder if that means that another wizard can learn to join their energies."

Alaan shrugged.

Tess rubbed the side of her panting cantigriff. Its flaps were slow and soft. Dre's cantigriff was struggling, too. He was losing altitude. The tops of the trees were less than a hundred feet below. Tess shouted over the wind, "They need to rest."

When they spotted a clearing, they landed. Knee-high grass covered the ground. Bushes, flowers, and vines flourished along a winding stream. Small fluffy-tailed creatures hopped away. As the cantigriffs lapped up water, Alaan searched the pouches on the saddles. He found bread, cured meat, raw fish, a small paper book, and five sets of clothes. He fed the cantigriffs as Tess changed out of her draftee robe.

Dre approached Hila, who paced around the clearing. "Can I see the map?" he said. All that he knew about Juli's plan was that they were to leave Lynit. He guessed they weren't traveling to another continent since there would have been no way to stay in contact with the Medina or Lynit. Magic couldn't span the oceans. That left them hiding in a nearby territory that didn't belong to any nation. He hoped that they weren't expected to camp in the wilderness.

Hila pulled out a rolled-up cloth without looking. The map was crudely drawn, but there were clear labels and landmarks, like the forest boundary line, a river that this stream likely fed into, and three towns.

"We know which way is East," he said as he dragged a finger from the Winder Plains. "We have to keep going that way until we hit the main road. Then follow it to Amade." It was the only town circled on the map.

"Do you hear that?" she said. She cupped her hands around her ears.

Dre reached out his wizardry senses but didn't pull anything. They shouldn't use magic around people unless they were in grave danger because they would be recognized as Lynitian.

"The Winder Plains has quitols. Doesn't this forest have deadly monsters?" Tess said.

Leaves rustled and branches creaked, but he didn't hear anything odd. He stared out into the forest for a minute before he relaxed.

"We'll probably hear all kinds of noises out here that we aren't used to," Alaan said.

Hila walked to a tree root and sat down. She dropped her head to her shaking knees. She was still worried about Lakree and Rye. Dre tried to distract her by telling her about how his father was in a coma. He explained that he and Alaan shared dreams. Tess gasped a few times, but Hila remained quiet. After Dre ran out of things to say, he signaled Alaan to jump in, but nothing he said seemed to relax her, either. Dre frowned as he glanced at the cantigriffs. They had finished eating and were lying down. It would easily be two hours before they were ready for the remaining leg of the trip.

Dre walked over to the supplies. Funk hit him as he peeled off his sticky armor. He hadn't bathed in several days and had been in multiple fights. He considered changing into clean clothes but wondered how easy it would be for Rish to track him on smell alone. "We should all wash the desert off or anyone we meet will know where we came from," he said. When he first met Lakree, Hila, and Rye, their faces were caked in dirt and sweat, but they thought their expensive robes would disguise them. He would not get caught by the same amateur mistake. "And I'll keep my helmet on. No one can see both Alaan's and my face." Not shocking the locals was the other key to not being found by the Guard.

He created a long tub out of dark energy and filled it with water from the stream. He warmed the bath with light energy and even created a privacy wall. After a few minutes of soaking, the water's surface was murky.

Bit by bit, he inched forward until he dipped his whole body underneath. He washed away the grime and the stress of the last two weeks. He was starting a new life. Outside of Lynit, he could start his suspenders shop and be confident that people were buying his styles because of the quality and not because of his name. He stopped short of envisioning a life without magic. He wasn't ready to deal with that.

He listened to Alaan's and Tess's conversation. Their voices were distorted but louder in the water. It was almost as if they were yelling. He heard Hila sniffling. And there was a barely audible hum underneath it all. He felt it more. With his teeth clenched, it vibrated his bones. He popped out of the water.

"There *is* an odd sound, Hila," Dre said. It was like a distant version of the guard's slowed-down whistle from when they were in the bar. "It's too consistent. It's not natural. It could be them."

Hila jumped to her feet and tired her hair up. "Let's go look."

Tess, Alaan, and Hila fanned out to cover more ground. The increase in volume was so gradual that it took a while to identify the general direction it came from, but finally, everyone heard the noise. The tone still hadn't broken or fluctuated. It was textured like an unnatural voice singing the lowest audible note. The rumble grew the more they walked. It vibrated the leaves and Dre couldn't hear his footsteps. Eventually, he covered his ears against the blare.

When they crested a treeless hill, Hila pointed. She shouted something, but he couldn't make it out. However, he spotted Lakree. He sat on the ground, his arms covered in blood. His eyes were transfixed and his lips trembled. Nestled between the roots of a tree was Rye. His body was still, almost like a picture. His chest didn't rise or fall and the roar reverberated from him.

Hila shook her head, lips forming, "No, no, no, no."

Dre almost tripped as he ran. He thought about the animalist that was hit and fell with Juli. He might have died. However, when Dre got closer, he noticed that Lakree was chanting a spell and that Rye's nostrils were flared. "He's maintaining a time dilation," he said, but no one seemed to hear him.

Alaan touched Lakree's shoulder, which caused him to scramble back. He was alert. His face melted into sadness as he mouthed something while pointing at Rye. When his spell was corrected, Rye's deafening noise shifted into a simple moan. He was still alive, though his breathing was faint. He didn't look much different than when he was frozen. The main movement about him was the crimson liquid flowing out between his fingers that he pressed against his side.

"Heal him," Lakree said.

The forest darkened as the sun set, but Rye glowed under Tess' red sphere. With the sound gone, tiny claws clattered on bark and critters chirped, but Dre couldn't take his eyes off the operation. Tess was a protector, but she was still a child and there was no Correction Factor here. All she knew was theory and how to heal creatures. Under the domes, enough Lynitian didn't get injured or sick for children to practice on them. The Guard had to train protectors by sending them on tours worldwide to heal those surviving in the wilderness. This was Tess' first real lesson.

Something bulged on Rye's side. It looked like a knot underneath his skin. He moaned again and it sent some nearby birds into flight. The bulge moved down his torso, growing in size. A desert rock about the size of a fist spilled out of him and his whole body shuttered. The wound then knitted itself close.

"The hard part is done. He'll be fine," Tess said. She wiped the sweat from her forehead.

Hila plopped on the ground. She looked more exhausted than Tess. She repeated "Thank you" as if it was a mantra.

"I panicked and started the spell," Lakree said. "I didn't have time to think through how you would find us."

"It worked. That's all that matters," Dre said.

Eventually, Rye sat up. He was weak, but he was alive. Lakree and Hila helped him to his feet. "We need to move. It's not safe out here in the open," he said.

"We know," Hila said as she hugged him. She wiped the tears from her face.

Lakree gripped Rye's head and kissed him on the lips. "I wanted to wait for you to wake up before I did that."

Dre glanced at Alaan, who was equally shocked. The last time they had seen these three together, Rye tried to choke Lakree to death.

"No, this should have happened years ago," Rye said. "I was the one pushing you away."

"I knew it," Hila said. "I always knew it."

"Do you feel left out now?" Rye said with a smirk.

"Oh, sorry, Hila, am I supposed to…?" Lakree said as he turned to her.

"No," Rye and Hila said. All three laughed. Then, they turned to Dre and Alaan.

"Don't mind us," Alaan said.

They found their way back to the stream, clothing, and only one of the cantigriffs. The other creature had flown off. Dre and Alaan made more tubs and everyone washed. Rye and Lakree changed out of their blood-stained clothes. They ate the remaining food, then headed East on foot. A soft yellow glow in the distance sharpened into a road lined with glowing stones. Wheels grinned on packed dirt. Lanky creatures with muscled legs pulled carriages of people in clean, tight-fitted clothing. They lounged, chatted, and ate. Others walked barefoot in ragged robes, carrying backpacks or pushing carts with their hands.

Alaan stepped onto the road first. A few people acknowledged him in strange accents and languages, but most didn't bother with a greeting. Lakree, Hila, Rye, and Tess slipped in behind him. Dre entered last. A woman with long blades of grass twisted in her hair seemed to comment on his helmet, but he couldn't be sure. He could only make out every sixth word, but he nodded back. No one said anything else to him after that. He was an ordinary person out here. He would miss being famous.